Volition

Book Two of the Torus Saga

Michael Berg

VOLITION

First printing (paperback): Amazon Publishing 2019

First published as an Amazon Kindle ebook Copyright © 2013

For all permissions contact: torussaga@gmail.com

Michael Berg is a professional writer residing in Australia. He dedicates this work The Torus Saga, to those with an open mind connected to the heart who seek the many mysteries and progressions of life.

Also in the Torus Saga by Michael Berg:

Book One: First Light

Book Three: The Last Year

VOLITION

Chapter 1

Human beings had become what they were through choice according to the issues of the time. They had always chosen during darkness and light throughout history whether it be for want, for need, or to satiate a hunger be it for lust, greed, selfish egocentricity, mania, or simple survival. Now in times near the end of the twenty first century, society was plunged into uncertainty and darkness where people struggled as if in times past living a life without so much they had taken for granted.

The machine billowed great clouds of steam, great clouds of dust, and great clouds of particles seen and unseen. Minds boiling with rage, boiling with contempt, and boiling with an endless quest for power, created the dust of humanity – its remnants blown away bit by bit to be carried on the howling winds coursing though buildings now pinnacles to darkness. As people went about their lives, those lives went about them in a continuous drain of both soul and of spirit – then gathered by the Agent to manifest as particles of dread.

In the three years since it had started, it had all begun to end, and yet there was never an end. Countless the ghosts of many were encumbered with despair between what was and dreams forsaken. Hope was but a distant filament of imagination – they had wanted this, accepted it, and now they would live, or die regardless if they still walked upon the face of the planet along avenues to oblivion.

Cities painted matte black with towers rising to laden skies cast gloom over all who dared look to the path of righteousness forgotten. It was a place where light only illuminated blackness within and of darkness without. Despite the sun of endless days there was no life just compliance, and the endless days bore on seemingly forever to nowhere. As kings, the towers reigned over the detritus of humanity below with their queens embroiled in the twisted shadows of memory giving birth to life seemingly already dead. Machines formed lives and machines deformed lives totally at will and then also in totality without will. Lines of humanity were all giving service to the beast – a beast from within themselves losing sense of soul.

Earth floated through darkness surrounded and bound to itself. As each cog turned within the machine planet, the inconsequence of lives was erased and others took their place to become the next gears of subjugation in realising the macabre art. A manifest of abundance, yet most were so hollow – their faces masked with loss, with habit, and with all of the dirt humanity created.

Eagles cast wings upon the winds to become the carrion of the ravens below. It was all far below, deep, dark, and utterly devoid of circumspect where nothing resides, where nothing was life. Inside these caverns of despair and of rabid fervour, was the Agent. He was not a leader yet he led. And as the vulture circles looking for prey, the Agent circled in his spacecraft dispensing horrors at will. Earth was his volition now...his will to change and send to oblivion should he choose.

He took them and he hated them as a man scathing in depravity and never hesitant to dispose. He could disgorge fractionalised memories only then to be re-cast his way. He was the Minotaur of the times with his labyrinth the endless wanderings of his mania.

He saw ends...to a means, and he destroyed means to ends. Lost as he was, he was founded and so founded was he, he let leash upon the lost Earth measures immeasurably miserable and intense as he slowly changed people.

The virus of his mind sent to many, reflected his inner workings so lacking compassion. He would send the virus to them for in a way they craved it and they needed it - the virus of humanity, yet not of humanity, setting humanity to task asking the deepest questions. His creations invaded bodies and minds of all who subscribed to deception and consumption, and the price was high, the contract endless. His hand would tremble with anticipation of pain, and anticipation of angst – it was all he needed to enliven his beast. Born from machine and beyond the bearings of most, he lubricated his thirst for blood through eternal suffering.

It hummed and cast glowing sight throughout – without eyes. Set against yet even more blackness than black, it stood as his power, again seen as an extension of himself. 'El tor exquisito' – the bull exquisite, as was the pain his vortex amplifier delivered.

He stood alone amongst the many as they stood not, for they were stooped, their heads bowed down in reverence to his methods. They complied free of will for he had their will and he controlled mercilessly with ambivalence. He was neither controlling nor wanting as he was merely a channel of hate without real ambition as it would define him in some sense as normal and as such would have to be expunged so his mania may express him as twisted and erratic being like the child of maniacal whims.

Chapter 2

Life and society evolved through adapting. It went on as it had always been this way. For many though, they were the unwilling minions of the Agent whose provocateur was the viruses he unleashed at will. To some who were full of hate for what he had brought upon them, they fed him in return with such hate as to almost transgress into mania with their minds churned seeking solace for their human spirit and comfort for their bodies.

Some bound to their way of life's progression through this mire, held dear to their hearts and to their life - a fire never extinguishable and a flame forever flickering.

She had changed since the time she let it happen. Unlike the Agent, she was in no turmoil and retained the determination to overcome adversity. Her living space coloured with life, set a contrast to the world beyond the gate where the tendrils of his reach were cast outward looking for victims – in any place, in every place. Her song came from her heart, whereas the Agent had no song and her body was far out of reach from him.

Carmel Madeline lived in the small house north of San Francisco, where she had been these past three years. She was free from all she had left behind, so long ago and so very distant since when it had plagued her conscience. She was herself. She was engaged in life and she was amongst a very few strong enough to resist the temptations.

The art of harmony was now her living where forms and flows were simply her way of being. Her body showed barely any ageing, nor did her heart. As she sang, her song was not of words for she was an instrument and her living the melody.

Now as she stood at the centre of the small town, she felt there was something calling her...summoning her. Not the Agent or the beast he used as his weapon, but a summoning from everywhere – it was a feeling. Her condition was one of being open to acceptance of these waves and she rode them. Unlike the others who were about the town, she would never sink and be drowned for her love was found. It had been a resurgence of memories almost forgotten when she felt a calling amidst a world in calamity.

It was a year since she last saw anyone she knew well, and despite her health inspiring heart and mind, she spent times in her life alone in body but not spirit.

Finding anyone to love was almost a lost cause in these times – so far apart people were. They were consumed and lost to it, and the Agent had sent out his viruses of fear, of pain, of suffering, and of oblivion. And so, people had forgotten themselves and without themselves, they had almost lost the love.

Out the gate and into the world beyond she took her love and her will, but so many others were not so free and nearly every face she saw outwardly expressed pain as a sense of nothingness. In the town centre she bought some food at the store – the only one still open.

When she arrived back home, her few flowers were again a reminder of life in progression and the ongoing reformations of which she was a part of…forever. Inside she lit the stove and prepared some food. There was warmth in the air but a distinct chill lingered. There had been nearly all those three years now.

Chapter 3

The Agent stood at the holographic bank admiring his vortex amplifier featuring three torus in situation atop an array of holographic image processors. Two horned torus flanked both sides of the Torus of Eternity diamond ring floating in the centre. He had stolen the ring torus from the previous leader of the dark sect he now controlled, where he then took it upon himself to indulge his whims through his amplifier technology. His fingers trembled as if pained when he controlled the beast. He was facetious as he laughed at the visions in his mind and on the holographic bank – his mania was he and he was it…simple. And through all of this, he barely ever remembered his name George Smyth, for now he was purely the Agent who was an agent of malice and he held most of the world to ransom.

He had held the authorities to ransom after returning with the stolen spacecraft from Mars almost three years prior to this time. The pathetic leader of the dark sect had allowed him to join them, and so over the following year, he had taken charge as malice like his was unequal in their ranks. First he replaced the leader who now served him as a minion without any choice. Then he had unleashed a swath of unstable viruses to affect systems and internal nanotechnology in people using the vortex amplifier containing two horned torus and the Torus of Eternity in the centre. It worked. With victory coming all over the globe, he despatched minions to control the cities and he had despatched his command for all people living under his control were to be denied technology. Then he chose to paint his world black with just a few red lights to mirror the spaceship he adored. They were not shiny black for it would cast light. Instead, he had ordered them rendered with a dull finish without depth.

He forced onto others his desire and his will for them to become a part of his plan with nanotechnology implants as their only saviour for their now technology deprived lives. And where he controlled them, he offered nothing to benefit them other than just a tether to actual living. This ensured their compliance as he held them, and all else in the world would have his face, expressionless and bland.

With threats and his amplifier he now controlled so many and his numbers were growing, despite the best efforts of the authorities. They fought and they struggled in counter attack, their dreams of efficiency almost lost. 'Their stupid minds compare nothing unto me,' he would think and in a macabre sense of pleasure, he would send them viruses. He could see them flail besotted with pain, so he would send out the viruses again and again. Terror was his way pierced often with the erratic natural behaviour of one prone to megalomania. His dominion was imminent in his mind and so he set about trying what he could to realise this as a planet.

Whilst the authorities had weapons, they stood as silent ghosts reminding them of failure. Vehicles too and the transit lines were unused standing silent like the other technology, their passengers restricted to the cities and the towns. The Agent's viruses kept them at bay where they relied on minimal secure operations out of his reach.

All across the west towards the east and beyond, the same state existed. People still worked for survival and the authorities had trimmed their ranks not by choice, but by force. Many were unemployed with status now a distant memory. The authorities needed them as did the Agent, so they were kept alive in body to service these needs.

Although blood was not a fascination of the Agent, the bleeding took on many forms of terror and of utter despair. Across the continents he could influence many with a virus and so he made incursions to places far-flung and wide. People would talk about him in the streets and in their homes – many trying to come up with ways to defeat him, but all futile. They dared not oppose through fear of losing access to food and resources, and those in the east, were forced to comply to meet the same needs provided by the authorities.

Living in the west within the Agent's dominion, the only thing to really trouble Carmel was the isolation. She missed the freedoms of life under the authorities despite their crackdown. She missed the tenderness associated with love and between friends. Her tenacity to persevere served her well through the winters and summers when she endured many times in isolation. These strengths extended to her ability to take care of herself during the instances when people affected by the Agent's viruses appeared about town. She had not seen into them as others had who had been close enough to see the vortexes forming holes in their bodies, but the sheer horrors she imagined was enough to find confidence in protecting herself when trouble arose.

During her lonely travels about town, she had found a small old steam engine at the derelict museum. She had repaired and restored it to a state of operation it had probably not seen for a long time. Brass fittings and working pressure gauges were restored to shine, and she had been able to restore the drive shaft to a balanced reliable condition. Whenever she felt inspired to, she would fire up the fuel box for it to chug along merrily billowing little puffs of steam she could watch. There was no real use or no real need other than to mirror her feelings, her tenacity, and her fascination.

In contrast to life under the Agent, there were those still with the technology of the late twenty-first century. They played and worked with devices electronic and holographic, but they had nothing new for nearly three years and they were becoming bored. Their lives were feeling the direct implications of the restrictions in place to avoid virus attack from their adversary.

Their technology served them, despite its propensity to some virus attacks from the Agent when he successfully sent the authorities scurrying to counteract his intrusion past their security systems. Their jets, their robots, and their networks, were mostly stood down, and those still in operation ran on minimal secure capacity. The two remaining spacecraft were vital in servicing mining operations on the asteroids as their means to energy recourses and in many ways, their means to survive. In consequence to all this technology loss, the regular updates to nanotechnology implanted in DNA occurred sparingly to mostly complacent and fearful populations.

Carmel decided to start her little engine today so she prepared the fuel, she checked its mechanical cogs and piston, and then she struck up a fire in the small box. She watched and she learned about herself unknowingly as it ran with all the parts working so well together and in sequence once the steam had built up enough pressure.

As it chugged making the sound the only one about the house, it sent puffs of steam to be cast upon the breezes created by Carmel's movements and she loved this. It was the main reason why she ever ran the little steam engine as mist to her always evoked a sense of mystery.

Carmel loved a sense of the unknown as part of living and she clung to it as her way and as her defence against the gloomy world. At times like these she showed it with the little steam engine. And then, when she sounded the whistle attached to the steam outlet, it gave a cheery sound in reflection of her inner self as if she wanted to tell the world how she felt. Her small voice was one small little voice in a world cast mostly silent in fear and sorrow.

Chapter 4

Driven again through mania, the Agent was beside himself with his own sense of sorrow had had given to the people. He was about to bring on his yet another type of deprivation and so powered up the vortex amplifier where the three torus came to life with sporadic static charge flowing over them and between them. Two horns and a ring in the centre – it was his centre stage from which he cast the play for every scene. He did not care of the instability of the amplifier. He did not care of the uncontrolled vortexes he had cast upon the world. And he did not care of any of the consequences, so long as he had power and he had dominance.

As he entered the sequence to render so many lives unliveable, his art forms began to take shape. The holographic bank showed them and the amplifier was about to send them. When the last few motions left his fingers and he stood back to watch it happen, many lives started to dissolve – slowly and surely dissolve. The Agent had sent a virus to bring the void unto them in a slow and painful way as people began to lose cell integrity and their life force was extracted. He didn't want their life force, it was not extracted for his use, it was simply extracted and they began to feel the extraction.

Soon they would become mere shells of humans and soon he would have killed so many there would not be enough numbers left for anyone to really resist him. Within their bones, within their hearts, and within their blood, they began to pass into non-existence as if they had never existed...as if their presence within the universe had never existed. And to these people, so many as there were, the loss of relevance through this ushered in terror as their escort to oblivion. The pains of torture and the pains of deprivation were nothing compared to the loss of relevance and the sense they feared of having never existed.

Their screams went unheard and unattended, for those to whom people were calling out for salvation were in fact stricken with the same screams and the same eradication of humanity on a mass scale. They twisted and heaved. They spoke yet no words could be heard – nothing aside from the screams...silent screams taking their breath away. Some would fight, tearing at themselves in a hopeless attempt to remove their nanotechnology implants, whilst others would cut ever so deeply inside using blades both sharp and blunted to remove it where to their dismay, it was all futile...hopeless.

The authorities scrambled to build anti-viral software and they had some success, but this was reserved for those of priority and so by the time they distributed any of it the public at large, many had already passed in to the Agent's oblivion. Many of those still residing on the towers became bodies within mausoleums of people stacked half a mile into the sky and towering over the streets of the poor below.

There were very few left by nightfall, and so as beautiful as she was and as vibrant with life she was, for five days she was stricken with gathering the dead and burying them. By the end of it all, the small town north of San Francisco now had only twelve inhabitants with most of the population now in graves. They were the fortunate ones.

Wherever there were people like Carmel who had neither technology or suffering in their hearts, they continued to resist as they listened to their elemental intentions. She sat in her lounge with the little engine silent. It could not give her what it did on so many other days – it was silent like the cities, like the towns, and silent like the hearts, except hers. Despite her weariness, she held true to her intentions, to the elements, and to progression.

Carmel searched around for solace. It was not something she regularly did for solace was always present in her heart. But on this day she needed solace for the heavy emptiness around her. When at last her eyes rested on the garden outside, the few flowers providing a glimpse of colour gave her an idea. She went outside and tended them, clearing away debris and turning the soil.

She paused at the arch along the pathway leading back to the house. Underneath it was a world separated for feeling more herself. Grapes upon the vine were ripe and ready to eat so she picked a few and let their juice slip down inside her. She toiled with their skins in her mouth and she tasted their sharpness in contrast to the juice. This was the world, as the depths of sweetness could never die despite the skin of the outside – dry and sharp. She would rid the evil wherever she encountered it. She would let the juice flow down the throat of the vortex and the vortex would balance, losing instability on a return to elemental manifest – a fait accompli.

Buoyed with these feelings, Carmel decided to again run her steam engine. In no time it was working hard and fast. It was lubricated by her love, lubricated by intention, and lubricated to progress. The little steam engine was at full power – the puffs of steam coming so regularly it looked now as if a fog had made its way indoors. Carmel spun and danced, sending the steam into eddies and currents. It would caress her and she would breathe it loving the gentleness of its touch on her skin and the warm moist feeling inside.

A knock on the front door suddenly sounded, startling her out of her dreamy state. Nobody had knocked on her door for about a year. She felt anticipation as an unusual sense as she walked the few yards to the front door. The notion or idea of being afraid did not occur to her. Nobody knocked on doors as the minions of the Agent would simply burst in and the authorities were long gone from these parts.

Standing there was John Matheson, a man she had met those years before when she was still an officer of the authorities. He looked at her as she opened the door. He was not suspicious, rather he was smiling, and the moment she recognised him was a feeling of relief neither of them had experienced in recent times. Despite the hardship of recent times, he looked well and he seemed strong to her as ever. She could sense this – it was not a physical thing, but an internal knowing of his intentions she immediately recognised. After half a minute just hugging without speaking, she invited him in. As she ushered him inside, he noticed the small steam engine still puffing away at full power, and was intrigued.

"Did you restore it?"

"Yes John. I love it. Do you?"

"It's great. May I look?"

"Of course, I would love you to look."

He watched it go through its motions again and again, admiring the restoration job she had done – it was flawless. He noticed how the brass pipes and iron cogs shone with lustre as if they had just been polished, and he noticed the way it seemed to effortlessly push the piston back and forth, back and forth.

"You know I have seen a lot of steam engines and other relics of the past in recent years with people turning back the pages in history as a means to manufacture and build these days, but I have never noticed one working so well and looking so good."

"It is a reflection of me John. It is how I am and so it shows me."

"It's beautiful."

"You are beautiful John because you are like me and not lost like so many."

"Oh I have been lost. It has taken me a lot to get here. I could do with a drink."

"Of course. I can offer you pure juice from grapes I have made…" Carmel said leaving him to watch the engine whilst she went to fetch the juice.

"Here." She held a glass out to him, which he accepted and then drank most of the contents.

"You haven't finished John," Carmel said seeing him hold the glass as he stood there looking as though he was thinking about something.

She had brought him back around, "I am never finished Carmel."

"Neither am I John."

He finished the juice and asked for another, which she promptly fetched from the kitchen. As she held it out to him, he appeared to again be lost in thought, "I think I know what you are thinking about."

"Oh…"

"Yes. You are thinking about what it took to get you here – to my house. And also, you are thinking about the time since we last saw each other."

"Hmm, you do have the knack Carmel – it was precisely what I was thinking about."

"I know."

"It was a long journey, and a hazardous journey."

"There are many hazards out there now John. Much more than those days around three years ago when we met. Do you remember?"

"Of course. In the warehouse under the Bay Bridge."

"It was a wonderful night."

"Yes."

"So here we are now. What are we meeting for John? I think I know it too, but I need to hear your words."

"Um, we need to talk Carmel…and act."

"I know. Too much suffering is taking place."

"The Agent."

"Yes. I am moved in such bad ways by him John."

"Why Carmel?"

"He is the nemesis of so many and if he ever finds me, he will be my nemesis too."

"Why?"

"I was his superior once – back in times I would rather forget. He is Agent Eight."

"Agent Eight!"

"He is so full of hate and now he is dispensing it all over the world. I feel it is partly my fault. He escaped his punishment and I think it is because I was not hard enough on him."

"How could you be hard?"

"I know it seems remote, but there was a time when I did not know myself and so I was acting a role…as part of the system."

"I guess we have all been those types of places. I too was once in the services."

"Do you know of Tobias?" Carmel asked him wondering if he had seen Tobias in recent times.

"Um…yes. I think he is in the east."

"Can we help him?"

"Maybe. I don't know. It has been two years since I saw him. I only know he was in the east…he could be anywhere now."

The steam engine let out a hiss, distracting them.

"I think it is building up quite a head of steam," John said.

"It does so at times. I love the way it hisses, like it is talking to me."

"Internal pressure. It has to release."

"Sounds like a metaphor John, for the world as it is."

"So much pressure."

"Yes. People are the steam and the hiss is their calling John."

They both fell silent for a few moments, thinking how exactly this was the way.

"And the others? Lorraine, Asper…?" Carmel asked, her mind turning back to their conversation.

"I don't know. I haven't seen Lorraine for a couple of years. And the rest…for even longer. As for Raynie and Jake, I have not seen them since before we met. They were in Australia last I knew."

"It is where the Agent lives."

"Hmm, unlikely place for someone with such power, but yes."

"He likes it there. He is free to do what he likes. He owns the entire country now. All who live there are under his influence."

"Surely there are some…like us there?"

"There must be. Not all people give in to him as easily or were forced to like so many were."

"Have you seen much of the world in recent years? I have been here at my house for so long."

"There is not much to see. Many places I have been have thrown back like this town, to times past. It is like the past two hundred years disappeared…except for their implants."

"What do you mean?"

"People are using machines from museums and relics to get by. It is as if the steam age is happening all over again in some places. But the authorities still have their technology in the east and some overseas I have been told. They still use technology and have transport but there is not much for the people at large. They are mostly just getting by. It seems as though progress everywhere has ground to halt."

"It is their nature. They are improvising I suppose."

"Yeah. They still need fuel and power and machines to get by."

"How do they eat?"

"Very much like you. They eat from gardens like yours and they get together and farm for produce. There are factories producing food stuffs. Apparently it is a mix of compounds designed to meet nutritional needs."

"It does seem to be a step back in time. Maybe they will prevail if they allow their elemental intentions to guide them."

"In some ways I guess, but there is still a lot of pain and suffering out there."

"Again, people seem to do such things. It can teach them the value of what they lose."

"I don't think the Agent is about teaching anyone except for their submission to him. He is like a lord or some deity of darkness."

"Yes I have heard about his viruses and the vortexes he creates."

"Very unstable using the amplifier with the torus the others found. Many of the repercussions are bad. Sometimes he brings in such a state of flux where he is affecting the very fabric of existence. It goes against natural elements creating voids dissolving relevance and casting matter into disparity."

"Do you have any technology implants John?"

"No, not since I had the device they put inside my head when they wanted to retrieve the flux mechanics information from me. I was grateful when the time came and it was successfully removed. The identification chip thing has fallen apart with the Agent on the scene. Their systems were so over run with viruses, they gave up on it. And there was so much international disagreement on administration of the security systems even before the time of the Agent."

"Yes, I remember the incidents…" she trailed off thinking of Tim and was tentative to ask John if he knew anything.

He saw her face lose some of the vibrancy within and took a guess, "Tim helped though. He took it out of my head and we were working on flux mechanics when he…when he disappeared. I am sorry Carmel, but I don't know what happened to him."

Chapter 5

He swept amongst the towers of a near dead city once full of life and beauty in the years before he arrived. On the second pass, he saw a few people struggling along street so he armed the laser weapons and vaporised them. Then for his own good measure he destroyed a few buildings he thought people might use as a refuge before flying out over the harbour with its broken bridge and half sunken vessels then onward back to his lair. It was normal for him to do such trips and to take more lives whenever he chose. Thirty minutes later, the engines powered down and he went underground deep to the heart of his underground hideaway.

The vortex amplifier housed atop his holographic bank and tended by those who suckered up to him in their own pathetic dreams of power, was alluring when he saw it upon return. There were only a couple of people about so he told them to get out and to leave him alone. After they had left, he went into one of usual moods of hate inspired mania. It was the mania of the stark manifestations from mania itself, permeated with mutterings of nonsensical matter others had often heard him yell from behind the closed doors. Such were his words and his moods, most of the time they could not determine what he was saying. He was insane and they knew he was insane, yet they too were of similar ilk as likes do get to know each other.

For so many years he had tried to get the amplifier to operate in a stable manner, and once again he was entirely unsuccessful. This bothered him. His mind would feel like it was on fire and his head would feel like it was about to explode, and in reflection of this he would have to deal with himself as the blood from his nose dripped upon the floor. His teeth did gnash and his body twisted as it always had, adding to his hatred and his quest for pain. But this time nothing would suffice. Not his own blood, nor the twisting and writhing normally sufficient to tire him and bring about some relative calm.

He linked into the vast global data network and then he hacked his way past the security systems into the research net. This net was primarily for use by scientists and was inaccessible by anyone else who still had technology. He worked feverously at the holographic bank entering sequences and cracking his way through the many layers of encryption protection. He had been waiting for this moment when he could access the machine using an amplifier in stable operation. Now with his most recent failure for stability, he did not care what the consequences would be.

After more feverish calculations and instructions were entered into his holographic array, he was able to bypass authority security systems. Without hesitation he continued, digging deeper into the machine until he found what he was looking for. And when he found it, he was abruptly cut off. His systems went dead, and his beast took to glowing – the static charge gone. Surprisingly he remained calm. He did not go into uncontrollable fits of anger and rage. No screaming, just calm. He had almost reached authority systems control and now he knew the path to them. Next time would be his time.

When at last after several days he emerged from his dark quarters, it was with a new sense of vigour. A new sense to wreak havoc and a new sense to deliver the worst human kind had to offer. His days alone served to refine his plans and soon he would destroy almost all of them. He would start by smashing them literally. No viruses - instead sweeping flights of destruction to physically bring their world down around them.

****

John was tending to some repairs on Carmel's house. It was late in fall and soon the winter winds would tear at anything not fixed properly. Since the days of the Agent, winter had taken on new dimensions – much colder and longer where many thought he had used the HAARP array to change the weather. They were wrong. He had no access to HAARP. It was the authorities doing this in an attempt to undermine the Agent by using adverse weather conditions as a means to slow his progress. All it achieved was to slow him a little and to undermine the people who struggled through long winters always short on fuel and always short on food.

John had just finished one job and was about to start another when Carmel appeared carrying a tray with refreshments of fruit and drink.

"Come and sit John. You need this. You have been working so hard."

He stopped his work and joined her at a table and chairs she had on the porch at the rear of the house.

"How do you come up with such good food? So many are starving yet you seem to have plenty."

"I guess it is just me. I grow some and I gather some. There is always the supply store run by the Agent, but rarely will you find wholesome food there."

"A strange attractor maybe."

"You could say so John. Things have worked out as such for me over these years."

Carmel had found even with many others around her suffering, she would help them where she could, and she seemed to flourish despite the conditions. She did not flourish with a wealth of material things – she simply flourished with life and with spirit.

"What can we do John? I feel like there is something, but I am struggling to see what the something is."

"I…um, don't really know. It is so difficult these days to get people together and as you know there is power in numbers."

"What about people of the scenes at the place where we met?"

"I have thought about there too, but with San Francisco in such a bad way, I can only imagine they are probably elsewhere."

"Seattle?"

"Very similar. I think the best option would be to get out of Agent controlled places and then look. Travel is not easy though. There are no transit links operating, there are hardly any vehicles in a condition to drive, and the few HyperJets flying if any, are not going past anywhere west of the fence."

"Doesn't the Agent's control extend further?"

"It is mostly his viruses making it past the dividing fence."

"So if we can get to the east, then…"

"Then we come up against the authorities and they are not allowing anyone to travel without approved passage – for official reasons."

"So the east is in lock down?"

"Effectively yes."

"Then we need to find a way. A way nobody would expect and a way not attracting attention. There are rumours of terrible things John."

"With this entire calamity, people can only be expected to get desperate. And…you would have to leave your house and your engine if we leave."

"I can leave the house as it is the spirit travelling with me. And as for my little steam engine, I can take it. It is small and can easily be carried. I feel it is the way ahead for us to leave. Something must be done to stop him John."

"So to the eastern sector then?"

"I think so John. I cannot just remain here wondering."

Carmel thought tentatively for a moment then decided to ask, "What about your son John? Could he help us?"

"He might. He is still with the authorities but now lives in Boston. I helped him out of London two years ago when the Agent unleashed some deadly viruses there. I still haven't brought him all the way back though, but I'm sure glad he had given up the nanotechnology."

"So he is free from implants?"

"Yes."

"Then he has begun the journey back. I am happy for you John, and for him. It takes courage to defy what you have come to know as the way ahead."

"Yeah. I am happy about it, but he is still quite dedicated to the authorities providing the best way forward."

"You can change him…we can change him. It is why he has begun the journey. His inner self is looking to re-align. Whilst it might take time, he is still heading there."

"But you cannot force him against his will…"

"Oh no, not at all. You can only do your best to show him the options and in time he will choose what he considers best."

"I suppose then we have decided to go east. Considering all things, it is probably best we try, otherwise we may just wonder," John was tentative himself knowing Carmel loved her life and travelling east would mean giving so much up.

She sensed this from him, "Don't worry John, it is all going to be okay."

"I seem to remember you saying so a long ago."

"I do too John – like it was yesterday."

In the evening as they sat eating a meal they had both prepared, their conversation reflected on those times three years ago when John had first met Raynie, Jake, and Lyle through a friend of his Jenna. They had just met a mysterious man Chan Lee who reminded them synchronicity can seem unreal at times when suddenly it launches a series of events in life. He had asked them to cross continents and study the waveforms and emotions of elemental geometry as it applied to the intentions arising from authentic human spirit. Dangers had become all too apparent soon enough as their movement in body, mind, and heart, was a strange attractor for those who the Agent now led, and the authorities in seeking knowledge of the Torus of Eternity – an object meant only to reflect awareness and not to be an instrument of affection as the Agent and the authorities saw it to be.

The essence of the learning then and since along with Carmel's personal journey, was the catalyst for activating the torus, then reflected in the technology John was developing for flux conversion of data transmission beyond light speed. This key knowledge he possessed was the most dangerous of all in the present circumstances where humanity was at the verge of incredible new technological possibilities and potential. It was of course the way though for some within humanity to see exploitation and so again they sought to repeat the loop of control but this time in such an advanced concept, people of reasonable dissent against such embellishment would struggle to overcome.

What both of them had learned was not essential to their survival together as it had been separately for each of them up to this time. Chan had discussed the application of self free from control mechanisms of the mind conditioned through societal influences and experiences often in reaction rather than in response. He had described and they had all felt the elemental intentions often delayed due to conditioned suffering, to be more easily attuned when the conditions of some egocentric traits have been permitted to simply slip away without thinking for the moment to be eternally authentic instead of being defined with thought. They all knew definitions were at the foundation of experience, yet he had allowed them each individually to find an easement within and reach conclusions as responses less prone to the errors of reaction.

"Imagine we are already on our journey ahead. We don't really know our destination when we set out, so the travelling itself might determine our plight," Carmel said calmly.

"Yeah, but you said already on our journey."

"Yes we are. See it has begun even with our urges to do something."

"I suppose. So you are saying we leave it up to fate then?"

"Not fate John. We consciously make it happen as we go. The progression will show us what it is we seek. Sure, we have our intentions of doing something but we cannot see precisely what it is perhaps until the time comes and then if we are clearer then the decision may well be clear too. I am thinking of going with our gut feelings even if it seems the wrong thing to do. Often they turn out to be the right things."

"I see your point. We will have to see. We should get going any day now..."

"Why not today? Why not tomorrow? We really don't have to do much."

"It is just the transport thing. Maybe we should go into town and see if we can find something...to give us an idea."

"Let's go now."

Searching around the town was like walking through a ghostly reminder from times long ago. They saw nobody else the entire time and it was haunting to see tools, food, and other things lying about as if everyone had stopped what they were doing and simply vanished. As they looked in buildings, inside the only shop, and around the streets, they managed to gather a few items they thought would be useful, but there was no sign of any transport. During a break to eat and drink, they decided to walk just out of town and look around the few rural properties just a few miles away.

At the second property they at last found something, though it was not what they expected. It was an old horse drawn cart – a relic too of times long past, but this one looked as if it only dated back about fifty years.

"Look," John said wiping dust off the side of the cart with a rag he found. "Horse Drawn Adventures. It was for tourist rides."

"It looks lovely John, but we have no..."

"Horse. We need to find one then, don't we?"

It took them all the rest of the day, and then almost all of the next until they found a horse.

"Frieda, what a lovely name," Carmel said looking at a name tag around the horses' neck. "She must just have been abandoned after the virus attack from the Agent recently."

"Her name means peace."

"Even more lovely John. And she looks peaceful too. Come Frieda."

22

Glad to see a human face after a long time alone, Frieda went immediately to Carmel. "We'll find some hay…"

"I have some," John had looked around the barn and was now holding out a handful of hay as he walked up to Frieda. "Hungry girl? We'll take care of you."

"Come on John, let's get a little hay and take it with us. Then when we have the cart, we'll come back and get more."

"Why not just take her and get the cart?"

"We will. I just thought if we take some, we can feed her again and it will help establish a bond between us."

"Good thinking. I'll get it. You get a bridle. Over there on the hook."

Frieda was roaming about the yard at Carmel's house by the evening as Carmel had the little engine powering at full steam. She felt buoyed by their day as she sounded the whistle every time she passed by on her way to talk to Frieda or give her something to eat. When she had remained outside to pick the last grapes from the vine on the arch, John came outside and joined them. "It's a beautiful evening with the sunset and the few remaining colours in the leaves."

"Yes it is John. I love these times. Over the years I have watched the seasons come and go and they are truly remarkable. I love it so John. I missed it all when I was in the city, working as an officer."

"I know what you mean. I was in Alaska – it was great up there. You know what though, when I found out you were the officer in charge when Raynie and Jake were arrested, it had me in shock for a moment."

"Yes, I did see it in your eyes John. But you quickly came to know the new me…the real me, and it's not too bad is it?"

"Not bad at all. Beautiful in fact."

"Thanks."

When they set out, Frieda was lively and alert as if she was eager to get going. The morning had begun misty and grey, though not a sombre mist, rather a 'mysterious edge' to it mist, as Carmel had said. They had packed what they had found about town, including as much food as possible and Carmel's little steam engine. John didn't even need to ask Frieda to get going once they had seated themselves and looked at each other thinking 'this is it then'. The moment they did this, she was away at a steady pace.

Through the town, the mist did evoke a slightly solemn edge as a shroud swirling on the slight breezes about the ghostly buildings. When they reached the edge of town on a heading east, they stopped to see the dawn sun break through. For a few moments, rays cast lines of light through the cloud before it was gone and they moved on, descending into the foggy valley below.

Carmel sat watching the trees mostly free of leaves, cast their fingers from the misty shadows out over the road, and at times letting go of a leaf sending it falling towards them. She turned and saw the swirling currents of fallen leaves they left in their wake. And she listened for anything – the odd birdcall was the only sound, aside from Frieda and the cartwheels.

John noticed all this too as he felt a sense of ease and yet he was alert. He was enjoying the ride as much as Carmel and together with Frieda, they set out feeling motivated to discover what lay to the east.

"I was walking mostly from San Francisco," John replied to Carmel when she asked how he had made his way to her house. "I had been there about nine months. Before I was further south. I walked along the old main transit lines north – they are pretty straight…and level. I didn't like the tunnels though. No lighting meant all I had were some phosphorous tubes I found before I left, so I took to walking over the hills they went through. There is still five left in my bag. Thought it was best to save them after the first tunnel."

"They are beautiful John. How they seem to emit the glow making it sparkle on the particles in the air. What did you see in the city?"

"Nothing much really. It is a lifeless place. A lot of people are just hanging on. No restaurants, no bars, nothing left of the old character. It just seems to exist – even far less than when the authorities were doing their thing. At least they had something, and it is just seems nothing now."

"It is what the authorities want too John. They want people to become stagnated in a way where they see progression only through status – but I suppose, like you said, it is not so relevant anymore."

"Maybe. You can bet they are working on getting rid of the Agent. It is just too risky though, and he has a hold on them with the viruses. They cannot even try to oppose him with the amplifier. Even their most conventional weapons rely on processors somewhere and he could probably hit them too. They are powerless, more or less."

"It is a bit weird John…powerless, more or less. It is a contradiction. If there is nothing... powerless, than it can neither be more or less John. So perhaps there is a suggestion, though only from you, where power or potential is always there. 'More or less' is acknowledging this as the leading words to the next progression – say an immediate correction."

"Um…yeah, I guess you are right. You get me thinking at times Carmel."

"Oh, it's just conversation John. These are just my thoughts. What happens next is anyone's guess…"

Frieda let out a light whinny and began to slow, "I think she wants a break Carmel. We'll stop just over there beyond the trees."

"We have covered about five miles since leaving town. From what I can recall, it is about another twenty miles to the transit line leading southeast. Once we get there, we need to keep going along the transit line for a while before turning east. I have heard it is not too pretty in the southern end of Nevada and down towards Las Vegas."

"It will take some time John. Those distances and places are much further apart travelling this way. It will be an adventure of sorts and I do like the thrill it has to offer, but…"

"We need to stay alert once we get to the transit line. People live inside them and if they are anything like some I saw on the way to your house, then we need to avoid them."

"Such things have happened in human history before."

"It cannot be all bad though. There are bound to be people who still have their heads up. Progress is human nature too."

"It is. I think I…we are such people, and Frieda such a horse." She was only a few feet away from them, feeding off the grass. Carmel reached into her bag and gave her a piece of carrot when Frieda had walked over to them – her soft nose velvety on her hand. She gave her a pat with the other hand, "Such a lovely nose Frieda."

A few miles on they came across a deserted farm and decided it was best to stay there for the night. Before sunset, they searched around the house, sheds, and barn for the best place to stay. The barn was almost full of old machinery and had no room, so they decided the best place would be in the shed and to stay close by Frieda for the night.

Whilst Carmel was organising some food, John gathered what he could to make a bed for Frieda. He had gathered some old straw he found around the place, some old blankets, and a bucket to put some feed in.

"Here you go Frieda," he said as he finished preparing the bed. She gave a slight sound, as she knew he was speaking to her. When he turned, he saw some old parts and electronics stacked on a shelf against the far wall of the shed.

"How are you going?"

"Good John. I'll get some food. Check out the gear over there. You might find something."

"My thoughts exactly."

"It is mostly parts, so not many complete units here," he called from the shelf. He continued to rummage around to see if there was anything of use, but it all appeared to be in such poor condition or for diverse purpose, he struggled to find anything. When he did see an old alternator and a solenoid, he decided they might come in use. By the time had had picked them up, he knew he was right.

"Carmel, I have an idea."

"What is it John?"

"See this?" he had returned to her side. "It's an alternator, and a solenoid. Now…if I get a light fitting from somewhere around here – the house most likely, then I can make this work, providing it still does work."

"And you can connect it up to my little steam engine?"

"Exactly. We will have a light. Also, if we find anything else to work, we might be able to run it too."

"Fantastic! See my steam engine is already proving its worth to us."

"Indeed. I'll just go and look for a light and come back as soon as I find one."

"Okay John. We can eat when you get back."

He returned about ten minutes later with a few light fittings, a few lamps, and a bag, "I found these so I thought it best we take them all."

"Good idea. You are always thinking well John."

"I've also found this. I had a look through the barn and there are mostly just the big farm machines. They are of no use to us. But this was stashed in a cupboard – it looked really old. It's a bag of coal."

"They stopped burning coal long ago."

"Yeah, so it must have been there at least forty years."

"And we can use it in the steam engine."

"Not all the time though. We need to save it as best we can. As we travel and come across more and more people, fuel will get harder to find. I'll go and get some wood now before it gets dark. We should save the coal – there is plenty of wood around here."

He returned a while later with an armful of wood.

"Here, eat this while you work."

He ate as he worked. He connected the light to the alternator, which also had a wired switch, and then he connected it to the solenoid. The most difficult part was to then attach the solenoid to the drive shaft in the engine and keep it in balance. He tried a few items he found as he went back and forth to the bench against the wall until he found a bracket he was able to fashion into something suitable.

Carmel insisted he stop then and finish his meal before they tried the engine. "I'll get the fire going while you eat. It won't take long. See how beautiful the little door is John? I worked and worked it to bring it up so well, it was very oxidised."

"Mm, it's great."

She lit the fire and then sat back beside him, "It'll be ready in a few minutes, and then you can switch on the light."

When the gauge on the engine indicated it had built up enough steam, John tried the light. "Okay, here goes." He connected the last wire between the solenoid and alternator, and then counted down from three. The light flickered for a few seconds and then as the engine let out a slight hiss, it became stable, and they had steam-powered light.

"It's beautiful John. You are so clever."

"It is, and so are you Carmel."

She couldn't help herself, so she let out a couple of steam whistles – drawing Frieda's attention from the feed bucket.

Their single electric light was the only one for miles in a place cast deeply into darkness where they also found themselves remote and disconnected from others. As the night went on, the stars provided only dim light in a moonless sky. Around them there were no signs of human life - there were just the elements in progression. A faint call from a creature, the sound of water dropping into a puddle, and the slight rustle of breeze amongst the gathered fallen leaves, were the only sounds amidst the silence.

Morning was silent, grey and full of little living. The farm seemed suspended within the tendrils of mist as if it was being drawn out of time and place allowing nothing to thrive.

"You know I think in my ways John."

"Hmm, yes."

"Well our cart has four wheels and so does my steam engine – but they are parts of the engine, not wheels for running along the ground."

"Yes."

"Then together it makes eight. I like eights John. They have no beginning and no end."

"Okay Carmel. How about we eat now? I'm hungry and we should make use of the earliest part of the day."

"Alright then."

Again, they started the day off amongst the mist as they rode out from the farm. Their passage sent leaves into the air fallen from the bare great Oak trees above them as John urged Frieda on. She was in her element expressing this without John really needing to encourage her much at all. Carmel and John laughed as they rode for the entire quarter mile before coming to a stop at the farm gates next to the road they were to take this day. Frieda was billowing clouds of steam into the chilled air from her nose as she stood there catching breath.

Ahead lay a seven-mile journey through the restored forest of sequoia and other pine, before the last leg to the disused transit line. As the road wound its' way around a few small hills and over creek crossings, the forest ahead began to loom larger and larger in their view. It formed a distinct line of tall trees covered in mist as they approached the edge where as they drew nearer, it became a great living thing with energy unique of itself. As it stretched into the distance, to then be lost in the grey, it beckoned them tempting their penetration of its' fringe where the forest soon took over land, sky, and mind.

It was here where they stopped to give Frieda a rest.

Carmel was standing beside the base of a large tree, "They are so beautiful John. All this majesty – you can feel their presence. It's invigorating."

"They are majestic – you are right. I loved spending time in the forests in Alaska, though not as tall as these. But you get a feeling there is so much going on around you, yet it all seems still, and silent, mostly."

"I sense it too John."

Inside the forest where light penetrated only along the course of the road entered and now was a small opening as if they were looking along a tunnel. Carmel noticed how the chill seemed to stop time amongst the trees.

"It's getting pretty dark in here. And the weather looks like it is not really going to lift much. We will need to go slow and take it easy," John suggested.

"Yes, I agree."

The trunks of the sequoias formed a hallway of misty columns as the single road took them deeper into the forest. The density of trees had become so thick it seemed as if they were in a great cavern with a roof high above them lost in the mist and dull light. An owl suddenly flew past very close overhead startling them including Frieda, prompting her to break into a pace for a moment before John was able to calm her down.

"An owl in the day time. I suppose it is dark in here."

"They have been seen as wisdom John."

"Many things have, whether or not it means anything…beautiful though. It was difficult to see with it being white in amongst all this mist."

"Yes and such flowing movement. Maybe people saw the owl as to remind them of wisdom. Anyway, it is a positive thing. They are such beautiful creatures."

As they went on the temperature began to drop even further.

"Gee, it's getting cold John."

"Maybe they are using HAARP again to try for a long winter struggle against the Agent."

"Yes, they have brought long winters."

Within an hour, the mist had given way to a steady wind, and light snow had begun to fall. Overhead, the snowflakes tumbled into view from above, falling between the branches of the trees in a magical sight to Carmel. She had never been in a place like this before and she felt enchanted. The soft caress of each flake as it landed on her face, and some on her tongue felt light and fluffy, melting in an instant. John watched her, fascinated with seeing her encounter snowfall in a forest – something he had experienced many times.

"They even taste magical…well in my imagination John."

"They do…I think we'll stop for a minute, I'll just put a blanket on Frieda to keep her from getting wet."

"How much further do you think? You said it was seven miles though the forest."

"I reckon we are about half way. It has been slow, but we are in no real hurry and we can't risk Frieda too much in this weather."

"She's so lovely. I'll give her a carrot."

"I think we should see what it is like when we get to the edge of the forest on the other side. If this snow sets in even only a little, it will make progress more difficult. At least with cover from the trees, we will not be exposed to the weather out in the fields."

When they reached the edge of the forest, there was three inches of snow on the ground and the rate of snowfall had not increased.

"I still think we stay here for the night. There is only an hour or two of light left. If we stay here, we can set ourselves up well enough for the night during the remaining daylight."

"I agree John. It is the most sensible thing. Frieda needs some cover too."

In a grove amidst the last few trees at the edge of the forest, the light from their small fire glowed softly on the tree trunk pillars surrounding them. They had chosen well as their camp site was surrounded by a wall of trees making for calmer conditions and a degree of security, and John provided them with a roof using a tarpaulin found at the farm. Now they were all asleep together with Frieda very close by as her head lay just at the wheel of the cart where Carmel and John slept.

By morning there was around an inch of new snow meaning they would still be able to continue. Frieda again was enjoying herself as she kicked up clouds of powder snow when John had her at pace. Then he slowed, pulling on the reigns to get her to ease off as they approached a left-hand bend ahead.

As they talked with Frieda at a trot, a feral dog suddenly leaped from the brush growing beside the road and went for Frieda. She immediately reared to a stop and stood as the dog approached growling and snarling. John looked for something to use to break up the situation and grabbed a stick of firewood they had on the cart, to use as a club.

The dog was almost at Frieda by the time he started yelling and threatening it with the stick. It wouldn't back off. He kept going at the dog, and even managed to hit it once when it started jumping around. It attacked him snapping at his lower legs to bring him down, so he jumped, but slipped on some icy snow. The dog immediately went for him, lunging forward, desperate and hungry rearing its teeth behind curled snarling lips, but John rolled over and the dog missed his target. It turned around not willing to give in, and lunged again. This time he was ready and as it came within inches of him, he struck it with the club, sending it yelping and scurrying away with a limp – John had broken one of its legs.

By this time, Carmel had settled Frieda and was holding her bridle and talking to her softly.

"Bloody thing was vicious," was all John could say as he straightened himself out.

"Are you okay?"

"Yeah, nothing bad. Is Frieda alright?"

"Much better. We should go on as there could be other dogs about."

For the remaining miles to the transit line, they were fortunate to see no other life. In fact, the area all around them was silent and white with a grey sky laden with weather and seemingly with a degree of sorrow. No birds, rabbits, deer, or wild dogs crossed their path and they were thankful for not seeing any other people.

"The line will take us down the valley east of Sacramento and then we need to follow it all the way to Bakersfield before we can turn to the east. Then we can stay away from the higher mountains and go for the pass through to Mojave."

"It still seems such a long way John."

"It will take us about a month."

"What about the desert after?"

"I know, but at least it will be winter by then so the temperatures will be down and a lot warmer than the mountains."

Time passed slowly and safely as they travelled the transit link for three days by driving Frieda pulling the cart along the service road built underneath. The tunnel twenty meters above them kept some of the weather away as they encountered rain and snow. Onward they plodded along for three long miserable days without seeing anyone or any buildings.

As time seemed endlessly to drag on, their conversation returned to what the others had done three years before – how they had gone to China, and how John had used flux mechanics.

Carmel had spent many hours alone thinking of those times herself where she came to realise how the time and place for their experiences in China had led them to her and her own subsequent realisations of self. She was enthusiastic in her responses and offered her own thoughts on the matters.

"Their journey was similar to ours and all other people. It was and is one of discovery. Isn't it thrilling? Seeing the thrill behind simple things is feeling in touch, and all else just disappears during those moments. No concerns, no fear, just being alive. I think they were learning to feel this leads to all the rest and to really feel alive is about being alert to all, not just some."

"Like the way the authorities want it to be."

"Yes. They want to hush this feeling so people forget. All the time, money, and efficiency – it all came undone so very fast. Money was…is…um, a tool. It is one of the many things we use. Water is much more essential, but for so long, the water was dirty and full of chemicals."

"It still is in many places I have seen. The Agent has brought a lot of damage to some places. People there live almost in muck, and they go to the city to get water. It is the only place he lets it flow, but it is not much better. Maintenance of plumbing systems is not his thing."

"He has brought so much pain. I think he has a lot more suffering in store to give to people. I saw a look in his eyes...he is a maniac. To him there is no end."

"I can only imagine he is planning worse based on the way his unstable amplifier gives him ideas. My own knowledge of unstable flux is enough to see how the potential of his viruses can undo matter and energy patterns."

"Try not to John. I am trying to avoid imagining such things. It is best we give it none of our energy I think."

"Perhaps some Carmel. It keeps me knowing what he could do and the authorities...for our own good."

Chapter 6

'So small. So small they are to become nothing,' the Agent thought as he worked on cracking the codes required to access the operating controls for the machine. 'With this, I will send them cascading…yes, cascading over the falls of oblivion. They will not be present then as they will never be. Such extermination of self and of soul must be my delivery of their salvation. I am not evil. I toil not with such things. I am just me. There is no issue other than my capacity to fulfil the desires of my amplifier, so starved it is of actualisation. When I have this complete, then I will give it birth and it will arise from conception into reality and so reality shall fall into misconception…and oh, forgetting, thus nothing and all traces shall be so cleanly discarded. Those fools will never break my codes. They will never be allowed to build strength. They will never be allowed to be people – I despise them all. And they will never be anything other than matter sent to nothingness. There will even be no blood to clean for it too will be lost and so their life extinguished. Ah, to be the Agent of…their seduction into destruction.'

He was beginning to show signs of yet more utter contempt and graphically, of a mind on the verge of destruction of itself. Madness was not a rage to him – it was his condition as it had always been since before he was born. For such people do not grow into these things in a life as short as a human life, despite the extra years nanotechnology offered. He was merely an incarnation of this…this madness, incapable of relating at any level to people through the burden of inability to see the elemental life and forces around them in compliment to life, rather than the fashion he saw these energies as dominion over lives. As there were anomalies in space, so too are there in manifest of sentient beings upon the Earth and as such, those anomalies whilst valid in all application, they are created often to interrupt the flow of waveforms.

The latest fluctuations in the amplifier did not trouble him. It was not stability he sought at present – he was looking for a way to get past the machine's defences. Destruction had been continuing and he assisted this by sending subtle behaviour changing viruses to people. He would taint their dexterity a little so as to cause what they saw as accidents. As they lost more, the people also lost care and as buildings became more and more ramshackle, so did their appearances. It was a slow grinding for the Agent but he was content with its pace for anything on his pathway to nowhere was part of the journey. It was ironic in a sense where the Agent did enjoy in his own macabre way, the journey towards an end of no end, for in contrast, many people had been overlooking this for the sake of instant gratifications in the recent years where they missed this journey and this unfolding of reckoning. For the Agent though, his reckoning was besotted with instability like his amplifier.

Times were proving as much more rewarding as he watched the pain and the suffering grow. This was his garden and so he would seed his crops to bear fruit in times of death. And…the equations and sequences were working well. He was making progress each day and even his pathetic minions sensed his mood change as they tended his every command. This also included the former leader of the dark sect who had taught him all he needed to know about making viruses and had foolishly allowed the Agent too much leeway leading to his own downfall and subservience. The man who he had summoned from space to bring his space craft to him, was now out of reach and saw the former sect leader as nothing more than any of the other pathetic minions around him.

It was the Agent's maniac self seeking the aspirations of power and self importance, yet he wanted nothing in recognition, no words, no ceremonies, for his recognition came from the people and the obvious negative effects he was having on them everywhere. Nevertheless he had installed idols – rank machines and buildings lacking in colour and lustre. These idols were not of him, yet they were of him. His presence behind the lack lustre life was enough for those affected to recognise his power as these idols reminded them of constantly.

It was his ungrateful gratitude, the suffering, the pain, and the destruction. Some would cry out in anguish when his viruses touched them, calling him the devil. But he was not the devil - he was nothing of such ways. For the devil wished life for itself, whereas the Agent did not even want such…but he was alive, and so he had to act, otherwise how would he manifest futility?

****

They had found a cave under a rocky outcrop in a field where they could spend the night out of the rain. It had not ceased since they had left the snowline days before. It was soaking them all and the tube overhead had not been sufficient to keep them dry when the winds were blowing. John built a fire at the entrance to the cave and they decided to wait at least a day to see if the rain petered out. They were patient as it was evident they needed to be and Frieda was glad to be dry. After two days of sitting around with her and the cart in the cave, the rain finally began to lift.

"If we can travel well, we should be east of San Francisco by the end of this day," John said looking out at the breaking sky. "The transit we are following takes a southerly route well to the east of the city."

"We will have to be alert John."

"Yes, I know. I am thinking of drifting away from the line and keeping to the foothills of the mountain range. Then we will be as far from the city as possible. There is a major junction of lines to the east and it is bound to have drawn someone."

"But they are not all bad John, as you said."

"It is not a fear thing – there must be others out there like us. It is just a precaution I feel. Also, there are bound to be people just desperately looking for anything...food, and Frieda would make for a lot of eating."

"Then I think it is best we go the other way John. Your feelings are normally correct."

"Who are you?" A voice suddenly came from within the trees. "Where are you going?"

"Who are you?" Come out. We cannot talk to someone we cannot see."

"I won't tell you my name, but I'll talk. I'm not one of those people you know."

"What people?"

"The ones who are appearing around here in growing numbers."

"How many numbers?"

"Dozens...but there will be more. This is just the start."

"Are they danger...hey come out and talk."

The stranger appeared, but was still hiding his lower half of his body behind a tree.

"Well...are they dangerous? You tell me. I've been here for weeks now and as far as I can tell, some are and some aren't. How many have you seen?"

"You are the first. John, I think we can trust him."

"How do you know Carmel?"

"His fear is based on being scared. He doesn't seem like a threat."

"And I'm not. If you want to survive out here, you are going to need to be scared. As I said, it is going to get worse."

"Why do you think so?"

"I just told you."

"No, I mean why do you think it is going to get worse? It might not."

"Look lady, my head is not in the clouds. I have seen a few things not far from here to make you change your mind."

"But if you fear other people, won't you come to realise those fears?"

"I hope not. I'm doing my best to stay alive and it means to stay hiding. I only spoke to you two because for some reason my gut told me you were alright."

"Keep going with your gut, it serves you well."

"All it mostly does is remind me how hungry I am. It is hard getting food around here, and dangerous."

"Then why not move on?"

"Where to? It has to be worse the further south you go. And me, alone? I don't have transport like you. I'm by myself."

Carmel looked at John and he instantly knew what she was thinking. He didn't mind but he looked back at her trying to emphasise they must be cautious. "Would you like to come with us? But only if we can trust you not to steal our things when we sleep. We'll be watching."

"I don't know. I don't know you, or where you are going. I don't want to go south, it's too dangerous."

"Okay, but think about it. It is up to you to choose."

"I'll think but one thing. You had better find somewhere safe for the night. And soon too. There is only a few hours left and you want to make sure you get well out of sight."

"Bye then."

"Good bye."

"He did seem alright," Carmel said when the man disappeared seconds later.

"A bit paranoid to me Carmel, but he was right, it will become more dangerous."

"We will go further east then. To the snow line is a good idea, and then stay with it as much as possible."

They drove on for two more hours before they decided to look for a place to stay the night. They had made good mileage, and could see the snow line in the distance.

"We will be there early tomorrow if we leave at dawn."

"We should leave earlier John. I feel we should. At least an hour or so before the sun comes up. Best if we leave before it gets light."

"Why do you think so Carmel?"

"I don't – I just feel it. That man we saw earlier was right. I could see in his eyes he was telling the truth. It was like they told me without him knowing they were."

"Do my eyes say things I am not actually speaking?"

"Yes. Often. I see thoughts behind your words, and I see feelings when we do simple things. You are most diligent in how you apply yourself John, and this is reflected in your eyes."

"As you are too Carmel. Take your engine for instance."

"I would like to run it again. It has been some time since the first night at the farm. Do you think we could run it tonight John?"

"Maybe. We'll see what it is like where we stay."

As it turned out, they managed to find an old roadside store with a garage out the back where they all huddled together around the small light generated by the steam engine. There were no whistles, or loud hisses of steam – just a gentle chugging for a low light. All three of them could relax more than they had for a while, enjoying the comfort of light and being in a building for the first time after many nights on the road.

When John and Carmel both heard a slight sound as if a person was outside the building, John was not concerned.

"Don't worry. I am sure I know who it is." John went over to the dirty glass window and cleared a section to look through. It was not who he thought.

Immediately his face changed to being very concerned and he quickly withdrew.

"It is a different person to the one we saw earlier. Just wait…"

They heard the person moving along the wall and then saw them try the door handle. It could turn, but John had placed some old furniture against it, so it could not be opened more than an inch or two.

"Open the door. I can see your light. You are taking a big risk with it on. Should have covered the window shouldn't you. Now you've done it. Let me…I want to get in. I haven't seen a light about these parts in years – expect for firelight. Show it to me…go on."

"Who are you and stop being so loud?"

"Just let me in. You'll regret it if you don't. Let me in!"

"Regret what? We don't do anything to regret."

"Let me in. I'll do a deal. You let me in and show me the light, and…give me something to eat and I might think of letting you go."

"How can you stop us?"

"I can. Let me in. I want to see it."

"Look through the window."

"It's dirty…and I want something to eat. You must have food."

John looked at Carmel as he considered what they could do. The person was insistent, but he was not violent yet. He could have smashed the window after trying the door, and fortunately, the large door at the other end of the building had a working lock on the inside.

John decided the window was the best option, "I'll clear a patch for you to look through, and you can have some bread and a vegetable. I…we don't want trouble, but we are prepared to fight if we need to."

"It will be useless if you don't let me see it. I can have many more people here tonight if I tell them what is on offer in this little garage. Show me the light."

"Okay…wait." John picked up the food and took it to the door first, where a hand was waiting. Then he went to the window and cleared one of the small square panes for the stranger to look through before pulling back in case he smashed his way in.

At first they thought they were only seeing part of the stranger's face behind the glass, but it seemed odd. As they looked a little deeper, they could see the man was missing almost a third of his face – actually it was almost missing. The affected portion of his head appeared to be in a state of flux. There was a definite fuzziness and as they looked further, it appeared as though it was gradually collapsing inward upon itself. It startled them. He looked as if he was being slowly sucked into a void appearing to come from the side of his face, yet it did not. Such was his state - the flux would make the void appear and disappear, as his very organic tissue seemed to phase in and out of existence.

Carmel placed her hand over her mouth not hiding a scream, but from shock. The man was so confronting in this state she was unable to take her eyes off him. John was simply staring – knowing what he saw, and knowing where it came from.

"Yeah, take a good look. And get used to it. There are more like me in these parts and not all of them give any hoots about a little light. But it is pretty. And hide the engine – they'll steal it, and some will kill for it. I'm warning you. Lucky I am not one of those real bad ones…I am just tired and this thing. The Agent…I hope I see him wherever I am going. He did this and he'll pay."

"I can help you…" John began.

"No you can't. Nobody can do anything about this. It is too late. I wouldn't trust you anyway."

"I can slow it down."

"How?"

"I have a little tech…"

"Yeah and you could make it worse too. I don't want your help. Save your tech…you will need it. Can I watch it… some more? I don't want to come in though. I feel better out here – more ways to escape."

"Oh sure. Perhaps you could move it a little John so he can see it better?"

John moved the light on its stand closer to the stranger, so he could see it more clearly. There he stayed until they awoke a few hours later and the engine had stopped – the light gone out.

Immediately John went to get a phosphorous stick but Carmel stopped him, "Frieda is still asleep. I think it is okay in here."

The stranger had left as soon as the light had run out.

In the early hours when it was still dark at around four in the morning, though neither of them was carrying a timepiece, they took a gentle walk away from the garage heading towards the snow line a few miles away.

"He was in an unstable state of flux. I have seen it before."

"A result of the vortex amplifier?"

"Yes. The effects are growing…getting more widespread. I saw it first near Seattle almost a year ago. I knew it was the amplifier creating the instability. The virus itself attacks the nanotechnology implants by changing a few sequences in their atomic structure causing the tech to mimic the white blood cells in the body. This overload of natural cells and the nano tech, eventually in a way, necrotizes the tissues. With the instability as well, the integrity of matter is interrupted, so you then so those holes."

"So it begins to rot?"

"Well not actually rot – it consumes itself and looks like rotting in a way. With the unstable flux created by the amplifier, the vortexes inside the cells are also rendered unstable and so the flux state begins to grow. There is no knowing where it could end…if ever."

"Is there really anything you can do John?"

"Very little. Like I said to him, I can slow the growth by stabilising the vortexes for a while."

"And they are progressive so the…"

"Stabilisation effect I render begins to breakdown and become part of the unstable vortex as it is consumed. And the virus is still there, but it too eventually fails. When I am not sure. It might take the whole consumption of the host body to eradicate it. With this, the entire host and virus disappear eventually I presume. I have not seen it in a state any more advanced than what we saw last night as yet. "

"Do you think the Agent knows this?"

"He might…maybe not. I don't think he would care."

"I think you are right there."

Chapter 7

For another day they had travelled with no further encounters. By evening after a few hours of worrying about staying in the open overnight, they found an overgrown ranch farm with a house, barn, and sheds. John did a check of all buildings before giving the all clear for Carmel to bring Frieda in.

Old fixtures and furniture on the inside of the nineteenth century wooden house made it look as if they were in a museum. Everything was covered in a thick layer of dust but was in still in the same place as it had been for almost a hundred years. They were looking for somewhere inside the house to stay as Frieda enjoyed time in the closest horse stable just behind.

"It looks strange John. There is the old architecture, yet it has this modern interior – for the time."

"Around turn of the century I think. There are still some places a bit like this in Alaska, but last time I was there, people had found them and well – it looks as if it has been deserted for a long time."

"There was a time when people were made to leave farm places like these so they could be left to restore naturally. It was as if they saw the interruptions to the ecology and they let it re-align. At least their intentions had some vision then John."

"I suppose people just abandoned places like this with the way things changed at the end of the fossil fuels era. It was also a land grab though. The authorities are never devoid of some other agenda, be it power, money, political favour…re-election."

"It was also the people's fault John. They kept looking to those leaders for guidance instead of listening to themselves. They would complain and hold no trust, yet they did nothing about it."

"Yeah, you can't expect people who seek power, to actually get it right…without strings attached."

"It was a cover John. They used the end of fossil fuels and these ecological restorations as a means to bring in new rules and regulations – like they always have."

"And then we were given more again with the security chip thing three years ago."

"There is a different type of imbalance this time. It is not the destruction of the ecologies so much, it is going within and this is why the nanotechnology is there. It reflects the focus of humans as they look inside, thinking about it and now suffering because of it. There was a lot of selfishness John."

"You're right. They lacked the giving nature you spoke about."

"Yes. Such inward focus often goes against the flow of life in progression. I tried it myself for many years and since I walked away, I have learned these things for myself."

"Well I am glad you are out, otherwise you might have become something going inward against the flow - be it the Agent with those vortexes or the authorities."

"As evidenced by this very thing, this house. Such waste and abandonment. It is not a healthy way to be."

"Yeah, they might have cleaned up the world, they might have cleaned up the efficiencies, but they still didn't clean up their minds."

"Because they are not talking to their hearts John."

"A heart removed from nature, becomes hard."

"I think I don't want to stay in this house John. It is nothing like my house."

"I can feel it too. It is like nothingness, bland and…let's go. I didn't want to clean up any the dust anyway."

They spent the night in the horse stable next to Frieda, deciding they were happier with her after feeling awkward leaving her out of sight. Now as they lay near her, the shuffles and soft sounds she made, comforted them as they fell asleep.

For the next three days, they were forced to stay at the overgrown ranch, due to heavy snow and howling winds. It had come early in the morning after their first night. John had gathered as much old wood he could find as he could sense the change in weather approaching.

"The authorities must be using HAARP and any other parts of the array they built. This weather is too heavy for this low in the valley."

"Yes, the Agent is likely to be the reason. He is strong John, but he is also weak. His is a maniac and it is his weakness."

"It's just he could do a lot of damage – a real lot, in the meantime."

"It concerns me too John. I think he will return here as he will get tired of being in Australia. There is likely no challenge left there for him and his inclinations will see him return here."

"Yeah, I suppose with Australia, he is far from this situation standoff here."

"It is more John. He will never be satisfied…"

"Never be satisfied…?"

"I think until he gets me John."

"Why?"

"I was condescending to him and I could see how much hatred he felt towards me. He is a maniac John, and he will never forget what I did to him. It drives him and whilst he hasn't found me yet, and is doing all sorts of other things, revenge on me is always there in the back of his mind. He will embrace it fully, if he is given the chance."

"Oh, um…"

"Can we have the light please John? I think I want to. It has been so long since I heard my engine whistle."

"Sure Carmel…we can use some of the coal too. Most of the wood is pretty useless anyway."

When the engine was running smoothly on a measured amount of steam, she sounded it once - only once.

Two feet of snow covered the ground on the morning of the third day, but at least the winds had gone. The early hours were a mix of cold and grey, with the soft white blanket of snow lost to the mist over distance. John had taken wood from some of the buildings at the ranch – there was not much, except for some beams and planks he had to strip bare so they did not burn paint. He had spent nearly all of one of the days doing this, and now with the potential passing of the snowstorm, he felt his spirits lift at not having to fetch much more wood.

"If the sun comes out, we might see a bit of melt as these lower altitude storms don't hold the snow for long. We could be out of here tomorrow."

"There is no hurry John, but I am thinking about moving on too."

When the sun did come out and there was sufficient melt to continue as the snow had rapidly decreased to large patches, they left the ranch after having spent five days there in total. It had taken two days for enough snow to melt so they could drive Frieda and the cart.

Other people who were much closer to the ranch than they had known were suddenly upon them before they had travelled two miles. They were riders on horses and stopped to form a line to block their way.

"We don't want your types in these parts," a woman said to them. "Look at you. You are from the city. We don't like city people around here. See your clothes – you are wearing those Geiga clothes. Fancy future suits…it's how I tell you are from the city."

"And you bring all the tech garbage with you. We don't like it either," a man said.

"We aren't from the city and we just wear these because they keep us warm. It's cold out here."

"You must be. It's only city people who come to these parts nowadays. Looking for whatever they can find, trying to survive. Well the technology isn't helping them now is it?"

"We are not from the city. We are hardly from anywhere…"

"You see, vagabonds. Those types who always wander and get into trouble."

"We ought to shoot them now and be done with it," another man said. He began to remove an old combustion weapon from a holster on his horse, and he noticed John watching him. "See. We have weapons. They might not be those fancy modern ones from the city. But, we all knew there would come a day when we would need these – so we saved them and lots of bullets too. You going to leave or what?" He now began to level the gun and point it at John.

"Please put the gun down. My name is Carmel and this is John. We are not a threat to you. We are just travelling…a long way. We only want to pass through. You can keep an eye on us if you like."

"We don't trust anyone but ourselves around here…"

"You can trust us."

The woman who had first spoke was looking at Carmel and felt a sense of ease, much more than her male companions, "Put the gun down, we don't need to shoot them. Look at them, they have a cart at least, and a horse. They might not be too bad."

"We're going to watch you though. No funny business or I'll shoot."

As they drove on, the band of riders kept a horseshoe shape around them with only the way ahead clear.

"You have any of the tech stuff, you know inside you?" The woman asked Carmel as she rode beside her.

"No. John hasn't either."

"Then you're lucky. There are some about these parts who have and it isn't pretty."

"We have been told…and we saw one."

"Lucky for you it was only one. We have seen groups of them – big groups. All wailing and moaning like they were zombies, but they're not. No they're living all right, just a warped way of living."

"The one we saw looked like he was disappearing and fading in and out."

"That's just the least of it. You wait…no you don't want to see what we have seen. They go all twisted and out of shape and the like. Then they start getting bad."

"How bad?" John asked.

"Real bad…hell bad."

"Huh?"

"Yeah, like I said, hell bad. They are not the devil, but they look like they are related."

"How?"

"They get ugly…real ugly. Their faces and their bodies begin to fade in and out so bad each time when they fade back in…well, they get all messed up."

"How messed up?"

"It's like a horror show. Their bodies and insides turn out and around, they look like they are melting in places…yes, melting. But they are still alive. We have seen them haven't we?" All the other riders nodded in agreement.

"They look dam ugly and they still moan and wail – it sounds like a horror show too."

"And they gather together so they can survive," another rider said. "You should see them then. They get all mixed up with each other."

"What?" Carmel asked.

"I reckon is starts because they are in such bad shape, they literally gather together – like a pile of people. It's then they get the runoff – it's what I call it."

"Runoff?"

"Yeah with their bodies melting into those weird shapes, they start to join together. They all get mixed up and there are those holes."

"What holes?"

"Those black ones. You can't see in them and they look bad. All the flesh starts to disappear when it gets to the edge of them. Worst I saw was this woman, young thing, not more than twenty, and she was on the brink. Her face…her eyes were disappearing and going to hell or oblivion or wherever, but she was still alive. The look in her eyes – makes your skin crawl right off you! The look was bad. I hope I never see it again."

"Sounds like the unstable vortexes are not reforming tissue and so it gets worse with each phase."

"Do you know this stuff then. Have you seen it?"

"Only the one man about a week back."

"It's the Agent. He is ruining peoples' lives everywhere," Carmel said.

"Yeah. He is bad but those technology people cannot stop him. All the stuff is their undoing."

"The Agent is undoing."

"You're not bringing it with you?" The entire group suddenly came to a halt and two riders positioned themselves at the front.

"No. I don't have any of it," John answered as the question was directed at him. He was lying of sorts as he was carrying the necessary equipment to still work on flux mechanics, but it was stable and so in part he was telling the truth.

"Maybe we'll check. Have a look you two," he directed two riders to dismount and check through the cart. A minute later they held John's bag open and had pulled the cover off Carmel's engine. "What's this then?"

"Just some gear I have – tools and stuff to help us."

"It doesn't look too much like the other stuff, let him keep it," the woman said.

"You just be careful won't you. No using this stuff to trick us."

"Never."

"So what's with the steam engine? It's a mighty fine piece."

"It's mine. I restored it after I found it in a derelict museum. It's my only thing."

"You did a good job. Does it work?"

"Lovingly."

"Ah, I guess that means good. What else is it for? What are these bits?" He was pointing at the solenoid and the alternator.

"I connect those up so we can run the engine and power the light."

"What do you want a light for? Just use fire, or a candle, and if you are lucky, you might have old kerosene lamps and fuel to run them like we do." He seemed pleased with this.

"Sometimes we can't and we want a light. So we use it."

"You need wood and there isn't much of it around. Fuel is precious see? And the trees, they are wet most of the time now with winter and all, so they are no good."

"We find bits here and there...and we have the coal."

"It won't last. Ha...you must have had some pretty long nights sitting in the dark then?"

"You could say. But not as long as those people you describe..."

This last sentence brought all of them to silence. The riders said nothing and parted to allow them to continue, but still rode in a horseshoe around them.

"So Frieda. Your horse. I can see its nametag. She yours then?"

"Um, well yes. We found her," John replied. "Where we came from, most of the people were suddenly killed by a virus from the Agent. She was hungry and we fed her and she liked us, so I guess she is ours. There was nobody else around for miles."

"You're not a thief are you?"

"No."

"I'm not either," Carmel said.

"How far you driving today?"

"As far as we can. We won't give you any trouble..."

"Yeah, we figured. You best be coming with us today. Our place is another nine miles. We can make it easy in time for you all to settle in."

"Why?"

"Why? We told you all. It's those people you see. They are about these places more than even we know, that's why we go out riding. To make sure they don't get too close."

"Are they worse south of here?"

"Oh yeah, much worse and much uglier. I haven't seen them myself, but I hear from other riders, they are bad. They even said they had seen them eating each other. There is hardly any food but yeah, can you believe it! Now what did he say? Yeah...they looked real desperate, worse than the girl he reckoned. It was like the Agent had turned them mad...insane, and they had turned into scavengers off each other, like they were trying to hold on...or something. He even said he saw one eating some of those melted bits like a wild dog that was crazy with rabies. People can exaggerate – but it won't work though. Anything they eat is infected like them and all they do is make a bigger mess."

Carmel was visibly sickened with what she just heard. Unspeakable horrors were beginning to unfold and they were so much in opposition to how she felt in her own life - and it was because of a person who she had once supervised. John felt sick as well. Not physically…he was thinking about what the Agent was unleashing with his unstable vortex amplifier.

Chapter 8

The Agent watched with macabre interest as he saw people drawn into the maw of their oblivion. It was pleasing to him how those last looks of desperation were so pathetic as he undone their grip on humanity and they fell in to the darkness of futility. He could see their blood and he hated his own. Their flesh torn and distorted as people began to blend into heaving masses of semi-consciousness, bound and to be fraught with the utter despair of irrelevance…of nothingness. And oh, the elegance in his mind of how in their last few seconds as they met their consumed fate – their eyes darting feverously side-to-side, up and down in a desperate plea at the moment of finality. As lives infinite, he was driving them to the finite end and no new beginning, no progression, and no elemental integrity on any level. He was like their atomic undoing as the viruses bombarded themselves with instability and so broke down the vortexes elemental in nature…almost forgotten.

The entire holographic array was alight with these visions of demise as he flew in his spaceship across the Pacific Ocean, higher than any HyperJet. He was flying alone as he always did on these missions, and would be there in a few hours, and so took to watching as he was waiting. His patience with the authorities was fast diminishing, as was his character, if indeed he had any. Their stupid weather manipulations had cost him too much in recent years, and now with his plans to physically destroy cities as well as lives, he had set out to rid himself of the nuisance HAARP array.

He knew where it was – everyone did. It had not been hidden to be kept a secret, but its operations had very much been kept secret. He didn't care for it then and certainly not now. It was a stupid instrument in his mind.

This time, this mission – he felt more confident than ever. They had fought him off previously using schematics they held for his spaceship, making him temporarily lose control before his viruses attacked them. Their HyperJets and mother ship aircraft bases in the sky had been futile deployments on their part, as again he would fire unstable virus weapons to interfere with their controls until the viruses broke down. And so back and forth, the battle had raged for years. His weapon this time was different and he knew they had no counter attack.

As he swung in low over HAARP, he fired a volley of laser pulses, each deflected by the force field the authorities had built over the array - but not entirely. It was designed to fend off attack from the air. They responded with a few bolts of their own, but to no avail. Under the guise of the lasers, he had sprayed the base with his latest weapon, and in no time it would take shape. At two thousand feet he brought the ship to a hover position directly over the array, eager to see it all unfold.

VOLITION

At first, those officers who were stationed around the facility, outside, and in the control room, thought there had been a slight haze in the air accompanied by the electrical burning smell as if the atmosphere was highly charged and about to discharge. Very quickly they realised it was much more. Billions of tiny nano technology bits were coming together to form larger machines. As each one took shape, the personnel could see this happening and so they began to feel an instance of terror inside as they contemplated their immediate fate at the hands of the Agent. Some tried to shoot them with laser pulse rifles, only for the pulses to be consumed by the robots forming in front of their eyes. As they finally manifested into hundreds of small robots each about five inches high, they commenced an attack in unison.

He had programmed them with all the hatred he could in designing their methods of destruction. The first personnel affected were quickly reduced to dust as the robots fired microscopic nano robots onto their bodies and immediately begin changing their very fabric of their existence. At first, it was as if they were being coated in something, but then it developed into a state of flux before seconds later they fell as dust. The nano tech were changing their entire atomic nature almost in an instant, turning them and their weapons into the atoms the Agent had programmed them to become. The unfortunate ones who took a little longer to transform during the heat of the battle, experienced the agony of their bodies changing whilst they were still conscious.

Other robots had been programmed to infiltrate the base and destroy the array. They were already inside before those present could really determine what was happening. Their holographic control panels were disappearing – even the walls were coming down. They were witnessing a quantum level destruction and began to panic and run from the building. For those who placed a foot on, or a hand against something already in flux, they quickly were afflicted with the same condition to then entirely disappear a few seconds later. Any who escaped, were instantly set upon by the robots outside for their atomic transformation.

Then to his insane type of glee, the Agent saw his robots destroy the array before they began to decay due to their own instability. After the passage of ten minutes, it was over and all lay silent. The buildings were gone. The people were gone. The array was gone. And the robots were gone.

But the Agent stayed. He remained there hovering for half an hour as he thought about what else he could whilst he was in the area. He considered playing a few games with Anchorage, but it was not enough. He thought about going east and doing similar, but again, it was not enough. Then he thought about Seattle and decided it was the next place to go. He engaged the thrusters and the spaceship quickly departed the scene. It was equipped with magnetic anti gravity force technology, so his ride was smooth, and very fast.

When he arrived one hour later, he landed at the HyperJet manufacturing plant on the outskirts of the city. It was under his control now and he was welcomed with open arms.

'Pathetic, the lot of you,' he thought as he was led to the main office at the plant, now a control room for his pathetic minions. They took him to their holographic bank where he told them to attend servicing his spacecraft to ensure it was flight ready.

****

"I guess the authorities just did not account for the consequences of their crack down. Such disruptions can let more disruptions in."

"The Agent?"

"Yes John. He is our biggest problem."

"The authorities cannot match him and are only holding on."

"He represents the worst in all and it is human nature to see such things. They have explored this a lot of times John. And you might soon start working John, on something, anything to do against him. The time is coming…"

"Yeah, I know…"

"Hey you two. We have a special night going on here. Come and join us."

"What do you mean a 'special night'?"

"It's party night. We have it once per month. It gets dreary these days, so we do this to keep our spirits up. Come and join us."

They had been offered to stay as long as they wanted with the riders, their families, and friends at the former equestrian centre where they lived. It had been four days now – the weather was clear and the snow had receded to the snowline they had made for days earlier.

"Is there music?" Carmel asked. "I love music."

"And dancing. Come on."

Carmel dragged John up from his seat by the hand and followed the man outside and then to a shed where she could music coming from inside. She had never approached anything like this before. The closest she had come was when she met John at the warehouse with the 'scene' groups – but it had been behind a closed soundproof door. It was alluring as the harmonies and melodies floated outside to her. She could not resist as she picked up her pace dragging John along who was almost at a run so as to not let go of her hand. As they entered, she was again surprised and enchanted. The music was live and being played by a few of the riders who had first met them and the woman was singing.

"Oh my…let's dance."

When they finally took to seats to rest, the man who had invited them in came over with drinks on a tray.

"We do things well around here. Drink madam, drink sir?" They laughed at his play on formality and took their respective drinks. "Watch out, it has a kick."

"What is it?"

"Tennessee whiskey…care of another one of our little stores of things we have here."

"You are prepared for a lot of things."

"We felt we should. It looked bad enough three years ago to make the move here. I'm not from around here myself. I just found this place after I arrived back…early?"

"Yeah?"

"I was on an assignment when the Agent started appearing in strength. I was just back in time. Soon enough my assignment was over and I was cast adrift some, so I came back to Earth. I have no family so I set out to find something, anything or place where I could live. It was bad near the coast, so I went east and here I am. They let me stay…maybe because I'm alright…well they thought so. I do help them a lot and earn my place here. They don't like people who just hang on and do nothing. Most here are pretty smart on what to do to survive."

"Sounds great. Where did you come from?" Carmel asked him.

"Mars. Yeah, I was on Mars when the big trouble started, so I came back here as soon as I could. We were supposed to take two weeks to get back, but he interfered with the ship and we were stuck at Luna One Moon Base for a week. It went into a state of disarray up there on Mars and the Moon too. They still have trouble getting mining materials back from the asteroids but the Moon is not so bad though. I made my way back…it was tough getting flights as authority personnel suddenly cut off from their work, were given nothing. No priority and all the checking. Luckily I was able to wrangle my way through to get back. I reckon it was my years in the service and how you get trained along with the experience where I learned how to get my way in difficult situations."

"Sounds like quite an adventure."

"Um, you could say so. Pretty nerve wracking at times and here I used to be a commander in the military."

"I was once hard too," Carmel said offering out her hand to shake, "I'm Carmel and this is John."

"Hi Carmel. Hi John," he shook their hands each in turn. "I'm Steve. Steve McCray."

"Oh…Carmel Madeline, nice to meet you Steve."

"John Matheson. Nice to meet you too."

"So you were a commander. Didn't they give all in the military identification chips? I was once in the services, but left before it all went down – I still had a chip though..."

"They did, but I had mine removed."

"Yeah me too. How?"

"I searched for ages, almost a year. I tried the city and all along the coast up into Canada. It wasn't until I was in Seattle where I found someone who then directed me onto Vancouver."

"What about viruses then?" Carmel asked.

"No problem for me since I never had the nano tech implants. Yeah...so I found this guy in Vancouver – he was pretty nervous about it. He didn't live there himself, he was like me and a bit of a wanderer at the time. He took it out. Bloody hurt though. Yeah, so now no chip, no nothing."

"Did you get his name?" Carmel was interested and John was thinking the same.

"Yeah. The Fixer I think."

"The Fixture!" they replied in unison.

"Yeah, the Fixture. A good bloke, even if a bit nervous. Do you know of him?"

"We both know him."

"Did he say where he was going?"

"No, he didn't have much of an idea when I asked him. He said he was going to find a valley to hide and he said conditions under the Agent were going to be a lot worse than under the authorities, and he was right. Up there, especially in Seattle, the Agent has taken a lot of strange people under his wing. You know the freakish ones who did weird stuff. They seemed to fit right in with his plans."

"Yeah we know a lot of what he does. They told us about the groups seen near here."

"About twenty five, maybe thirty miles away is the closest of them. I haven't seen any of the real bad ones...fortunately. From what I have been told, they are not something you ever want to see."

"Did he say anything else, the Fixture I mean?"

"Not really. He did say he was looking for some people he knew and then lost contact with them not long after the Agent arrived. I guess he is still looking for them..."

"And us, for him."

"Huh?"

"The Fixture is a good friend of mine, and Carmel...well they were lovers for nearly a year - pretty well up until the time you saw him."

"Yeah, he did mention he had to leave down here and go back to Vancouver in a hurry. Didn't say what for though."

"Probably the flux mechanics. It is very sought after. I worked on it for a time with him before we were separated."

"Is it how you know him, with those mechanics?"

"Well yes, and more."

"So you are looking for him. Where will you go?"

"East, but we need to go south first and take the lower pass through the mountains to Mojave."

"Oh, I wouldn't be going there. From what I was told by someone who recently returned from the area, it is not worth going any further south than Fresno – after there it gets real bad. I mean bad, hell bad, from what he said."

"Hell bad. We've heard it before."

"Well, it's right. I suggest you wait here for a few months until the worst of winter is over. Maybe then you can take a mountain pass closer by. There is no way you can get through sooner either. It is still a mess around Tahoe after the detonation three years ago. There isn't even any of those people there I believe, nothing. I suggest you try the river though to Yosemite, but you have to wait for winter to finish."

"And you Steve? Are you going to stay here?"

"Me? No, I could be coming with you…in a way."

"What?"

"Well, if you wait until winter is over, you can travel with us. All of us here…at this centre, are all planning on going through the mountains in spring. Less population on the other side means less trouble. It is going to get worse around here as soon as the weather lifts. We are too close to Oakland and San Francisco. The cities will drive them out here, as their conditions get worse, and people will want to survive, um, those who are able to and don't have those holes in them. This is where they will come. You wait and see…no, actually don't. You are best to leave as soon as spring thaw allows it or maybe sooner."

"How sooner?"

"I forgot to mention. There are people attached to this centre who are out looking for any machines we can get running…"

"So you can plough your way through the snow?"

"Yeah. Let's hope they find one, or more, and fuel as they are bound to be old. Getting a few weeks ahead of the pack, so to speak, will only increase our chances too."

"Do you think it will get real bad Steve?"

"Sure do Carmel." They fell silent for a moment. "How about another drink? Let your hair down for a bit. I bet it has been ages since you did it last."

"Sure has Steve, sure has."

As Steve went to get three more drinks, Carmel asked John, "How come it is taking so long for the people to get to these 'bad' conditions? The Agent has been at work for years now."

"I suppose it is the unstable vortexes. They are only small fluctuations so maybe they take a long time to manifest to a size where they increase and grow faster and faster. Plus, the viruses he has unleashed in the past year, are much worse than when he started."

"I do wonder John, how he became so good at making viruses. He seemed such a bland person when I knew him – only capable of hate I thought. He was not a good operative."

"There have likely been others around him to teach him. I suppose he had nowhere to go once he came back to Earth and so he joined them, and it looks like he was smart enough to overtake whoever it was in charge at the time. Once you get a feeling for making viruses, it is not too difficult afterwards to make more…new ones."

"Here we go. I'm just going over there for a bit. We'll talk later no doubt."

"Yes Steve…and thanks."

"No problem."

He left them to sit by themselves, but it was not long before they were up dancing again – perhaps it was the alcohol, but regardless, Carmel loved to dance.

By around two in the morning, all had gone quiet at the centre – their party for the month was over. Carmel and John had decided to see how Frieda was doing before they went to bed. As they walked along the path in shadows beneath the large oaks, Carmel felt a sudden chill. She didn't say anything to John and she knew it was not the air. It was a different kind of chill.

"Oh there you are Frieda," she said keen to change her thoughts and feelings when they arrived at her stable. "Nice and warm girl?"

Chapter 9

Winter conditions began to ease back to the normal climatic fluctuations of the season now the Agent had destroyed the array in Alaska. The snow line had receded up into the hills in only a few days, making conditions warmer for Frieda and the others. Whilst in a way this was welcomed, with it came the risk of the Agent's minions being able to continue with more of their destruction and make incursions into areas previously impassable due to snow.

From further north in Washington State, it was precisely what he instructed them to do. The Agent was determined to destroy as much of the west coast as possible this time, and then…amongst the rubble he would make it take shape in his way. He was tired with attending to the needs of the high-rise and across the outer buildings in the cities. He had grown impatient with their fumbling and pathetic struggles. He would not kill them all, but he would ensure they were entirely his – in service to his desires and his sick taste for suffering.

Without warning, he suddenly made for his spaceship and took off. Some hours later, he had arrived back in Australia and then set about dismantling the beast of three torus – his vortex amplifier. They had made a special box for him to place it in with soft linings and a secure lid. And when he had done all he wanted, with the amplifier stowed inside his ship, he departed for his new headquarters back in Seattle at the HyperJet factory, along with a small group of passengers.

Immediately when he returned, he barked instructions to those who were present. He ordered them around almost as if he was a commander in the services, yet he was really the superior of none – it was just those minions who aligned themselves with his ways, simply reacted to each command in servitude… mostly from fear. By the time he had made it back inside of the control room, he had decided to build another arsenal of nano robots for a destructive attack on San Francisco.

"Get me all the information on whatever remains of the authorities in this area," he said to one of them as he swept his hand over a holographic map of the entire west coast. "I want numbers and installations from here to San Diego. Don't overlook anything."

There was no verbal response – they barely ever gave him one. Rather, they simply followed his commands with only a nod in acknowledgement of them. Some would take to giving a slight bow, and although he hated them and saw them as pathetic, some part of his megalomania had begun to depend on this, and soon, they would all have to bow.

****

As Steve walked up the main entrance to the equestrian centre, he was suddenly confronted with Carmel riding Frieda. Such was their bond, the horse had taken to the saddle without an issue and now Carmel was out exploring the place after the snows had all melted.

"Hi Carmel. Nice ride?"

"Oh yes. A lovely ride thanks Steve. Say Steve?"

"Yes?"

"It was nice speaking with you the other night."

"And you."

"I am wondering what plans the group here has once they get through the mountains?"

"I'm not entirely sure – it is a lot of wait and see what conditions are like. There is no news of anything further east, except the rough divide between the authorities and the Agent."

"I feel there is a lot more trouble in those parts than most of us think. I have been riding and thinking there will be a mix of those who are supporting the Agent, and those who wander aimlessly, looking for something...anything. They will bring out even the worst in our group Steve."

"How do you mean Carmel?"

"People who get desperate, either in looking for something or protecting something, can lose sight of why they are doing it. Rage takes over. It is a primordial thing Steve. We need to be careful of this and be able to see it coming."

"Oh I see," Steve was a little baffled by Carmel's words, but he did get the gist of what she was saying. "Um, where's John?"

"John is in the main shed, working on his own little bits and pieces now, after he finished repairs to the snow-damaged roof. Go and see him if you like. He would surely love to chat."

"Okay. I might do so. I'll see you later Carmel, when we all have dinner together."

"Alright Steve, see you then. Bye." Carmel rode on, but only at a walking pace as she continued to carefully consider whatever thoughts and feelings came to her. She stopped a short while later - remaining astride of Frieda, to gaze out across the valley from a small hill. It seemed still and quiet with only the odd faint birdcall to be heard. She felt all was not what it appeared to be, and could sense a growing tension in the valley although they were the only group for miles. Then, in the furthest distance about eight miles away, she noticed a flock of birds rise from behind a hill and fly east towards her, and a minute later, a thin wisp of black smoke appeared from where the birds must have taken off.

Over dinner two hours later, there was a general meeting for everybody at the equestrian centre. Others had seen the same black smoke as Carmel, and this was the topic for discussion.

"We don't have anything to plough snow with, it will be too tough in the mountains."

"But the smoke. It is a bad sign. We should leave now."

"It might just be something small. There's no telling from this distance what it could have been. From what I saw, it could have been at the old produce distribution depot – maybe something there just went bad and caught on fire."

"But there was a disturbance," Carmel said. "The birds did suddenly take to flight as if they had been spooked."

"An explosion?"

"I didn't hear one."

"Me neither."

"Perhaps something fell and knocked something else starting the fire, and this scared them off?"

"We cannot be sure, but either way, we do need to respond to this. We cannot just sit here and wait for them to arrive, whoever it might be."

"I think we should go. It is obvious we are not going to find any machines nearby to help us, but we might if we leave now and go through places we have not searched as we get higher into the mountains."

"We could organise a scout party to go ahead of us," Steve McCray said.

"A good idea Steve. Then we can get advice of any machines they find, and if there are any of those people about."

"What about sending some riders out to look around just before first light tomorrow?"

The entire group was silent for a minute or so whilst they considered this option. It would mean staying a little longer to check the scene of the fire, or leave as an entire group at first light and not look back.

"I say we send them out, but also prepare to leave. When they report back, we will at least have a clearer idea on what or who it is."

They all took a vote and decided to go with the idea of sending riders out – just three, and then preparing to leave upon their return.

"One thing though. I suggest the riders leave in the middle of the dark morning hours. If it was at the old depot, then it is at least a sixteen-mile return trip from here. They can ride by kerosene lantern light until it gets to daytime."

Around three in the morning, each of the three riders were fixing lantern holders on the saddles of their horses so the light would shine over the horse's head creating a small glow of about ten feet in front of them. Then, as they rode out, everyone else was busy packing belongings and essentials into their own carts, and those without a cart put theirs into packs for their horses to carry.

There were seven wagons and five riders, who each had an extra horse now saddled with two large packs hanging either side of its back.

Eight miles out from the equestrian centre just outside the perimeter of the depot, three riders could see a type of machine they had never seen before. It appeared to be a collection of different machines and odd parts, and was painted all over in a dull black finish. It looked a bit absurd and ungainly but they remained cautious.

"I think we have enough. Obviously it is responsible – there are charred remains of something not far from where it is now. We should go." The other two agreed.

They rode off then leaving the machine to blend into the darkness. After two miles with the first light of the day now adding to their lanterns, they suddenly heard the machine behind them. They had been unaware it was following until it was within one hundred yards. This time red lights at the front were on, styling it in such a way it appeared to have eyes and horns.

Instantly the riders broke into a gallop, but the machine continued to follow them and gain ground. On they rode at pace, their horses panting loudly and beginning to sweat but the vehicle kept coming, remaining about fifty yards behind.

"We should lead it away from the centre," one of the riders shouted as they came to a fork in the road. They took the left turn to ride along the floor of the valley – the machine still came. They galloped on, but it remained at fifty yards behind, not closing and not falling back either. Still they rode for at least another mile, and still the machine was there silently following. It was obvious it was trying to get them to lead it to where they had come from, but the men knew this and were willing to keep leading it away. Another left turn, leading away from the side of the valley where the centre was. Then another and they were now effectively doubling back to where they had first seen the machine.

Unfortunately for them, the driver could see this was happening, and through with the chase, engaged the weapons array by firing two laser pulses twice. The first struck and vaporised two of the riders who were close to each other. The second pulse focused on the third and remaining rider obliterating him and his steed in a second. The driver then brought the machine to a stop and considered the course the riders had taken him over the past ten minutes. Turning around, he had decided to back track and take the opposite direction at the first left turn.

When the machine arrived at the equestrian centre, everyone had left. The group had decided to leave when they saw the laser pulse lights for an instant. They had a head start of fifteen minutes and were taking an old dirt track through the forest behind the centre on a heading straight into the hills. Their head start then extended to twenty-five minutes as the machine spent time surveying the centre looking for anyone to kill.

"Quick, bring these old trees down and block the trail," a man shouted as he directed to three others who had fallen back from the main group to delay the pursuit. "This might slow it down for a few minutes."

They felled three old trees and then rode on.

The machine came in silence floating a couple of feet above the ground. It reached the fallen trees and only stopped for twenty seconds as it blasted the tree trunks to oblivion. It was catching them, and now they were only one and half miles ahead.

"Set these and wait," John said giving two other men a small package each – he held a third package. "They are explosives I made. Gunpowder mostly. This might stop them." The two others were a little surprised to see what John had made.

"Go!" he yelled and they went about setting the explosives in shallow holes in a group on the trail. Then all three of them retired to some trees to hide and wait. They saw it coming, so they lit the fuses – the old burning type smelling of black powder. It was now a game of timing and they watched hoping the machine would be in the right place at the right time. They could see the small fuses glowing orange in the early light, burning their way towards the explosive packs.

John realised he had made accurate calculations as he watched it begin. When the machine reached the place where the explosives were buried, all three bombs almost went off in unison with only a one second gap separated the first two and the third. The machine came to a stop but with no visible signs of damage. It was however, unable to proceed as the explosives had damaged its vulnerable underside. John and the other two, immediately then raced to their tethered horses and rode off in pursuit of the main group.

"We were able to stop the machine," John said when he and the other two riders caught up with the lead riders of the group. "But there will be others and no doubt they can communicate to each other."

"What shall we do then if they catch up to us?" another man asked.

"We cannot let it happen. All we have are a few explosive packs left and some guns. They will be no match for more than one of them."

"Should we split into two or three groups?"

"It might be a good idea, but they will send more machines and so likely they will track all groups. No. I think we should stay together and keep pressing on into the mountains."

"We could become trapped," the lead rider said.

"We are going to have to take the risk. Surely even above the snowline, we could find a trail still passable at reasonable speed. Those machines won't be too fast. They only just fit on this trail. Any wider and they would be hitting the pines. But…we need the lead scout group to leave now. Three riders together."

They had already chosen who was to be in the scout group, so the lead rider indicated they should go on ahead with a wave of his arm.

The group continued on eager to put as much distant between them and the stationary machine. It sat still where it had come to a halt, but was now resting on the ground with its sole occupant seated inside. He was waiting for others to arrive after directing them to his position and advising of a potential larger target moving ahead.

A strange effect was beginning to take hold on the location where the now motionless machine sat waiting. As the winter sun caressed a pale sky, it would normally encourage signs of life in places below the snow line, but here it was absent as if the machine itself cast a sombre presence of dread chasing away all signs of living. The usual hub of life living just below the snow line was absent and the scene for a hundred yards around was silent.

Three hours after the incident, two other machines stopped on the trail to the rear and all three drivers were discussing their options.

"We cannot just destroy it, the Agent will hate it. He wants results and he wants us to capture anyone we can so they can join him. If we get this lot, then he might see us favourably. We could use their animals for food – even horse meat has to taste better than the crap we have been eating lately. I suggest we blast some trees so we can get your two machines around, and then continue to follow them along this trail."

"What if they take another trail?"

"Follow them there too. Their horses are going to leave marks for us to follow and they won't be stopping to cover their tracks. We have them scared. I'll ride with you," he said pointing at one of the drivers. "You blast the trees now," he said to the other. Both of them did what he said, and within five minutes they had cleared a passage around the stationary machine. "We'll come back for it when we can."

Fifteen miles ahead of them, the group was still on the same trail as the machines. There had been no other trails branching off, so they had continued along the same way as fast as possible.

"We need to find somewhere to get off this trail. I wonder where those scouts are?"

"There! Look!" One of the riders was pointing to a gap in the trees where they could see the trail about half a mile ahead on a ridge.

"Everyone, pick up your pace for a bit if you can. We need to meet those riders as soon as we can."

The riders had seen the group as well and had met them halfway between.

"See anything?"

"Yes. There is an old farm about five miles ahead. We checked it out and found a vehicle and some fuel cells. The vehicle looks pretty dirty though and will need some work to get going. And the fuel cells might need some refurbishing."

"Okay everyone," the lead rider said. "Five miles as fast as we can. When we get there, only John and Steve will go in. If those machines catch up today, they will go through the place...literally. We need to outsmart them..."

"Shouldn't be too difficult..." someone shouted.

"Yeah. They are probably not so smart, but they have machines with laser weapons...and communications. The remainder of us are to continue. If we see a fork on this trail, we take the right turn and keep climbing into the mountains. The others will catch up."

"It's in the shed," one of the scout riders said pointing it out to them. "We are going to keep going and find somewhere for the night."

John was going over the vehicle checking it for damage. It appeared to be in reasonable shape, despite it being a large utility he estimated to be about fifty years old. He rubbed a small section on its side, "F350," he said. "Right, I'll check the engine while you check the cells Steve."

"It's good in one way how these places were just abandoned. Who would have thought back then, these cells and the light truck would come into use all these years later."

John had been trying to clean the electric engine which had not run in so long. He was thinking it was likely to be inoperative and seized but after another hour he managed to clean it up as much as he possibly could. His next job was to restore the electrical fuel cells Steve had piled up next to the vehicle.

"I found what looks like a metal sheet we could use for a snow plough. It must be – look at those fittings on the front there." Steve pointed at what looked like mounting brackets.

"Okay, here we go," John said as he crossed the ignition wires – there was no key to be found. The engine didn't do anything aside from a few clicks.

"Oh shit – the starter must be dead. I filled it but it looks like it is a no go." He thought for a moment. "I know." He went to his bag that he had taken with them and removed a small energy cell he used to work on flux mechanics. "If I can connect this and modulate the output to match the voltage for the starter then it might work." He quickly set about doing this and was finished within a couple of minutes.

"Right this time." He crossed the wires again and started it but only a few slow turnovers of the engine sounded. "Well, at least it sounds like it is not seized...pray tell me how it isn't. These things needed regular running to keep them going. Okay, another try." This time it was a little better, but the engine would not start.

On the fourth try, the engine turned over and then stopped, so John tried it again. It coughed and let out a bang, and then it slowly wound up. John gave it a rev and it wound up some more. "It's not going at full idle speed yet, but this will have to do. Maybe it will get better while we are driving."

A minute later, John engaged the accelerator. "Alright, hang on."

They drove out of the shed and left the farm as fast as they could. The engine did gradually warm up and soon began to run better though still rough. As they exited the property, John swung the steering wheel hard to the left as they set off to catch the others.

By this time, the machines were only a few miles behind, and the vehicle John and the others were driving, suddenly appeared on their holographic sensors. They could see it was not too far ahead so they increased their speed as much as possible along the wooded trail.

John had a plan. He knew their pursuers would not be far behind and the silent machines could be on them before anyone in their group realised. Also, as it was the only trail so far, there was no means of escape along this single route.

"We are going to start a wildfire. Here's what we do." He pulled the light truck to a stop. "I'm going to make a few more of those explosives. Get some fuel and start soaking it over the trees either side of us. When I have finished making these explosives, we need to set them one on the trail and two either side of us."

Steve set about splashing some liquid fuel he had found as they were leaving the old farm, on the trees, whilst John made the three explosives from gunpowder he had been given at the equestrian centre.

"Lucky you lot have been so prepared – those bullets and gunpowder are coming in use. Without them we wouldn't have many options."

A few minutes later John was setting them under an inch of soil on the trail – the others did the same at the base of trees Steve and the others had splashed with fuel.

"Well, no time like the present. Drive up there about fifty yards. After we light the fuses, we run to the truck and get out of here."

A minute later both men were sprinting towards the truck as the fuses reached their end. Three small explosions rocked the scene, immediately setting the forest alight and bringing down a few of the pine trees lining the trail. When they had jumped in the back of the truck, they looked back to see a fiery barrage across the trail and extending into the forest.

"It will hold them up for a while," Steve said. "Hit the accelerator John, we need to catch up to the group."

Ahead of them, the main group had seen the fire erupt from the trees and they hoped it did not mean the demise of their companions. Their fears then were quickly waylaid as the truck appeared around a corner a few hundred yards behind them. All felt a sense of relief at both the men's survival and the appearance of the truck itself – meaning there was now a better chance ahead as they pushed on towards the snow.

"They won't stop for long, as they have lasers and will clear a path around the fire. It just means we get some extra time. So we need to keep pushing on," John told the group the moment the truck had caught up to them.

Just then the three scout riders also returned from yet another advanced scouting ride. "We have seen the trail split into three a mile or so ahead. It is good for us – so long as we choose the right trail to take."

"We won't know until we take it," one man said.

"Again it is another chance we take on getting out of here."

At the triple intersection, they decided to take the middle trail, hoping it would lead them higher. The left side looked to traverse the mountainside and they assumed the right side trail would be similar – just in the opposite direction. Before they moved on, the lead rider instructed a couple of horses to go down both the left and right trails to make some tracks as a decoy.

John took the lead role once again, "Double back but keep to the trees beyond the verge. Make it look like tracks only going one way. It will make them think for a few minutes. And make some dummy cart wheel tracks too – use the spares on those two carts over there. Then hurry back on the verge and throw them in the truck. John, you and the others following in the truck, need to make a bit of a mess as we go and cover our real tracks. Grab some broken branches and old growth and spread it over the trail as you go. It might make them think it is an old disused path and may again help us get a little time."

Their plan had worked. The two machines were indeed stopped by the wildfire now extending about sixty yards either side of the trail. They decided to focus laser fire from both vehicles together to clear a trail around, but it would take them at least twenty minutes to clear enough for the machines to move on.

The group ahead had their horses almost at a gallop going as fast as they could push them, with the truck at the rear. Fortunately they had chosen the correct trail as it continued to wind its way uphill, and then it met another, wider trail looking like it once may have been a better road as there were broken bits of tar seal in many places.

"This is good," the lead rider said as the decoy trail riders arrived back with the main group. "We can make better time and distance on this solid surface now there is snow about in patches. As we go on, it will get thicker until there is a consistent cover. Those trails will be muddy and very slow."

By the time the machines had cleared a path around the wildfire and had arrived at the triple intersection, they had gained a considerable amount of time and distance. The machine drivers had also fallen for their decoy and had taken the right trail, thinking the group would not have taken the way directly ahead as it looked overgrown and strewn with debris and would slow them down. And despite tracks leading off to the left, it looked as though the main group was going right as they could see a few different cartwheel marks.

"They won't fool us. They went right, those tracks on the left are a decoy to try and slow us down." Such was the relatively low state of alertness of those in service to the Agent, they failed to consider all the options as the group ahead had considered.

When the group had travelled three miles along the partly sealed road, the scout riders again returned to them – they were now going slower to give the horses some respite.

"There is an abandoned settlement ahead. We should stop there for a while and figure out what we are going to do. The snow is more consistent from there on and the road will need to be cleared as we go."

"Did you see anyone at the settlement?"

"Not as far as we could tell, but they could be hiding. We still need to be very cautious."

By the time the entire group had reached the small settlement of half a dozen houses and a few farms, they decided they would spend the night there as it was only a couple of hours until dusk.

The pursuers had taken the right trail but quickly discovered it was a decoy as the wheel tracks suddenly disappeared, leaving only horseshoe marks continuing on. "Damn it! Double back. We need to take the middle trail." They reversed each machine back to the intersection, as there was not enough room either side of the trail turn them around. When they had made it there, they cleared the debris on the trail and quickly discovered the tracks left behind by the group.

By the time they had reached the broken tar seal road, the day had turned to dusk. "Keep going until we find them, even if it takes us all night," their leader said to them - the driver who had first lost his vehicle.

The group at the settlement were all located at the one farm property on the fringe of the village and could see the lights of the machines slowly winding along the road a few miles distant.

"It is going to be a standoff – we are going to have to fight," John said as they discussed their options. "Take the women and children, and the horses into the barn over there. Get all the weapons we have and all the gunpowder. We'll need them. If they catch us there will be no more use for it ahead, so we might as well give it our best shot now."

Steve had a plan for the coming assault. "First we set up some barricades using anything we find suitable – wood, metal, wire...anything. While you men do this, John can make us some handy little bombs we can throw. But he also needs to make a few packages we can set in the ground with fuses as well. This is where the barricades come into it. We need to narrow the access into this place. After, we fall back and locate ourselves in a broad semi-circle around there where we want to stop them." He pointed to a place a hundred yards away where the path into the farm went between some rocky outcrops. "If we can hold them up there, we can open fire with guns and the bombs John makes."

"What if they get through?"

"Then it is open warfare – we are going to have to do our best to defeat them. I know it sounds bad, but if we don't, they will kill us or try to make us a minion of the Agent. Find some places where we can hide and fire at them from. Make sure they are good too – those laser weapons can have a devastating effect."

"What about if they check the town first, can't we get them there and save them getting close to the majority of us?"

"I thought about it, but I think by channelling them in here, we can have our best shot at taking them out for good. So let's get to it. I reckon on them being here within an hour, even if they check the town first."

The first mistake their pursuers had made was to keep this chase for themselves and not advise anyone else. They had foolishly decided this was going to be their prize and it would be seen well by the Agent. And yet, foolishly they did not realise the Agent would not have done this even if they had been successful at any time.

Their second mistake was to look around the village for the group. There was simply no room amongst the houses for them all to hide with horses and carts. And their third mistake was to underestimate the force they were about to encounter.

John had been cunning making the hand held bombs. He had fashioned a dozen hand grenades with fuses and they were affective at halting the machines. He had told the men to aim for the underside of the machines where they were exposed to damage, as the upper side looked like carbon nano fibre and would repel the small bombs.

The planted explosives had missed their mark – going off behind the machines as they entered the property. When their machines eventually came to a halt from the barrage of grenades, their drivers emerged – each of them in a rage. Such was their state, two of them failed to focus on their own strategies and despite having laser pulse rifles, they were no match for the group of determined men using weapons of times long passed. Steve took a run and rolled a grenade under the two machines. He sprinted away before seconds later, both machines were lifted a little off the ground - the explosion underneath rendering their driving gear useless.

Covering him the entire time, were the other men with rifles rapidly firing bullets. Under their barrage of fire, he was able to achieve this upper hand relying on his tactical skills from years in the service and the sheer determination of those men who brought two of the drivers down. It was not a killing for they acted in defence, yet those men took none of it lightly despite the situation being a fight for life. By the downturned looks on their faces, any victory was not at all apparent on their hearts.

The leader took a different approach as soon as he was out of his machine. He had been sneaky enough to avoid the volley of gunshot and had successfully made his way around the men by first doubling back, and then taking a wide route towards the barn.

When he arrived there, he found it undefended and could hear noises coming from inside. Carefully he picked his way through the piles of old derelict machinery at the rear of the barn towards a small door. When he burst inside, unleashing laser pulses, he injured three people before they really knew what was happening.

The men outside heard the commotion and rushed back to defend the barn. The intruder looked frantically for cover and unable to find any, he seized Carmel as a hostage. It was a standoff. The men stood, their guns at the ready watching him, looking for any opportunity to take him down.

"Don't make a move or she gets it."

"You are not going to get away from here alive," one of the men said.

"Oh yes I am and I am taking her with me. Now lower your weapons unless you want to see her dead."

They had no option – his laser weapon was held against her ribs. Slowly he stepped backward aiming for the small door he had entered through. He went through the door dragging Carmel with him and immediately pushed her onto the ground. Some of the men rushed to the exit, whilst the others went back outside and around the barn to cut him off. The intruder was surrounded and became agitated realising his situation.

"I'll kill you! I'm not going to leave this place empty handed."

"Why are you doing this?" Carmel asked him from her position on the ground.

"None of your business. You'll soon see the darkness of oblivion when the Agent takes over…"

"But he already has."

"Not enough for him. He is never satisfied. Now shut up and get up!" He looked around for options and decided on cover behind an old machine about twenty yards from the barn.

John was watching and he saw Carmel being pushed along, the laser rifle stuck in her ribs. "Let her go," he shouted.

"No way. She's my ticket out of here. Don't move or I'll kill her."

When he made it to the machine, Carmel slipped and began to fell. This destabilised the intruder and his rifle went off, striking her in the leg. Immediately she fell to the ground in agony.

"Screw you!" John yelled and charged towards them.

"Watch out John!"

The intruder steadied himself and fired, but he was off target and the laser pulse struck the side of the barn. John was in a rage and kept coming. He tackled the intruder then set upon him. He didn't shoot - instead he began a fistfight. First he struck the intruder in the head with a decent punch, but the intruder was half ready and was able to fight back using his rifle as a club. He struck John in the torso, causing him to bend over with the pain, but only for a second. John fought back and knocked the intruder over. This was all he needed as he set upon him again and lay a volley of punches into the intruder. He kept punching him – he had him pinned down. On and on and on, John kept punching, his rage growing. He felt as if he would teach this intruder a lesson and make him pay for the suffering he had brought as a minion of the Agent and injuring Carmel.

By the time had could punch no more, the intruder lay there, his face bloodied and swollen. Not satisfied, John picked up his fallen laser weapon and fired twice, killing the intruder.

John turned to look at Carmel, who was being helped by some of the others. He was seething and angry, his chest heaving and his rage barely subsided. "Screw the lot of them," he yelled and turned back to the intruder firing again into his dead body. When at last he did calm down, he dropped the laser weapon and went inside where the others had taken Carmel.

She lay on a bed of straw with a large gaping burn in her right leg, "How is she? Will she live?"

"It looks bad John, but I think if we treat this wound, she will make it."

"Man, you gave it to him," Steve said. "Quite a fit of rage there."

"Yeah, I've bloody had enough. Those bastards are everywhere and it is time they began to pay. I'll take revenge on any of them for this."

Carmel's eyes turned to look at John - they were not eyes of pain, but of sadness. Although John had saved her and she was grateful, she was upset at his rage, and his temper. 'It makes him look beastly,' she thought. Then she passed out.

Chapter 10

The group decided to stay at the farm for at least the next week to provide enough rest and recovery time for those who had been injured. For the first few days, John was going through the broken machines looking for any technology they could use for themselves. He was still in somewhat of a rage – the injury to Carmel and his tiredness of running from the Agent, fuelling him. He was not seeing what was apparent before his very eyes. His rage and anger was blocking his vision, both in sight and in heart.

"John?" Carmel had surprised him.

"What are you doing out here Carmel?"

"It's okay John, I can walk with the help of this crutch one of the men made for me today. What are you doing?"

"Just going over these machines to see if there are any parts we could salvage."

"You still look angry John."

"Yeah you could have been dead. And I am sick of this running. It has been years now."

"But I am here. He didn't kill me."

"Thankfully. I don't what I would have done if he had killed you."

"John…you need to calm down."

"I can't calm down Carmel. All this seemingly endless struggle. Constantly moving on, constantly keeping out of sight. All these years…and the violence now with the Agent. It was not as bad when the authorities were in charge."

"It was as bad John, you were just seeing it differently. It was a challenge to you then, only now does it seem like a struggle."

"It was a struggle then. But you are right in a way – it was more like a challenge. It was as if I was being called…called to do something to help people and to actually live. Now it seems just a case of survival. Everything is gone…"

"What about Chris, your son? You helped to have the implants removed."

"But he is still with the authorities."

"At least he is not subject to the viruses from the Agent."

"True. But it is not so different. He is still far from me and far from living. It is as if he…we, are existing and not really living."

"It does appear so John. We are not often living as the people we thought we were and we are being subjected to things making us spend our time where we would rather be somewhere else."

"It makes me angry Carmel. I am getting tired and angry. Angry with the running. Angry with those people I am close to being threatened or disappearing all together. Angry at not having my place to live where I can choose what I will do on any given day to make a real contribution to the world. Sometimes I just want to rage and fight it all…destroy it all so I…we can live. It is like my life is not my own and I am just a pawn in the playing out of this game. I even question why I bother at times. It might be easier to just give in, be ignorant."

"But it is not your way John. You are not such a person to give in. You have always stood up for your way, your feelings about life."

"And look where it gets me - constant struggle and nil return. It seems futile. Look at me, at us. We are fleeing the tyranny of the Agent just to get closer to the tyranny of the authorities and there is no end in sight, no objective, other than survival. We are at the mercy of those few who play these games to control people."

"It is not entirely as such John. Sure, you see many people who give in and just become part of the game those players play. They want to forget the struggle to survive and just take it easy. You are not like them. We are not like them. You are a beautiful soul John. Please don't let anger and rage take the place of what is truly in your heart. You are a leader too, it is just you do not see yourself this way. Your struggle is one in oppressive times. Many times humanity has been led away from oppression by people like you. Individuals who care enough to do what they can, in their own way, to make changes. And unfortunately, many of those changes get slapped in the face because they do not suit the agenda of others. Don't let yourself slip away to this anger and rage. Remember who you always are and be that person. It does not matter if many don't see this. You know inside you are doing the right thing – it is your way, and your intentions are are key here. Never lose sight of it John. People and things may fall by the way side and at times you may struggle and it can look as if everything is against you, and us, and this is the time where you must draw upon your inner strength and not lose sight of yourself. If you do, then those who oppose you, oppose your ways, will win and all this will be in vain."

"I know what you are saying Carmel, but I feel as if it will be anyway and they will win. My work is insignificant…even with the flux mechanics, because one day someone else will do it, or do it better and so I am nothing…"

"It is never the case John…ever. You can never be nothing. You can never be insignificant, despite what you may think being small and they are big. Be relative to yourself and focus on this as your centre. It does not matter what anyone thinks…even if some person says your work is no good. Their view is for them. Your view is for you. They are no more correct for you than yourself. If you believe, you will create."

"But I feel so angry. Often I feel as if I just should not bother and I may as well be dead myself…for all the difference it will make. People will still carry on. Chris will be alright…after a while. It's not like he thinks much about me anyway."

"You may be very mistaken there John. Chris is your son and children never forget who their parents are, despite distance or time. And you should never consider yourself better off dead. You have life and it is so much more than most people on this planet care to think about. They are consumed and have been for so many years. This latest consumer thing…the authorities and the Agent, is the manifestation of this, and of the inwardness prevalent through consumption. Don't be too inward John."

"Yeah…um…"

"You said to me not so long ago you were glad I had left the authorities because I might have ended up as something resulting from all this inwardness."

"I remember."

"Yes, do remember John. Whatever comes along and however down about it you may feel, there is always you, the elemental you and the intentions in your heart."

"You are right Carmel. You do get me thinking at times."

"You said so before too."

They both laughed for a moment in recollection of this.

"And one other thing. Why don't you look at these machines in a different way? Perhaps you can see something you can build from them. I did notice you seemed to be guided a bit by your rage tearing them apart."

"You may be right. I was looking at it as salvage and out of desperation. Maybe if I approach it with the idea of building something new."

"Of course you can. You always have and you always will John."

"Thanks Carmel. Can I help you get back to the barn?"

"No, it's okay. I think my leg needs to work a little anyway."

"Well, I should get to work on building something."

"Yes... sounds like a good idea."

John busied himself over the next hour or more, realising the letting go of his anger as he looked for components to build something. He was a little amazed at how he had lost control of himself a few days earlier and since, considering the degree of focus he could hold. As he exercised his mind drawing upon knowledge he used to assess the components, he could feel this direction of energy help him realise the errors of his anger and how much Carmel meant to him in assisting his reckoning of self during these difficult times.

"So, how did you go John?"

"You were right Carmel. I was looking at it the wrong way. I have come up with an idea I would like to discuss with the whole group and see if they agree."

"Okay John. You make me happy," Carmel said this smiling as she realised the look of release from anger in John's eyes. "Can I ask something?"

"Sure, ask away."

"Can we use the light? I am happier now and I want to run it."

"I think it is a good idea Carmel. Sort of reflects our breakthroughs. How is your leg?"

"It is feeling good."

"What about the burn?"

"I have some antiseptic cream. Mostly it is to keep it clean and free of infection."

Later as everyone was situated in the barn talking, they all sat together in kerosene lantern light at the fringes with the steam powered light at the centre. John was about to gain everyone's attention, but Carmel took charge letting of a few steam whistles to quickly bring a hush over them all.

"I have been going through those machines we have acquired from those who pursued us, and I have some good news - thanks to Carmel." John said as he gave her a quick glance and smile. "Thanks to her, I have looked at what we can do with the machines and I have decided there are some options ahead for us by using them. As you probably know, each one individually is pretty useless, as our little bombs have rendered them un-drivable. Instead of just stripping them for parts, I have come up with a plan to re-build a machine."

"But they are all damaged underneath in the same way. What can you do?" someone asked.

"I am going to reconfigure some of the parts and add some to the truck we have acquired. This means we will be able to run the truck using the fuel cells from the machines. I am also going to use other parts and make a machine to use as a scanner so we can detect any other people or machines in our vicinity. This trek to the east is our only way to avoid the legions of people who follow the Agent, and we must keep going, otherwise we may as well give up now and just subject ourselves to his motives. And I for one am never one to give up – neither are any of you by the impressions I get."

Five days passed by as John worked on converting the fuel cells for use in the truck, and as he built a scanner device to alert the group to any presence of technology. On the morning of the final day the group had decided to remain at the farm, he was happy to have been successful as he tested and demonstrated both the truck operability and the scanner, to them all gathered together. Carmel stood watching him, pleased how far he had progressed from his rage, and she admired his strength and confidence as he detailed his achievements. Notably, she thanked him for his grace and humbleness in acknowledging the help he had received from others during this time.

When it came time to depart and continue their journey east, John and Carmel were once again in the cart with Frieda at the front. It made obvious sense for the entire group to continue with scout riders and for the truck to lead them along whichever path they took, clearing away snow as they went.

Winter was now taking a grip on the mountainous terrain and they would require the truck to clear snow almost all day as they travelled through the deserted regions of both the Sierra Nevada ranges, and then onward towards the Rocky Mountains further to the east.

"We need to stay south of the Tahoe region, as there is still too much residual contamination from the explosion three years ago," Steve McCray said as the entire group stood together ready to depart.

"What about going further south?" one man asked.

"We are going to have to stay as northward as possible," another replied. "There are too many of the Agent's people combing the south looking for people and anything else they can use. With less snow and warmer conditions, they are still fairly mobile."

"We need to skirt as close as we can around the south edge of the affected area surrounding Tahoe, and then head north-east again towards Utah," Steve added. "Let's just hope the Agent has not been able to make use of the facilities around Salt Lake City and Denver. I am sure they would have been sealed off and a lot of the technology removed before they were forced east, but you can never be sure. If the Agent gets hold of anything from those underground installations, everyone could be in for a hell of a time."

"Why Steve?"

"The technology developed there was the cutting edge machines they were using back when they tried the identification chip. Robots, military vehicles, and jets, you name it, and it probably came from the installations near Denver and Salt Lake City."

"So it is north-east then, through Utah. At least we will have some easy going through Nevada…"

"Isn't there still a lot of damage from Carson all the way through Reno?"

"Yes, but as they used delimitated weapons back then, we are safe by keeping just out of the affected zone. We'll follow the circumference and take a north-east heading as soon as safely possible."

"Is everyone clear on our heading?" Steve asked addressing the entire group. Everyone acknowledged. "Let's go then."

Carmel gave John a soft look. She was not holding any fear but she knew the danger ahead would come. She was not looking earnestly at him for protection though she knew he was of the mind to protect the three of them. And she was not feeling any sense of desolation despite the lack of living and the running they were doing – her house held appeal, but she knew this appeal was for another time as she felt compelled to be with John and Frieda and the others, and do something to help change the circumstances for so many under the Agent who she had failed to reprimand sufficiently in her former life.

He returned her smile – they were friends of personal confidence and both felt at ease to share their own resolutions as he did now with a look of determination in his eyes.

Chapter 11

It could never be enough to simply meander about commanding people to do as he wished – he desired to affect his minions so they would reveal their fear to him. He could not sustain his desires based on mere compliance, as this failed to feed his hunger for his type of power. The Agent had ordered them to gather information and now as they reported back to him, his impatience took hold.

"I told you I want numbers and I mean more than just who or what is out there. How many people have been brought into my service? How many have you destroyed? Basically none. And now I get this pathetic report of a group of less than thirty heading up into the mountains going east. What relevance do they have to me, unless they are either dead or in my service?"

"They fought against us…"

"Many do. It makes no difference."

"They defeated our people and they have use of our machines."

"What machines?"

"Some damaged personnel transporters."

"Then we must pursue them and take back what is ours, as well as take them. Who are they?"

"A group of travellers with horse and carts, and an old automobile they use to clear snow."

"And we…you fools were defeated by these people!"

"They had weapons and explosives…"

"Where are they now? How long ago was this failure?"

"Somewhere north of Yosemite I am told. It happened two weeks ago."

"Then I am going there…now, alone. I don't need any useless minion like yourself or those others who fail me."

The Agent ran to his waiting space ship and immediately took off such was his impatience. As he arced out across Seattle, he admired the dour look of the city, and especially how gloomy the central high rise was, painted in a matte black finish. He could see people below on the streets and they looked glum to him, something he found pleasing. The entire city looked downcast without any sense of vibrancy, and it was precisely how he wanted it to be. Inside the pressurised cabin, there was barely any effect as he accelerated to ten percent power - enough to take him to California within fifteen minutes.

It was imperative he find this group as soon as possible, as something inside his maniacal state was sensing both urgency and elation. This for the Agent was not the joyous feeling of genuine elation at a beautiful apparition or positive injection into life. It was more of his macabre sense of power mongering. He could feel it though, as it was impossible to be entirely devoid of any feeling, for the human body is of such construct where some in the least has to occur at some operational level. His feelings drew upon his foundation of anger and hatred, and so his response was a reflection of this inner turmoil.

The area to search was provided to him and he set co-ordinates for the mountains south towards Yosemite. Snow was everywhere as winter had now set in as he set holographic scanners to maximum. They would be unaffected by the snow or any weather. He would have them soon enough, and then he would realise why he felt as he did at this time.

This unknowing was exciting to him this time as it presented a situation not common enough for his distaste. Too often he had grown bored – administration was not really his thing and so to command was not in his interests. It was more of a realising his mania requiring him to act and make plans. This time he felt some type of experience similar to an emotional drive. Normally he would just be plagued with hatred punctuated by manic urges for power. Now it was different as there was something fascinating, some intrigue, and whilst his impatience normally demanded any uncertainty to be erased as soon as possible, he had the notion of a chase and pursuit entering his mind.

As he piloted the ship in a low altitude trajectory over the foothills of the mountains with its scanners running at full, he began to touch a place in his mind he cared not to venture very often, if at all. Then it struck him, causing him to sit as upright as he could in the pilot seat.

He recalled the feelings he had when chasing those dissidents into Reno years ago when he was an Agent of the authorities. How he had captured them and he had felt similar when taking them back to the facility near San Francisco. Not since then, had he felt this way. Many times over the years since, he had subjected many people to arduous torture, taken lives, and dispensed horrific computer viruses into injected nano technology using his unstable vortex amplifier, but none of it was like how he had felt then and how he felt now. There was no way he could precisely pinpoint why, and there was no causation from the information he had about those he was seeking alluding to any clue as to their identities. But there was definitely something different and he wanted it. He wanted to relish in its outcome, for his intentions were malicious, and he could feel the ever-present hunger require satiation through acts of malice and observation of suffering.

After an hour of searching he was not irate, he was not losing control, nor was he randomly carrying out destruction based on frustration. He was continuing on methodically without hindrance from ill spent angst or feelings of deviousness. It was as if he held himself in character almost respectable in a strange way – a way entirely rare to him for most of his life to date except when he first joined the authority ranks and showed his keen youthful exuberance. It was then he knew of the path he currently travelled – the way into the ranks was not the beginning for him as one might regard in circumspect the Agent's way as having begun before his birth as a deliberate catalyst of nemesis. There was a regal air about him, a sense of upmanship and of astuteness – traits normally so very distant to his meandering states of megalomania. He continued on carefully plotting the search areas and setting the co-ordinates in the holographic scanner.

After a little more searching, he came across a collection of farmhouses in a small village and his scanner sensors lit up in an array of positive results. They told him there were machines amongst the buildings below, so he entered a request to provide more than just the details of their presence. The results came through an instant later and he immediately knew he was on the right path and closing in on those he sought.

'So you think you are clever using my machines to build something for yourselves to use on your pathetic escape,' he thought as he observed the scanner results. 'We will see who is clever and who is submissive very soon.'

He felt a surge not of gravity or acceleration, but of a sensibility to embrace chaos in a state not thinking contempt but merely acting. This positive result brought him out of this calm collectiveness some. Holographic readouts told him there was a trail leading east away from the village, and deeper into the mountains without any other trails leading off the main trail for many miles. It was simple to him. He would follow this trail and even if the group had travelled and taken another trail, he knew he would be closing in on them.

John observed the presence of the Agent's ship on the scanner device he had built and then turned it off. The truck was clearing snow for the entire party of travellers and their horse drawn vehicles were making good progress despite the depth of snow as they crossed the mountains north of the Yosemite region. He could see the space ship twenty miles behind them and he knew it would be the Agent.

Everyone on Earth was aware of the fact he had stolen the ship many years before and had returned to Earth from Mars. Many had witnessed his attempts at coercion with the authorities when he arrived back, before he was mysteriously drawn away and disappeared. Then everyone knew of his resurrection and the calamity he brought upon the Earth using his craft to travel wherever he wanted as he released viruses to create hurt and pain whenever he chose.

Now John was very worried as he was realising their worst fears coming into being. Many years ago he had learned from Chan Lee of the power fear has to attract instances into one's life based on such fears. But now with the conditions imposed by the Agent and the state of chaos and anarchy in most nations across the globe, it was difficult to remain entirely free from fear. There was so much imposition wrought into so many lives with the regular instances of horror from the Agent along with the restrictions and fighting against him from the authorities, the Earth had become a place where people were driven by fear, driven by compliance, and driven by dependency and need.

He told Carmel the Agent was near and asked her to call out to those travelling ahead for the group to find somewhere and assess their situation. She immediately passed on the request without any of the fear she saw on John's face, and the word soon carried to the front of the group. The scout riders were sent ahead and within ten minutes they returned to advise there was an old camping ground where they could stop less than a mile away. Another ten minutes passed by the time the entire group were stopped and gathered in a tight circle amongst the stands of tall Sequoia pines.

"The Agent is nearly here," John told them. "We need you Steve. Work out a strategy whilst the rest of us prepare for him."

"We still have some incendiary devices we made but I am not sure they will do anything against his space ship," Steve replied. "We are going to have to rely on tactics alone this time."

"Keep some handy though. Knowing him, he will be alone and armed with a pulse rifle. If we can draw him away from the ship, then we stand a chance."

"Do you think he will let it happen? He is most likely just to blast this place."

"Yes, but work out a strategy. He will need to do a lot of blasting if we are in small groups."

Steve set to work on devising a strategy based on the terrain they were located within. The camping area was beside a small river mostly iced over and covered in snow, with the tall pines throughout. Their only choice would be to stow the wagons and take the horses with them for a trek through the snow to various locations scattered in proximity to the camping ground.

"We need to hide the truck. If we make it past this situation, we are going to still need it to clear snow. The Agent is sure to just destroy it as soon as he detects its presence and location."

"I thought so," John replied. "I'll deactivate all the energy cells on board and establish a resonance field around each of them as I hide them around here. Then he will get an approximate reading but there will be no definitive or precise location on each. We can hide the truck under some snow and fallen branches and I'll set up a similar resonance field. Hopefully, this means he will have a wide area to cover if he wants to randomly blast away giving us time to move on in the least. It would be no good to leave it all behind, but our lives are worth saving in priority over any of the technology we have."

"What about my steam engine?" Carmel asked.

"We'll have to stow it too. It should be okay as it will only show up on his scanners as a metallic object should he actually detect it. We can't take it with us…yet. But we can come back for it."

Steve had finished mapping out a strategy by this time and he went about directing all in the group to re-locate in various surrounding areas – all within a mile of the camping ground.

"We meet back about half a mile back down the road we came on to get here. But I want you three," he said pointing to three men standing as a group. "Come back here and assess the area then wait for us to return. Hopefully there will be something left for us to return to."

The Agent was close now. He had scanned ahead and saw there was a fresh track through the snow recently cleared. His scanners had faint readings of technology in the vicinity, but no definite leads or details showed on the holographic array. A few moments later, he began to see life sign readings in several areas scattered through the forest up ahead. Whilst his pleasure at being so close was evident to him, he was put off by there being so many tall trees in the area preventing him from a clear view to the ground. He liked to see his pray when he hunted. He liked to watch their efforts to escape, and he thought it marvellous how at the last moment before he killed or captured them when they would look frantically for the last futile means of avoiding him.

Within minutes he was upon the campground, hovering just above the treetops. He could see the evidence of their recent presence by the many tracks in the snow. But nobody or no thing was evident. His scanners showed faint technology readings in various locations around the area, but these did not really concern him. He cared not for seizing the technology they had stolen from him. He cared for seizing them in the least, should he decide they were worth more to him alive than dead.

Frustration began to take a hold. There was nothing in view he could terrorise or destroy and his patience receded in rapid succession as more indefinite readings came from below. He had to do something, so he blasted some of the trees around the campground and they erupted into fire. This quickly became a blaze and was not a good decision for his motives as the heat from the rapidly growing wildfire began to interrupt any clarity in his readouts - in-turn fuelling more of the mania state within him.

"Screw them," he said aloud to himself. "I'll fish them out." He took the craft to five hundred feet and fired a volley of laser pulses into the trees in a broad circle, causing them to alight and join in a growing fire.

For some on the ground the fire immediately became a concern as it was quite close to their hiding positions. But as it was with the trees being mostly older specimens, they had no lower branches and so the fire failed to make it down to ground level, instead leaping from treetop to treetop.

There was nothing they could do to escape, as the Agent would detect them on scanner the moment they headed away from the fire in any direction. So they just waited, avoiding any burning wood falling from above.

After ten minutes of firing the Agent stopped and surveyed the scene below him. He decided he would land the craft and so fired a concentrated volley of laser fire into the campground, obliterating any of the remaining trees to clear enough space for landing. As he gently touched down inside the ring of burning trees still standing on the perimeter of the cleared area, he armed himself with a laser pulse rifle and prepared to look around.

His sense still alluded to some degree of fascination and he felt determined to find out precisely why. It was obvious the group had split up as he could see various tracks leading away from the location in different directions. Without any sense of hesitation, he chose one of the sets of tracks and followed them beneath the fire and onward into the forest. After about twenty yards, his portable scanner told him there was something underneath the snow just a few yards away, so he fired at it until he finally saw a small explosion erupt from beneath. He had destroyed a fuel cell. Continuing on, his sense of anticipation grew and this puzzled him for a moment as he was really not sure on why this would be happening. Another fifty yards and it felt stronger.

John and Carmel were holding Frieda behind a boulder they had fortunately come across in the forest. They could see the Agent barely thirty yards away and almost held their breath, not daring to make a sound. But it was Frieda who gave them away with a slight whinny.

The Agent turned but could not see them. He followed the sound and approached the boulder where they were still standing on the other side. Before he could realise what was happening, John had rushed him, tackling him onto the snow. John punched and wrestled with him as they both struggled to gain the upper hand. With a large swinging punch he knocked the Agent down, and then gave him a few more punches to try to knock him out, but he failed.

Although he was unable to get up, the Agent was still conscious and from his position on the ground, he could see John leading a woman away with a horse in tow. When the woman turned to briefly glance back at him, the Agent was almost overcome with exultation. He immediately recognised Carmel as his former Superior Officer. Immediately he struggled to get to his feet and as he did so, he realised John had taken his rifle and so he was unarmed. But oh, to see his former superior, the one person he had vowed to extract all he could in revenge. To see her mere yards away from him was enough for him to overcome his immediate setback. He had found her and he now knew why he had felt they way he had on the chase leading up to this time.

"I'll get you. You will not escape me…ever," he shouted after them. Then he turned and hurried back to his space ship, determined more than ever to catch his prey.

Fortunately, the other small groups had witnessed his landing and his trail into the forest, and whilst he was gone, they had gathered contrary to previous agreement, and were busily uncovering their wagons and hitching their horses. By the time the Agent had arrived back at the campground after stumbling the few hundred yards back to his ship, they had mostly gone, with only one pair left who were trying as best they could to leave the scene.

When they had finally hitched their horse and started on their way, the Agent was back inside and sent a laser pulse after them, obliterating them in a second. His mind was primarily on the capture of his former superior and this momentary distraction was just a part of the swelling rage inside him. With a swift movement, he motioned for the craft to rise above the trees and head in the direction he thought Carmel and John had taken.

John and Carmel had actually doubled back, feeling confident such a simple ploy would be sufficient to avoid the Agent, at least for a few minutes. They were right. As they uncovered the last of the fuel cells and were hitching Frieda up to the cart, they could see him a few hundred yards distant, firing laser canons in rapid succession and heading away from them. By the time they set off, the Agent was nearly half a mile away, searching frantically.

They quickly caught up to the other groups who had gathered together on the trail beside the river.

"We will have to come back for the truck if the Agent does not destroy it. Steve, I suggest you lead the group on whilst Carmel and I take another route along this more narrow trail here. It looks like an old hiking path, but I am sure our cart will fit. Fortunately the snow is much thinner on this path due to the overhead cover from the trees. It should help us. He is after us first and foremost – I could see it in his eyes…"

"He recognised me," Carmel added.

"I know. You others need to be vigilant. He will not give up easily. Consider there may be no turning back either and we may have to abandon the truck, but I hope not. I have a little plan to buy enough time to go back and get it. Here, take these fuel cells and re-install them." John handed the cells to one of the men who had helped install them back at the village.

"Steve, do what you can and we will re-join this trail as soon as possible. Carry those old maps we found back at the village and stay on the trail as far as possible. Then we know your heading."

The Agent was getting nowhere. He had not seen Carmel again and was growing tired of retaining some element of composure. So bereft of logic and sense when his mania took hold, he began blindly firing all around him. Simple reasoning associated with assessing the situation was absent as his hatred for his former superior reined over his senses.

Now John and Carmel were moving off in the opposite direction along a narrow trail making it hard to see them from the air. They knew the spacecraft had sensors on board for detecting them, so John was busily working to circumvent this as Carmel drove Frieda. He was building a resonance device to mask their location by sending out a scrambling signal to confuse the Agent. His sensors would detect them in various non-specific locations and John thought this would at least buy them more time to escape. And now, with the light of the day fading, the Agent would have to rely only on his scanner outputs to make any headway on their location. When after an hour of travelling without any direct sign of the Agent, other than some distant explosive sounds, they came across an old stone bridge crossing the same meandering river running alongside the trail further back at the camping ground. The view overhead was almost entirely obscured by overlapping tree branches, and so they both agreed this would make a good place to stay the night. John immediately set about clearing a space for the three of them underneath where they could remain hidden. Carmel stayed with Frieda just holding her bridle and making calming sounds. Frieda made a few soft sounds in response and nuzzled Carmel with her velvety nose.

"Oh John, you've done such a good job to make us a dry place in all this snow."

"Frieda can lie down on the tarpaulin and we can have a small fire if we really need to. I'll park the wagon just a little to the left under those trees. He won't see it there."

The Agent was now furious. He had been ever so close to capturing his former superior and now all seemed to be going wrong. He had almost exhausted the energy banks for the laser canons, resulting in a large forest fire. Unsure of what to do next, he hovered a hundred feet above the forest, as the sunset gave way to the first stars of the night. He had tried to circle the area a few times to carry out scans searching for human life signs, but nothing had shown up. In one instance he saw something, but the signal was so faint, he decided against pursuing it, as he was certain they could not have made the seven miles distant the reading showed. With a burst of expletives, he turned the craft on a sweeping arc and headed to Oakland where he could stay the night and re-charge the energy banks. He had not given up the chase, as he would spend most of the night planning and having bouts of absurd behaviour before returning to the forest as the sun rose the following morning.

Chapter 12

The eastern sector beyond the dividing fence was the main centre for combating the influences of the Agent on Earth. Most nations were now divided into sectors due to the influx of the Agent. Scientists from across the globe had gathered in this eastern region to work together on developing anti viruses to gain the upper hand, and restore their sense of order. To this time, there had been barely any success, with only a few advances over some of the minor viruses he had sent out using the vortex amplifier. Their systems were running at limited capacity in order to isolate them from attack, so they were unable to control a lot of the aspects of life for the populations who were located within their administration.

Whilst those in office and their associates lived almost entirely free of the Agent, many people still suffered the horrors of the viruses sent to affect their injected nanotechnology. Many called for the authorities to help them by removing the tiny robots, but the authorities were unwilling to assist, as it would expose their systems to the Agent. In growing numbers, people began to experience the horrific effects as parts of their self were being lost to the ugly oblivion brought on by the Agent. With an increasing state of paranoia, the authorities had no compassion for those afflicted so badly and anyone with viruses was banished to the western sector.

It was during the transportation of a large group of people from the east to the western sector, when Tobias Engelmann thought he recognised someone he knew. He was watching from a window in his small house near Omaha Nebraska as the transport unloaded just inside the boundary dividing an entire continent. He could see the looks on the faces of those to be sent into no man's land. At the fringe just inside the fence, it was safe for people like him who had none of the technology the authorities had forced upon people. Very few people came to or wanted to live in these towns and other places due to proximity to the western sector. Tobias and the few others about the small town were able to choose at will where they wanted to live. Life was relatively untroubled unless someone came looting or there was an incident at the gate. He was glad to leave the chaos of the larger cities and so he lived a normal existence getting by any way he could. He could do work here and there based on the requirements of the authorities needing someone to repair a device or machine, and he also took on a little gardening growing food. This is why looters would come calling. Material goods unless they were useful, were of no value. Food and water were of the highest value – everybody needed them and wanted them. Those who went hungry and thirsty soon began to feel these ravages as they joined the ranks of virus afflicted people on a slow path to death. Tobias kept a very close eye on both food and water ensuring he was never in danger of running out or of having them stolen.

His small house was away from the high-rise in Omaha but it was not far enough to stop those people from the city who saw the fringes as easy targets. Their struggle in the towers was worse Tobias thought. He could not imagine being confined in these times of survival so far above locked away and slowly dying in the cold grey blandness. Their lives had become meaningless and at least with his survival out here, Tobias could draw some purpose from each day...some purpose to his self.

Tobias could hardly believe what he saw on the faces of those who were being sent away. The looks of desperation in their eyes, gave way to the maws of vortexes on their bodies, as their very being receded into oblivion. He had avoided seeing these times during the many previous transportations in the past, but on this day, he was drawn to the process. When he looked harder at the person he thought he recognised, he saw it was a guard who had detained him at the facility near San Francisco eight years before. As the guard was quickly ushered past him towards the large metal gates blocking the roadway ahead, Tobias turned away in disgust at the spectacle. Officers herded the people with laser rifles using the rifle butts to strike the heads of those not moving fast enough. As the gates opened, several people from the western sector rushed through – they had almost made it and were past the security systems. For a second or two the escapees were confused seeing their path ahead was blocked by the oncoming group. At the last, they went left and right of the group only then to have an officer shoot them dead. After mercilessly shoving the people through the gates, there was a long groan and then a crash as the gates then closed behind them.

Tobias could hear their screams and pleas. He was very unsettled and wondered why he had chosen to see this, as he had never done so previously. He struggled internally himself at the sheer horror of the sights and the looks on the faces of those being sent away, and he knew this would resonate with him through time.

He fixed himself a hot drink and sat down alone to contemplate his feelings. His life had become one of survival, and even with a sense of purpose through survival, it was not enough. He remembered days long ago when he would enjoy the openness of the wild, the sparkling waters of San Francisco Bay, and the social times by the wharves.

'Where would Asper be?' he had thought many times 'I wonder if she is still alive.'

He had fallen in love with Asper Carter during the time they had eluded the authorities and when they had escaped the facility. They had spent some time together, until the day came where he never saw her again.

While he sat there, a news broadcast began to show on his holographic projector, "The authorities advise there has been a recent breakthrough in the fight against viruses from the Agent. Recent developments in technology have enabled us to take another step towards eradicating the potential threat from the Agent. Members of the public are advised systems will soon be brought on-line for servicing nanotechnology. You will be able to rely on the authorities to provide the protection you need."

Tobias wondered what the developments in technology could be as the last he knew of the most effective way to counteract the Agent's viruses was through the use of balanced flux mechanics. He had discussed this with John during their last contact over a year previously where John had told him the authorities still had not been able to glean any information about flux mechanics from him.

'I wonder if they have caught up with John?' he thought. His last meeting was a hurried affair, where they had talked over a beer - something increasingly difficult to obtain. John had told him he was going west to find The Fixture and Carmel. Neither Tobias nor John, had been in contact with the couple for well over a year prior to their brief chat, and they had both speculated on their whereabouts and their lives.

'Could I go and find them? It will be risky.' He speculated on this for a moment, wondering if there was any sense to even giving it consideration, and after a while decided there would be almost no leads to go by other than Carmel's house north of San Francisco if it was still there.

Tobias knew the conditions in the western sector were bad. Aside from the regular propaganda style reports issued by the authorities, he knew enough to see the devastation the Agent would have wrought upon the people, places, and the way of life in general. He had now seen it written across the faces of those being transported today. For many their faces met an end to nowhere, and so Tobias decided a journey to the west, may well be the same.

His mind turned to the others he had met three years ago when the authorities first began their clamp down on civil liberties. He had not seen Lorraine, Raynie, Jake, Jenna, or Lyle for nearly the entire time. In fact, he had only seen Asper and Lorraine since their escape from the facility and the dreaded robot chasing them along the transit way.

He felt sad as he loved the others as friends and had grown close to them during those times. Since their parting he had felt this way often at first, but it had tapered off a little as the years passed by. He had absolutely no knowledge of their location or if they were alive, so his sadness deepened as he sat there alone in the ramshackle house.

To him, at least he had his spirit and his way of endurance. Despite the hardships and tribulations of the recent years, his times of sadness often ended with his recollection of his inner strengths, and so they would lift him so as to not keep his feelings and his head down. Being solemn had never been his way, even though he would often be seen as the quieter one who seemed to be at the fringe of a group. Tobias was an observer, a thinker, and a feeler, and so whilst he was silent, he always took careful note of what was happening and how it made him feel.

After the news bulletin had ended, the projector went back to the entertainment program it has been previously showing – a rather shallow episode featuring a dramatisation of life better lived with the authorities as providers. They had largely continued on with this motive since the breakdown of the identification and security agreement between nations in the short time after the year twenty eighty eight. Two years later, the Earth was a quagmire of dissent, both from governments, and by the Agent, and as a runoff effect to this, the authorities had lost some of their grip on the people. Many people who were seen as of less status previously and who had lived on the fringes of the consumption, were not nearly as affected as those who had seen the authorities as the sole provider for their lives.

The failure to counteract the many viruses sent by the Agent, and the shutting down of central systems where support and upgrades were no longer available, had left many with diminishing technology implanted inside their bodies. As the technology began to decay, their bodies began to decay reflecting their inner selves.

A flaw in the nanotechnology was its requirement for regular upgrading and support in order to maintain its integrity, so with the very limited services now available, people began to experience entirely new illnesses brought on by the implants, in addition to the effects of viruses. Imperfections began to erupt in bodies where lesions would appear on their skin like the tip of an iceberg, a mere indication of what lay beneath. Some suffered from the technology being expelled by their own body's resistance mechanisms, resulting in unsightly lumps and skin conditions never healing and often necrotising as their flesh dissolved and fell away. Others would be subjected to the pain so very deep inside themselves they would beg for attention, beg to be helped, and beg to have the technology removed. But the authorities were adamant bringing nanotechnology services back on-line would make their central systems far too vulnerable to their adversary.

And so, society was rapidly descending into a plethora of the few well off and the rest who were left to suffer and make do where they could. The authorities still had the view of there being too many people for an efficient society, and so they made no special cases, no considerations, and had no compassion for those who suffered.

There were the robots previously used to round up dissidents and these were still functional in a limited capacity. When they would appear out of thin air from being disguised to reflect their surroundings and thus render them invisible, they instigated the same fears as they did when they were first deployed, and so anyone seen as a nuisance was collected and simply disposed of now.

Tobias switched off the projector and went over to the window to see dusk was fast approaching. He had watched it many times before as the last rays of the sun shone on the dust always seeming to hang in the air around the thirty foot high wire fence. There was nobody to be seen there for the authorities ensured anyone on the western side, could not come within fifty hundred yards of the divide. Anyone who tried was simply shot with a laser canon from one of the many towers forming part of the fence every three hundred yards. It stretched the entire length of North America from the Gulf of Mexico all the way to just south of Hudson Bay in Canada.

The dust never seemed to settle and Tobias had often wondered why it would just hang in the air, seeming to defy gravity. As he watched, a person from the western sector came running towards him - it the first he had ever seen.

'They must have made it past the canons...' he thought.

At the moment they made it to the fence, they were electrocuted to death as their body twitched and convulsed. The sight of this shocked him – to see a person go through such a torturous death right there was upsetting. He turned away as he could not look at their motionless body, realising the electric fence must have something to do with the ever-present hanging dust.

'I have to do something,' he thought as he walked back over to the sofa. But he did not know what he could do, or why he suddenly felt this way again after having thought he could do nothing. He was unsure yet he was sure on one thing - it would continue to plague him until he responded somehow.

Chapter 13

John had spent most of the night keeping watch night as Carmel slept. Now and then he slept only to wake again with a start as he realised his lapse. When he woke her at around three in the morning, he quietly suggested they should leave their place under the old stone bridge and make as much ground as they could before the light of the day came upon the scene.

Frieda towed their small wooden cart along as they walked beside her, making it easier for her through the snow. They had a kerosene lantern given to them by the others which he kept down low so Frieda could see a little way ahead and avoiding showing too much of their presence in case the Agent was already about. The old map he had studied showed the trail meandering through the forest and then joining up again with the trail the main group were following after about five miles.

John told Carmel they should continue on as the walking trail would provide cover as it traversed a cliff face, before venturing up through a gap in the edifice, and then winding on to meet the others.

"We need to go as fast as we can to make the Agent guess at where we could be," he said, responding to her questioning look.

"John, I do like the light. It gives me a sense of comfort when there is very little. And it makes me feel warm. It is so cold now."

"We should warm up a bit as we walk Carmel."

As the hours rolled by and the sun appeared illuminating the whiteness all around, they made progress without any sign of the Agent. The forest was still and quiet, with the crunching of their footsteps and the sound of Frieda drawing the cart being the only sound to be heard.

"I have the scanner but we cannot use it, as the Agent would detect it," John said as they stood resting for a while at the junction of the walking trail and the larger trail the remainder of the group had taken. Their path was very evident as they had managed to re-start the truck and had cleared the way ahead.

"He will find this track won't he John?"

"Yes. We can be sure. But if the others have made good ground, they will be waiting at a section up ahead where the trail splits as it goes deep into the forest. If we can get there before he appears and if we can all keep some cover, he might not find us easily."

Two miles ahead, they met up with the others, but they had bad news. The truck had run into some mechanical trouble and could proceed no further. If it could be repaired, it was going to take some valuable time, and it might expose the group to the Agent.

"I'll have a look at it," John said. After a few minutes, he turned to them all who were eagerly watching and waiting for good news, but he could not give them any. "The engine has seized. Such an old electric engine only had a little life left."

One of the women in the group became very worried calling out, "What will we do? He'll get us in no time."

Carmel walked over to her to reassure her and help to calm her down, "Don't worry so much dear, or you will help the Agent to find you. He thrives on the negativity people can project. I know this sounds silly to you, but he will find us much more easily if we project negativity because it will affect our actions and this could lead him to us."

"Well, what can we do then? This snow is so deep and now we don't have a plough to clear our way."

"We can always find a solution. Ask John. Look, you can see he is trying to think of one now."

The entire group turned to look at John in expectation of something they could do.

"Um, we will have to go on as best we can. It is not so bad. Up until now, the plough has made our path very obvious to him, but without a cleared path to follow, it might make him guess a bit. I suggest we split up and take different paths from this intersection. Here, look on this map. We could agree to split up and make our way to the town of Bishop on the eastern side of the mountains. At the lower altitudes, there will be much less snow, if any as we head into the town."

Everyone gathered around as near as they could to see where John was indicating on the old map.

"We should meet there in five days. There are bound to be other people about the town and it will give us some cover. Anyway…" he paused and looked at Carmel. "I really think the Agent now has a specific target amongst us in mind. It is best we split now and head for Bishop. If we are not all there within five days, then those who have made it should then take this route up to Tonopah and then head north-east from there."

Everyone agreed John's plan was their best option and so without delay, they all said goodbyes and good luck, and then split into three smaller groups who each took one of the four trails leading away from the intersection. John and Carmel were left behind then with only Frieda, their cart, and Carmel's little engine.

****

The Agent was in the sky above where he had burned the forest as soon as daylight allowed him to see the ground below. He could see nothing of interest, except for the wisps of smoke winding their way skyward as trees still smouldered. He liked the way the smoke snaked its way carrying the remnants of what once was with it to be lost to the sky. It made him feel good as if he had destroyed something and the something was no longer there to now be lost to oblivion. But soon enough the sensation was lost to him, and he recommenced his search to find his former superior.

After many low sweeps of the surrounding area he grew tired of achieving nothing, and so decided to look further to the east. Within minutes, he found the plough trail and his senses picked up again. As he followed the trail, his anger then arose once again, upon seeing it disappear at an intersection. He saw the abandoned truck below and so blasted it a few times until it erupted into an explosive fireball.

"Where have you gone bitch?" he said aloud.

Without enough room to land the craft, he was forced to hover and try to see where the group had gone. After scanning he area, his mania made its' presence felt when he was dismayed at seeing four separate paths with footprints and cartwheel tracks leading away. He chose one. He followed it until he saw a person on a horse below for a fleeting moment between the tree branches. Without any thought, he immediately turned to his holographic weapons array and blasted them until they were no more than a stain on the snow below him.

"I'll kill all of you!" he shouted.

But he was wrong. In fact, he killed no others this day, instead flying his space ship over the forest frantically looking for them, and finding nobody. Not even his scanners brought him success, for as soon as he received advice on human activity below, it would disappear amongst the thickly wooded forest. He had no time to randomly burn forests as he was after his former superior, and so by the time dusk came, he had left the scene and had made his way back to Oakland to devise a better plan for capturing them.

Carmel and John had seen the Agent fly overhead so they had left the trail to hide amongst the trees. He flew past three times in total before the light began to fade and he left the area. Night was now their ally, and so they continued on in the still coldness under the stars they could see now and then between the trees. Once again, John had rigged the kerosene light for Frieda to see ahead as they walked beside her - often giving her a pat and words of comfort.

She was as much to them as they were to each other since they had first found her, and she had her own affection for their company. Fortunately, the snow cover was not as deep as it had been higher up in the mountains, meaning there was less struggle for her with only a few inches covering the most of the trail. Then they would arrive at a deep drift and John would clear some of the way through.

Like their first time in the forest, an Owl suddenly loomed into their low sphere of light startling them. Again, Carmel took to seeing the bird as an indication as if the presence of the Owl was a talisman of wisdom and power accompanying them during their journey.

John could feel her. He could sense her presence whenever she was near, and so thought of her as one of the most unique people he had ever met. Despite the trials of their recent experiences, she held her senses and composure in a way he could not describe, though he had tried working on a description himself quite a few times now. She was an apparition to him – the way she looked, the way she spoke, and the underlying sense of resolute calmness she nearly always seemed to carry, was having a growing effect upon him. He was able to see why his friend Tim, known as The Fixture, had fallen in love with her. It was as if she cast a spell on those around her, on those to whom she spoke directly, and against those like the Agent who opposed her. Yet, he knew this too was a danger, for the Agent could be drawn to her now he had seen them in the mountains, and her alluring aura was one so very special, the Agent would not be able to help his macabre sense of intrigue should he ever detain her.

Amongst the tree trunk walls of timber with their sole light falling upon the white snow just in front and a little beyond them to the sides, they continued well past midnight and onwards towards dawn. The day was soon to break when as they rested, John asked Carmel what her thoughts were on what they should do. They were still amongst the tall timber without any clearing, and so they felt safe about stopping for a time.

"John, you know I hold the deepest trust in you and I can feel you have the same for me. It is with such grace how you speak with me and never to me. It is with such flow how our words carry back and forth upon the air to each other - our intentions so aligned with the elemental connection of love in our hearts. And it is with such reverence, I place dear to my heart, to be in your presence during our journey, for I know you feel the same towards me and it is something we can both cherish and give outward…even to Frieda." She giggled a little then. It was almost a childish giggle, but in being so, was a sound of innocence and of purity, and of love.

'She is a blessing,' he thought. 'Here we are being pursued by the Agent, and yet she can give such grace and feeling…'

"Well. What do you think? I am thinking we should stay here and rest until it is late in the day. The hours of light are not so long during these winter days, and Frieda could surely use some rest."

"Then you have answered for us Carmel."

Frieda was slowing turning over some straw in her mouth John had given her, when the Agent was seen for a brief moment overhead. It was then obvious to them both he was getting angry at not being able to find them, as they heard some explosions a few hundred yards away when he had taken to obliterating some trees out of frustration. He was not aware of how close they were, but he could see there was a trail of some type below him. This trail along with others all heading roughly in an easterly direction, were his targets. Still, he had failed to make sightings of John and Carmel or of any of the others who were making their way towards the township of Bishop. His scanners had failed to give accurate readings and he knew nothing of John being the cause of this. John had disguised his data so well, even the virus bound Agent was unable to detect his intrusion.

Frieda barely lifted her head in response to the sounds as she continued to chew the straw. She too felt comfortable and not at all troubled by the snow. Carmel had draped a woollen blanket over her as a layer against the cold.

The Agent took to a few more flights over the area, before again, being forced to retire for the day. The forest was on their side, not his. His instruments only gave him ideas of life forms now and then, and the vastness of the forest, meant indiscriminate firing at all the readout locations, meant he would need to methodically plot out the area and cover it with laser fire all day long.

The Agent was a megalomaniac and methodically plotting was not his strong point. He had his ways and they could be se very devastating, but the patience required to work through the forest this day, was not something he could draw upon. He left the scene without success and took to those who were awaiting his return to Oakland. He barked commands at them upon arrival and surprisingly to many, he actually asked a few of them to help him devise a plan to find his former superior officer.

When the light of day once again receded, John and Carmel took Frieda on a night trek through the forest and through a decreasing snow pack. At times, the trail would be entirely clear of snow, so they took to covering these sections as fast as possible to make good time. As morning neared, they decided to take one more rest stop within the forest before they would leave it behind to cover the open ground beyond the trees. The snow was still all about, but there were much larger areas of the trail clear of snow, and the distant view had revealed only a few drifts were clinging to the walls of the valley below.

"Carmel, I am going to take these looking glasses to see if anyone is in the valley. I suggest you stay here with Frieda whilst I go back up to the ridge point so I can get a good view."

The day was a few hours old by this time, and there had been no sign of the Agent.

"I think so John. I can trust the wisdom of your decisions. Take the time you require. We are sure in remaining together here, Frieda and I."

"I'll be back in about half an hour."

When he did return, he had some news. John had seen a few of the group travelling along the path beneath the transit way a few miles to the east. The journey to Bishop was then about another twenty miles south, and so he was sure the people he had seen on horseback, were from the group they had travelled with.

"Surprise though…no sign of the Agent. I thought he would have worked out we are travelling east and we would end up on the fringes of the forest, to then make for the transit way. There was no vehicular traffic, just those on horseback I saw."

"He does know this John. He wants me much more than those others, and despite his absence, we can be sure he will be upon us again. I would say he is planning his next move. He will want to make a fast decisive action John. He is not one for patience and methodical thinking. He is devious and he has his own methods and they are never well thought out but they can still work. We must be careful John."

"We will rest for all of today and then head off after dark. Lucky there is no moonlight, but he will have his scanners and they will be effective in the open countryside beyond here."

"Then I know you will come up with a means to buy us time. A means to distract him John."

"Hmm, you do know me don't you."

"Of course."

They slept the remainder of day, even Frieda. She was content to lie upon the bed of pine needles free of snow and close by to the others who were asleep underneath the wagon. Nothing disturbed them the entire time, and so when they awoke an hour before sunset, they all felt refreshed and alert. Carmel took the lead as she harnessed Frieda to the cart. For a moment she looked at her little steam engine stowed at the rear and longed for a time when she could run it again and let off a few whistles. John was going through some plans in his head, and she could see this, so she chose to leave him to his planning as they made their way towards the edge of the forest.

"I'm going to turn the scanner on for a while," he told her as they paused just a few yards from the last trees. "We will benefit from anything it shows us as we head out into the open country. The range extends to around five miles, so it will give us a warning if he is approaching."

"He will be able to detect it though won't he?"

"Yes. Whilst it gives us five miles of detecting range, it also will give the same to his scanners, so if he sees it, he will come straight for us."

"What if we try it in small bursts every now and then?"

"Of course! What a great idea. Can't think of why I didn't think... You truly are marvellous Carmel."

The transit way was just a mile ahead when John tried the scanner for the first time. He left it on for the next few hundred yards before switching it off again after seeing nothing showing on its holographic readout. By the time they reached the transit way, they had encountered nothing and so they paused for a while underneath. The transit was high above them, but still low enough to keep them mostly from sight should the Agent fly over at a few hundred feet.

"We will follow this until we get to Bishop. If we travel fast, we could be there by dawn."

"Well, let's go John. Frieda is keen."

It would have been around three in the morning when John briefly saw the Agent show on the readout a second before he switched the device off.

"Can we go faster girl?" he said to Frieda as he tugged on the reins. Without hesitation, she increased her pace and they continue on almost at a gallop.

"She is such a fine horse John."

"She is."

"The Agent will track us John. He saw us on his display and I think he would be going into one of usual states by now. He always becomes a maniac more so when he gets close to his targets."

"Yes I know, but I have another plan. There is one other device I have in my bag we can use. It will mean leaving it behind but it is worth it."

"So you are going to set up a decoy."

"Precisely. It is a smaller hand-held scanner I found back at the farm. It only works now and then as it is a bit faulty, but I hope it is enough to distract him. We just need to stop at the next cable node we come across and set it up. There, we can make a little cover so it will require to him to land and get out of his ship to investigate."

"It will buy us some time."

"Hopefully enough to at least almost get to Bishop. I think we have at least another hour to go at this pace."

"Then prepare. I will guide Frieda. Do what you need to do."

When they left the next node behind at a near galloping pace under the cover of the transit way, the Agent was a mile behind and closing rapidly. His readouts showed them to be stationary and he laughed to himself as he thought they were trying to hide from him. When he arrived at the node, his scanners told him the source of the signal was amongst the various structures featured at each node, so he brought the space ship to a gentle landing and approached the site on foot with a pulse rifle. He had taken a hand held scanner with him, and half way to his target, the signal suddenly disappeared.

"Too little far too late. I knew you would resign to me," he said aloud, quickening his pace.

For a few moments he searched around the node amongst the various buildings and cable conducting boxes until he thought he had found what he was looking for. Quietly he approached as he was keen to instil the most in fear through surprise the best he could. When he reached his target, he found it was a trick. John had carefully placed a few items in the dark shadows appearing from a distance to look like the outline of a wagon. He was not pleased, so he shot it until it was ablaze. Then after regaining some of his senses, he ran back to his ship to continue the chase.

Carmel, John, and Frieda were well ahead of him by this time and only a mile away from the township. No lights offered them respite as this was a place under control of the Agent, and so all were extinguished, except for a few in the very centre of the town. When at last they entered its outskirts and took to a shed for cover, the Agent was almost overhead.

"He knew we would come here John. To go north towards Reno is too dangerous, so this was our obvious choice to him. We need to think about what to do. He will not go through this town in the dark, and his scanner will pick up the life signs of other people here, so we at least have some cover. But in the day, he will order everyone out and then he will come for us John."

"Perhaps we still have something to work with yet."

Chapter 14

Dreams cannot turn to dust, nor can they be forgotten forever. Dreams can change and can be overlooked, but somewhere deep inside they always remain waiting to be realised. Inner turmoil can mask the view into dreams, and clouds can weather away the spirit leaving one to feel wanting. But so long as the spirit is keen and therefore to be lived, then dreams will again arise to the fore and they will become life.

It can become the ways for the mind to be disconnected from the heart, where life takes on existence rather than living. Conformity to learned ways where the learning has not always been so beneficial to the heart, can lead to pain and to the apparition of hardship, and so a person can cease to be their self intended as their self intends to be, thus the pain also can permit an uneasiness to enter and despair can follow. But these notions are only 'cans' and 'learned ways'. Those of wisdom realise there is always learning leading to further learning of intentions for wisdom is like the cosmos – infinite and never ending in concept and in matter.

This is how it was for Tobias, as he lay awake late into the night just outside of Omaha where the curfew still remained since its inception three years before. The streets were empty as they were every night, and there was barely any sound aside from machines making living possible - keeping the air artificially fresh. His sense told him there was something stirring inside, but he was unable to determine its cause and its effect. A sense of purpose other than to exist and solely rely on your outlook – action had to be taken. He was unable to fathom what it was somewhere inside him wanted to do, or where to be. His life in the house was not one of reward where one enjoys the mere comfort of being at home. It was one of mere existence as if he was in waiting for a moment as a catalyst providing him with the vision on where he should be in order to feel alive.

He was alone. Asper was just…nowhere. He had no child or parent – he was entirely alone, and he felt it so very much on this night. It was difficult to socialise for many who lived in fringe dwellings as he did. With survival so central to life, barely any room existed for people to meet and develop relations as friends. Some did, and Tobias had a few acquaintances, but he could barely count them as genuine friends like the others with whom he had shared so much a few years ago, and for a time afterwards. Even John could be lost as a friend, for contact had simply ended after the brief meeting over beer, and Tobias put it down to the conditions of the times where many people simply disappeared, similarly as Asper had also disappeared.

She had been so dear to him and he to her. Now with it all so much a part of history to him and with nobody to turn to for company, or to share a meaningful conversation with, or to share feelings, he felt as if he was but one small insignificant molecule coursing through the veins of infinite embodiment without a destination. For Tobias, thought at times in abstraction seeking to find a type of art as an adventure into the realms of expression, was a release for him to go beyond the mundane and to embellish himself a little in the full emotive relationship.

As it is when the brain takes a stronghold over the toroidal flow of existence, a person can be in isolation, yet be surrounded by others and by the very nature of elemental creation containing many waveforms. Dominance by the brain is quite different to an egotistical sense of desire and power, but dominance none the less, and so the eternal flow becomes disrupted, causing angulations within where angulations conflict with the rounded nature of those elements of water, of air, and of the great vortex – the heart. Inside it awaits the dream of dreams, the message to express, and the blueprints of manifestation born from loving intent – an intent Tobias had always felt yet struggled to actualise through experiences.

He lay awake nearly all the night, choosing not to view any holographic projections, and choosing not to read any material available via the holographic library – it was mostly authority driven propaganda anyway.

He also chose not to listen to anything other than the calling inside of himself, around him, and throughout. Tobias felt connected somehow as if he was aware of his place within everything and he chose to explore this rhythm, to explore the questions he was being asked by himself, and to explore why he had chosen to watch the transportation event where he could see the looks of utter despair on the faces of those doomed to oblivion in the western sector.

He rubbed his arm where the two tiny scars from the two identification chips he had received in life, had suddenly began to itch. His mind again turned to his friend John and how he had been such a willing companion to help escape those many years ago. In contrast to his earlier mood, he let out a small laugh as he recalled the hair raising flight in John's plane all the way from Alaska to Vancouver. This led Tobias to other thoughts, more specific about the journey from Vancouver to San Francisco, and their meeting with the others, and of course with Asper and Lorraine at the wharves by the bay.

In reminiscence of the night and the sparkling lights upon the gentle waves then, a spark ignited inside and made its way to his eyes, where it was wrapped in tears to then slowly roll down his face. They were tears of joy, tears of the deepest sentiment in recollection of the strength within the relationships he had back then, and they were tears of yearning – an expression of his inner most dreams as Tobias began to awaken and take the path towards where he was to go and what he was to do authentically despite the nature of any circumstances.

Such is the strength of these things, adversity then is never any measure, as restraint is only a temporary distraction however long it may last, and sorrow just a shallow breath barely drawn. Without knowing what he was to do, or how, Tobias felt as if the answers were there, they were flowing to him from within him, and they were all about him as in any eternal flow as waves forms manifest in his actions based on intentions. He was not a man of malice in any sense, nor would he extract vengeance when he had clearly been wronged by those who sought to depose and subjugate the elemental nature of his spirit. Tobias was a man of recognition and of grace, as he was one who in essence, lived the appreciation and invigoration of life given, and the ever-changing progression of nature within and around. This was his strength and without conscious thought, was why he survived so well there on the fringes not far from the fence dividing the entire continent into two sectors.

He rose out of bed, but there was nowhere much to go other than within the small house or outside into the fenced small back yard to the shed at the rear. He decided he would go there and at least gain a few precious moments outside beyond the curfew hours. He had often wondered what it would be like for those who lived in high-rise apartments with no access outside at night after the cut off time. Very few of them had balconies, and even with such small allotments of outdoor space, Tobias had never considered a balcony much of a place to enjoy the outdoors. Outside in the yard he could look up to the sky and set himself free, he could feel the Earth beneath him, and his spirit for wild places free from all of the restrictions in life, could maintain its connection, however faint.

As he stared up at the stars always a little obscured by the ever present dust in the air, he could see a few space vehicles slowing traversing the sky. For some years now, the night sky had progressively lost many of the space craft people in times past could look up and see on any given night. The authorities had switched off most of their vast satellite network to avoid attack from the Agent. Since the curfew came into being, the skies no longer hosted the many HyperJets crossing the nations and the oceans, and so the night sky had returned to what it must have been like many years before the latter half of the twenty first century.

He dared to take on some deep breaths, knowing there was dust in the air, but not concerned with it at this time. The only lights he could see came from the sole lamp switched on upstairs in his bedroom, and from the amber glow of the lights atop the sector dividing fence almost half a block away. All of the other buildings adjacent to his were in darkness as they had been unoccupied for some years now.

His memories returned to the event of his escape from Alaska and how he had ridden the motorcycle through the outskirts of Seattle late into the night with his headlight amongst the mesmerising flickering amber streetlights. Then, he was driven with the purpose he was beginning to rekindle now, where he had an objective in mind and he had given all he could to make it happen. With a sudden thought of realisation, he turned and entered the back yard shed.

Inside there was a jumble of mostly inoperative electronics and machinery parts, some his, and others already there in the shed when he first found the house. Dust was everywhere, and as he searched around for the device he wanted, the dust stirred and swirled through the air illustrating the currents and waves he was creating with his cause. When he finally found the scanner device he had been searching for, he lifted it close to inspect its condition.

Immediately he could see it was not going to be a case of simply switching on. First, he would have to make some rudimentary repairs, and the he would have to find a power cell. Tobias was still unsure what he was going to do, but he was doing something. He felt confident as he worked with the device where one thing would lead to another as a course of action on the way to realising an objective.

As he sat inside at the kitchen table working on repairing the scanner, he again thought of John, and how he was so highly skilled at repairing and reshaping technology to make it work for him. Tobias had spent enough time with him to learn about how to work on technology and design it for specific uses.

It was near dawn when Tobias awoke at the table after having fallen asleep while working. On the table in front of him lay a half completed device. He had put the basics together for something he was uncertain of what it was. For a few seconds he considered picking it up again before realising he needed more sleep for a clearer mind, so he left the kitchen and went to bed. Then he would return to the device and make it work for him.

Chapter 15

Darkness shrouded the town of Bishop with black ice covering the streets, when John and Carmel awoke a while before dawn after Frieda had stirred and made a few slight sounds. In contrast to his normal flat black desires, the Agent's ice covered space ship glistened as it stood motionless in the town square under the few amber streetlights. It was an ominous sight representing what was to come this very day when he would do whatever he considered worthy to extract Carmel from within the town's perimeter. He knew they were there, so he too was awake early to devise his methods for the process. The cockpit was the only other light on the scene as its multicoloured holographic arrays sent beams outward in rays through the misty tendrils hanging around the space craft.

They knew he would be waiting as they sat quietly discussing what their plans for the day would be.

"I feel as if he knows we are here John. His presence has found its way to me and I am so sorry I cannot do anything to prevent his sense of me in this place."

"Don't apologise Carmel. You are yourself and you should always be expressive of who you are. Consider it an asset for us against the Agent."

"Do you think any of the others from the group will be here? Perhaps they can help."

"I can imagine some would have made it by now, but I am not sure what they can do to help us."

"We don't want to hurt them if the Agent is after me John."

"Yes, I know how you feel Carmel. We need to make a plan of escape. This is only a small town and the country surrounding is open and vast, but there are some ranges to the east, and it is there where we should head."

"He will make the townsfolk here help him John. We will have them all against us."

"Then I think we should run, and do it now. I will reconfigure my scanner into a device to temporarily scramble his spaceship sensors. It will be based on the flux mechanics I know. You will have to drive us fast Carmel. And Frieda…" he trailed off as they both turned to look at her where she appeared to be listening to them.

"She is with us John. Frieda is peace and her determination is in her name. Do not doubt her John."

"I don't. It is I just feel for her and how much work she has to do."

"Then think of it as her destiny if you will John. Perhaps it is why we came across her as we did, as we seek peace as well."

They had taken the fringe roads around the town to avoid creating any disturbance in the early hours, and after crossing the river to the east, they drove on at a full gallop to cover half of the distance to the ranges by the time dawn

VOLITION

was upon them. John had managed to reconfigure the device and now he steered Frieda to give Carmel a break. "We will only use it if we have to. I think I made a mistake yesterday…"

"No John, it was a wise thing to use the scanner. Otherwise the Agent could have been upon us before we knew he was there. It was a risk, but one we had to take. He had surely made a plan to cut us off, or find us at Bishop, as travel there would have been the only viable option for us he could determine. Remember John, he is a maniac and so thoughts of logic can also elude him at any time."

Carmel was right as logic was lost to mania as they rode the cart eastward away from Bishop. The Agent had woken all the townsfolk early, first by destroying a couple of buildings at the centre of town to draw them out, and then by commanding them to find the travellers. Unfortunately for him, the frantic search immediately after had brought no results, and so his impatience took hold. He was uninterested in the few horse riders who the townsfolk had found and offered to him – he didn't even bother to kill them. The Agent was only interested in Carmel, and so now without any sign of her, he began to lose control of himself.

He blasted a few more buildings the moment he was back inside of his spaceship, and then he fumbled his way through the holographic controls before lifting off to hover a hundred feet above the town. He could not make a decision for a time, as he was lost to his rage, until during a fleeting second, he noticed the human scanner readout showed a fluctuating presence. He knew it must be them, for the townsfolk were all gathered below, and back in Oakland his minions there had assisted him by stabilising and increasing the power to the scanner.

Without hesitation, he turned the craft on an easterly heading towards where he thought they were going. The White Mountains loomed just ten miles away and he knew they would try to hide in there after their successful avoidance tactics of the previous few days in the mountains and forest to the west.

"He has found our signal John."

"Yes, I can see he has left the town, but he cannot be certain on precisely where we are. We should be into those foothills in ten minutes according to this old map."

Frieda could sense there was trouble coming as she hastened her pace without John prompting her. They covered the distance in less than ten minutes.

"It will make it harder for him to see us. These hills provide some hiding ground."

"But he will come John. He must be furious by now."

"Then we need to be extra careful."

They had not seen his spacecraft at all since the escape from Bishop began, but this did nothing to alleviate their concerns about the Agent's proximity.

After driving on for another thirty minutes deeper into the ranges, they rounded a corner to see the Agent's spacecraft in the middle of the road. He had landed just minutes before and was now bringing the ship out of invisibility and revealing it to them. He was ever so pleased to see the look on their faces as they rounded the corner – the look of surprise, and the look of desperation to escape. They were not stricken with fear though, and this slight detail troubled him much more than it should have. He fed off fear, and now as he was about to apprehend them, they appeared resolute and not in fear of him, and he hated it.

"Don't move or you die," he said via the ship's external communications. "You cannot escape. As you can see, these mountains have no forest around here for you to hide in, so there will be no stupid cat and mouse you tried on me recently. There is no purpose in you bothering to consider escape, because simply you cannot. But I will not kill you. No, in-fact, I am going to let you go…well one of you. The other, and it means you bitch, is going to come with me whilst I enjoy the notion of your friend's despair as he travels away all alone with your horse and your little wooden cart. Don't try anything either or I might just change my mind and destroy you both now. But please, do not make me do such a thing, for I have so much to show to my former superior officer. Now come over here by yourself."

Carmel gave John a deep look prior to leaving him behind. It was a look of determination without fear or sorrow fear or of sorrow, and whilst he felt for her, something inside him told him this was not the end.

"It will be okay John. Keep going east. It is where our answers are. Don't follow me, but please do seek me when you have some answers."

"Oh Carmel…"

"Quiet dear. Don't show him anything, as it makes him worse. I know you will find some answers John. I can always trust you. We will meet again and please take care of my lovely steam engine and Frieda. I do so want to make my engine whistle again and find a time when I can ride her in the grass."

Carmel left him and walked over to the Agent who had disembarked the ship and was standing with a laser pulse rifle pointed directly at them.

"Now get in, we are going to Seattle. And you," he turned to face John, "Go and get yourself lost and suffer. You are all alone and there is nobody out here to be with. I control this place and for hundreds of miles to the east. So, I am sorry, but there is nothing for you I'm afraid."

Something in him was telling the Agent to spare John's life. He had no sense of it. Rather it was now just the way he was seeing. He let out a maniacal laugh and then boarded the craft to immediately take off on a heading straight to Seattle.

"You have already helped me you fool," John said as he stood alone beside Frieda. "I'll find you."

He had no other option than to continue east as Carmel had said, for the town behind him was an alias to the Agent and he could not expect to be welcome. The day had started with a clear blue sky, but as a wind gusted throwing Frieda's mane around, John could tell the fine weather was about to end. He was confronted with a choice as he stood on the road, yet he did not feel alone as Frieda was with him and Carmel's steam engine was still in the cart. For a time, he looked at the engine pondering how it represented Carmel's spirit to him now, and he too longed for the time when she could make it whistle again.

When he came around, Frieda was standing there staring at him as if she was waiting in expectation to get moving. With a skyward glance, he sat in the cart and steered her back towards the main transit route. By day's end, they had covered over twenty-five miles, and as he sat looking at his old map, parked beside an old sign reading 'Welcome to Nevada', he mapped out a more direct route towards the east.

"We'll stay here tonight girl. You could use some rest."

Over the following week, he met no other travellers on the road as he journeyed – there was nobody he knew in Tonopah where he wondered what might have happened to the others in the group he and Carmel had travelled with. When he took the left turn transit towards the old state of Utah, he thought he saw someone up ahead on the road, but by the time he reached them, it became obvious they had been there some time.

'Must be the Agent's doing, or his people,' he thought when he ambled by the wreckage of an old vehicle and what appeared to be the very decomposed remains of the occupants.

It was not until well into the second week of travelling as he approached Salt Lake City when people began to appear. At first there were some fringe dwellers to the city who looked to be very badly affected by viruses from the Agent. He found it hard to look at some of the faces pleading for food from him. Parts of their bodies were being drawn into oblivion, whilst other parts of their bodies were covered in weeping open sores and lesions.

He found what he thought was an abandoned farm closer to the city than he expected, but when he entered the barn looking to find a place for Frieda, all he saw was a mass of bodies where some people were still alive. All of them seemed to be disappearing into a large vortex or void, with their bodies joining in a tangled mass of ganglia at the edges. This site was far more disturbing than any others he had previously seen, and the smell coupled with the sounds, made him vomit until he was well away.

When at last he arrived at the city, there was nothing there to appease what seemed to be a growing sense of dread. People were all about in survival mode – some feeding off the corpses of others, and yet some trying to feed off the living. What the Agent had done was to turn humanity inside out and unearth the darkest corners of fear, anxiety, and of behaviour seemly even beyond the most savage found in the wild. People were losing their minds, they were losing themselves, and they were becoming a mess and a scourge unto their own existence. Life nearer the cities was the worst examples of the Agent's undoing, and so he decided to find what he could to keep him and Frieda going, and then to leave as soon as possible.

The effort to find food was not as difficult as he had imagined, due to the loss of sensible mind amongst the population in general, and due to him being able to find a very few people in Salt Lake City who were not affected. They were glad to see him, and glad to meet someone who was of strong mind, alert, and not there to steal from them.

"You are best heading towards Denver if you are going to the eastern sector. Then, take a turn and head up to Nebraska. Keep well clear of the south before you get to the east, it is bad down there. You think Salt Lake is bad, but you have seen nothing yet. People down there…well, there are so many of them, and they are eating pretty bad stuff. Each other, excrement, raw flesh. You name it, and they eat it. Those holes are much bigger too because there are so many of them, and they are even worse than those twisted ones around here. You can hardly recognise them as human, so disfigured they all are. And then there are the ones with the real big holes looking like only half of a person. Suddenly they erupt as their bodies smash into little pieces with mess everywhere. Apparently they are still conscious for a few seconds as it happens. Don't ask me how, but it sounds bad."

"Um, thanks. I intended to head in the direct you say. Is there anything I can do for you? You gave me this food and some hay for the horse. You must have something I can do."

"Only if you know electronics. I have some machines here to help my pals and I stay alive and keep those others at bay."

"Yeah I do know electronics. Show me and I'll see if I can fix them."

The man took John to a small warehouse. When they arrived, he saw other unaffected people about obviously positioned as guards and lookouts.

"It should work without a problem," John said as he finished work on the motor the man had shown him. "What are you going to use it for anyway?"

"Oh, we have a little transport machine we can hitch it up to. We can get about a little faster than all the others on foot. You are lucky to have a horse – not many of those left around Salt Lake. Keep an eye on her when you leave though. Out to the east of the city, there are some who will do what they can to steal anything, and a horse would sure be a prize possession and good food. And those Geiga clothes you wear, well they'll even try to steal those. Trade you see. Anything they can trade for food or fuel, they'll take."

"Thanks for the advice, and again, thanks for the food. I guess I will have to leave tonight…"

"Yeah, best you travel at night. Without any lights or much fuel to burn, they are not party to night raids. You have one thing on your side there."

John had stayed two days with the people he had met in Salt Lake City, and after he had done what he could to repair their machines, they gave him a little more food when he departed.

"A little bonus for you in there as well. A touch of whisky for the cold nights."

"Thanks mate. If I ever come back through Salt Lake, I'll be sure to come visit."

"You are welcome any time my friend. Good luck on your travels, and keep a watch out too at the transit way. I heard there are a few nasty folk up east somewhere along the line."

John was on a heading northeast towards Nebraska and the divide between the western and eastern sectors almost one thousand miles distant. By the time he reached near Denver, he had seen far too many people for his liking. Most of them were affected by the viruses from the Agent one way or the other, and others had scheming and troubled looks in their eyes. Twenty miles out from the city, he decided to skirt around its northern side and take a path through the ranges, then to re-join the transit line forty miles to the east.

It was hard going alone through the mountains with Frieda as the snows were deep and at times he was only able to cover a few miles each day. Without Carmel for company, he was left to long winter nights where he would talk to Frieda now and then as he sipped a little of the whisky he had been given. When at last he descended to the lower altitudes and joined a roadway coming from the north, the travel became a little easier with the thinning snow. It was a beautiful place, with great stands of Aspen trees, frozen creeks and waterfalls, and a feeling of purity. At times it became a little eerie to him, with barely any sound, no signs of other humans, and almost no sign of wildlife, other than rabbits, which he caught a few of to keep as food. He saw a couple of eagles circling high above one morning and thought of times he could fly in the Beaver. He missed the peace where he lived in Alaska for a time. Those seemingly endless days of almost nothing but the woods around him and the river flowing by, were visions of paradise compared the time since he had left with Tobias.

Nine days after taking the route to avoid Denver, he could see the main transit heading east, in the distance. He had covered half the distance to Omaha since leaving Salt Lake City, and as he studied the old map, he calculated there would still be another two weeks ahead of him.

"Well at least the snow will give way soon girl," he said to Frieda as they had re-joined the transit way after having skirted around the town of Sterling.

He had thought of Carmel every day since the Agent had taken her, and whilst he felt she was quite a capable person, he was stricken with worry about what he might be doing to her at times. John had travelled alone quite a few times in recent years, partly as part of a plan as he sought out anyone he knew, and partly because circumstances and troubles had forced him to keep moving. He had not encountered many of those badly affected people when he had stayed in the north, as he had remained mostly out of sight and secretive, but ever since venturing south into California, the sights of the degenerating virus affected people began to instil a sense of foreboding as he realised just how bad the effects were.

Fortune had always seemed to be with him in recent years. And now, since leaving Salt Lake City, he had found enough resources to feed himself and Frieda, and so far he had not encountered any real trouble or threat. But as he approached the junction of the easterly transit way with one running north south about two hundred miles from Omaha, he felt something strange. It was if some inner sense Carmel may have passed onto him was speaking, and it was telling him to be wary.

The last snows were now a few miles behind as he drove Frieda on towards the intersection underneath the transit way tube. Taking the road through this intersection was a risk he had to take as the lesser roads and tracks all around would prove impassable or too much work for Frieda and the cart.

As he approached the intersection, his level of caution found new heights. At first he was unsure what it was inside the tube twenty meters above him, and then it soon became apparent as more and more faces appeared. The transparent tube was mostly opaque now as it had not been cleaned or serviced for years, resulting in a murky surface mostly obscuring the people inside. John immediately responded by urging Frieda to go faster towards the intersection. They had speed on their side as Frieda was now at a full gallop towing John on a wild ride while those in the tube could only run. He kept her at full pace as they neared the intersection, but to his dismay he could see there were people lingering where the off ramps from the transit tube descended to the ground.

"Where do you think you are going?" one of them yelled at him as he slowed a little whilst looking for any means to avoid the group. "We want your horse to eat."

John could see those in the tube were gradually catching up, meaning there would be too many people for him to physically take on. He calculated at least twenty in all, with eight ahead of him standing at the bottom of the access ramp and around a dozen in the tube. With only fifty yards between them, he had to devise a plan, so he pulled hard on the reigns bringing Frieda and the cart to a stop.

"Don't try and escape or it just means a bad outcome for you. We are hungry and we hurt, so let us have your horse."

John did not reply. Instead he remained silent as he reached into the cart to his bag. Whilst keeping an eye on the people ahead and those who were rapidly approaching the exit to the transit way, he carefully rummaged through until he found the only incendiary device he was carrying. Frieda then shuffled a little as she could smell what John could also smell. It was a scent similar to death striking both of them at the deepest instinctive level. John felt a little sick and he could see Frieda wanted to go as soon as she could.

"It's all or nothing girl," he said to Frieda as he straightened up in the driver seat whilst concealing a device in his hand.

The others had now begun to emerge from the tube and it only took one brief glance to know they appeared even more desperate than those already outside. Their faces and bodies were massively disfigured with gaping holes to nowhere and large oozing lesions, and a look in their eyes John thought was of pure carnal deposition unaligned from normal human integrity. He was convinced they would not hesitate to kill and eat Frieda, and he was quite sure they would do the same to him the moment they discovered he was not afflicted as they were. As he prepared to make a charge, he could see there was a wide enough area of clear ground for him to drive the cart around or through the group should they disperse in an attempt to form a barrier.

"Give us your horse! We are hungry and so are they." When the person said this to John, he indicated to the tube where there were at least another fifty people rushing to the scene from the opposite direction.

"Oh shit. Frieda this is it!" He lashed the reigns and immediately they set off at a slight angle away from the tube. When the timing was right, he activated the fuse on the small bomb he had. At barely twenty yards away, he threw it at the main group. Instantly they were thrown into chaos as the explosion killed a few and sent others flying, whilst at the same time, John corrected the angle and headed through the gap in their defences created by the bomb.

"Come back! Come back!" he could hear some of them yell as he drove Frieda as fast as he could.

'No bloody way,' John thought, and as he cast a glance behind him to see how close they were, he could see they had resigned to his escape. Some of them lost their wits at losing a potential feed and set upon each other. With flashing glances forward and to the rear, John could see they had begun to tear at each other. It was as if the loss had sent them into frenzy so very shocking to John, he thought wild life would barely engage in such crazed behaviour.

People lost their senses smashing each other with whatever weapon they were carrying, then gorging upon the ruined mess of flesh, and upon screaming people as they ate them alive. He could not understand how human beings could behave in such a way, particularly the immediacy of their state of frenzy given just prior they were acting as a gang of desperate people. Then he thought of the Agent for a second and realised some answers. The people well behind him now had crossed a line into chaos growing at an unstable and exponential rate taking them into an abyss devoid of reasoning and integrity.

Half an hour later, when at last he felt he was far enough away to stop and give the panting Frieda a break, he studied his old map. With just under two hundred miles to go, he decided to head for Fremont where he would find somewhere to stop and plan a way to cross into the eastern sector.

For nine days John played it safe. People were appearing more often the closer he journeyed towards the dividing fence. More were in the small towns, so he took the lesser roads around them. He drove Frieda mostly at night using only the moon and stars to guide them. Any sign of a light would only attract attention, and so they were forced to keep mostly away from the main roads.

On the ninth night he sat with Frieda quietly as she lay down on some hay he had arranged for her.

"Well girl, we have almost made it. But we still have five days ahead if we can keep our pace up." Frieda was a strong horse and so covering nearly twenty miles per day along the roads was within her, but by the time they reached the outskirts of Fremont, they had both run out of food and Frieda had begun to weaken.

John had her hidden in a deserted barn when he went out to look for something they could both eat. Most of the town was deserted, except for a few people here and there, and luckily, they appeared to be unaffected by the Agent's viruses.

"Do you know anywhere I could get some food," he asked a woman who herself was out looking for the same thing.

"Not sure honey. I need some too, but it is not easy to find in these parts."

"In any parts," John replied. "How long have you been here?"

"All my life. I like the country air, the cities are not my thing, but there is nothing much out here these days. As soon as you try to grow something, those other people come along and steal it."

"Other people?"

"Yeah, the bad ones with disease, but there are others too. They just steal because they are too lazy and so unwilling to work to survive. You're not one of them are you?"

"No. I have travelled all the way here from California. I want to go to the eastern sector, and I don't have any of those viruses."

"You best try and survive here. Getting through the fence is nigh on impossible. Anyone who tries, they laser them dead if the electricity doesn't get them first."

"Have you thought about it…trying to get through? It is bad west of here, and I reckon on it getting worse and worse."

"I have thought about it, but I am all alone you see, and such things just seem too difficult for me."

"Maybe we can try together?"

"Maybe. You seem all right, and not like any of the others at all. What's your name? Mine is Kerry Ann."

"I'm John, nice to meet you Kerry Ann. Where do you live?"

"In an old house…well, it looks old, but it is not so old. I have always lived there, but I keep very quiet you see. I don't want any attention, so I stay in my basement mostly."

"Perhaps we can look for food together. I have a horse to…"

"You have a horse! Lucky you. There is not much stock left anymore as they have eaten it all. You had better keep a good eye on your horse, or you will lose it. What's its' name?"

"Frieda."

"A pretty name for sure. I am on my way to a place not many people around here know about. It has some food…it grows a bit wild you see. Some grains, and some vegetables and the like. Seems like it comes from nowhere, but I reckon on there being wild seeds about from the days when people used to farm around these parts. We could get something there for Frieda, and with the grain if I get enough, I can make flour. I have an old millstone, but it is heavy. Maybe a man like you will find it easier…if only I had something to drive it."

"I might be able to help you there. Let's go to this place you speak of. Then we can go and get Frieda and go to your house."

"Okay then, but we better hurry. You should not leave her alone for too long."

John left to get Frieda and then returned a few minutes later. Kerry Ann was nowhere to be seen causing his heart to sink.

"Hey. Over here honey. I keep to the shadows for safety sake. Hurry now."

Kerry Ann took John and Frieda on a course through town she knew was the safest way during dusk before they arrived at her small house. It appeared to be deserted and unkempt on the outside.

"As I said, I live mostly in the basement, but tonight with you and Frieda here, we can be upstairs."

"What about Frieda?"

"There is a rear brick outhouse big enough for her. I think it might have been an original stable or something long ago."

Chapter 16

Tobias had been successful with working on his device. As he admired his achievement, he wondered why he had never had the motivation to do something like it previously. He thought how John might be impressed with his work for a moment, but then was lost again. Now he had made it this far, he had come to another impasse – what would he do next?

Outside the air was still dust laden with its familiar orange glow feature during every sunset when the weather was clear. As he stood by the kitchen window looking west, he thought of his companions again – the first time since the night when he had laid awake for so long before venturing out to the shed. The distraction of creating a scanner had allowed him the space to forget the disconcerting memories of those he had held dear, and still held in such a way. But now, those feelings returned to him stronger than ever, increasing the degree of speculation within as he had always considered himself resilient to sombreness or despair. As he continued running it through his mind, his connection with his heart was once again being realised as it had those years before. Tobias was not consciously trying this or aware of it, but his feelings were unleashing the potential of who he actually was again, as if it was a memory lost for a time but never forgotten.

He took a deep breath and turned away from looking out the window, when a realisation suddenly came to him. The stirring inside was indicative of his passion, and he could feel his passion pointing him back towards the shed in the backyard.

"I'm going to build myself a ray gun," he said aloud.

Tobias was not suddenly feeling a passion to shoot at anything or anyone. His feelings were about the protection he knew would be required in the confrontations soon to be faced, and so the decision to build the gun was an instance of resolve. Tobias knew he was progressively building more towards an outcome he was realising as he went.

Amongst the dusty boxes of wires and parts, he came across a power unit he had never noticed before, and it was an ideal place to start building the weapon. After thirty minutes he had gathered the power unit, some wiring, a few parts he was sure would make for the gun housing, and an electronic switch for use as a trigger. This new challenge excited him, making him feel determined as ever to continue on and follow this feeling.

The authorities permitted only a limited power supply to those dwelling in the fringes of the cities, and his allocated supply would be enough for him to keep working and test each stage of the ray gun he was building.

When at around midnight, he decided to go back to the house for some coffee, he switched on his holographic projector as he waited for the water to boil. Another announcement came on a few moments after he had turned it on.

"The authorities advise the Agent is attempting to increase his impact on people living in the eastern sector, through a new onslaught of nanotechnology viruses. His use of the unstable vortex amplifier to accelerate atoms is causing some malfunction in some of the central systems, and citizens are advised further restraint of services is now in place. All procedures for treatment of viruses affecting the operation of public use machines have been cancelled until further notice. Citizens are advised they are to proceed to their daily work places as normal, but interruptions are to be expected. Any failure of infrastructure transport systems must be endured to ensure the on-going efficiency of systems, and therefore the public are advised they must ensure adequate means to travel to and from their workplaces on time. Any person not fulfilling their obligations for compliance at work could have their employment terminated."

The authorities had often told the public of their requirement to fulfil their obligations and comply with the law as a means to eventually overcome the Agent. In such unstable times, nearly all employed people had become ever fearful of losing their work. Many had heard the stories of decline experienced by those who were unemployed, and how eventually they would move to the fringes where survival was much more difficult. This new heightened fear, aside from the general dismay and disarray life had become over the past three years, had served to actually strengthen their hold over the people, despite many instances where the efficiency of central systems was undermined by viruses.

This news did not bother Tobias as he was already in the place so many feared to tread, and he had often thought of how soft many were and not resilient, considering although survival was a struggle, it was not actually much worse than employment in the cities. Many of the items of affection people had grown to adore and many of the facets of their consumption based life were gone, but many held on to the belief eventually the authorities would eventually re-establish the life they used to have.

'What's the use in holding out for false promises,' Tobias had often thought when considering his place west of Omaha in comparison to those just down the transit way in the main city. Transport was more difficult in these times with restrictions placed on use of the transit way tubes, and the confiscation of most private vehicles by the authorities. Times saw most people movements restricted to necessary travel mostly back and forth to work. A lot of time was just at home and at work as the curfew in place restricted the evening hours. This combined with restrictions placed on private ownership where many business owners, restaurateurs, and others, had simply given up and forced to vacate their premises.

When Tobias had made the coffee, he returned immediately to the shed and continued working on his ray gun. By dawn, he had tested all of its components and was satisfied as they had all proven to be operational. Tired from his long night, yet happy at the same time, he decided he would rest all day, and then put the components together the following night. Without deliberate intent, his life was changing from the emptiness he experienced killing time most days, to a night time existence where he would become more secretive than he had been previously.

When he awoke in the afternoon, the first thing he did was to go and find a large amount of food for a stash much larger than he had made before. The authorities still provided outlets to purchase food, but they severely limited the supplies to just enable people to survive. Often, many people would make raids upon others, or simply scavenge for anything edible they could find.

It was just prior to the close of trading hours, when Tobias exhausted his allocation of food he could purchase in one single transaction at the local store. Lucky for him, the authorities had not pursued the injection of identification chip technology on those in the fringe areas, and so he was able to go to another outlet, where he made it in with just a few minutes to spare. Again he purchased the maximum food allowance. Those with identification chips were automatically detected and they were required to use them for payment, where the system would then register them as maximising their allowance. People like Tobias were still able to use cash, though it had nearly been completely phased out, and so without the registration in the system, they, and he, could go to several outlets per day. The authorities were not even aware this was going on, as they were far too busy working on counteracting the Agent, rather than finding people who exceeded their food allowance.

On his way home, Tobias decided he would take a route to the north and see if there was any wild food growing there. Not many people lived in his area and there were even fewer to the north, and with winter at its peak, many did not think of going to the wild fringes to find food. There was no snow about, but he was confident he would find some winter berries and vegetables, remnant from the farms in the area, now long deserted. At one old overgrown farm, he found what he went looking for and extracted a bag of berries and a few vegetables, along with some wild grain seeds. On his way home from there, he came across a wild boar foraging in soil underneath some Oak trees. Without a weapon, he was unable to catch and kill the boar, but he was lucky enough to unearth some truffles the pig had been looking for.

Satisfied with his haul, he hurriedly travelled the rest of the way home, to avoid any of those people who lurked about in the few dark hours between sunset and the curfew at ten. When he arrived there, he immediately set about safely storing the food to prevent it going off, and to hide it in case he was robbed. After eating, he went out to finish work on his ray gun. Tobias had the only lock and key he had seen for ages, and was thankful to see it intact when he arrived at the door. Within five minutes of going inside, he was back to working on building the gun from all the components he had laid out carefully on the workbench.

"Now to test this baby," he said at around three in the morning when he had finished assembly.

At first, it just crackled and hummed, and then it stopped altogether. After a few adjustments, he tried it again, and it was a success. With a few sporadic bursts as he tried the trigger a few times, it then emitted a constant beam of electricity reaching about twenty feet. It was quite a spectacle as the beam erupted from the muzzle like a bolt of lightning then striking the wall he was aiming towards. Each time he released then pulled back on the trigger, the ray gun responded as he had intended and this made him smile. He a also thought of how John would have admired his ingenuity and skill.

A ray gun and a scanner were much more than the authorities would allow citizens to possess, and for the first time, it dawned upon Tobias how he was beginning to fraught with the common law now governing life even out in the fringes. People were allowed to carry personal holographic devices, but these were limited to basic communications and for viewing holographic news broadcasts. There was a strict compliance in place, where all citizens were prohibited from possessing and carrying weapons. Anyone who was unfortunate enough to be caught was immediately transported to the western sector, and so they had become rare due to the fear of transportation held by many.

Tobias was never one to give in to fear, nor would he readily comply with regulations as set out by the authorities, and so after a few moments of consideration, he thought all he would have to do was to be careful and keep the devices in a safe and secret place somewhere on the property. The shed was not secure enough despite its working lock. If the authorities ever tried to find his weapon, it would be the first place they would look, and with operating security still in place, he would have to keep the weapon entirely out of sight, should there ever be a chance occurrence where a surveillance camera detected something. After an hour of deliberation, he decided he would have to extend the basement under the house. Fortunately, it was well concealed already, and now all he had to do, was to hollow out some more space beneath and make a door easily disguised, yet difficult to uncover.

Chapter 17

The Agent was not concerned with making life for Carmel comfortable, or pleasant, nor was he of the mind to torture her, or to kill her. Rather, he was set on making her suffer as she witnessed his malicious intentions.

"You see my beautiful amplifier, so exquisite in apparition, yet so deadly in purpose don't you? And…of course, look upon the torus. All three aligned…"

"They are not aligned."

"Don't interrupt me…ever! My three torus aligned…and so lovingly amplifying the vortexes I so choose to create. Surely you can admire the beauty before you. See how the ring torus just floats there between the horns?"

"It looks like a beast, as you are."

"Oh yes, my former superior. I am a beast. I am a nightmare, and I am the fulfilment of oblivion, if such a thing can be. My intent is not to rule, despite those pathetic minions of mine who see me as such with their worship of my presence in cities and towns. No, my intent is to rule out! Rule out the cognitive perception of existence being worthy of recognition. Yes, I seek to unravel all held dear and to create a machine…a world succumb to me."

"You are mad!"

"Yes I am and I know I am, so please do not state the obvious to me, for I already know and your weak expressions fail to capture me as the epitome of such things. I was made to be this way and to undo many other ways. But oh, do not despair my former superior, for you too will soon realise any little dream you ever had of just about anything, is irrelevant. There cannot be any justice either, nor any instance of love. For this world beckons unto me, and as you are aware, I am unearthing the deepest desires for this within humanity."

"Those torus will be your undoing. They are unstable. Look at how it flickers…like you. You are unstable."

"And so where is there a problem? Why, former one…former superior officer one? Is there anything you consider better than I? Surely not, for as it is obvious, even I can hold the authorities at bay. I can hold them to ransom, and I can disrupt them into oblivion."

"I have seen your ugliness…"

"Yes. It is beautiful is it not? Back when you were my employer, you could sense it then and I will give you credit for your senses are strong indeed."

"Why do you keep me?"

"A good question, for I am not even sure why. But something in you intrigues me, and so I keep you. Now watch. I am going to send out my latest virus. It is a sensation, but not one to revel in. No. It is a sensation of undoing and one to enhance the emergence of the worst in those who you seem to love, and in people for whom you have adoration. Will you adore them when you see what they are capable of? Will you want for salvation in those who suffer at my hands?"

"I never look for salvation. I am resolute to learn."

"Yes you are my former superior. But...no such resolution can be nearly so great as mine, for my resolution will bring an end to resolution. Now get your mind around such concepts if you can."

Carmel could not hate the Agent as she watched him enter a sequence via the holographic array. She never held the concept of hate. She could not feel bitterness as he powered up the amplifier to bring the Torus of Eternity into an electro-static state so removed from the warmth it had given to others. All she could do was to remain determined to overcome this beast before her, both in person, and machine, and as she watched his devious quirks and heard the manic laughs, she focused not on the machine, but through it where she could feel as if the torus was itself released from the Agent's bind.

Within moments, those unfortunate enough to be susceptible began to feel the affects. Millions of hearts across the world began to dissolve as they were drawn into oblivion, with people everywhere feeling emptiness beyond anything previously conceived. The Agent had targeted only the heart this time with specific nanotechnology types, and whilst their injected technology strived to counteract the effect from the sudden loss of the body's centre, they remained conscious as the core of their being slipped into oblivion. Aghast with a sense of shock so severe and so sudden, they cried to the utmost of dismay as they slid into nothingness and into irrelevance.

"Now watch," he said to her as he engaged holographic cameras located in various cities within places he controlled. Instantly, the images came across clearly showing people collapsing into themselves and taken to the verge of destruction and whilst they gasped their last few breaths, the Agent's virus instilled the last hope to them and so their final actions in desperation were to set upon each other tearing and maiming in an attempt to reconstitute some type of physical being. Then with explosive delight, the Agent began to laugh almost endlessly as he forced Carmel to watch people dissipate into the growing holes of their bodies. Screams and moaning in ways so horrific could be heard and as they came to her, it was the most sickening experience she had ever encountered. Then a few seconds later all became silent, as all had simply disappeared and their existence was no more, and nor had it ever been. The Agent's unstable viruses were opening holes in the fabric of space and of time sending people beyond the conception of both to have their atoms taken entirely out of this dimension's existence. There was no fire, no flame, and no embers. Just a coldness of nowhere and it was unfathomable to Carmel. How such things could occur in defiance of the progression in nature and the changing of forms, she found difficult to accommodate. Yet before her eyes, it was as if the very foundation of elemental natural characteristics of existence were being lost – all done by a man she felt could not be given the grace to describe as human.

"Now watch this as well. Watch my robots take San Francisco. My tiny nano creations will wreak havoc upon anyone in their way."

The Agent engaged the command to send out the robots similar to those he had used to destroy the HAARP facility. Via holographic cameras installed throughout the city, Carmel could see the robots consume people on the streets, instantly turning them into piles of dust and puddles of ooze. It was one horror after another and she felt ill, yet resolute she would somehow overcome the Agent for the disturbance he created.

"Now, come with me. I have someone for you to meet," he told her after a few minutes of his maniacal laughing. "I think you will find them interesting."

The Agent lead Carmel out of the room of his headquarters near Seattle, taking her deep underground to the furthest reaches of the facility. When they arrived outside at a long ill kept and very dirty room, he paused for a moment at its door where he flicked a few switches.

"In here is what I want you to see."

He opened the door to a room now emblazoned with bright light where Carmel could see a small group of people sitting against the far wall. Each one of them had their hands covering their eyes, indicating to her they had been previously been held in total darkness. When she had adjusted to the light herself, she saw a couple of the others had taken their hands away and were blinking their eyes as they looked to see who had arrived. Carmel immediately recognised them.

The Agent noticed this, "Ah, don't speak, they'll barely respond. Just look at them. See how pathetic they are? See how weak they have become at my hand? Oh, and see how utterly powerless they seem? Well they are, and they have been. Think of this my former superior officer one. These people have been asleep for most of the past three years. They have barely been outside of a room at all, and they have not had any contact with the outside world...none. See what I can do? And they thought I was a powerless fool when they first met me. But I put them in darkness you see, and I made them sleep for such long periods of time, with barely enough intravenous fluid to sustain their pathetic lives."

"I do so like to have them near though, so I brought them with me when I came to this facility, and now I can enjoy their suffering...and yours. Yes my former superior, you know who they are don't you. You also know at one time, I interrogated two of them whilst you watched over me, and you were condescending to me. I have kept you here in isolation these last few weeks because I wanted you to witness the worst of my viruses before you met them. And now I have destroyed the hearts of so many, I do feel so inclined to include just a few more, but...not as fast as what you have just seen. No. I intend to break these…and yours ever so slowly, so I can indeed enjoy the destruction I will make apparent."

When he had finished, he ushered Carmel back out of the room, and then flicked the light switches back to off, before he demanded she follow him to the quarters he had held her in previously. When she sat there alone a short time later, Carmel felt such dismay and sorrow, causing her to cry. The Agent was slowly destroying the very people whom at one time she had apprehended, and then she had seen as those who had inspired her to leave the services of the authorities. Raynie, Jake, Lyle, Jenna, and Chan Lee had been captured in Australia when the former leader of the dark sect had stolen the torus of Eternity, and then after the Agent had returned to Earth in the stolen spaceship to take over control of the sect, he had delighted in keeping them.

Carmel could not tolerate this position for herself and certainly not for the others. As she lay awake for hour upon hour, she grew ever more determined now was a time she could do something for them, and so she set about attempting to devise a plan to undo all this horror.

Chapter 18

Kerry Ann delighted at John's strength as he ground the wheat grains into flour with the old millstone. They had accepted each other as friends since the day he had returned to her house with Frieda, and since then, they had continued to build a relationship they both knew could never be forced apart. When he had ground enough flour for Kerry Ann to make some dough, he went to check Frieda - something he did a few times per day.

Kerry Ann had told him of the desperation some had to find food, so he went to check on her regularly. She was fine and again, welcomed his visit.

"Well girl, I have made a little motion sensor device so I can keep an eye on you when I am not here. Good girl."

"How is Frieda?" It had become a regular question from Kerry Ann.

"She's fine. What are you making there?"

"Oh, just some flat bread. I think we are going to need it, and it keeps well without going stale."

"Need it? Sure we need to knead it to eat it and yeah to bake it…"

"I think you know what I mean John."

"Oh yeah. I was going to discuss it with you tonight, but it looks like you needed to beat me to it."

"Ha ha, mister funny."

Before long John could smell freshly baking bread. It was astounding. He had always loved the smell and now here it he was being reminded of this smelling such a simple yet desirable scent for the first time in years. It reminded him of childhood and the smells from the bakery two blocks from where he lived with his parents. For a second he embraced this memory and then it made him think of his own son Chris. In an instant he began to worry and feel a deep sadness over the potential opportunities they had missed as father and son.

"Hey, you look a bit glum honey. What's the matter?"

"Oh, I was thinking about my son Chris. I hope he is safe."

"If he has anything of you in him, I'm sure he'll be okay."

"Thanks Kerry Ann."

"No problem honey. If you want to talk, just ask me anytime."

"Okay. You know I am thinking with the pressure coming from the Agent, we could have to consider moving on and trying to cross the fence any day now."

"I knew it was coming John and I am a bit worried. You know, leaving where I have lived for so long, and trying to get to the eastern sector. The fence runs the entire north south of the continent. We surely cannot go around."

"No it is not possible. By the time it runs out in Canada, there is nothing but cold wilderness in winter and hordes of pestilence in summer. Humans can't survive there without a lot of equipment. We need to get through at Omaha and I am thinking about how we might do so."

"You have a plan?"

"Well, sort of. I have a few ideas. It is just getting through the fence or the gates will be our biggest problem."

"What about the laser canons and the electricity?"

"I have an idea there. In my bag is a few items I have been keeping for many years now, and I think I can fool their automatic sensors."

"So you are going to use some of those electronics you have?"

"Sure will. That part is easy."

"Perhaps I can help."

"How so Kerry Ann?"

"You know I have the stable out there."

"Yes."

"Well, I bet you don't know what is underneath it."

"What do you mean? I didn't see any door or hatch when I set it up for Frieda."

"Because it is hidden."

"Why didn't you tell me before Kerry Ann?"

"Um…I had to get to know you. Sorry John, but you know how it is. It is only tonight…now, when I spoke to you, when I thought I could tell you about the stable."

"Okay, I understand. But what is it? Something good I suppose."

"Oh yes, but we will have to be careful John. We can only use it at the moment we are ready to go from here. Once we do, there will be no turning back…it will be too obvious."

"Let me guess, you have some transport?"

"You guessed right, but you need to take a look at it first John. I have had it here for a long time. I am not even sure if it will work."

"So you haven't used it for years then?"

"No, not since just after the Agent started making himself known around here. Since then I have kept it in hiding."

"But how will we get it out?"

"Oh, no problem we can just drive it out. There is a ramp leading to a trap door underneath the grass you see in the front of the house. I planted it there when I decided to hide the transport."

"What is it?"

"A common vehicle people used to own…from about ten years back I think. But it needs a charge John. I think the cells would be flat by now."

"No problem there. I already have a plan worked out to re-charge them."

"How?"

"Well, you know Carmel's steam engine?"

"Yes, but…"

"Yeah, I thought it too, but I don't think she would mind for this, and it won't damage it if we just charge the cells and then shut it down."

"What about Frieda?" John asked, suddenly remembering her and horrified at the thought of leaving her behind.

"I already thought of her," Kerry Ann smiled at him, and John wondered how she would have. "It is a utility type of vehicle John. She can ride in the back, if she is prepared to cram in for a while and lie down."

John laughed a moment, "I'm sure she won't mind."

After dinner, Kerry Ann showed the vehicle to John and he was elated to find the vehicle was almost a small truck larger than the F350 he had restored for a time back in the mountains and it was still in good order except for the power cells needing an overhaul and then a re-charge.

"I'll get to work on it straight away. We can fit Frieda and the cart in here. Carmel's engine can go in the cab with us."

"Yes, I think so John. We should go tomorrow if we can. The others are getting closer each day and we cannot afford to remain here much longer than a day or two at the most."

Kerry Ann brought him some refreshments a while later when they took a break to discuss their plan.

"The fence is electric John."

"Yes, I am going to work on it. Another device I have will be able to create a reflex static field neutralising the charge over an area big enough for us."

"So we just drive through. Do you think the vehicle can get through the wire?"

"Only if we attach something to the front. Do you have any ideas?"

"Well, there are some metal pieces we could sharpen and attach above us in the shed."

"Yeah, I thought about them. Perhaps you could get to work on filing the edges, while I continue here. Then I'll reconfigure my devices whilst the engine charges up the power cells."

"Good idea. I can file them to an edge."

"Bring them down as soon as they are ready."

A few hours later, their vehicle was charged and had the cutting plates affixed to the front. John brought Frieda down the steep stairs into the lower room to get her used to the vehicle. He showed he the rear space inside where he had stashed some straw and some blankets, and comforted her as he helped her into the space for a try out. There was enough room for her to lie with her head up, but it was too small for her stand as they drove. She seemed okay, he thought, and he speculated about all they had been through together - she was likely to accommodate whatever it took to remain with him.

"You are remarkable girl," he said to her when he took her back upstairs to rest until they were ready to leave.

"I have put a lot of supplies together John. Food, blankets, and other things we might need. I think we are ready to go whenever we decide."

"Let's go in one hour. By then, dawn will still be a little way off, but there will be enough light for us to drive without using the headlights."

The drive of twenty miles from Fremont to the fence took them only fifteen minutes as John drove as fast as he possibly could in the low light. They encountered nobody during the journey, and now they were parked within sight of the fence, but just out of reach of the sensors and scanners.

"As soon as I have these devices calibrated correctly and switch them on, we have to go."

"Is there anything I can do?"

"Um, go to the back and give Frieda a pat and a few words for me will you?"

"Sure John. I'll put a blanket over her – the bars over the back will protect her from debris when we smash through, but a blanket will be there for her."

Kerry Ann returned a minute later. "She is fine. Quite calm for a horse in the back of a utility."

"Good. Well, we are right to go then. I'll switch these on...now!" A second later he pushed the accelerator to full and sent them headlong towards the fence. Within a few seconds, the vehicle had reached eighty miles per hour where John kept it, save for going too fast and losing control at the moment of impact.

"Well, here go your cutting blades Kerry Ann."

With a screech of metal and a few serious jolts, they burst through the fence, and continued driving. Alarms began to sound and laser pulses erupted from the canon the instant they broke through, with officers appearing from nowhere to attend to the commotion. They saw nothing besides a large gaping hole in the fence. John's devices had worked perfectly - they had avoided the laser canon, and the electricity.

Without hesitation, the officers tended to at first guarding the hole, then others arrived to mend the hole. They could see a few people running towards them from inside the western sector, so they shot them whilst the others attended to the fence. Within ten minutes the repairs were complete and there was no sign anyone had made a hole just shortly before.

John had driven on for half a mile and then parked the vehicle inside an abandoned shed where they just sat there for a minute coming to terms with the fact they had made it through successfully.

"We cannot keep this vehicle Kerry Ann. They are forbidden in the eastern sector," he said breaking their silence. "The authorities will come looking for us and..."

"Don't be too sure John. Whilst they keep the fence and the gate, they don't have the resources to patrol these places. Maybe we should hide the vehicle all the same. We might be lucky and be able to come back for it."

"Good idea. I'll take Frieda out of the back."

She was in a relatively calm state and as soon as John let her out of the back, she began to eat some of the straw he dragged out with her.

"She is beautiful," Kerry Ann said as she came around the back of the vehicle.

"Indeed," was all he could say.

****

Tobias had wondered what all the noise was when heard something going on at the fence just a short distance from where he was sitting having a coffee in his house. It was still too early to be out due to the curfew, so he could only speculate someone may have tried the divide before dawn and had been caught. He decided he would go and have a look as soon as the curfew lifted – in about an hour. Until then, he thought of trying out his ray gun again as he was now wide-awake and certain he would not go back to sleep. It was there in the hiding place he had made underneath the basement and he gave it a few test runs to see if it was still working. Its' now familiar hum sounded first and then when he pulled the trigger, the bolt of electricity shot out again and hit the target tin can he had set up to test its accuracy. The air around him smelled a little of burning electricity.

"All good," he said aloud. He tried a few more times, before deciding it was time for coffee.

When the curfew time passed, Tobias left his house and went towards the fence to see if there was any traces of the event an hour or so before. When he arrived and stood as close as was permitted from the eastern sector, he could see no evidence of activity. Slightly disappointed, he decided to take a longer walk home to soak up a little time.

When he noticed two people inside the abandoned old shed just down the street, he thought of his ray gun...still at home. He knew the shed had been unoccupied for years, so he was immediately suspicious. There was nothing in there of interest – he knew because he had looked inside a few times over the years and found nothing aside from a few old broken tools.

As caution was the way to survive out on the fringes, he took to hiding himself as he dared to get closer and check out who was inside. When he had reached a corner where he could slink along the wall and take a look through the dirty glass window, he felt somewhat at ease. This was a complete surprise to him. What was even more surprising was when he looked through the window, where he could see John with a woman he did not know, and a horse with a cart.

Tobias could hardly contain himself as he ran to the front and burst inside. John reacted as if the authorities had found them and he pushed Kerry Ann to hide behind their now covered vehicle, before he did the same.

"John? John, it's Tobias. John…it's Tobias!"

"What?" he said as he came out from hiding, hardly believing his eyes. "Tobias! Man, am I glad to see you. Kerry Ann, it's okay. I cannot believe it, but this is a friend of mine. Come out and meet Tobias."

Back at Tobias' house shortly after, the three of them shared a meal of berries, truffles, breads, vegetables and meat, whilst Frieda was content with some fresh feed and comfortable lodgings in one half of the rear shed where they had also stowed the cart. It was a celebratory feast as the two men caught up on everything since their last meeting over a year before, and where Kerry Ann joined in with the feeling of being with people she could trust.

When it came to John telling of the conditions in the west, Tobias was dismayed to hear of the horrors he had encountered, and of Carmel's capture by the Agent.

"I have a feeling I am about to do something, but I am not exactly sure what it is."

"There must be a meaning behind our meeting here after all I have done in coming to the eastern sector. Carmel and I agreed there was something we needed to do, but like you, we were unclear on the precise purpose of our travels, besides just to make it to the east. I am thinking we need to go and get her somehow. The Agent is in Seattle, so I am thinking at some time it could be our destination."

"Back west?" Kerry Ann said. "But we just made it through the fence."

"Yeah, it seems a bit absurd to come through and then go back, but we won't be able to do it straight away. You will not have to come with us Kerry Ann…"

"I'm sticking with you. I have nobody here in the east. The only people I knew were lost somewhere in the west. So where you go, I go."

"Are you sure?"

"Sure as I can be, given the times of late."

"Great, because we need to be all in for this as travelling to the west is going to be more and more confronting the further we go."

"You'll need weapons then…"

"Hey! I've already started with one."

"What do you mean Tobias?"

"I'm sure you'll like it John. Come and have a look."

Tobias fired up the ray gun and took a few shots at the target, impressing both John and Kerry Ann very much.

"It is a great gun you have there. You guys are geniuses. Being with you two makes me feel safer by the minute. What do you think John honey?"

"I'm impressed. It looks like you really did learn a few things off me all those years ago." He gave Tobias a friendly punch on the shoulder, and Tobias pretended to point the gun at him. "Hey, don't point it at me, it might go off."

"No, I killed the circuit, it can't go off."

"Well one thing sorted, but we will need more weapons. At least one each and one spare just in case. Do you know any leads there Tobias?"

"None really. It is pretty deserted in these parts, and where there are authority outposts, they are heavily guarded."

"Any cache or stores around?"

"There is one alongside the old highway going towards the middle of Omaha."

"Then we need to focus on there. Have you seen anything there we should know?"

"Not really. You know, I haven't really scoped it out, or even thought about weapons at all until just a few days ago."

"I think our first plan of attack is to find out how we can make a raid on the place. I have some of my devices…you know the type. We can use them to help us get past their systems."

"It's about five miles from here. Maybe we should go now."

"My thoughts exactly."

Tobias threw a glance at Kerry Ann who had been listening in as she sipped a cup of coffee. "Oh, don't worry about me. I'll take care of your place. You can trust me."

"She's okay Tobias."

"Hey, don't take it the wrong way, but you know…"

"Sure do. How do you think I survived these years in the west?"

"Check on Frieda for me while we are gone, won't you?"

"No worries honey. She'll get the good treatment from me. You two go off and see what you can find. This is kind of exciting, don't you think?"

"You could see it as so Kerry Ann. Tobias, what tools do you have? Something to get us through wire fences or similar?"

"Come to the shed. I have a few to do the trick."

They covered the five miles in good time, encountering very few people on their way.

"See, I told you it is fairly deserted around here. Too many just cannot seem to endure too far in the fringes. They need the authorities I guess and the authorities are spare on technology, provisions, and personnel in this place. These caches are their only means to enforce anything if they have people to use them."

"I bet they never figured on anyone breaking in."

"No way. Their systems are well beyond anyone in these parts hacking in."

"Except us Tobias."

"Except you John."

"The first thing I need to do is to run a scan of the systems they have guarding this place."

John calibrated his scanner device via the holographic controls and quickly intercepted the data they required.

"Gee, you were quick."

"Yeah, over the past few years I have been honing my skills."

"What about flux? I heard the authorities are developing something to counteract the amplifier the Agent has."

"They didn't get it from me. I can only speculate on where it came from or what they are doing. I suppose it is just a progression of what they had when they were trying to get the information out of me through the device they implanted in my head."

"So they are basically lying in a way."

"More or less. The flux technology is still cutting edge. In all the years since those days, I have not met even one individual who had any notion on how to make it work, besides Tim."

"I wonder how or where he is."

"Beats me, but Carmel was a bit upset. She has not seen him in a long time. Okay, now I have the readings. With this data I can decode their security and fool their sensors."

"What about locations? We need to know where they keep their weapons."

"I'll have it in a minute. We just need to wait whilst the algorithm aligns with theirs."

A few moments later, John had what they required, "Right. We need to go to the northern side of the building and find access there and get to the weapons store. We are going to have to be fast though. I am going to take video surveillance off line in the section we enter. You can be sure they will be onto any discrepancy in a flash. I estimate we will have about three minutes."

Tobias cut through the wire perimeter fence as John attended to maintaining the correct data feed to create false readings for the sensors. As soon as he had cut through, they ran to the doorway John was already opening as they approached.

Ten meters onward, they reached the weapons cache doorway where John entered a sequence to open the door. Inside was an array of weaponry.

"Just grab some rifles and power cells, while I make sure this data keeps working."

Tobias took four rifles and filled a bag with power cells.

The moment they had made it back to the external doorway, alarms began to sound throughout the building.

"Grab the tools," John said seeing Tobias about to bend over to pick them up.

They ran through the hole in the fence and then headed to the east to give the impression they had come from there to anyone who might have caught a glimpse of them by sight, or through the surveillance system.

"Keep going this way," Tobias said as they ran as fast as they could. "I know a way we can circle around and then go back to my house."

Two hours later, they arrived back at the house to see Kerry Ann had organised a stash of supplies and was waiting for them in readiness to leave.

"Did you get us some weapons?"

"Sure. We are going to have to move fast though. We might have tricked those officers back there, but soon enough, they could be around here looking for anyone they suspect of stealing weapons from them. How's Frieda?"

"She's great, and ready to go. I harnessed her and packed the cart with food and blankets...and Carmel's engine. There is a bit of straw, but we don't have a lot."

"We'll head for the old farm where I found those truffles and stay there for a while. We can get some of the wild grain there."

"What about the authorities, won't they go there?"

"It is a risk we are going to have to take...as if life these days is not full of risks anyway. Besides, if we go and establish ourselves, hide the weapons, and look as if we live there, then it could increase our chances. We need a base to plan our next moves. Staying here is just too risky, and with so few people about, they are bound to scope all the houses in the vicinity."

Just before sundown they were at the farm and Frieda was happy to be inside the barn eating some wild grains. John decided it was best they all stay with her so they could be close and also to give them a tight close knit area should anyone visit them.

"We should take a heading to the north and then attempt a crossing there," John said putting his finger on Jamestown in the old state of North Dakota.

"It will take us far too long honey," Kerry Ann replied. "Why don't we go back and get my vehicle. It will be much faster then. Surely you can use the brain of yours and come up with some device thing to help us on our way. Travel by foot with Frieda is just too slow...even with the cart. It would be too much to get her to haul us three along as well."

"She's right John. Maybe we should go back for the vehicle."

"I had considered doing so, but the risk driving…"

"You said there is going to be a lot of risk involved. Why don't you and Tobias go and get it. I'll stay here and see what I can find on this farm."

"There is another road we can take it along from my house back to here."

"Okay, you've convinced me. I guess Frieda has done a lot of work by now."

"So what do you have in mind?" Tobias asked John during their eight mile walk back to his house.

"A shielding algorithm. It should work, but it is not a guarantee. We are going to have to be very careful and travel mostly at night without lights. The authorities won't be expecting anything like us so near the fence with all their efforts concentrated on guarding the permitter."

"How long until you have it up and running…the algorithm I mean?"

"About a minute. It is just a few configuration parameters and floating calculations changing in real time as we drive."

Around midnight they were gathered again in the barn with the vehicle parked inside. John and Tobias were working on some modifications to the rear compartment to give Frieda some more space.

"Look girl, they're making some room for you. We can't have you lying down all the way."

When they had finished, John suggested they hide the vehicle in the old shed a few yards behind the barn with a cover and by scattering old debris and broken machinery over and around.

His thoughts had proven worthy, as the next morning when the curfew hour passed, two officers of the authorities had arrived, waking them all from a deep sleep.

"What do we have here? How come you are living here? Why aren't you in town?"

"There is wild food here. It just seems like a good place to stay."

"For how long? When did you get here?"

"A few weeks back."

"This horse. Who gave it you?"

"It's mine," John said. "I've had her a long time."

"We can take it. Any reason why we shouldn't?"

"None I can think of. But I was going to ride her to have my identification chip update according to the advice the other day."

The officers stood silent for a few moments considering the merit of this statement from John. "Why don't you walk? A lot of people do."

"I have a sore leg and it is much more efficient for me to ride. After all, I want the update as soon as I can for protection from the Agent. I was going to have it done today," John said whilst showing them an old scar on his leg – it did not affect his ability to walk at all.

"How did you get a sore leg?"

"I've had it for years. It happened when I was helping an officer like you apprehend a dissident non-complier when the chip first came out." This lie seemed to have some merit with the officers.

"Do you have any weapons?"

"No. What for? Life on this farm is fairly safe so far and we thought being here as responsible citizens would be okay. Anyway, weapons are illegal."

"Indeed they are. We need to take a look to make sure. Is there anything you would like to tell us?"

"Um, only to say I hope they authorities can get rid of the Agent. He is making life very difficult for all of us." The others nodded in agreement.

The two officers looked around the barn without finding anything, and then they went outside to look in the shed. When they went inside, this instilled a degree of nervousness in the three of them as they stood at the door to the barn watching.

"Stay calm," John said. "Give nothing away."

"Come here," one of the officers shouted.

"What is it?" John asked.

"Did you know there are illegal machines in this shed?"

"What machines?"

"These farm implements and the old produce transport."

"We had seen them, but we are not interested. They are of no use to us."

"Have you tried to operate them?"

"No, they look broken." John was thankful for the extent they had gone to in hiding their vehicle, as it was stashed behind a pile of machine debris and so well disguised and out of reach to the officers, they simply looked in its direction, and then moved on.

"You are clear. But…make sure you all get your chip upgrades as soon as possible."

"We will," they all said in unison.

After the officers had gone, the three of them could take a few deep breaths.

"You know how lucky we are?" John said as the officers drove away from the farm.

"What do you mean?"

"They were absent minded enough not to scan us for chips with their hand held scanners after I said the lie about the upgrade."

"I entirely forgot," Tobias said.

"I'll make some of those dummy chip devices I built years ago now, in case we need them."

"Good idea."

As he worked, his thoughts drifted at times to Carmel. Something inside him, told John there would be no requirement for hurrying to the aid and rescue of Carmel. He could not exactly tell what it was giving him this confidence, as he felt sure she would have the strength to survive. Perhaps it was her essence as a person prevailing for her through these times of travesty brought on by the Agent.

The three had agreed they would stay a while at the farm to prepare plans for the mission to Seattle, and to lay up for some time before the arduous conditions of travel in the western sector. It would take a concerted effort to make it to Seattle and even more so to rescue Carmel and take back the Torus of Eternity. Nevertheless, they would not delay and as soon as they could move, they would.

When he had finished building the false identification devices and had tested them thoroughly with dummy signals he generated through his scanner a few days later, John joined the other two in living a little at the farm. Winter's grip was still holding strong with each morning an icy start to the day, giving way to clear sunny weather and for the first time in ages, all three adults finally relaxed some. As reliant as they were upon their own individual types of ingenuity for survival, they all felt free of the burden of running, of hiding, and of worrying for a time, enabling them to feel more alive than they had for weeks.

Tobias no longer felt alone as he had for so long just surviving in his house on the fringes. Kerry Ann finally had the company of people whom she could trust and who lifted her own spirits and John had time to contemplate how long he had been running up until this point. They had gathered as much of the wild grain they could find, each of them enjoying the activity and each other's company as they scoured the open fields in search of food.

As John rode Frieda through the windy grasses at full gallop, she seemed to have a renewed spirit as if she felt similar to the others and for all he could tell she was thoroughly enjoying the ride, despite her heavy breathing and the strain of her muscles. She let out a heartened whiney as she reared up before they were off again, on a return route back to the farm buildings.

A few minutes later when they pulled up at a gate, John could see the weather would soon change when he felt a gusty cold wind hit his face.

He looked to the northwest where a cloudbank was building as he talked to Frieda, "Come on girl. One last run."

With a pull on the reigns, they were off again, headlong towards the barn amongst the stand of old Oak trees.

By midnight, the weather had closed in, bringing freezing temperatures and a gentle snowfall. Then by morning a few inches of snow lay upon the ground under laden skies of grey. This cold weather lasted for the next few days, bringing constant snow, and a bitter wind coming in from the north. On the fourth night, Tobias and John discussed the technology options they had and what they thought would serve them well along the journey ahead all the way to the Agent in Seattle.

"I still have the flux resonator and the teleport configuration. If he or the authorities ever got hold of this technology, we would be in much more trouble than we are now."

"They would use it to accelerate atomic resonances wouldn't they?"

"Yes, and if the Agent was able to do so, he could unleash viruses with much more devastating effect than he has so far. And, the authorities would have sufficient technological advantage where no-one would ever be able to challenge them...or even come close."

"So, it would stabilise his amplifier?"

"Precisely. The unstable nature of his beast is what makes his viruses have only limited impact and it is why they only last for short bursts before breaking down. With the flux algorithms, he would be able to open up voids in the continuum and then he could end up sending the entire planet into oblivion. It is fortunate he is not aware enough of its potential and also to go after it. Lucky too, he knows nothing of my ability to make it work otherwise I would also be his captor and be forced to work for him."

"What about the authorities and their capacity?"

"Limited. They are still probably at the pseudo flux stage where they rely on theoretical physics, rather than actually working with the real thing. I have a fair idea on what they are missing, but for them to get it would mean they would have to change their intentions...or the way they look at it. You see, you can only access the pathways to the algorithm based on your instigating angle. A bit like how at the quantum level, particles respond to the investigation placed upon them and so they change relative form and resonance to show the intended test results."

"So they would be able to accelerate atomic fields and open up connections through dimensions?"

"Yeah. It is pretty simple after you get the algorithm. One thing leads to another basically, and then you can control the vortexes. My worry is what the Agent might be doing with these unstable viruses. Those holes I've seen in people and how they tend to congeal together, means there is a sub-atomic squandering happening, and it could lead to unstable vortexes basically disrupting the integrity of time and space. He doesn't know what he is doing, or care about it. But if he continues, then literally all hell could break loose."

"Seems like it already has. Those people you told me about, and the looks I have seen when they do the transports at the gate, make for pretty horrific experiences."

"I've seen a few of them too," Kerry Ann interjected. "They look pretty scary to me and in such misery too. It is hard to imagine human beings appearing like they do and seeming to be so miserable. It puts pay to any misery I have seen before."

"What I saw near Salt Lake City was weird in the least. The fusion of organic mass and the entanglement of their atoms," John said feeling a shudder at the memory.

"So their bodies begin to blend with each other?"

"More or less. I can only guess it is due to the viruses loosening the integrity of their cohesion and so they literally float about until they re-attach with other organic matter, which then leads to issues of bodily rejection and the formation of bad lesions, and the fetid smell...hey, let's change the subject, I think we get the picture."

"Yeah I'm with you there honey. How about a nice hot drink with a touch of the whisky we have?"

"I love you Kerry Ann."

"Aw John honey. I love you too."

Chapter 19

Winter closed in across the north bringing snow, ice, and terrible winds for the next two weeks. Whilst people throughout the west suffered due to the Agents' afflictions, so too did those in the east where cities and lives were drawn to a standstill making for harsh conditions the authorities did nothing to ease. Where in previous times they would ensure the on-going efficiency of society by responding to the weather and making it possible for people to continue their daily work life, they were simply disinterested now, leaving many to suffer and fall by the way side. It was becoming the severest winter of discontent since the Agent had begun to have influence, and even worse than the storm brought on by the authorities when they had used the HAARP installation as a weapon to battle him.

People froze in the west, deprived of energy to keep them warm, and people froze in the east without the systems being maintained by the authorities. It was as if they did not care, and they didn't. Their focus was on the Agent and so any lives lost were considered the price to pay for them to be able to reconstitute their grip on society as a whole.

In the west, he sat in front of his amplifier sending out more and more viruses to make matters worse. Alongside the roads, inside of buildings, and between the sheets of ice layers, bodies froze, they fused, and they formed a sufferance of humanity, in stasis until the seasons brought forth the thaw.

In the skies over the great cities on the east, there still flew some of the machines of progress. HyperJets streaked the skies now and then as they were deployed to control those who sought dissent brought on through hardship. As they heightened their push to gain supremacy over their adversary, the authorities began to completely disregard humanity with missions of destruction. Entire towns burned bright in contrast to the chilling white of the snows. Sectors of cities were marked as off limits and their tenements were blown to ashes. Gatherings were dispersed, their occupants sent to scatter in fear. Where once they were providers, now the authorities were seen to be in disgrace to the fundamental values all for the sake of power and control.

There was one thing and just one man who knew the secret desired by the authorities as they began to change technology away from the public view, and so they began to make plans to find him, to take him, and to use him. As this man sat in the barn with his friends, he was aware they would want him. He knew they knew his knowledge was key to any truthful success and he knew once it was revealed, both the authorities and the Agent would clash over him.

He felt a bit cold and a little hungry as wintery conditions stipulated they be mindful of their supplies, forcing them to ration the food and the fuel. Tobias had tried his holographic projector a few times to see if there was any news about the weather, but broadcasts were limited to a few items advising there was no reprieve in sight for the next few weeks.

News was increasingly becoming difficult to obtain as the authorities placed further restrictions upon citizens. The use of holographic phones was restricted to communications only in places where they had isolated their systems from attack by the Agent. Using any device for any other purpose was now strictly forbidden in case of contracting a virus from him and this virus entering central systems via the phone.

News from other nations was virtually non-existent as across the globe they were implementing similar restrictions reigning in the operations of their vast networks to only service only the essential for the limited functioning of society.

The Agent knew no bounds as he sent his virus attacks out across the network of transmission hardware under his control. Fortunate for him but not so for the authorities or his victims, the central systems established in the years leading up to the identification chip implementation, had seen vast capacities realised where data could traverse the globe in seconds from almost any location to another. And he continued to use the network – again and again sending out viruses to bring about suffering. His motives were to bring them all to their knees and then to gain an upper hand where he could make inroads into places not under his control. This included breaching the dividing fence across North America.

He sent his minions to gather up those afflicted so grotesquely and then bring them in vast quantities inside transport vehicles to his Seattle base of operations. Inside transport jets he placed them, and then gave the orders for their re-distribution into the eastern sector. Showing no remorse, he then enjoyed the visions relayed back to him as his squadrons ventured into eastern airspace where they dumped the masses – individuals and those joined through atomic meld were thrown out of the jets to fall to the cities below in a rain of horror.

Bombardment was his new weapon to aid the spread of displacement and the spread of dismay. For many below, the clusters of twisted humanity suddenly cascading from the skies, made them fearful of being outside, and it made the authorities care even less for many places they had already considered inefficient to their goals. The Agent knew no ends, yet he sought an end. He knew nothing of what it was to hold compassion, nor did he care, for to consider such a thing was never within his constitution. And ironically, he held no regard for constitution, as such was his intentions to bring horror, oblivion, and deliver futility as his spectre.

There was no more George Smyth, Agent Eight from authority central, under the command of superiors. He regarded himself as superior, yet he struggled with the true meaning of such notion for he held no real regard for himself at all. His megalomania was his character in each and every breath, and in the way he laughed, how he toiled with the holographic controls for his vortex amplifier, and when he marvelled at how destructive his beast could be.

At times, he would seek to further this act of vengeance, and so would gaze at the two horned torus suspending the ring torus between them. He would search for answers wondering what it would be like if his amplifier were stable. He would engage himself through mannerisms and expressions at times so inward he was…as were his viruses. He would yearn for a time for it to stop flickering and deliver a splendid apparition of eternal nothingness to his soulless endeavours. Seeking further extrapolation of his mania and rage, he then expressed this enacted in response to heavy industrial music played at volumes loud enough to vibrate the room. This would stimulate moments resulting in fits of physical violence as he flung furniture about and flung himself about.

For most he was far too distracted to care, far too distracted to think, and far too distracted to know he held a vital key within his compound – a key to enliven the beast into complete furore where he would be able to dispense with this world at will enacting his volition.

Carmel stood beside him now in witness of his latest measures of attrition, for he wanted her to show him her difficulty with such things. He wanted to slowly break her as she had done to him all those years ago. And he wanted to then make her suffer at his hand where her acts of condescendence toward him would not compare to the hatred coursing through his veins.

"Show me some blood you fools," he suddenly yelled at the holographic images showing on the array before them. "I want to see the fluid of their lives wash down the drains. I want to see their essence be cast into the filth and the mire of their remains. I want to make them all nothing…"

"Shut up you sick…sick…oh what is it you are called?"

"Yes my former superior, I am sick. And…I am becoming sicker. Why? Don't you like it? Are you not impressed with how I can dismember them? How I can tear at their very souls? Oh please, do not hold back. Please tell me of your distaste, for upon it I will feed. I am distaste and soon enough, you will be like those others whom I hold deep below this factory. And in there, I will machine and shape you all to be delivered unto me as my minions. For I am sorry to say, there is simply nothing to be done about it."

"Don't count on it. People will challenge you. You are disgusting."

"And so are you." He said smiling in a smug resolute way. "Your pathetic love for things and your pathetic caring for those who are barely alive is meaningless. Now watch as I take yet another step towards this end lurking so very near."

He engaged the array once more and sent out a new virus he had been working on for the past few days. It was unlike any he had sent previously, for it struck at the authorities and at their machines with more effect than any previous time. His holographic imagery relayed the impacts back to them as they stood watching.

The matte black high-rise buildings collapsed and crashed to the ground killing people outright. Machines everywhere at random became dysfunctional causing mayhem, with the largest impact being upon those for processing and manufacturing foodstuffs.

"Now they will starve," he said as he turned to Carmel, "And so will you. Take her to the room with the others so they can all share in their demise together. And don't let them have any light for five days. By then I will have prepared my machines for them."

Inside the room, it was pitch black to the naked eye of normal sight, but to those inside, there could see an aura field around each other. Chan had instructed them on how to focus on their auras as a means to counteract their long periods of being held in darkness, and so each of them could see the light of each other at the time Carmel was sent to their room. As she entered, they all felt a simultaneous uplifting in their spirits – a moment Chan had told them would come soon. Since their initial contact when the Agent had shown them to her, Chan knew Carmel would be returned. He saw as it as the elemental natural flow of progression. The moment she entered they remained in silence, bringing her into their circle of light to welcome her and embrace her.

Carmel was of similar feeling as she had spent most of her time concentrating on the group of five since their first contact. Immediately and without word she sat with them, embracing their love and their visions of light. She focused on giving to them as it was her way to give, and they could sense the resurgence of strength she offered. When it came time for them to finally speak to each other, it was not a discussion of the past, and it was not a discussion of what was happening in the world outside – it was a discussion of progression.

"His mind is so very loose and distracted from any connection to his heart," Chan said. "He is and will be his own undoing and now he has sent you here Carmel, as a means to bring this about. His senses are not aligned with the intentions of progression and so he thinks only through his mania, and by doing such things, it will see him struggle eternally with his issues."

"He thinks by making us weak and by making us desperate, he will be able to control those he does not understand and through this misalignment and desire to control, he will overlook the connection to all sufficing to bring about change. It is then with this change, where he will be brought to reckon with his own self, and be brought to reckon with his deeds."

"We are not alone Chan," Carmel replied.

"There will be many who are willing to listen once again to their hearts, and there will be those who we know and will be most instrumental to bring about this awakening. They will arrive to us."

VOLITION

"Are you speaking of John?"

"Yes Carmel. I speak of John. I speak of his very being as the representative of the human spirit and the will to awaken through his actions…as he has often done in the past, the present, and will do in the future. All of these times align despite their seeming to be in lineal passage. The nature of intentions in their true elemental state is one not bound by such ways for they come laterally from beyond the material aspiration of consciousness."

"The Agent told me you are all so very weak and would be unable to understand me if I spoke to you before."

"He is blind through his ways, for you spoke very clearly to us when he presented us to you, and it is through these actions, the Agent was polarised in his very intentions where he sought to endear suffering, yet he did precisely the opposite. We have strength as you can feel, he cannot understand. Our bodies may be weak but our hearts remain strong in feeling, for the Agent cannot afflict us through his efforts with starvation of both light and food. Even our deaths would serve no progress for his wayward intentions."

"We will have to escape from this place."

"Yes. John will help."

"I know. The day I was captured, he gave me a look of such determination I was confident in his strength to find us and avoid the guile of the Agent."

"So very true Carmel. An appropriate choice for both yourself and for him. Such communications can be the strengths of indication leading to the response through actions of those very intentions elemental in nature and therefore of progression in return to the aligned position instead of the mind casting doubt or any issues interfering with this flow."

Chapter 20

By the time the arduous winter conditions had eased with sufficient thaw to allow passage, John and the others had taken to driving the vehicle at night as fast as they could manage towards Jamestown. They broke through the fence in the same way they had near Omaha, and then had driven onward underneath the transit way on a heading towards what was once known as Montana. Driving though the mountains had been difficult due to the amount of snow and ice, but their use of a snowplough blade the two men had fashioned from some old metal before they left the farm, had been adequate to get them through. After five days in the western sector driving carefully to avoid any people, they had made it through the mountains and had stopped to make a plan of attack, at a place called Spokane in old Washington State. Kerry Ann was tending to Frieda as Tobias and John discussed what they would do when they approached the Agent's lair at the jet manufacturing plant further west.

Considering the nature of horses and their propensity to being flighty and nervous at times, Frieda had endured well riding in the modified rear section of their vehicle. They had fashioned a space for her to stand up or lie down. Now as she grazed outside the shed where they had decided to hide, she was as content as any horse when left to roam a field of ample grass supply.

Kerry Ann was walking with her and supplied a good number of comforting words and the occasional pat in reassurance. Their hideout was in a valley to the west of the town where the steep sides shielded them from the incursion of bad weather, and also provided only one access point through a small canyon. They had considered this aspect of the natural geography as an advantage should anyone try to visit.

Conditions in the western sector had continued to rapidly decline under the Agent, but in one way this helped them as many had become unable to move about due the wintry conditions and their state of physical health. When Kerry Ann grew tired of walking the fields and thought Frieda had settled, she walked her back to the shed to join the two men. She was not much of the mind to tackle concepts involving technology or strategy but did hold the will to survive and what it meant to hold dear to those she saw as trustworthy and genuine. She considered herself to have an important role, which both men agreed upon. They saw her as a good friend with input into ideas and a sense they respected. Without realising it, they were forming a sense of reliance on Kerry Ann – something she was well aware of.

"How is Frieda?" John asked seeing her return with Frieda walking behind.

"She's great honey. It's good there are some open fields here free of snow with ample grass. I'm sure she feels right at home. What are you guys doing? Are you hungry?"

"Um, just some technology work, and yes, I am hungry thanks," John replied as Tobias nodded in agreement.

"Good. I'm starving, but don't you go start thinking I'm here to fix you meals."

"Never Kerry Ann. Hey I'll fix some food if you like," Tobias offered. "I think John can work alone for a while."

"Sure Tobias. I'll help you though."

As they sat eating a dinner of wild vegetables Kerry Ann had found, some berries, and the last of the truffles Tobias had found, they talked about what lay ahead. John was intent on letting Kerry Ann know the full details of the plans he and Tobias had begun to work on.

"Tobias and I are going to scope out the facility at Seattle. It should take us about two weeks. When we are there, I am going to take a few scanner readings to see what systems the Agent has in place. Tobias will help and keep an eye out for anyone and anything."

"So you would like me to stay here and take care of things?"

"Yes please. This place is a good base for us and we are going to have to rely on you to keep it so. Without you, we would be out in the open in a way."

"Yeah, I figured you might be. When are you two going?"

"Tomorrow before dawn. We thought we would hitch up the cart and get Frieda to take us."

"What about our vehicle?"

"Too risky I would say. If the Agent has any sensors on the lookout, he would find us in a flash. Tobias, do you think you could make a few repairs to the cart after the damage it sustained on our drive? I want to get a few of these calibrations sorted out tonight so we can head off with everything at the ready in the morning."

"Sure, I'll get on it now. There are only a few little repairs to make to one of the wheels and to the harness."

In the early hours they left Kerry Ann under a cloud laden sky void of stars.

"You are sure about the plans on what happens if people come and how to use your weapon aren't you?"

"I can handle the plans John, and the gun. If it gets heavy, I'll take the vehicle up the track. Don't worry. I've seen my share of country roads. You can count on me honey."

"Are you scared Kerry Ann?" Tobias asked.

"Sure am Tobias, but it will keep me alert. I'm not going to give in to any fear."

Two days out from Seattle, John and Tobias encountered their first obstacle – a group of four people who had watched them approach and then had stopped them in their tracks.

"You cannot go over the mountains with your horse. There is too much snow. Anyway, what makes you think we are going to let you past?"

"Look, we don't want trouble. We just want to get to Seattle. How deep is the snow?"

"About three feet, maybe two in places if you are lucky and we let you past."

"As I said, we don't want trouble. We are going to try the mountains anyway we can. Where else will we go?"

"With us."

"What do you mean?"

"We could stop you. Look at the horse. There is very little to eat around here, and sure it is not as good as beef, but a bit of horse meat sure looks tasty considering the rubbish we have eaten lately."

"You cannot have her. No questions. Let us past."

"No. Who are you to make demands? In case you cannot count, there are four of us and just two of you. It makes for two on one you see."

"No it doesn't," Tobias said as he revealed a laser pulse rifle to them. "I think this puts the odds in our favour, don't you think?"

"Yeah. I bet it doesn't work. We have some weapons too. A few bows and arrows. They'll sort you out."

"It does work. Now let us pass."

"Prove it, otherwise the horse is our dinner."

Tobias shot at the feet of the four men making them jump as the laser caused a small explosion on the ground in front of them.

"Now let us pass."

"Yeah you win, but watch out. Others around here are in bigger numbers and there are even more the closer you get to the city."

"We'll take our chances."

As they passed through the mountains, they found the group of men had been exaggerating, as there was barely twelve inches of snow on the road. A few laser blasts took care of the deeper snow, so the journey continued on as per their planned timetable, where they arrived in the vicinity of the manufacturing plant and home to the Agent, on time.

There was very little evidence of any activity on the outside of the plant. Tobias and John took their chances as soon as they arrived by setting a camp on its permitter out of sight of all of the main buildings. They could see the large hanger used to store completed HyperJets – they wondered if there would be any working planes inside. John had never piloted anything so large, but he was willing to take his chances with their mostly automated systems.

"I think we need to consider any aircraft available Tobias. I am confident I can fly. It might just take a bit of getting used to."

"But we won't have enough time to do so."

"We could. Listen." John told Tobias of how he could use the flux mechanics he had brought with him to over ride the systems the Agent would have in place. He detailed what it would take to create enough diversion for them to have time to find a plane, spend some minutes analysing its systems, and then a little more time to power it up and take off along the runway stretching from the main hanger to the field nearby where they were hiding.

"This could be what we really do need to get an upper hand on this entire situation. If we can steal a jet, then we will be free to go just about anywhere."

"Yeah, but the systems are a lot more complicated than your old Beaver plane."

"Sure, but remember, you are talking to just about the only person around who knows how flux mechanics work, so it is not like I am inept at technology."

"You have a point. What about fuel?"

"See over there?" John pointed to a large storage area nearby the hanger. "There will be fuel over in the building there. These jets only take relatively small cells for their size as they rely heavily on pre-plasma rocket thrusters. I reckon we could put four or five of them on this cart."

"Can we land back at Spokane though?"

"The landing strip is smaller, but I think if we come in on a steep approach then we could pull up in time."

"Hey, they are not like beavers you know. You can't just fly in and fly out of riverbeds in a HyperJet."

"Sure, but I think I can try something close. We have to think about it Tobias. Travel is just too slow otherwise."

"Okay, we'll scope it out and then when we come back with the vehicle to get Carmel, we'll try then. It's really going to get the Agent angry though."

"We just have to stay a step ahead of him. He might know a few things, but in reality, he is an idiot. If we have the means, we can defeat him."

Their success was happily reflected on their faces as they departed Seattle the next day after spending almost a whole twenty four hours camped and watching. John had all the data he required, and they had found three HyperJets in a shed just off the main hangar. The Agent had destroyed those in the main building, but such as it was with his attacks of mania, he had left the scene content and laughing, having completely overlooked the other jets in a shed he had likely considered not worth his efforts.

"What about those people around the place. They all look so sad, yet they were not afflicted with any viruses."

"Probably his servants or some type. I guess if you work so close with the Agent, you are not likely to be a very happy person."

Frieda took them willing at pace back to Spokane over the mountains and back to the valley over the next few days. They encountered a small group of virus affected people wandering the road at one time who were so weak all they could do was slightly motion towards them as Frieda took them at speed. Aside from the odd sighting of aircraft piloted by a minion of the Agent, no other obstacle had appeared in their way.

Kerry Ann was delighted to see them coming down the valley on the day they were due to arrive back at the farm.

She ran to greet them, praising them as she went, "I knew I could trust you honey, and you Tobias. You two are the greatest men I have ever known. And Frieda, look at you."

She gave Frieda a hug around her neck as John and Tobias jumped down to return her greeting. She gave them hugs in turn repeating her accolades for their successful return.

"Okay, let's go inside and Tobias and I will tell you all about our little journey."

"Not so little honey. You've been gone over two weeks and it's more than five hundred miles return since you left here. I'll take Frieda to the shed first."

When they sat eating together, Kerry Ann felt safe to be with the two men once again. John gave her a summary of what had occurred during their trip to Seattle and how he was set on stealing a HyperJet.

"So we're going to fly. Wow. Last time I flew in a jet, I was a little girl. I haven't even been in one of those new fangled HyperJet things. How fast do they go?"

"Fast enough to get us far away from Seattle. They can go to around four thousand miles per hour."

"At least Frieda will get some rest. She has been great."

Yes she will," John reflected on his time knowing Frieda so far, rekindling memories then further back as he thought of Asper and Lorraine, and then of his son Chris. He wondered where they all were and if they were alive. He could not be certain. Times were so uncertain, anything seemed possible, yet so much of life seemed out of reach.

"So what is our next move?" Kerry Ann asked interrupting his thoughts.

"Tobias and I are going to take the vehicle to Seattle and do three things. Rescue Carmel, steal the torus used by the Agent in his amplifier, and then we are going to take one of those HyperJets and come back here for you Kerry Ann. You will need to make it to the airport in Spokane with Frieda - we are not leaving her behind, the cart, or Carmel's engine. If we cannot take the jet, we'll come back here via the airport in the vehicle and then we will have to keep going."

"We can count on you honey. I'm already thinking long about flying out of this mess."

Their time together again was only brief as John and Tobias agreed it would be best if they went back to Seattle immediately to avoid problems driving through the mountains from any new snowfall.

"I'll be waiting with Frieda at the airport just like you said," Kerry Ann said hoping they would be back sooner rather than later.

"Make sure you go to the place we told you. Tobias and I checked it out on our way back here, and it looks safe. Be there in nine hours. It will be five hours drive there for us two. We'll allow an hour in Seattle just to be sure, and then the drive back will be another five so this makes it better in case we are able to take a plane. You might need to wait around a bit if we are late driving back. If we fly, then we will wait around for you. I guess we would be there in about seven hours to be sure...maybe less."

"Don't worry, we will avoid any trouble," Tobias added.

They had decided their first objective would be to investigate and prepare a jet if they could. Once the melee of rescuing Carmel began, they would need a fast escape. This objective proved to be successful when they were able to free a HyperJet of its holdings and load five fuel cells on board without being detected.

"It will take a bit to get it going," John said as he studied the controls. "At least we have it ready to pre-flight stage. If we make it back here, we'll have to do the pre-flight checks and then power up for a few minutes. This shed has kept these planes in good condition even though they have not flown for years. We can thank the authorities for the lengths they went to in keeping this place at the ready and free from contaminants."

The readout on John's scanner looked unusual for what he was expecting as they stood a few minutes later in hiding just outside the main building. It showed an installation in a room at the rear of the main factory building with six machines producing a constant stream of input data. From what he could tell, the readouts were similar to the nanotechnology update chairs he had encountered years before – notably at his son's Chris' residence at the high-rise in London.

"The Agent must be using some of those implants. I wonder why. They'll only affect his own people if he sends out another virus or mess up his own systems."

"It must be part of his madness. Maybe he is using them to test some systems."

"I'm going to focus in on those readings for a minute. Keep a watch out and use the scanner you made – it will show if anyone with weapons are closing in on us. Once I have enough data, we should make our move." John calibrated the readout for a few minutes to zero in on the room. "Yeah, I was right, six people by the looks of it, all undergoing something nasty from the Agent."

"So where do we start?"

"In the main building. My readouts show his main operations are there, along with his amplifier. We need to disable some codes and falsify others, before we can move in."

They armed themselves each with a laser pulse rifle, took one spare, and Tobias's ray gun. Kerry Ann was left with the remaining rifle in case she ran into any trouble. As the two men approached the doors to the main building, they only needed to avoid a few of the Agent's minions who were milling about looking lost for something to do or focus on. When they reached the main doorway, they paused for a moment as John fine-tuned his scanner readouts.

"Okay. There is definitely a strong signal coming from the far side of the room, which I am sure is the amplifier. I am going to send a flux signal to it now. This should enable us to penetrate the electro-static field and take it from its position."

John entered a sequence to disable the charge field leaving it to appear as though the field was still physically in place according to the Agent's readouts. The effect was sufficient to make it appear as though the three torus were still active and the amplifier charged.

"I suggest we change tactics and take it as the first thing. With these other signals, we can make our way around avoiding the sensors. When we get to Carmel, we can then leave without having to go back for the torus. He'll be nearby, but most likely working alone, as Carmel told me he preferred to be alone when she was his superior. Keep your rifle at the ready but don't fire unless you have to, otherwise his minions will come running."

They entered at a run with John immediately going to the holographic array where he took the Torus of Eternity. His algorithm was working as the readouts continued to show the amplifier was still operating with the torus in situation.

Next move was towards the rear where two doors were located side by side, but their footsteps had brought attention. At the moment they were about to enter through the right side door, a minion of the Agent burst through the left side.

"What's going on here?" he demanded.

"Nothing," Tobias said as he shot him with the rifle at stun setting. This served to bring more people from inside the room, and so both John and Tobias shot them as they appeared. When no others came through the door, they were about to run in through the right side doorway, but they held their ground. Tobias looked at John questioningly as he swapped from his rifle to his ray gun. "What...?"

"Left door. Go in," he said as he began to run at the doorway just a few yards away.

"Who are you?" the Agent demanded of them the second they entered. He was standing in front of a row of chairs occupied by people with their heads bent low.

"Never you mind who I am."

"You!" the Agent identified John an instant later.

"Yes me. You little bastard. Where is Carmel?"

The Agent did not hesitate a moment longer and fired at John, but Tobias had covered him and before the laser bolt could strike, an electric blue bolt erupted from the ray gun burning the air and causing static to flicker about. Tobias had shot the Agent in the hand. It didn't stop John from being hit though as a laser knocked him to the ground where he cried out in anguish from pain in his shoulder.

"Carmel! Hey Carmel, it's Tobias." She was the first person he saw in one of the six chairs lined up against the far wall. A second later he realised the other five were people he had not seen in a long time. "John! John, are you Okay? They are all here John."

The Agent was whimpering from the severe burn to his hand, and for a moment was disorientated from what was happening around him. When John responded to Tobias, the Agent came around with his attention on his attackers once more. He launched at them in an attempt to inflict injuries, but the two men were far too strong for the small man, and after a few seconds of scuffle, he lay on the floor unconscious. Without delay, both John and Tobias turned and ran to the chairs.

"Careful. If we disconnect before switching this off, we could hurt them," he said as they set about freeing the six adults linked to nanotechnology injection chairs. Within ninety seconds they had freed all of them from the tentacle like injection and data lines.

"John, we knew you would come. The others are so very weak though."

"I can see, but we need to be quick. There will be people all over here at any moment. As fast as they could, Carmel, Tobias, and John led the others out through the doors into the main control room.

"Just a second," John said letting go of Raynie's arm. He levelled his rifle and fired a volley of six shots all over the holographic array, destroying the vortex amplifier and most of the other equipment. "Right, let's go!"

When they arrived at the doorway leading outside, the Agent's minions had come rushing. There were at least thirty people all intent on stopping the attackers any way they could. Some had pulse rifles, and others were armed with whatever they could find. The scene quickly became a battleground of cross fire laser shots, and objects being thrown around. Tobias now had his moment with the ray gun. Shooting the Agent had not been a pleasure, but to shoot the Agent was a breakthrough. Now he took to the minions sending bolts flying where at times they flickered from one attacker to the next. Carmel took a ricochet shot in the lower leg but remained at Tobias' side managing to stun three of their assailants with the rifle he had given her.

John was firing and helping the others by trying to shield them as they slowly moved in the direction of the shed out by the main hanger. He watched Tobias use his ray gun and saw him smile as his weapon had full effect upon those whom he aimed for. Amongst the melee, John was impressed with its results and for a moment he even managed a slight smile.

As they finally approached the door to the shed, there were only four armed minions left, with the others doing what they could to prevent escape. At the last moment before they went inside, Jake and Jenna both took laser shots, their cries sounding out through the din.

Tobias then let forth a volley of ray gun bolts taking out another three of the minions.

"Keep them back while I get the others into the plane," John shouted.

"Oh we will," Tobias replied. Both he and Carmel kept firing at and around their pursuers until all the others had successfully boarded the jet. As they gradually retreated towards the ladder to go inside themselves, John powered up all the systems and pre-flight checks. Within three minutes he was complete and the jet was ready to go, but the Agent had regained consciousness and was himself running towards his waiting spaceship.

John powered up the four engines and they slowly taxied out of the open end of the shed and onto the runway. As soon as he was aligned, he pushed the throttle to full power and the jet reacted instantly, pulling everyone back hard into their seats. Take off for HyperJets was normally a gradually process in order to minimise the effects of forces on passengers, but now circumstances demanded John give it maximum power.

Within half a minute they were airborne and as soon as he could, John turned the jet on a hard left heading straight for Spokane.

"We have to make a landing for two more passengers, and then the sky is the limit."

Ten minutes later John took the jet in on a steep approach to Spokane airport for a landing to pick up Kerry Ann and Frieda. He was concerned though as the Agent would be following in his space ship at any moment and the wait at the airport for Kerry Ann to arrive would be stressfully long. As he pulled up at the main terminus, he was surprised and immensely relieved. Kerry Ann had taken the initiative and arrived early to wait the time out at the airport. He did not even cut the engines as Tobias helped her bring Frieda and the cart inside. Kerry Ann had thought ahead and so Carmel and Tobias were able to help her pull up a ramp she had found. As soon as all was secure, John turned and then took the jet skyward again on a heading east at maximum speed.

The Agent was beside himself with anger and hatred. He was almost at his absolute worst and he was almost unable to control his space ship. He was flying but erratically as he entered sequences again and again in an effort to track the

HyperJet. Each time he tried, he failed, and so he would try again, only to get the same result. John had used his clever stealth like device he had first used when he and Tobias escaped from Alaska, and so the Agent had no idea where the HyperJet was, or where it was heading.

He started screaming, and then he could not stop. He was screaming words indiscernible as speech. They were rants and babbles screamed incoherently at the top of his voice. He blew up buildings, bridges, houses, transit tubes, and trees.

He was utterly beside himself and unable to deal with his failure, so he finally landed back at his base and decided to send out as many viruses he could, thinking he might affect the lost HyperJet. But he couldn't as John had destroyed his array, and the moment he discovered he was powerless, he descended into his mania again and held it for the entire night until the next morning where he fell asleep on the floor of his control room and was lost not to dreams but nightmares as dreams in the sense of mania for within his sleep, George always retained this element of consciousness.

Chapter 21

The authorities tracked the HyperJet since it left the manufacturing plant at Seattle. Despite their knowledge of his whereabouts, they had remained powerless to do anything against the Agent. They were baffled why it had stopped at Spokane, an airport not equipped for large jets, and then taken off again shortly after. They watched the readouts as it headed towards them in the east, only to then turn away on a new heading towards the north. A moment later as it disappeared off their scanners, they were convinced John Matheson was piloting the plane.

The authorities needed him if they were to dispose of the Agent for good, and so were prepared to do whatever it took to finally recapture the only man who could help them develop true flux mechanics as an insurmountable technology for managing planet Earth. An emergency meeting of those who made decisions was convened at authority headquarters far below New York City. They were continuously assessing the situation battling the Agent, and now a renewed sense of hope for dominance had come to them. When all required to attend were seated around the large oval table inside the central meeting room, they began to analyse the situation and make proposals.

"We have to see this as an event of significance. If Matheson has taken a jet from the facility, then it must mean something has changed. Matheson must have done something, and I am willing to bet he has interfered somehow with the Agent's operations capacity."

"How can we be sure though? If we take it on your advice and go ahead with the premise he is now less capable, what is going to happen if the premise is wrong? Bringing major systems online is a risk. If he unleashes a virus using the amplifier, then we are wide open."

"Why would Matheson have gone there at all? The torus is surely not the object of his intentions. I can't see him as wanting it in the same way the Agent did. Perhaps he just wanted a jet."

"You have a point. His service record was exemplary. But...he is the expert on flux mechanics, and with the torus he could realise a lot of power."

"Yes, but look at this," the officer said as he displayed John's record via a holographic projector in the centre of the large oval table. "If we look at all these records of his thought patterns we took at the facility near San Francisco, and all the other data we have on him, there is nothing to suggest he is anything like the power mongering Agent."

"So what do you suggest his motives were?"

"We have conflicting data and reasoning here. We don't really know if he has the torus as the data we have only just received indicates changes coming from the Agent. It is not enough to be certain. But...Matheson could have an objective and with his success, it has caused the Agent to go haywire. Look at these reports of what he did immediately after the event. Flying around with no clear objective…"

"It's because Matheson used the stealth device as he calls it."

"Yes, but for the Agent to even bother giving chase...there must have been something major happen there at the jet factory."

"He's a maniac where even the slightest little thing could set him off."

"Sure, we've all seen examples of his behaviour. But I think in this instance, if you consider the knowledge Matheson holds, then he would have been sure to wreak some type of havoc upon the Agent during his visit…whatever it was for. I suggest we run some test of the major systems. Make it look as if they are online, but actually run some dummy test scenarios. If there are any new viruses coming out of Seattle, then they will be picked up immediately and we will have a result. But if nothing new is being generated, then the anti-virus measures we have in place should hold."

"What about these unstable vortexes he has opened up? Some of those are getting too big to handle. If we cannot do something about them soon, then these issues will fade in comparison to the problems we'll have."

"Therein is a reason why we should at least try the dummy tests. If it turns out we are not going to encounter any new viruses, then we can go ahead with counteractive measures to treat those vortexes. Otherwise, we will sit around here at the mercy of whatever happens."

A general consensus was being reached at the table as they all fell into line with the idea of at least trying the dummy tests.

"If we get Matheson and we have systems in place ready for his work on stabilising these vortexes, we have a winning situation."

The order was then given to proceed with the test scenario for bringing some of the major central systems back online.

Even further beneath New York City, the authorities operated their central systems inside a complex stretching for two miles. It was filled with vast holographic arrays, personnel at holographic stations, complex secret machinery, and a legion of newly developed robots on standby. Travel tubes reached out from the complex on north, south and west headings, where anyone could travel beneath the great city. Destinations to installations located underground were in place to service the anticipated resurgence of dominance as they saw the demise of the Agent.

They could see their future – George Smyth would not last forever and their certainty including something they all actually believed as a means to escape.

An entirely new level of technology had been secretly developed at the expense of the population for a new version of their take for a mechanised planet and mechanised human race. This time they would not seek the compliance of people or of other nations – they would enforce compliance where choice would be the most sought after element of human nature they would seek to smother. Their intentions were to wither away those very last vestiges of natural intention and alignment of person with heart and soul, and bring about a sophisticated machine based reality where human beings were to service the system and themselves for trans-human survival.

Technology development scientist Eric Gunter was at his command post ready to analyse the results from the test scenario. Eric was a leader amongst the new type of officers the authorities had determined would be best suited for the new efficient machine society. He was one of the first to take on the advanced nanotechnology implants developed in recent times free from the Agent's viruses.

A look into Eric's eyes revealed his internal mechanical presence. One would see they were in fact mechanical and as such were a window into the soul of a man losing himself seemingly to his inward self focused take on reality. Without reason, embracing such enhancements was an embrace of self and where they cast a peculiar light when viewed closely, his eyes showed a sense of self lost to this embrace as a type of infatuation. Yet in contrast, the very motive for these implants was to lessen the effect from erratic thinking and emotions for the pursuit of efficiency.

Behind them was a complex array of both physical and holographic components forming an integrated circuitry linked to his brain and deeper into his thoughts. Eric was human and machine much more so than any previous enhancement or medically required procedure. The very moment the opportunity had arisen to uptake the technology, he did not hesitate to undergo surgery required to replace many of his organic systems with mechanical systems.

"Set output parameters at maximum. This test must completely engage all possible weapons systems contingencies for offensive operations at a city-wide level." He issued the command in a calm yet direct manner, rather than with the nature of egocentric superiority an entirely organic officer could do given the situation.

As part of his new, and some would say, enhanced constitution as a mechanical trans-human officer, mannerisms were programmed to be direct without any hint of emotion. His subordinates were programmed to react only to his orders, hence they too as examples of the new trans-human being, were given to only respond with compliance.

As the test commenced, the holographic array lit up with data statistics and imagery constructing the scenario being tested. Eric watched the weapons systems engage active mode as they were directed at their target – a group of dissident citizens gathered at a subversive meeting. He saw the ultrasonic pulse as the holographic beam was directed at them, and he observed a slight sense of enjoyment as he watched the result where the people were immersed in a wave of nanotechnology programmed to activate on arrival at its target and immediately commence reconstitution of vital human systems into mechanical systems. The tiny robots were directed to re-establish atomic form where they transformed organic matter into machine at the atomic and energetic levels.

He still retained an element of the facet of humanity known as enjoyment, for the authorities had deemed it essential to the growth and therefore progression of efficient officers and citizens to particularly focus on enjoyment for successful outcomes at their work. As he watched the test scenario, he himself was a subject of testing as authority scientists marvelled at how they had constructed such efficient human systems from their studies of elemental geometry and waveforms within the human physical, emotional, and energetic experience.

After running three other test scenarios, Eric instructed all officers to disengage and stand down. The results automatically compiled into a report where it showed there had been no influx of virus data coming from the Agent. Eric then immediately left to discuss the report he had just sent to his superior.

He proceeded along the passageway to the meeting without delay as he had seen positive results and thought the most efficient decision would be to proceed further. Other officers he encountered on his way were a mix of the new trans-human type and of the preceding officers who had not yet taken the machine technology to such an extent. Those who were not yet fitted with mechanical eyes, looked at him as they passed by, noticing the shallowness in his. Some wondered if it was the right thing for them, whilst others were envious of Eric. Soon they would no longer be envious, as envy was not programmed into the new trans-human ways. Yet little did they realise, indulging the new technology for efficiency sake, would come at such a deep personal cost revealed as a misalignment within not only their bodies, but also striking at their very essence.

Chapter 22

The fence ended well into an area barely hospitable to human beings. Great expanses of forest, marsh, tundra, ice, and pestilence kept nearly all away. Only those few desperate enough and either foolish or wise enough, dared try round the end of the fence not far from the southern shores of Hudson Bay. Since the coming of the Agent, and the erection of the dividing fence, people had abandoned the region for warmer climates and more populous cities in the search for food and fuel. In a city called Saskatoon just inside the western sector, around one thousand locals who had spent all their lives there remained along with those who periodically visited as they tried to go around the northern end of the fence and passed through the city on their way. Finally, for those who did make it to the northern end, there was a minefield to negotiate, meaning very few ever made it around.

Landing at Saskatoon airport had been hazardous in the icy conditions without any upkeep of the main runway, but John had skilfully brought the HyperJet to a stop, and then parked the jet inside the main hanger. Conditions in the city were calm when they had arrived under a pale blue sky. Then shortly after, the weather set in forcing them to accept they must remain in Saskatoon until it cleared enough for flight.

"The stealth device works, but…if we were tracked up until I was able to engage it, we can be certain the authorities will be onto us."

"Where do you suggest we go John?" Carmel asked.

"Well… the sky is pretty well our limit. This jet can fly us anywhere in the world, but our problems are, one…the authorities will track our movements, two, we are bound to create attention wherever we go, and three, the Agent still has his spaceship and he will come looking."

"Yeah but he'll have a very wide area to look for us. I'll keep him at bay with my ray gun."

"Ha…I bet you would give him a decent run for his money Tobias, but he can modify his instruments to find us, if he is smart enough."

"The Agent and smart just don't seem to go together."

Up until this time, Chan and the others who were held captive had remained silent. During their years held together mostly in darkness and being forced to sleep for months at a time, they had become distant to the outside world. Now they needed the means to recover and gain health to again focus strongly on what they had begun three years before. Despite what Chan had taught them in focusing on their internal light as an aura to retain strength of heart, their bodies were weak, and required solid nourishment,

"This tastes so good," Raynie said in a low shaky voice.

"I'll bet it does sweetheart."

"Thanks Kerry Ann." Raynie spoke for the other four who were also eating the mixture of wild vegetables and grains Kerry Ann had prepared.

"Don't eat too much though. Your bodies will not be used to much food yet."

Tobias and John went to scout around the airport to see if their arrival had drawn any attention. Frieda's appearance inside the plane was odd, yet she had happily rested in a place Tobias and Kerry Ann had cleared for her during the flight from Spokane. Carmel was very glad to see her and equally pleased to see she had carried her beloved steam engine. Without second thought, she considered the effort of John and Tobias worthy of celebration as she prepared the firebox, and then when enough steam had built up, she let off three whistles.

When the two men returned from their objective to ensure they were secure in the hanger, Chan, Raynie, Jake, Jenna, and Lyle were asleep. It was not an Agent induced sleep, but a natural response to their tiredness and to their full stomachs, and for the first time they could rest much easier than they could almost remember.

"It is all clear out there. Tobias and I checked around the entire perimeter and we also looked inside the passenger terminal. This place is deserted. It does not look like anyone had been here for a long time, but we will need to post two guards the entire time we are here."

"I'll take first watch," Carmel claimed.

It was after an hour later when she watched as a group of people approached the hanger.

"John. John, wake up. There are people coming,"

"Where's Kerry Ann?"

"She's at the foot of the ladder. Come on. They will be here soon."

Tobias woke up when Carmel stirred John, and readied his ray gun as John took the only remaining pulse rifle. As soon as they had reached the bottom of the ladder, they could all hear a commotion less than one hundred yards away.

"It does not sound good. Tobias and I will take a front position while you two stand here by the jet. Did you see how many there are?"

"I think about a dozen honey. Be careful."

John and Tobias took up position at the centre of the large open hanger doorway, standing a few yards apart with weapons at the ready. As the group approached, they could see them in the moonlight as Tobias counted twelve – seven men, three women, and two children. The moment the group saw the two armed men, they stopped and began to talk amongst themselves.

A moment later, one of them called out, "Where did you get the jet? And how did you fly it?"

"I'm a pilot. Why do you want to know?"

"We saw you fly in. Why did you come to Saskatoon?"

"To escape."

"Escape hey. Well, what were you escaping from, the Agent?" The other people with the man broke into a short laughter until John answered.

"We did in fact, where else do you think we were able to get this jet?"

"From the authorities. You're not the authorities are you?"

"No. But they might come visiting here soon."

"Well we don't want them here. They abandoned people long ago. They don't care what happens to people. We don't have viruses. We are clean."

"So are we."

"How many of you are there?"

"Enough."

"What do you mean enough?"

"Just enough." John knew they were analysing what they might be up against.

"Look. We are not after any trouble. We are clean as I said. Survival here is tough though. We thought you might be able to help us."

"Why would we do so?"

"Um, because we are not a threat. We just want some food or anything to help. This weather is bad and the food is running out. We want to get out of here."

"We can't help you with either of those. We only have enough food for ourselves."

The leading man then walked towards John, leaving the others behind. As he approached, John felt strangely at ease and although he held his rifle in position, he did not become edgy and ready to fire.

"Stop there. Don't come closer. Who are you?"

"We're a group of travellers. We thought about going around the fence. Look, we only want to go to the eastern sector and away from the Agent."

"You won't have to worry about him too much for a while."

"What do you mean?"

"Let's just say, we gave him a setback."

"Well, there's some relief. Please don't fire. We are just travellers. A few weeks back, we came through the mountains east of San Francisco, heading for Omaha, but there were some real bad people in our way, so we came up here into Canada."

"Yeah. Well, as I said, I cannot help you."

The man began to approach again and was within thirty yards of where John and Tobias stood. When he reached the light coming from within the hanger, John was surprised to recognise him as one of the group he and Carmel had travelled with.

Immediately he lowered his rifle, "I know you. We were travelling together through the forest."

"Yeah. Is it you John? I wasn't sure about your voice."

"Sure is."

The man turned to the group behind him and called out, "Steve! Steve, it's John."

"John? Where's Carmel?"

"She's back near the jet. Come here out of the weather – all of you."

The others joined Steve as he ran the one hundred yards into the hanger. "Mate, it is so good to see you," Steve said shaking John's hand.

"Good to see you as well. Why did you come up here?"

"Like he said, there are a lot of bad people at the main transit. It seems as though some type of movement was on. We saw at least two to three hundred."

"Where are the rest of you?"

"The Agent shot two men on horseback and we lost four others to those infected groups. It was gruesome…"

"Don't tell me about it. I've seen and heard enough. Well, come in all of you. We have a bit of food, but it is no feast."

"Thanks. So you stole this jet from the Agent."

"Yeah. Hey Tobias, go and tell Carmel it is Steve."

Tobias ran off and then returned a few moments later with Carmel and Kerry Ann.

"Hi Carmel. Where is the little steam engine of yours?"

"Inside Steve. How good to see you. All of us should go inside the jet, it is much warmer there."

"How long are you going to park this thing here?" Steve asked John as the entire group sat together at the front of the HyperJet eating a meal.

"As soon as the weather clears, I'll take her up again. The authorities will have tracked us for a while before we landed. Keeping on the run is our best option, so when the snow stops, we are going."

"I have to say this meal smells good. We've had to eat raw horse meat recently, but back on topic. Can we all come with you?"

"Sure. But what about your horses."

Steve looked downcast and when John looked around the group, he could see they all appeared the same. He was able to guess they had eaten them to survive.

"Frieda is here. She is up the back."

"A horse on a HyperJet, now who would have thought."

"Have you seen many others here about Saskatoon?"

"Only a few. Some like us, and some of those with the holes. I reckon we've seen around fifty or sixty in all, but there must be others around. We asked those who were not infected if they wanted to come with us, but they were not interested and just said they would stay here and do what they could."

"Well it's good in a way. We could be pretty safe here for a while. John and I were discussing it before," Tobias said thinking again of his ray gun.

"Yeah, but remember we still have to think about the authorities Tobias, so keep the ray gun ready."

Tobias laughed and took the gun out, "A few well aimed bolts from this might make them think twice."

Later after all the others had retired to sleeping in the passenger chairs inside the aircraft, John, Tobias, and Steve were talking about tactics the authorities might use to find them, and the risks of showing up on scanners.

"They'll be looking for this jet using fairly wide spectrum analysis, so we will have to leave tomorrow regardless of the weather."

"It seems to have levelled out at least," John replied. "The only thing is the winds. They can change in an instant."

The morning dawned very cold with icicles along the edge of the hanger roof and a few on the jet as well. Everyone from the newly arrived group was out clearing snow from the runway, with a few taking to de-icing the plane. When they had cleared three narrow tracks along its entire length, John was satisfied there would be enough traction for takeoff.

"Everyone ready?" he asked as he lined the jet up at the end of the runway ten minutes later.

Three seconds later, he engaged full thrust and they headed into the steely blue sky.

"Um, this is John, your captain speaking. Our flying altitude will reach approximately forty thousand feet today at speed mach two on a heading towards somewhere warm. I like you, am sick of this cold and think it is time we all thawed out."

They had not decided precisely where to go, but all had generally agreed they should head towards South America and re-locate a long way from the authorities in the United States, and from the Agent. John's address shortly after takeoff did a lot to lighten the mood amongst all on board, including those who were beginning their recovery. He had engaged his stealth device prior to leaving Saskatoon to cause some confusion for the military aircraft searching for the rogue HyperJet and of course for the Agent if he was able to track them.

The authority planes were flying in wide formation flying over Calgary when three separate readings appeared on their scanners – each of them showing a heading in all directions except for the actual direction John and the others were taking. All three pilots then boosted their signal receivers and scanning output parameters to confirm readings it was the HyperJet. Their new scanner was able to determine the actual position of the jet and not just a dummy signal as had been experienced a few years ago when John had escaped Alaska.

John had anticipated their capacity to see through his mirage. His last measure and hopefully a failsafe one, was to reconfigure his stealth like device a little the night before using flux mechanics he knew was still unavailable to the authorities. This enabled him to project readouts showing their pursuers a HyperJet yet flying on a course at angle away from the actual course John was flying. Over time and due to the high velocity, he was certain of piloting away from them sufficiently to avoid their detection entirely. He knew they would be closely guarding their secrets from exposure to the Agent, so any widespread use of essential systems was still far too risky for anyone, even those other nations detecting their flight.

Eric Gunter had been watching the pursuit since the few hours had passed by when he had arrived at work. He had been instructed to monitor the situation involving the newly upgraded scanning capacity they had just tried and failed with for locating the jet John was piloting. He was not impressed, as he knew reporting this failure to his superiors was not going to be a welcoming experience. They were demanding results considered necessary for re-establishing sufficient strength in defeating the Agent, and whilst this was not Eric's fault, it could make life for him difficult for a time, despite the impartiality within him from his mind based nano mechanics.

Eric decided to investigate the situation further before having to report this mission failure. He instructed the pilots to take a southerly heading and scan the skies until they had further progress to report. It proved a futile measure though, as John had taken the aircraft beyond the reach of the pilots - by this time he was flying over Mexico leaving their pursuers behind as they turned back when they encountered Agent controlled air space. He felt safe and comfortable at the controls. For a time John enjoyed being a pilot again before he was reminded of why the authorities tried following him.

"They will come eventually Tobias."

"They want the flux algorithms from you. It is the only way they can gain the upper hand."

"The Agent is inevitable too."

****

Speculation by the authorities on how disabled the Agent had become since John destroyed his vortex amplifier proved to be correct. It would take him at least a month to build another, and then it would not have the Torus of Eternity at its centre, so it would be a weak device, capable of only small intrusions into the eastern sector. The Agent had set about building himself this new device, despite his mania and despite his losses, for to him, it was an instrument representing his self, and soon he would fly his spaceship and take this new version with him so he could still spread his mania.

His anger was at the front of his mind. It drove his determination and along with his pure hatred of John, the Agent's anger was now his catalyst to begin the unparalleled journey into the abyss. Prior to this moment, George Smyth had retained an element of stability being a link to the person who his mother had named some thirty eight years prior. Now he easily resigned the last vestiges of person to this void as he lowered the mask of his conditioning to reveal the utterly contemptible mania of his disposition.

To lose those people...the supervisor bitch. To lose the torus and see Chan Lee escape. He spat in disgust at the thought of their purity gaining any place. He was sickened with images in his mind of their happiness and supposed tenacity to survive. And he longed to exercise his own will...his volition to dispense finally with everything.

George no longer – he would despise his own name too. He would set about finding Matheson and when he did, he would meet his end after volunteering his knowledge of flux mechanics. Yes, he would volunteer for what would be in store for him as an alternative, dug deep into this abyss George had become to unearth the terrors deep within the core being of a human.

Chapter 23

John had flown them south to Peru. The city of Arequipa was set amongst a dramatic backdrop of the snow capped jagged peaks of the Andes Mountains as John lined up for landing. Everyone aboard the jet had discussed this place as an option since leaving North America as it was rumoured there was the least authority control and influence from the Agent in regional South America. Local inhabitants were subject mostly to the whims of the authorities in Peru, but with very few having ever taken up the offer of injected nanotechnology to maintain their bodies, it meant the number of virus affected people was significantly lower.

Known in the past as the city of eternal blue skies, the small city of Arequipa enjoyed a clean life free of the drawbacks from the larger cities. With the city at an altitude of two thousand meters, many lived long and unhindered existences in clean air and open vistas to the snowy peaks and volcanic cones to the west.

After landing and parking the jet in a hanger, they were welcomed by a number of spirited people who were enthusiastic to hear of any news.

"Please tell us what is happening. You must know...you have this jet," one of them said.

"There is much trouble in the north," Tobias replied. 'We have come here to live in peace away from the sickness."

"Ah si. We have heard of the sickness. Very bad."

Without the strict rules of compliance from the authorities regulating the city, they did not even encounter any officials demanding information when they proceeded through the customs check area. When they arrived at passport control, they were given passage without so much as a check of their documentation, which most of them did not have anyway. The authorities of Peru were like many other nations across the globe where they focused on maintaining a level of control in battle against the Agent's viruses, thus issues like passenger documentation were not even being attended in many instances.

John had parked the jet in the mostly vacant hanger beside one other HyperJet appearing to have been there for a considerable time. The officer in charge advised them they could leave the jet there as long as they made regular payments, so John gave him enough cash to last at least one year of fees.

The officer was more than pleased to receive this from John, "You are most gracious. My superior will be very pleased to receive such a large amount of cash. It will look like he is running a very efficient office here at Arequipa, and it will please his superiors."

"You are most welcome. My HyperJet is my prize possession. Please take good care of it for me."

"Certainly sir, it will be locked in the hanger. I would be very happy to assist you in any way I can."

"Thank you and here…take this extra cash for yourself and your family. Times have been tough and I am sure it will help you."

"Indeed it will, and thank you for your kindness. Please feel free to go. We mostly check people's character. Just remember…no trouble or the police will come. We just want people to do their best."

"A sentiment we all share," Carmel replied. "Thank you."

"I have a feeling we will be here for a considerable time John," Carmel said as they walked towards the rest of the travellers who were gathered outside a hotel across from the airport terminal.

"I think so Carmel. It was a good decision to come here. I am sick of running – it has been for so long now. This city is a long way from the Agent, and the authorities will have to search far and wide to find us here. We also need to give the others some time and space to recuperate. Some of this clear mountain air and these warmer temperatures will help their recovery."

"And ours John. The running has taken a toll. It is time we started to live again. One thing though, will they be able to track us somehow to here at Arequipa? I know the device you used will have fooled their scanners, but there are the authorities of other nations and people who would have seen us arrive."

"It is certainly worth considering, and it is a tangible reality, but I think they will still be counteracting the Agent for some time, and so we have to hope there is not some planned objective to find us yet…but it will come."

"Don't be concerned John. It is inevitable they will want you. Both of them. We know now we must accept these events. How we respond is key."

"If we can find some type of residence here for a while with a bit of peace, we can all work on what could be ahead."

"The Agent is a miser John. He thrives on depravity. But I think you are right and we can stay here. It will be much better for us in the long term, if we can settle and focus ourselves for some time."

"We are fortunate the authorities here are relatively lax. No passport control, no questions about the jet, and not so much as a reason for our being here."

"They are spirited the people from these parts John. I could sense their type of living and approach to life as soon as we arrived. It is just we have been misfortunate to have been in places for many years where control is much stronger. Perhaps now with the troubles caused by the Agent, they have allowed the people to return more to their true selves in places like Arequipa?"

"I think you are right. I can sense what you speak of as well. It is as if there is a calm air about the place, and the fear factor is far lower."

"Indeed John, there is much less fear. In time, the 'air' as you say, will also allow us the clarity we require to push on with our understanding. We have much work to do John, and now we are in a place allowing us to focus, I feel we are going to make some great progress."

"I think Chan would feel similar to how you speak. I caught a twinkle in his eye when he disembarked and looked around. It was as if he sensed it as well."

As the group wandered through the centre of the city, they began to realise many of its inhabitants were living mostly free from technology. Very few of the establishments open for trade featured the arrays of holographic entertainment and broadcasts seen in northern hemisphere cities. People on the streets were engaged in life style barely changed for a century. Only a small collection of tall buildings and apartments modernised over the recent decades stood at its centre, with no hint of the joined towering high-rise seen in so many places globally.

Jenna came to life a little when the group found themselves in San Francisco Street with its bars, restaurants, and clubs. Whilst most were only trading at a limited capacity and some were closed, there was a definite feeling to the area reminding her of her home thousands of miles to the north.

Chan noticed her mood enhancement, and so asked John if they could all go inside for a rest to discuss what they were going to do and where they were going to stay. He considered it an opportunity for them to rekindle some of the worldly spirit found in public places and venues. The Agent has suppressed them for so long they needed now to draw upon elements of stimuli amongst people to further their awakening.

John agreed, as did Carmel, who had been a little concerned over what they were all going to do and how they were going to accommodate Frieda. Tobias had been leading her as she towed the wooden cart with Carmel's engine.

"Go in and ask if I can tie her up at the back. I saw a lane and a yard behind. Perhaps they won't mind," he said to John.

John went inside and then returned a minute later with good news. Tobias could take her around the back, as there was a yard and a small shed where she could stay whilst they were inside. "Only if we order a meal and some drinks, the owner told me."

Inside they all talked about what they could do next, over a meal of potato cakes and cheeses. Aromas filling the air were of spices and meats, vegetables and grains. These fresh cooking scents so normal in times past were now realised for their simple honesty and invigoration to the entire group and not only those recovering from the Agent's afflictions.

"We need to find somewhere to accommodate all of us if we want to stay together," one of the travellers they met in Saskatoon said. "Otherwise, we will have to split up and find smaller establishments."

"I'm sure there will be enough room for us. Don't worry, they are likely to need the cash," Kerry Ann replied.

"We don't have any. Only John has cash."

"Don't worry. I have enough to pay for all of us. But, such a large group draws attention. They are not likely to see large travelling hordes in single groups these days. I think we need to find somewhere out of the main city. A rural place would be ideal. Then we can stay free of the bustle of the city and out of sight should anyone be looking around or asking questions."

"I don't agree. You can go to the farmlands if you want. They look a bit desolate to me. Did you see the desert to the east of this place? I cannot imagine they are too plentiful. I would rather stay in the city and blend in. Who is with me?"

Most of the others they met in Saskatoon declined John's idea of seeking a rural location, and voted for staying in the city.

"There are some nice old houses and apartments here. We could look for work and find a place to live."

"Work is not going to be easy."

"I'm willing to take my chances. So what will it be, city or farm?"

In the end only Steve McCray decided on somewhere rural with the others. Those who were to stay, had voiced their opposition to the farmlands, saying they had been in deserted places far too long and they wanted to be amongst the people here who did not appear to be a threat.

Whilst John agreed their ideas had merit, he was secretly pleased the group of twenty-one and one horse would now split up. His reason for rescuing Carmel and taking the Torus of Eternity, had not involved the others.

"Okay, then it is settled. I suggest if any of you ever want to contact any of us, then we come to this place and leave a message. I will talk to the owner and tell him we are people looking for a new life here in Arequipa and from time to time, we might meet here, or leave messages for each other."

When he returned a few minutes later, he advised the owner had agreed so long as any of them made a purchase each time they visited, as he was not a meeting house, but a business and life was a struggle. All agreed this was a good plan and if ever anyone required contact from either group, then they would come to this place.

John gave them some cash they were very grateful for, before they split into two groups and went their separate ways.

As they walked away from San Francisco Street, Chan approached John speaking softly to him, "You have been wise in understanding of the choices ahead of us. It is best for our intentions to maintain our objectives and to not be distracted through doubts coming from the others. They are not aligned as we all are as a group for they have been running and they have done this in fear. Such things are not our calling to dispense now. The other people are embarking on overcoming this for themselves, though they do not have this in their thoughts. It is for their basis in understanding to pursue their path as they have chosen today, and similarly, the path we have chosen is for similar reasons. We do not hold the fears the others carry."

"Thank you Chan. I feel it is best to assist their recovery in a place where they can focus once again on what they experienced with you three years ago and since. The distractions of the city here just did not feel right despite the easy going nature and low level of threat about."

By evening, they had reached the outskirts of the city and took lodgings at a roadside inn also equipped to accommodate horses. Carmel, Kerry Ann, John, and Tobias were on foot as Chan, Raynie, Jake, Jenna, and Lyle rode along in the cart. The going had been slow as nobody wanted to make Frieda strain with five adults and Carmel's engine in the cart.

"We can't go on like this honey," Kerry Ann said. The others are too weak, and I am sure we'll find one somewhere about."

"I would agree there John," Steve added. "We are not going to make it very far like this."

"How about we ask around the inn tonight…for somewhere we could go?"

"I think it is a good idea honey. Steve and I were just talking. The others look beat. I'm sure they could do with more rest and this slow thing is too much. Even Frieda looks weary."

"You're right."

"Maybe we could have a chat and work out a plan John."

"Good thinking Steve. Aimless wandering is something we came to avoid and were only talking about earlier."

The inn was an old wooden building with a musty smell of history, cooking oils, spices, liquor, and smoke. Lights were dim. There was a low fire burning in the lounge room and it was here John, Carmel, Tobias, Steve, and Kerry Ann sat to discuss their options. The others had already retired immediately after dinner – declining any offer to sit and have a drink.

John had bought them each a whisky on the rocks and as they sipped its' fire, their minds found a little reminiscent there in the old surroundings as if they could each sense this moment was more of the release from times of running.

"I think it is up to us again Tobias. Just the two of us and we know how we work."

"I agree John," Steve added. "Two is best. Makes for more speed and less weight for Frieda."

"Place some faith in yourself too John. Have surety you and Tobias will find something…meet someone. These instances of coincidence are synchronising. Life works this way."

"I am feeling more of what you say each day Carmel. Since this plight began at your house, I have felt a sense of knowing the path is there and needs to be revealed."

"Like Chan's words of allowance."

"Do a broad scope around each place you visit and watch out for thieves."

"Oh don't worry. John and I are used to getting through trouble," Tobias added laughing a little as he recalled the close situations they had shared.

After breakfast, John and Tobias left the others to spend the day at the inn. This area of Arequipa was a mixture of people working, people going to and from work, and of sellers with wares haggling prices as they walked beside them.

When a man grabbed John's arm, he was startled.

"Hey...what?"

"Oh sorry sir. Can you and your friend please help me. I need you two to hold up my cart so I can re-attach the wheel pin."

"Oh...take the weight of the axle?"

"Yes yes. Thank you."

A few seconds later the job was done.

"Thank you kindly. I am most grateful."

"Our pleasure. Is food scarce here?"

"Yes and no. Sometimes there is plenty, and at others there is not so much food. I would say for you to go to the river valley if you want to find a place for food. The farms still sell produce in the city but don't go stealing anything. Nobody ever tries to steal from the farms because we all need to share what they provide for us in these times. We all need them and the farmers have enough security to ward off thieves. You will find farms there. Wheat, rice, fruit."

"We are honest and have no intention of stealing or hurting. Thank you."

"Oh no need to thank me. You will find there are plenty of friendly people here. We are not so affected by the authorities or the Agent. People are peaceful and they are often clear of mind. But watch...there are still the odd ones who will steal and try to trick you."

"Thanks for the advice."

For the remainder of the morning, both men asked people about the farmlands whenever they could. They gained a few favourable responses in support of their idea, whilst others warned them to stay way and the city was the best place to find work.

"They know who they are dealing with. It has been the way for some years on the farms. You can't expect nobody to come calling. If they don't like you then you will soon see the consequences," one woman told them.

"Okay, thanks for your help."

John turned to Tobias looking a little frustrated.

"This could go on all day. I suggest we go back to the inn and then all of us leave tomorrow and go find somewhere. I don't want us to run out of money paying for too much accommodation."

"How much is left?"

"A bit. But we need to be mindful of making it last."

"I see your point. Let's go back then."

After a lazy afternoon where they had discussed John's idea, dinner was early around sunset as they watched the distant ochre sky from the rear porch of the inn where they all sat eating.

"We are really beginning to feel better John," Lyle said speaking for the others. "Getting this travel out of the way sooner sounds good."

"Yes John. Lyle is right. We need to recuperate as soon enough the Agent and the others will come into our lives again. It is best we endeavour to be our best," Chan added. He had spent most of the afternoon in quiet contemplation appearing as if he was meditating. His thoughts though not conjured, had come to him through effortless allowance where he felt the strength returning to his own sense of intuition into their situation.

After Chan and the others had gone to bed, John, Tobias, Carmel, Kerry Ann, and Steve found themselves again by the fire sipping whisky.

Tobias and Steve were discussing their experiences three years earlier at HAARP where Steve had taken over command from Tobias after the authorities had attempted to remove him.

"The irony is, they tried the same thing with me, but I was still of the mind to continue my service. I guess I just didn't have the same insight you suddenly realised when you led them on that chase. Shunting me off to Mars was not a good outcome though. After my failure to successfully escort the Agent to the Asteroids, they did not look too kindly on me considering the trouble he made stealing the spaceship and killing twenty one people at Mars One base. Then we have the havoc ever since. I guess you could say his rise to power or whatever you may call it, was my fault in part."

"Don't be too hard on yourself Steve. The authorities should have taken him there all the way themselves. Changing him over to the transport you were on, just so they could use the ship to steer the asteroid into Earth, was their doing. If they had proceeded as planned, a lot of his catastrophes may have been avoided."

"I suppose you are right. Their pursuit of efficiency certainly let a lot of people down and set them back years."

"The identification chip would have never worked. The reports of Russia and China and some African nations not holding up to the regulations coming mostly out of New York, was a catalyst for its undoing. It was bound to come unstuck."

"Besides, they were always going to be looking for me as well," John interjected. "Until they obtain true flux mechanics, there will always be to be incursions into their systems. Perhaps not by me, as I was not really interested with involving myself, but at least from others like Tim…" He trailed off as

Carmel approached them, not wanting to upset her by mentioning the man she had had grown to have a close relationship with and had not been seen in a long time.

"I'm glad Chan and the others have gone to sleep. They looked so relieved to find comfortable beds to rest overnight. It is still difficult for them."

"Yeah. Thanks Carmel. I meant to help but I was distracted. Where did Kerry Ann just go?" John asked.

"She's taking a shower, and will be back down here in a few minutes. It is so lovely to be here tonight John. Staying here at the inn with all those troubles thousands of miles away makes me feel like myself again. It was trying being held captive by the Agent, and if you had not rescued us when you did, I'm sure we would have all been injected with nanotechnology."

"I wonder why he didn't do it previously. He had the others for three years."

"I think we can only assume John. He is a maniac. He told me the capacity to deliver the technology into human cells had eluded him until some of his people recently had raided the authorities. It must have taken him a long time to develop the viruses to get past their security. Anyway, we are here now, thanks to you and Tobias, Kerry Ann…and Frieda of course. Chan said your strength would endure when I was first sent to join them. He was right John. He is a most insightful man."

"Yes, I see things in his eyes prompting questions you want to ask him. Unique indeed."

"He told me to speak to the locals here at the inn John. Chan reckons on there being a purpose behind our travelling to this region aside from just leaving the Agent and the authorities far behind."

"Did he suggest anyone in particular?"

"No. He just said it would be of help to us to understand what the people are really like and what the places are like so we can find somewhere to live appropriate for us."

When the hours had passed by and it was nearing eleven at night, a stranger arrived as a late traveller looking for accommodation at the inn. Shortly after being taken to their room, the stranger re-appeared and ordered a drink at the bar. John and the others watched them for a while looking for any sign the traveller was approachable, but they sensed nothing.

"I am sorry, but I accidentally overheard your conversation. I hear you are looking to locate somewhere in the farmlands," the stranger tentatively said to John. He was immediately surprised they had been overheard and cast a suspicious look at the stranger.

"Thank you," Carmel replied sensing an impasse for a few moments. "We are surprised you knew what we were saying."

"Oh, I am sorry, but I practice listening well and I could not help but…"

"Look. Are you trying to deceive us?" John asked. He continued to eye the stranger with an air of suspicion.

"Oh no sir. Please believe me. I just thought considering what you were discussing, I might be able to help you."

"How can you help?"

"Just to say take the roads towards the winding valleys to the north. The people out there are honest farming people and would welcome a group of honest workers."

"Thank you again for your help." Carmel replied looking calmly at the man. She could see he was genuine without any sense of deception she could determine.

"Any time. I am just passing through. Perhaps it is meant to be yes. Me seeing you here tonight when you are looking for some information. Perhaps you have some spare cash? I am not well off."

"Of course," Carmel smiled and turned to John. He was already reaching into his pocket where he took out a cash note.

"Here you go. And thanks. Carmel seems to like you so I am going to go with her now," John said as he handed over the money.

"Oh thank you kind sir. This money will help me for a few days. You are gracious."

"Perhaps Chan was right...again," John said to Carmel when the stranger had returned to his drink leaving them in silence for a few moments.

"I think he might be."

They had travelled a day out of the city along roads winding along valley floors towered over by large hills and distant snowy peaks. When after a time where they rested at an intersection, it was then an instinctive decision Carmel felt to take the left hand fork in the road. A river bordered by trees, shrubs, and grasses accompanied the road as they ambled along.

By midafternoon they had veered away from the river to traverse some steeper hills forming a narrow section to the valley.

"There looks like some more narrow sections ahead John," Steve said. "Do you think we made the right choice back there?"

"We can't know Steve, but I trust Carmel's feelings. We have nowhere else to be and at least this valley appears safe."

After another hour, they saw a local farmer and decided their only option was to talk with him.

"We could do with some extra hands at our community, but there would be no payment, just accommodation and the food you can harvest," he told them as another man ambled into the scene. "You are welcome if you are honest, but we live a simple life, and you must be trustworthy. We can deal with you if this sounds alright but we will watch and if there is any trouble, then we can even deal with a group as large as yours."

"We are not looking for any trouble sir. John honey and the others here know how to work. We just want to rest and live for some time. We won't be any trouble," Kerry Ann replied.

"Our simple life is like a life from the past. We need you to have faith in what we do. We need some people to help with the harvest soon enough but some of you look like you cannot even walk or work."

"We are all seeking to live away from the city for a time and your offer sounds good. Our friends on the cart are recovering and soon will be able to work. We are most grateful and will immediately prove any worth to your cause," John said speaking for all of them.

"Then if you all come to our community farm, understand we do not have much technology. Such things are scarce in these places. You need to understand our way of life is not focused on what you would have been doing before. Our life is not just of survival either, but one of peace and as I have told you, it is one of faith in ourselves. When I say faith, it is the faith in all who live there, to be honest and to work creating a good life without any disrespect towards anyone. We all need to work to make a contribution."

"It sounds ideal…exactly what we are looking for, isn't it honey."

"Sure. It will be a good place for the others to recover and for us just relax…and work. We would like to accept your offer, but please tell us your name. We have not introduced ourselves yet."

"I am Juan and this is Diego."

John and the others introduced themselves to the men in turn, and when they had finished, there was already a warmth between them all. John then told them of their friends who were already asleep and how Frieda was a good horse for life at their farm.

"So many of you. Ten in all and a horse. Our farm will be very productive. You are lucky, for we live in a hidden valley and there is plentiful water and the soil is good. We do have some machines, but not like you may be used to, for they are old, but they are strong and work well."

"Great, we are all good with our bare hands."

"You will need them to work the land and to work our machines. But do not be concerned for our machines."

Juan then took out some paper and a pencil and drew a map showing the route to the farm.

"Diego and I are going to the city for supplies we need. Not all we use is from the farm you know, but maybe one day we will be able to be self-reliant. Just arrive there and to say Juan and Diego sent you. From this the others will know it is okay."

"It's a secret valley, so please do not speak of this to anyone else," Diego told them. "There are some simple and honest people in these parts, but there are also those who are desperate. Many are not interested in the hard work we do to live, but some of them would be quite willing to steal from us."

"Yes, you see desperate people in so many places. Thank you Juan and Diego. We are very pleased to have met you, and please be sure all of us will do our very best to help on your farm and to be trustworthy."

"Yes I know. I can sense the values of you John and the others," Juan replied. "Be safe and arrive before dark. Diego and I will see you when we return."

The map directed them to follow a dirt track at first following an old railway line, and then a small river into a valley. When they arrived at the entrance to the valley, there was barely any sign of what lay beyond the narrow chasm in front of them. To a casual passerby, it would appear as though the river emerged from the hillside, and they all agreed the location was indeed a hidden and secret valley suited to them. When they passed through the opening, all could sense an uplifting feeling releasing them of any burdens they were carrying. Amongst those on the cart, Chan lifted his head at this moment, and Carmel noticed a slight smile come across his face.

She walked over to be beside John, "See?" She indicated towards Chan.

"I have a good feeling about this too."

After journeying on for another five miles, the narrow valley opened out into an area of flat lands bordered by steep peaks on either side, with the small river running down the centre. The far end of the open area was a further mile onward, where the valley once again narrowed in as it continued its way climbing towards the rugged high Andean peaks they could see in the distance. Massive formations of rocky outcrops made for impenetrable country beyond the valley ensuring there was no access from its western end.

Upon arrival, they went to the large farmhouse to introduce themselves and tell the people there Juan and Diego had sent them. A woman came out to greet them, followed by a few men who gave the group a suspicious look.

"Hello, I am Lolita. Who are you?"

"Hello. Juan and Diego sent us. They said it would be beneficial to your farm for us to come and stay. We are honest people and peaceful. I am John."

"Hello John. And the others?"

Each of them introduced themselves in turn as the group on the cart had sufficient strength for walking over to where John and the others stood with Lolita. By this time, the men behind her had eased and greeted the group more openly.

"Hello, I am Pablo. It is good to see you all. We have only a few of us here and now with such numbers, our farm will thrive so long as you are honest people. It is good Diego and Juan spoke to you, otherwise we might not be so welcoming now. They would never have told you of this place unless they could sense your honesty."

"It is good to be here Pablo," Kerry Ann replied. "I see there is a mill house here. I do love grinding grain, and John here is good at it too."

"Oh yes, we have a mill house for the wheat, and we have other things too. But there is no need to grind by hand...the stone is so heavy."

"Do you use a horse or a mule then?"

"No, no. Come see." He led Kerry Ann over to the mill house where they looked around for a few minutes before returning. The others were in conversation with Lolita and the other men, who had introduced themselves as Manuel, and Ricardo.

"Hey honey...and you too Carmel! You're going to like it here. They have a steam engine out back of the mill house to drive the shaft connected to the stone."

"Really Kerry Ann! Oh fantastic. My engine will be right at home here."

"Yes, we have a few steam engines at the farm," Lolita added. "You could say we live in an era from long ago."

"Juan did mention old machines," Tobias added. "I guess he meant steam engines. Where do you get fuel?"

"Yes, yes. Juan is very proud of how well they operate. He restored them himself, and he keeps them in top condition. We only use them when we need. Fuel can be scarce but we manage to find what we need and keep a store. There are some old stands of wood long forgotten in these parts and they are too far away from others for them to come looking. But...for now, you all should settle in and relax. We do not have any room for such a group as you in the house, but you can choose either of those two barns over there. They are clean and weather proof. Sorry we cannot accommodate you in the house."

"Oh don't be sorry Lolita," Carmel replied. "You...and everyone we have met this past day have been so gracious. We will be very happy to live in the barn. All the other travellers agreed life in a barn in such warm and peaceful surrounds was precisely what they wanted.

"Okay, it is settled then. Take your time and feel at home. Come to the house any time, if you want anything."

"Thank you Lolita, and you Ricardo, and you Pablo, and you Manuel. We are so very thankful for such kindness." Carmel had spoken for them all, as they all felt exactly how she had said.

"We will have a dinner to celebrate tonight and get to know each other, though I can already tell you are reasonable people. Dinner will be around six. We will see you then."

Lolita and the three men then left the group to find their way to whatever barn those chose and settle in.

Sunset spectacularly illuminated the peaks surrounding the valley casting a gold and orange glow over the farm. Chan remarked on the essence within the light bathing the scene as the group walked to the house for the celebratory dinner.

"It is with reverence we must take in all this from our very first times here in this valley," he said to them. "Circumstances have brought us here, as they do to any place, and the strengths in all of us, even when Raynie, Jake, Lyle, Jenna, and myself appear weak, are of noteworthy significance. Simplicity is what it takes to recall those elements showing us the beauty within and beyond this valley, and this notion is the underlying aura properties of all we are and are yet to recall. This light is like so many things, as it reflects back to us our intentions and so we are placed here so far from the adversity of recent times."

"I can feel strength returning almost with every moment Chan. I have not felt like this since many years ago when we first travelled and your guidance awakened more human spirit of living within."

"Yes Jenna. I can see in your eyes, the essence of what you speak. Hold on to this, but also release it and cast in outward beyond you as far as you can imagine."

When they arrived at the house, dinner was prepared and they were invited to come in and eat immediately.

"You look ravenous," Lolita said looking at those who had travelled on the cart. "Have you not been eating enough?"

"You could say," Lyle replied. "We have been starved for years."

"They were prisoners of the Agent. He is an evil man."

"Oh yes, we have heard tales of his doing. You must be very relieved to be free from him. Sit. We can all eat together."

As the meal commenced, Juan and Diego arrived back from their journey to the city, and Lolita immediately ushered them to the large bench table.

"So you found us. Diego and I thought about our meeting and we talked all the way into the city and nearly all the way back here again. We are very happy you have arrived as you are honest and give us the numbers and strength for our farm work. How has it been since you arrived? Did you find a suitable place to live?"

"Oh yes thank you Juan," Carmel replied. "Lolita was so graceful to offer us a choice of barn, and we all agree it is a very fine place for us to live. As soon as we can, we agreed to get to work here so we can re-pay the kindness from you all."

"Ha. It is good to hear from you. We have a lot of work to do. There is grain we have harvested for grinding to become flour, and soon, our summer vegetables will ripen."

"Do you ever get any trouble here?" Steve asked.

"Only once," Manuel replied. "The authorities came here two years ago to see what was going on. But we are just a small group, and they decided to leave us alone. There was nothing here they could use."

"So they didn't try to take over and send you to the city?"

"No. They are not so worried with such things. If there is anything they want, they would come and get it, but we are peaceful and simple, so I think it is to our advantage."

"Anyone else…um, try to steal or take over."

"Some people did come looking a few months ago and they had weapons with them, but we have a few of our own and we sent them on their way."

"What do you have?"

"Ah, this may seem a little out of place, but we have some of those laser rifles the authorities use. It is one of the reasons we went into the city. The power cells for them are low, and so we obtained some more. We have a contact who provides for us now and then."

"Can they be trusted?"

"I suppose. They are not from the authorities, but they have links to others in Lima. We have to trust them, but we are wary. Weapons are not our thing, but we have to be realistic and keep some for protection."

"I can help you there."

"I'm sure you could Tobias," John said. "We have weapons too. Like you, we do not like to use them. You can hold them for us if you wish, in case you think we cannot be trusted, but…"

"No, no, we trust you. We can feel you are peaceful people. It is good you have some weapons, as it will add to ours and we can feel safer should we need to use them."

"Are there any special places nearby this valley?' Chan asked, changing the subject.

"Oh yes, there are some very special places. In amongst the Andes Mountains here there are avenues to what some say are places of spirit. Not far from here is a place called Tora Muerto…"

"Dead bull," Lyle said.

"Yes, dead bull. It is an old place of special significance. It has petro glyphs of times past. Some say they are of things said to be unworldly."

"Petro glyphs…um ancient images?" Kerry Ann asked.

"Yes they are images of times long ago Kerry Ann. They are not so far from this valley. You could easily travel there and return the same day on horseback."

"What are they of…these images?"

"As I said, some say there are images of people not of this world. But also, there are pictures of life from times long past. Of animals, daily life, spiritual, and village matters."

"This is very adequate for our understanding," Chan said. "Consider what we have done to come to this place, and there is now a destination to visit during our stay called Dead Bull. Our…"

"Of course! Dead Bull. John here killed the beastly amplifier thing the Agent had. You're strong honey."

"Killed the beast? Whatever do you mean?" Pablo asked.

"It was a machine the Agent used called a vortex amplifier. It looked like a bull with two horns and a centre ring as if it was a nose ring."

"It sounds very bad. We have legends of similar things in places near this valley where lines and stones were used to summon unseen forces. This beast may have been a similar thing."

"Perhaps, but the Agent was using it to create bad things. There are many people in North America and other places with holes…"

"Oh. No, do not speak of those things. There have been a few of those people seen in Arequipa. They look like horror has been planted into their hearts. Many people are wary of them and if they ever see them, they are outcast to the desert. There it never rains and food is almost non-existent. A few of those people you speak of, tried to attack people at the edge of the city, and whilst it seems awful to abandon them, it is all they could do. We do not have any machines to make them well again."

"I'm afraid nobody can make them well again. Even with what I know about technology, I tried but there are simply no answers."

"You have done what is required to further progression by doing this with those afflicted people. There are elemental disparities within them created by those holes you speak of. When we were within the Agent's grasp, he told us of the devastation he was doing to people in their bodies and their souls. It is okay for you to have reacted this way, otherwise there would have been growth of the disparities and then many more would have been afflicted," Chan said and as he spoke, his words drew the attention of everyone present.

"You sure speak a bit funny Chan," Kerry Ann remarked.

"Oh you get used to it. He's a lovely man," Raynie replied. "We have known Chan a long time now."

"More food anyone?" Lolita offered. "I have prepared a special feast to celebrate, so please eat as much as you can. We cannot let it go to waste."

The entire group continued the feast well into the night, and although Frieda was not beside them, she too was enjoying the fresh hay and grain she had been given, along with the company of the other three horses living at the farm.

Chapter 24

Further testing under the guidance of Eric Gunter revealed there were no new viruses coming from the Agent. As he processed the information appearing on the holographic array with his part human and part mechanical mind, he began to envisage the near future when he could deploy many of the new systems he had been testing over the past year and a half. Gone was the notion of compliance through identification chip technology, and gone were the ideas of dependency as they had stood three years before. An entirely new set of arrangements for the population at large had been developed, and soon Eric would be in charge as they were rolled out across the nation and further across the planet...but only when they were certain the Agent was no longer a tangible threat to the security of authority systems.

Eric's next duty was to report the latest findings to his superiors for their assessment and decision on how to proceed further. When he arrived at their office, he found they were looking into their latest quantum-computing calculations for the deployment of pseudo self-realisation robotics. Being the next level in technological robotic surveillance, these machines were programmed to rely on authority driven parameters, yet also to have an element of self-determination for making decisions. Studies into the elemental properties in self-awareness had developed to a stage where these new robots were equipped to anticipate the actions of human beings in any given situation. Subtleties of the human experience were in part also accounted for where this new technology held the capacity to read into situations and into responses and actions by people. Fifty of these robots stood waiting in the warehouse below authority headquarters in New York City and soon according to Eric's assessment, many of the people above would experience the true force of the authoritarian intentions commenced those years prior.

"Sir?"

"Yes Eric?"

"I have the results sir. It appears as though we have a positive result for proceeding."

"Do you have the holographic data report?"

"Yes sir."

"Leave it with me, and then you may go. Oh...and well done on your initiative. I look forward to more efficient outcomes from you Eric."

"Thank you sir. You can expect nothing less."

Constant music sounded throughout the main authority complex. Further studies conducted over the past three years, had shown with the right type of rhythmical constant, human beings could sub-consciously connect with the tones where their actions and thinking were affected for enhancement to their output at work and as a person generally. The authorities took this current drive to compliance and efficiency to the extent of influencing people at all times in life as they saw better efficient thinking generally, contributed to more compliant outcomes in all activities and decisions. It was not really music, rather a mixture of tones and rhythm sections played at low volume to avoid any distraction. Senior officers and officials were not subjected to the subliminal suggestion of the constant tones, remaining free from the ever-present drive for efficiency as their status was seen to confirm their capacity to operate according to objectives. Only those ranked at the elite level were given this consideration as a degree of relaxation from the strict rules of compliance enforced upon all sub-ordinate employees.

When Eric arrived back at his workstation, his heartbeat had risen along with his adrenalin levels from a mixture of the walk and from the subliminal tones. Immediately he set about his next task without any moments taken to consider his place, or himself. As part man and part machine, the technology systems inside of him were connected to a real time status holographic readout. Eric and many others involved with taking up the advanced nano implants and systems mechanics could be prompted by subtle internal system changes made by executive science officers who could re-direct their focus and return to work.

The trade-off for accepting the implants was the promise of a longer life span guaranteed beyond one hundred and forty years. Specific care was provided in these early stages where the technology could experience errors. As more people pursued the technology, ongoing development was challenged in accommodating new actions and thoughts then incorporated into learning heuristic algorithms in real time. In time, the authorities would aspire to make them mandatory for all employees and those who among the population were seen as assets to the efficient drive, would also be made to comply whilst being made offers of benefits too alluring to refuse.

Inside Eric's brain, millions of the tiny robots worked to enhance his neural capacity as he collated data on the possible locations of the rogue HyperJet. With such enhancements in place, he was capable of processing considerably more information than those without the nano inserts, and also to make decisions based on projections contained within the data. His superior had permitted him to continue with this objective using whatever resources he deemed necessary to find John Matheson. As he analysed the data, he was able to gather information from the jets deployed to chase John on his likely heading and the signal from any technology John uses.

The holographic array at Eric's workstation contained a new type of quantum computing processor providing each officer access to pseudo flux capacity. Pseudo was not the real thing. Eric knew this as he entered possible scenarios based on the telemetry readings. The array lit up showing possible outcomes for the HyperJet taken from energy capacity to show a comprehensive estimate of possibilities. John's personality traits from the data obtained during his incarceration at the facility three years ago also appeared, and artificial intelligence generated scenarios and projected outcomes based on John's decision making traits when he was under tense conditions began to unfold as the algorithms set to work making assumptions of his behaviour.

Heading projections the jet might have taken given their requirement to remain obscured from detection, provided several destinations on a three dimensional Earth globe. Locations within reach of nominal HyperJet energy capacity and one with potential power enhancements John could make were everywhere – Eric had to narrow the search knowing John would have likely travelled far from any trouble to escape and feel some of the remoteness he had enjoyed prior when living in Alaska.

He determined John would likely not want to remain airborne for too long knowing the risk of detection would be foremost in John's thinking. His service records showed he preferred solitude and the company of only a select few. They knew of him as they knew of all the ex-service personnel. Had never been a concern and was seen as a loner staying out of trouble and content to have a few whiskeys after flying his plane. The records revealed nothing of John's expertise with algorithms and electronics but Eric knew otherwise after the experience where John had managed to avoid the probing mechanics in his mind. Eric knew John was an authority on flux and knew far more information than Eric had successfully retrieved during those mind sessions three years ago. Aptitude tests had shown a level of skill but they were mostly aligned for efficiency in addressing specific criteria for a position and so failed to reveal what Eric suspected – John was the key to stable technology. Eric had succumbed to less than he would have liked with the deployments then and now and with the new level of robotics at the verge of deployment, it was essential he find John to ensure success and prevent any gradual problems arising from instability.

Eric considered how these factors and the information on those associated with John, could affect his choices. Realising the skill John possessed in covering alluding authorities, Eric knew the task ahead would require testing of the enhanced critical thinking and lateral interpretation algorithms of the mechanics interacting with his mind. So lost was he to this process of analysis, his emotive self had receded almost to the destination so aspired to by the Agent as if Eric's loss of self was also a willing passage to oblivion.

He had also projected some data involving the Agent into the sequence, and this was included within the results he was now analysing. As he entered information, the holographic projections updated within the second, yet it was not as instantaneous as it would have been using flux mechanics. This began to bother Eric as he studied the reports in front of him as his desire to be ever more efficient taking hold in his mind for a few moments. His internal mechanics sensed this, and so they eased his angst through deliberate manipulation of his synaptic processes for him to gather focus only for the task at hand.

Eric's sight was not susceptible to the subtleties of normal organic based sight where the blink of eyes, a speck of dust, or the loss of focus, might affect his capacity to continuously view and thus analyse the results as they appeared. His eyes retained a constant fix on the array spread before him, but somewhere deep inside his self, inside his brain, there was a misalignment of the nuances within the human experience. Unknown to him, and to those who were also monitoring his progress, they began to create a disassociation similar in ways to the unstable vortexes created by the Agent. In time this mechanical art would render an elemental disturbance to the normal patterns of life during the evolution of the integrated trans-human.

After a five minute effort at compiling sufficient data to complete a report for consideration on how to pursue John, Eric noticed his time was up for work. Without any sense of relief or any feelings of excitement about what he could do during the non-working hours, Eric simply logged out of his workstation, and then left to go home. His place of residence was not above ground – it was at the same level as his place of work, and so he only required boarding the electric transport and standing patiently on its carrier platform for the ten-minute ride through the tunnel to his allocated abode.

Upon arrival he sat in the specially equipped chair for the automated daily injections required each day for the first two years of his new trans-human life. The medicines stabilised the endocrine system until his body had adjusted to the implants. Each implant was a hexagonal design of technical marvel, constructed as a result of studies into elemental geometric forces, then compiled into form through data spectrum prototyping. They were designed to operate as a framework integrating with his physical structural integrity, and also as a conductor for processing data throughout the body.

Ten seconds after the injection procedure, Eric felt hungry so he ordered his once per day meal from the food dispenser. Dinner for Eric was the same food substance every day – a mixture of compounds with alternate flavours each day designed for compatibility with his nanotechnology implants

After eating, Eric disposed of his utensils via the built in laser dispersal unit, and within a second of engaging the holographic control, his waste was reduced to a small mass of densely packed atoms to be taken away via the garbage chute.

Entertainment was not something Eric chose each night during those hours between working. Most evenings he would exercise his trans-humanism to sense the internal workings aligning his systems with efficient processing of both organics and data. It was an entirely new experience for a human being where one could feel their internal processes, described by those with the implants, as a feeling of warmth. These moments were the only time Eric came close to feeling pleasure, yet is was pseudo in nature and his robots manipulated his remaining natural self. When the sensations ceased, Eric would then analyse all the information he had collected for the day, in pursuit of creating further technological developments to please his superiors. Finally, the systems would tell him he was tired, and at almost the precise same time each night, Eric was sent to bed.

The very next morning when Eric awoke as he had done at the same time for one and half years now, his mind immediately switched to efficiency awareness. He washed efficiently, he dressed efficiently, and then he made his way to work efficiently. When he arrived back at his station, the night shift officer handed operations over to him for his daytime twelve-hour stint. Two shifts per day were all the authorities required from enhanced personnel to ensure their facilities ran nonstop without any downtime.

Prior to commencing work, Eric instructed his backup officer to be at the ready. Next he downloaded all of the considerations he had made at home the night before into his holographic array by sending a command to the wireless transmitter at the base of his skull. Then as he resumed actual work on the developments he thought would be required to apprehend John Matheson, the quantum computer once again provided him near real time statistics and results.

As he continued processing the information in front of him, Eric felt a slight surge of excitement as if one of remaining organic neural pathways came to a sudden realisation. Before he could recognise this in himself for more than a fleeting moment, the implants took over. They both analysed the response and then adjusted his thoughts to send him once again into primary efficiency status.

Further investigation revealed nothing from the scenarios in front of Eric with no real tangible data on where to find John. Consequentially, Eric immediately moved on to other considerations with his goal to eventually determine enough information for a physical search and apprehension. His biggest problem was John did not have any technology implants himself, nor did he have the identification chip still found in most of the population.

****

On the opposite side of the continent, precisely the opposite was occurring in respect to efficiency and focus. The Agent went about re-building his vortex amplifier between spasms of manic behaviour between flights to destroy buildings and people in his space ship. One thing did occur through all his episodes of mania, and construction and destruction - he was creating a plan. It was a plan not so well planned, but nevertheless it would come together in what he saw as his way of creating an axiom of apathy – a turning point of oblivion and non-commitment. The moment he was able to connect his repaired amplifier and then make the connections he had designed for allowing him to use it in his craft as he flew, then he would again have his time. All those who ever dared consider him a failure, or who had ever dared now thinking his power was lost, would suffer unimaginable despair through his new creation. But…time was on their side as he was still largely manic, and so progress was slow.

Seattle had turned to ruin in the days after John had stolen the torus. The Agent's first act of vengeance was indiscriminate as he set about flying over the city picking off groups of people and laughing as he watched occupied buildings crumble to the ground. The laser cannons on his ship were glowing red from his countless firings he rained down on those below by the time he was finished with each flight when the charge ran out. Forced to return to his base at the jet factory, he would relinquish to the inevitable with bouts of manic flying in and around buildings whilst feeding his hatred and deciding on targets he would return to the next day. When he was finished, the central high-rise contained only two full towers of the original eight, with the others left as smouldering wrecks of both rubble and bodies.

On the fourth day, he decided to spend more time at his base to work on his new amplifier. Given his propensity to mania and without a means to dispense suffering through flights spreading viruses, he reverted to long periods of sheer madness where even his minions could not approach him. Each night was spent on the floor of his main control room where he would fall asleep wrapping his body around the loose components and the partially re-built vortex amplifier.

After two weeks of this behaviour, he considered his task of re-building complete. The amplifier stood once again at the top of his array but it lacked the vital ringed Torus of Eternity in the centre, so when he engaged it for the first time it gave him no satisfaction, instead fuelling his hatred for John.

His focus had turned to him now as he had stolen the torus and his prized possession former Superior Officer One. Nothing could alleviate his mind from images of the man he now hated more than anything he could ever remember. It drove him to senses and to madness where his work was a mire of utterances punctuated by bouts of concentration as he adjusted controls and output for the new device.

Chapter 25

In the evening of New Year's Eve twenty ninety one, everyone at the farm gathered to celebrate in the one remaining vacant barn. Festivities amongst the sixteen adults living at the farm began early prior to the sun setting behind the rock formations at the tops of the peaks behind the valley. They all had reason to celebrate their settled lives and wellbeing now as they counted each other as friends.

Chan and the others had made significant progress in their recoveries, and were now able to contribute to working the fields each day and other general farm duties. On this day, they had all worked in earnest preparing to celebrate life and also have a day or two off from working afterwards. When the sunlight was low near the horizon, the valley took on a soft orange glow surrounded by the towering peaks around them still bathed in rays of golden light.

Carmel sounded five whistles from her steam engine they had situated in the middle of the barn to run an array of lighting John had built. There was no electricity other than what they could generate themselves, meaning on most nights they relied on light from candles and fires. Juan had been particularly interested in Carmel's engine where they had spent many hours discussing what she had done to restore it to such grandeur, and about what he had done to restore the three larger steam engines on the property they used to drive some of the mechanisms. Then as if precisely on time, the last filaments of sunrays filtered through the trees reaching out to illuminating the steam as it wafted about already creating atmosphere.

Carmel was in high spirits, and upon seeing the transition from day to night, she went about organising the last few things at a table against a wall whilst singing a soft melody.

Only John had heard her singing for a brief time before they set out from her house north of San Francisco, but this time he and the others were captivated by the angelic essence in her voice. Without thinking they were compelled to stop what they were doing to just listen. Her song was from the heart with words of connection to human spirit, of endurance, and of uplifting awareness.

Chan was listening the most intently. Since their meeting at the Agent's lair, she had moved him much more than at the time they had encountered her as Superior Officer One in Germany three years ago. Back then he knew something was stirring within the group and within her as they extended their awakening outwards where she could feel similar during their encounter. Now he was certain on his intuition upon hearing her song. He could feel the song as an outpouring of giving to all present then added to with their feelings and responses. Carmel was affecting them without effort and they received her without effort. She established a harmony entirely suited for the moment and for their presence together.

Without looking, Chan reached into his pocket where his hand found the object he was subconsciously directed to retrieve. When he revealed it to himself, the Torus of Eternity radiated its brightest pink hue yet. As the others sensed his movements, they turned to see Chan holding the torus in front of his face. They were drawn somehow deeper into the moment, and those who had not yet been shown the object, were immediately entranced with its beauty.

During her song, Carmel realised something had changed in the barn, and so she stopped her singing and turned to face all the others. Then she looked at the torus - her very first vision of the eternal object. Inside she felt a knowing and a connection...growing as did the smile light up her face almost like an angel.

Lolita, Kerry Ann, Pablo, Manuel, Juan, Diego, and Ricardo marvelled at the object Chan held. They expressed their wonder at seeing an object of such beauty offering warmth yet without touch, and knowledge, yet without instruction. To each of them, the torus was immediately a connection of within and of outward in fulfilment of eternal experience as if their lives were given a deeper sense of purpose and intention and allowed to be represented and thus confirmed.

Chan noticed how they simply stared at the torus as he held it, "You see what is before you as an object, yet it is not so much an object as a reflection. For all life is of a torus in nature with infinite progression connected in an electrical and dimensional field. Such is the progression of our very natural elemental intentions for us to gather here and experience this moment together."

He turned to Carmel, "And Carmel, how graceful your song to enlighten these moments for us all to share."

She was a little shy of this attention for a brief few seconds but she knew Chan was right. It was not an egotistical assertion within her – it was a realisation and a comfortable acceptance of her place, and of her intent. She was glad to be able to share this with the others. For a moment her thoughts were afar and of Tim, wherever he was – far or near, for to her their connection was an eternal entanglement.

"Shall we eat then?" Raynie asked.

"Of course," Lolita said coming out of her trance-like state. "Let our celebrations begin."

Pablo, Ricardo, and Manuel performed a collection of traditional Peruvian songs and musical pieces to entertain them all after the dinner had finished. Lyle and Jenna took to dancing as they rekindled spirits of moments past and present. Tobias and John were a little reminiscent watching them dance together, as they too though of times they had spent with Asper and Lorraine at the wharves by the bay.

Chan could see their downward trend, so he prompted Carmel and Raynie to take flight with them on the dance floor and help them dance away their worries. Steve grabbed Kerry Ann's arm giving her no choice in joining him to move with the excited salsa rhythms. Lolita took Jake's arm and Juan, Diego, and Chan began to talk quietly amongst themselves.

For a couple of hours, the scene was one of swapping dance partners, laughter with broad smiles, conversations, and some drinking. Chan was even coaxed to join in by Raynie. She held the man dear to her as did the others, but she felt a sense of connection from how he had helped her the most through those dark years with the Agent. He had felt she was the most of the five to be susceptible to the burdens of life he had placed on them, and so he had taken to giving her special guidance and inner strength. Now he joined her and the others in the abandonment of the night letting memories and thoughts slip away.

When the music ceased through sheer exhaustion felt by all and they had taken to sitting quietly in a close huddle around the steam driven lights, they pondered what possibly lay ahead in the newly arrived year of twenty ninety two. Chan had asked Juan and Diego more about the nearby petro glyphs and proposed they all could take a journey to visit the site sometime soon.

"It is a journey of at least two days return by horse and cart," Juan told them. "We have been there before. It is an interesting place to see, but I think it best some of us remain here at the farm whilst the others travel. There is work to do, horses to feed, and we should remain vigilant against unwelcome visitors. Perhaps if you go as a group of ten, it might serve us well?"

"Perhaps it is best if a few of our group remain here as well, and then the others can return and tell us all about it," John replied. "I have some things I want to look into now we are established here and there is a little spare time away from farm work. What do you think Tobias? I would like your help."

"Yeah, sounds okay to me. Anytime you might want me to help you with a bit of tech, just ask."

"Sure mate thanks."

"And you Steve? You look a little like you don't want to go." Chan remarked.

"Hmm. It sounds interesting, but…maybe I'll stay. You guys will likely glean more from such a thing as I would."

"So, it is no then?"

"I'll think about it."

"And you Kerry Ann? How do you feel about travelling to this place?"

"I'm with Steve there Chan honey. I like this relaxing atmosphere, so the thought of more horse and cart travel does not sound good for me at the moment. Another time maybe." She gave Steve a quick glance and a smile. Kerry Ann was growing to be very fond of the onetime military man who had softened to become more gentile whilst holding onto a sense of determination.

"It is probably best only a small group goes anyway," Diego added. "It will be easier attracting less attention as there can be thieves or others. They have always been there really but now with times much harder...well."

"I see," John became a little concerned at this news, as did Steve. "Take a pulse rifle with you just in case Carmel."

"Okay John. We'll be careful. Chan, I suggest we leave in the morning and make the first day of the new year an adventure of sorts."

Chan glanced around at the others who were intent on taking the journey, "All right Carmel. In the morning then."

Frieda led the way towing their cart, as they all walked beside her out of the valley the next day. The journey ahead would see them arrive at the ancient site by days' end if they made good time with a plan to spend an entire next day there, before returning on the third day.

Their travel was uneventful aside from an encounter with a snake causing Frieda to come to a sudden stop. Their road was remote yet posed a danger demanding they remain alert despite the relative serenity mostly by a river amongst trees and around hills where they caught views of tall jagged mountains stretching beyond the horizon on either side. Ahead the road could be seen to gradually make way uphill away from the valley floor, so they decided to rest for a meal and to give Frieda a break before the climb. Their cart was light with provisions only and so far the road had mostly been level. Most of the way they had walked – their strength now returning. It was only when Jake felt a little worn did Frieda take on a little more load to drag.

After the climb and spectacular views to the mountains now ahead and on both sides, a brief stop to catch breath was all Frieda seem to need as she stamped her feet a little eager to keep moving. All present could sense a feeling as they went further into the mountains where their concerns slipped away and the energy of the great towering peaks capped with snow, drew their thoughts. They glanced back the way they had come searching for signs of the farm but found no trace and could not even see an approximate location.

After another stint, they rested at the start of the white pathway marking the start of the road to Toro Muerto – their destination. Carmel had taken to reading some of the material Diego had provided about the site.

"It is said the Huari, Wari, and Collahuas people were likely to have made the petro glyphs. Some of the images carved into the stones have lost parts of their face, or all in some instances. Other petro glyphs were carved over and around them. Apparently the loss of the faces was symbolising a 'loss of face' of those who carved the first sets of imagery."

"There is an uncanny link there between the 'loss of face', and the 'dead bull' name for this place, if you consider the recent events in Seattle," Chan added. "The bull was the Agent's imagery and now we travel to a place known as dead bull where there is also the element of losing face. This can be considered as losing honour, yet the Agent has no honour, but…he has lost face in regards to the amount of fear he is now able to generate."

"He could never be attributed with such grace as honour Chan. I discovered the geometric figures of symbology and people interacting refer to a more universal idea. This could be a very interesting destination."

"I think there is some reason for our travels as yet unknown to us, but known. If like in previous times, the reasons may become apparent as we explore."

"There are the lines of Nazca not so far from here as well I believe," Lyle added. "From my recollection, the descriptions of those petro glyphs and lines are associated with the geometric flow of water and rituals to summon water. Some are even said to be astronomical calendars."

"Yes, this region does appear to be one where the people were quite eager to illustrate their relationships with nature."

"The Toro Muerto is also the largest rock carving site on Earth, and there are said to be instances depicting a head figure known as the Doorway God."

"Ah, this Doorway God may perhaps be something we could consider in context like a metaphor and not literally. With all we have learned and practiced through activation of the torus, again we find there is connection through representation, and so the relationship may not appear direct. As we have discussed previously, there are instances from cultures in many places where they each form a part of the understanding common to humanity and expressing experiences many may have shared."

Ahead of them lay the ascent onto the desert plains of volcanic rocks and ash surrounded by distant conical peaks capped with snow. When the day was near its end, they had been welcomed by the owner of a farm very near to the site who offered them a place to stay as long as they chose.

"It is not very often I see visitors. Most people are too busy just trying to survive. I welcome you so long as you are not here to steal from me."

"Oh no. We are interested in looking at the petro glyphs. And thank you for your kind offer."

"You are welcome, but I can only offer you to stay in the barn with your horse. My house is much too small to accommodate so many."

"Your barn is fine thanks."

Despite the chill in the air, they had all chosen to sit around a small fire under a vivid array of stars. The view to the heavens was stunning as the Milky Way formed a ribbon studded with thousands of glittering lights from horizon to horizon.

As they sat quietly talking about where they had been in recent times and their strengths to survive at the hands of the Agent, what potentially lay ahead of them and their relations with Carmel took on new meaning. The irony of her now with them in contrast to the times she was Superior Officer One in charge of the Agent, was not lost. Chan had remarked on the activation of the torus being more than just the physical object where it was a reflection of the energy and intentions they were sending far beyond their own physical bodies. He had shown the others the way to this understanding in being compassionate to Carmel when she had encountered them in Germany, explaining the sub-conscious construction of events many saw as coincidence.

In response to the meeting at the fringe of the Black Forest, Carmel had seen the path of circumstances leading to the very chance event, and in herself, she had begun to understand the giving nature of self realisation. Raynie and Jake had given to her despite their arduous incarceration at the facility deep underground. They had not realised this at the time, nor had Carmel seen it unfolding before her, but regardless of anything their minds attributed to their paths in life crossing, their eternal hearts spoke a language of alignment and of endearment. With their gathering under the splendour above, they all could feel the connection building upon the essence of their intentions, and so in part the beauty of the cosmos above was a reflection of themselves.

"We are all actively choosing this as we proceed," Chan said, breaking the temporary silence as they all gazed skyward. "The stars above us are connected. The winds gently caressing our flame are winds eternal in progression, and the beating of our hearts as a torus is aligned with the wave forms and geometric vortexes encompassing the energy field of all reality. Beyond here is simply not a place in time or in situation, for beyond is a notion of awareness and intentional alignment with our true giving nature."

"John is a person for endearment. His strength when we travelled from my house towards the eastern sector was our greatest asset."

"Ah, what you say Carmel, is true in a sense, but think too of the strengths of intention from both of you, for you both took on such an undertaking through your intentions of continuing progress without really thinking of it as an idea. So often in these times many are forced as they think, to survive, but there always remains the elemental intent to progress. It is just so many overlook this as their minds are dominated with pressure and fear, be it the Agent or the authorities. Now our travels and ordeals have brought us all together..." Chan trailed off remembering those missing, especially Tim.

"There has been a lot of healing as a result. Lyle and I have talked about how even the Agent whilst depriving us of so many things, he has actually invigorated out bond and our strengths," Jenna said seeing Carmel pause for a moment looking distant.

"The Agent is a catalyst unknowingly successful in what to him would appear to be the opposite of his intentions. Elementally he is not aligned yet he is for an expression of such mania as his, is simply another one of infinite universe expressions. He strives to overwhelm all with his state of discord by using his stolen spaceship and up until recently, his unstable vortex amplifier, to wreak this havoc as a means to discharge some of his personal electrical circuit."

"Do you know much of what vortex amplifiers can do if they are in alignment with stable flux Chan?" Jake asked.

"Yes I do Jake, in part. These instruments are still mysterious to me somewhat, but I do know of their potential to accelerate atomic energies including the electrical and space time elements of information creating atoms forming matter and so on."

"Like a nuclear…"

"No. The invention of nuclear devices is for the splitting of atoms and to disperse the integrity of structure against the natural flow. This is why they are so dangerous because they are opposite to the alignment and of acceleration. The amplifier can accelerate atoms and this can be used as an energy source for the machines people build in reflection of their inner knowing and inner seeking. This takes an understanding though. As with quantum mechanics, intention is key to shaping the results. A result of stable flux and vortex amplification may well be the construction of machines taking humans beyond what they call light speed where they can accelerate atoms for transition of matter between places almost instantaneously. Remember some years ago when I said sprit sets the path for light to follow. Well this spirit is the pre-empt to light and so if you look at technology the same, you can see how the flux can be the spirit of intention and then the inter-dimension energies being the light in this case. It remains to be seen if people who control such things, look to this type of progression, or if they look to control and manipulation based in ego and exploitation. Such a device would strike deep at the heart. This is all I can say…perhaps talking to John would give you more information to put into a physical context."

"He has advanced knowledge of flux mechanics," Jenna added.

"And this is both an asset and a cause to be wary. At such times with both good and bad influence at at the brink of actualisation, we must be vigilant in remaining alert to allowing John to progress with this knowledge without again losing the torus."

"Could the Agent's vortexes have any on-going effect, even though they are unstable?"

"In regards to this, I can only offer a suggestion indicating they might have an on-going effect. Again, without being knowledgeable sufficiently, I suggest speaking with John may help you, but consider, the vortexes he creates destabilise matter and they also open pathways perpendicular to the natural flow where access to other dimensions might be found. We can only assume the consequences, but such assumption in this instance is not from blindness, for our knowledge whilst in its infancy, comes from collected awareness not only for us but others in other places. We reach out to acquire the nature of influence brought on by our presence in and as the universe beyond the physical along with other people. Our relevance is because of our holding the torus and the implications of the knowledge of flux John has."

Amongst the hills shaped akin to Toro Muerto the bull - for the hills did look like such a beast in the low light of dawn and dusk, Chan, Carmel, Jenna, Raynie, Lyle, and Jake had awakened prior to first light with clarity of purpose to match the emerging sky.

In heart and mind, they set out to explore the petro glyphs after breakfast with their host who was about after hearing them. There were carvings everywhere of images on almost every stone within the broad expanse of the site. Pictures of animals, of people, geometric patterns, and representations of ceremonies from long before, could be found indiscriminately. They saw some figures of people adorned with symbols they recognised as having seen in other places, especially Jake and Lyle. They pondered the similarities between the shapes of the figures and the properties of electricity and plasma energised at certain frequencies. The two men had shared similar talks over time after finding they could relate based on their occupations and their understanding of the properties of electricity seemingly reflected in the ancient art around them. They had seen this similarity and speculated on the somewhat mythical nature of their observed carvings and images. Agreement on the possibility of myth founded in truth yet abstract had spawned previous conversations during their captivity by the Agent and since now with their returning health.

Carmel, Jenna, and Raynie stopped at one large stone featuring dancers appearing to be moving despite the many centuries since the carving was made. The others walked over to see what had captivated the women, and they too were drawn in by the image.

"It's like their dancing onward and eternal," Lyle said.

"Most people do this dancing, yet they do not take it in stride," Chan added. "It is…um, how would you say? Ah, it is like they are out of step with their dance of life in so many instances."

"Dancing is a celebration of life. It is a responsive embrace to rhythm, and often it is giving through creativity and for lovers in close relations, especially physically as embrace," Carmel said thinking of her love for music and dance.

"Yes Carmel. What you say is significant. It is the progression of lovers to embrace physically and then to dance. This motion and embrace, opens up the energies of creation and the eternal knowledge connecting self to the universe. It is a continuation of the energy and not cut off or separated. There is geometry through the motions made to the rhythms, and it amplifies the feelings between couples."

"Yes, but not all couples dancing are in love."

"In essence when those two people choose to dance together, their creation is not so much different from the lovers. The intentions are elementally similar creating progress in a different way in context for their relationship whether it is once or ongoing."

"And don't forget the dancing just for fun," Raynie said with a wink as she gave Jenna a dig in the ribs. "Look, you can see a type of ceremonial head dress and the line of people appear to be in celebration of something."

"Again there is significance. With dancing there is response to the elemental rhythms created as sound waves then invigorating more than just auditory senses."

Lyle was eager to show the interpretation of the images from his once professional perspective, "The dancers here in these images are surrounded by representations of important facets of life. They would have danced to celebrate their animals, the environment…especially if water was scarce, and the elements giving life. This occurs in many of the older cultures all over the Earth, where people danced the dance of animals and elements."

"There is the connection to aligning as it resonates within the entire energy field of existence. There is no real space. Always matter…energy in some form is present. It is as if all life is in a continuous dance."

"So keep in step," Raynie said. "If it falls out of the rhythm this can be reflected in the heart and the mind…"

Chan could feel this sentiment from Raynie along with the others who had been held by the Agent. They had each endure personally and as a group during these times where Chan had suggested they focus on thinking and seeing the aura of each other to maintain a sense of this rhythm of life.

"There can be reflections throughout with implications projected outward where the mind manifests the misalignment and so many things are done and created seen as out of step…say of character. This is out of the flow yet in the flow for all makes relevance. Seeing this relevance authentically is the elemental way without pressure and so clarity could be better," Chan said before pausing a moment to consider where he was going.

"People have long forgotten this in many places. Even before the Agent, there were changes as cultures blended more into a planetary consumption model. People lost the will and with restrictions and regulations seeming to kill the atmosphere of places and social life became smothered. We are social beings but it is sad to say a lot of our technological progress has brought us undone in ways. Places like Peru here and many others with strong indigenous cultures don't seem as consumed. This rock art, their art designs, dancing, and music combines to show this deeper connection many others have failed to understand."

"Let's move on. There must be other things to discover amongst these thousands of images," Jake suggested.

A petro glyph featuring humanoid beings standing atop a platform riding through the sky was the next to catch their attention. Immediately Lyle thought of the Nazca lines and the speculation of how some of those were thought to be messages sent to the skies. He told them in times during the latter twentieth century, many groups had thought the Nazca lines were runways for ships coming to Earth from the stars, and books had even included this in their discussion of the idea of extra-terrestrial life.

Carmel once again referred to the information Diego had provided to her, "Same here as at Nazca Lyle. People deliberated over whether these images we see today depict beings from space, or if they are more dancers in worship of celestial bodies. I think people were a little carried away with their visitors from space thing."

"Is there any difference?" Chan asked. "Really, if you consider this in a different context, you can ask this simple question. Thinking of other life coming to this place aboard spaceships is somewhat a lineal thing, as if they come here from there. Even if these are depictions of dancers in worship of the celestial, then can you see both instances are virtually one and the same? Regardless if the elemental soul comes from another world, or from this world, there is a connection through the intention of awareness of life within the celestial apparitions, be they space travel, or simply to be amongst the stars upon this planet, in this location."

"Yeah, but space men are a bit removed from ancient peoples worshipping the celestial elements. I find it difficult to see these images as actual depictions of aliens. I see no sense in the concept of aliens visiting here...well, mostly," Jake said looking defiant on any idea of alien visitors.

"In essence of intent, they are of the same thing. What I am saying is, not to focus on whether they are from space. Thinking this instigates the notion of removal and separation. Consider them as purely of the same elements in a metaphorical sense. I agree on the idea of aliens being absurd, yet we are not of all knowledge and so it is best to remain a little open to possibility without being carried away. This serves us not so literally in the sense of subject matter, but also in the way of opening the mind allowing the moment to take place from the heart rather than the moment taking place so much through the thinking and analysis of the mind. This is to see with the heart or the body and not seeing with the mind and thought. After all, the beings here worshipping the celestial bodies are also space travellers as are we upon an Earth craft speeding through the cosmos. It has mainly been the limitations associated with the lineal approach where the sense of separation and removal from has been evoked and so we often see toxic ways emerge as the very Earth craft we rely upon has been disregarded along with the minds and hearts of the many people. To allow the imagination without construct...just to flow is the beginning."

"Invasions took place over time as well. Look at the behaviour of many who changed South America," Lyle added.

"Yes, and this is likely from their disassociation from heart and mind, as they have sought to dominate. Such dominance is not the natural flow of human elemental intent. As you have experienced, it comes from the egotistical need to place this information into a controllable set of circumstances for exploitation rather than best use."

"During my time as Superior Officer One, I was feeding this beast born from paranoia. Control mechanisms come from insecurity along with the need to dominate and this arises from the fear of not being in control and fear of the unknown."

"Yes it does Carmel."

Jenna had walked a small distance away from the group, where she had found a peculiar carving showing what appeared to be dancing human figures with energy shooting from the top of their heads.

"Come and see this. Perhaps it is more of what you are speaking about Chan."

The others all walked over to where she was bent down closely examining the carving. Immediately, they could all see what she meant seeing energy rising to the celestial heights above the heads of the dancers.

"You see? Perhaps what we have just discussed, has now lead us to reach further confirmation of our thoughts. One thing is leading to another."

"And another," Jake said noticing a similar petro glyph just a few yards away.

"Notice there is the symmetry of life and of the surrounding influences all over this region. The peoples of this area from long ago were leading simple lives, yet they were in harmony with these elements and they recognised how they all played a part in their daily lives. This is an essence many people of the Earth have been overlooking for many years. Instead of synchronising with the elements of life and the progressive nature within its intentional manifestations, many have struggled to control and fight against the elements. It is not to say one should just merely cast their life upon the wind to see where it ends up, but...there is a degree of truth in being with the flow of such wave forms where it is the expression of this constant progression connected."

"Also, see here where there are inscriptions and geometric shapes," Chan lead them over to another group of nearby carvings. "These people were aware of the intricate nature of elemental shapes playing a part in the cycle of life as it progresses. We cannot read this writing, but one could say or assume, it is likely to be in relation to the shapes with meaning expressing their awareness of the intimate relationship they shared. This comes as we are all elemental organic beings requiring this fulfilment on many levels, not just the mind and certainly not just desire. From this relationship come our thoughts...our intentions and then our actions."

"Are you saying their awareness did not require any measurement by the mind, rather the heart and mind accepting it as the way of things was all they needed to fulfil their elemental intentions?" Lyle asked looking a Chan as if he just made a breakthrough and wanted Chan to share this moment.

"In nature all elements are perpetuated by progression in many forms. Simply allowing this through acceptance removes pressure from the mind to constantly decipher...um, measure information as the way of things."

Just then the prevailing winds of Toro Muerto returned. It had been calm under a bright cloudless sky until this time, and whilst there were no clouds carried by the wind, the stirring of dust made for a feeling of haste – it warned of wilder conditions to come.

For the remainder of their day before deciding it was time to leave ahead of the approaching weather, they examined art and discussed themes associated with the meaning and psychology behind each. As a group again, they were rekindling the connection they had formed three years earlier. As each moment or conversation passed, they established momentum through exchanges where at many of the glyphs they determined further meaning and began to feel an energetic resonance together.

"It is important we retain this composure as its' residual affect will help us in ways we cannot yet determine. It will also be of benefit in our coming times where its' authenticity to each of us will naturally be tested," Chan said as he and Carmel examined one rock together.

"John will need what we can establish Chan. It will have to be so as his work will only come if we are there."

"So true Carmel. His understanding is perhaps the most important of all as he is the bridge between our focus of intentions and the manifest of physical intentions through flux technology and the torus."

When they had gathered from the far reaches of the site towards days' end, the weather was changing to a steady wind blowing the ashen white soils in swirls making conditions unpleasant. Everyone agreed the conditions were telling them it was time they left the petro glyph site for the short journey back to the farmer's barn for the night.

As it had been before, the heavens were once again aglow from the thousands of stars as the ribbon of the Milky Way caressed the sky from horizon to horizon, but this time clouds were gathering. They sat around the small flickering fire talking about their day, the meaning of the art, and what it meant for them.

"This is further activation," Chan said. "As bearers of the torus, it is our path to invigorate activation of the allowance of elemental intentions. We see this reflected through the increasing hue within the torus. It is our confirmation. Nothing of aspiration, rather something to let go and it is here reminding us of this. As it continues to increase in colour, we will notice harmonising nature through sub-conscious suggestion. Remember…the torus is not an instrument for this awakening to occur within people. It is a representation as the activation of this object is a reflection of the activation within people, within self, as all is of a torus. This awakening is simply mere allowance of energy already available so perhaps one could say re-activation."

Jenna was looking to Chan and then to the stars, then back to Chan, and again back to the stars as Chan spoke. He noticed her and knew she was up to some suggestion.

She spoke softly, "The torus can be an instrument as well. Um…it can help with awakening as we realise the release of pressure from the mind and simply allow the natural flow to occur. Perhaps those rock images where they seem to bare themselves to the heavens similar to what we are doing now, is this pressure release as if there is a crossing of the boundary between dimensions physical and energetic."

"Yes Jenna. You have observed its scientific properties and we all know of what it could do for the Agent. As I said many years ago, given the right place and circumstance, it can be seen to amplify energy as the very construct enables it to harness the wave patterns and project them. For the stability of flux technology, energetic responses flow through the toroidal waveform allowing the creation coming from the intentions. This is the place of the physical and non physical and both exist equally."

"So then if people awaken and remember their elemental intentional flow of life patterns, what will the torus be then?" Raynie asked.

"The torus would be activated as a reflection of the activation within…hmm, which is re-activation. Then it could be used for the intentions arising from the heart and mind connection of those who choose this use of the torus. Then again…it may well also serve to show beauty, like you three lovely ladies here tonight."

"Hey, does it mean we men are ugly then?" Jake asked.

They all laughed and Raynie replied, "But I still love you sweetie."

Chapter 26

His flight took him beyond the atmosphere into space on a heading towards the Moon. His mania was determined to unleash havoc upon the lunar installations – three in all and time was apparent to show the authorities he was still a threat. Instability of mind and body was now his most regular state. Despite this behaviour, the Agent had been successfully re-built a partially operational vortex amplifier. It sat near him reflecting his mind. As it failed in most instances to send out his intended horrors, so too did his mind fail in maintaining awareness considered even remotely stable. It was his avid reflection, his conjuration, and his madness. Incapable of the devastation he sought to send across the Earth, it was now merely an instrument to apply in a localised sense with range limited to the immediate proximity.

Three hours after departure from Seattle he arrived and took a low orbit around the Moon, one hundred miles above the surface. He was in no hurry to immediately set about releasing his fury and his hatred. Instead he carefully plotted his course to take him on a sweeping flight over the widely dispersed lunar outposts. His first target was the far-flung station where the far side of the Moon converged with the side viewable from Earth at the Rumker Plateau. From there, he would proceed to his next target at the northern end of Mare Serenitatis, the Sea of Serenity, and then onward to the largest of the three located at the Sea of Tranquillity.

He had the benefit of equipment the authorities had installed in the spaceship prior to him having stolen it from Mars. Their latest pulse weapons and the capacity to create a defensive energy shield meant it was still sufficient for him now. He had never made a return to space since first arriving back from the red planet as his methods had been divisive enough for the Moon to be of no consequence. Now upon return, he would surprise them with this attack using a little technology of his own.

The authorities had detected him in orbit and placed all defences on standby and readiness. It was Eric Gunter's first failure as a development officer and a sign of the inefficiency of his internal mechanics. His organic and mechanical mind relied on what was known about the stolen craft. Contingencies, psychological data, projections, and calculations, were all made on this knowledge and from artificially induced assumptions. He had envisaged the Agent on a rampage and to this extent, Eric was correct. It was the failure to recognise the potential of the Agent's mania where it took him to new heights of erratic behaviour interjected with bouts of intense focus.

The Agent could hear transmission from the first lunar outpost he targeted, "On priblizhayetsya s temnoy storony na zagolovok pryamo dlya etoy bazy."

'Ah, so they know I am approaching from the dark side on a heading directly for the base,' he thought as the systems translated Russian into English. 'Good, so they are aware of their nemesis coming to destroy them.'

"Bystro okhranu vse oruzhiye oborony!"

'Yes, yes, quickly arm your weapons defence systems. Your panicking will do you no good.'

He swept into across the plateau barely one hundred feet above the lunar terrain with all weapons firing. At first the Russian officers witnessed their systems begin to experience data disintegration. Then as the first laser pulses began their destruction, they screamed in anguish as their life support systems went off line and they lost pressurisation. A few seconds later, they were thrust into the vacuum of space as their base erupted into explosions and was entirely destroyed.

'Now. My exquisite bull shall rise again,' the Agent thought as the automated systems took the craft to its next plotted destination at the Sea of Serenity.

Again, the voices of panic could be heard, but this time they were in English. The Agent laughed at the futility of their defence systems only momentarily affecting his laser fire, before they too experienced the same losses as the Russians. He watched as the officers were cast into the vacuum whilst their base became a brief cloud of fire before the airlessness of space extinguished the flames. And then he laughed as the ship took a steep banking turn on its way towards his final target.

The situation at Luna One was of a base at high alert status. Defensive systems were operating at full capacity and officers manning the holographic control arrays were on full alert unaware of the virus weapon the Agent was bringing to them. They watched his approach as he covered the distance between targets at great speed giving them barely any time to prepare their minds for the onslaught.

Eric Gunter was watching the events unfold from his array deep below New York City, and after the first successful attack from the Agent, he was beginning to feel a degree of unease – something his internal nano mechanics were trying to rectify.

When the Agent did arrive, he brought his craft to a halt, hovering about three hundred yards from the base and about three hundred yards into the lunar sky. The ribbons inside the nano mechanics were working as fast as possible to assist Eric in anticipating and calculating the next move by the Agent. It was obvious what he would do, yet there must be a way to do something. All the work Eric had done under the tyranny of this beast who was now looking almost directly at him as the camera angle lined up with the view into the cockpit of the spacecraft, had to come to something. Surely this fool of a man could not continue to threaten the system Eric and others regarded so highly. He stared at the array's three-dimensional holographic projection as the Agent stared straight back observing his final and largest target.

Then in a moment where a tiny filament of collective reason flashed across the Agent's mind, he abruptly dismissed it as his mania tore into him, prompting him to unleash all the weapons power he could.

Eric saw the systems at the base go haywire. He watched as defence systems could barely make any sense of the incoming craft - firing with no effect on their target. Eric knew then his defences against the Agent were failing.

He saw the looks on the faces of those at the base turn to horror when all of their life support went offline, and Eric watched as the de-pressurised environment was torn apart and they were thrust into the vacuum. For a moment he gazed at their bodies as they drifted away at first with a backdrop of the grey distant lunar terrain, to then fade away as the slid aimlessly into the great black void. Then Eric watched the Agent's moment of maniacal glory as he flew close to unleash volley upon volley of laser pulses reducing the base to nothing.

When the cloud of ashes, smoke and dust had cleared, Eric could see nothing as the Agent had terminated all transmissions from the lunar surface except for one. Unknown to the Agent, the mining operations outpost at the southern lunar pole was still operational, and so he had left the Moon behind with the lonely outpost still intact. Immediately Eric began to calculate possibilities for this last remaining outpost.

The Agent streaked across the sky during re-entry on a heading directly to his Seattle base. Such was his sense of jubilation he destroyed a few more of the city's buildings on his approach to landing. When he arrived back to his minions, he immediately dismissed them as insignificant whilst ordering them to leave him alone.

"Oh my tor, so exquisite you are to rise to me again, and so exquisite to end their meaningless existences. Oh my tor, those bastards could never break you. You will always be my own agent. Tomorrow my rise on Earth will resume with you as my instrument of futility," he spoke this to nobody as he was alone aside from his device. It hummed and glowed with crackling orange electrical charges coursing around and over it. Deeper inside it glowed the familiar red of his previous amplifier, of his lights, and the red of the eyes for his spacecraft. For a time he kept repeating those four sentences as if it was an incantation. Bereft of any real meaning, the sect he led was barely this at all, yet within the character of each member or minion, and the Agent himself...George Smyth the rather lowly Agent Eight of three years prior, an evil like enchantment was held where they could attune to energies through their determination to create darkness...and redness.

The next day George blasted away all signs of the gates near Omaha dividing the western and eastern sectors, and almost as soon as he did, scores of afflicted people crossed the line into the east. He flew on over the great cities of the east towards New York, and destroyed anything he possibly could. People ran in fear, screaming as they went, but those in his sights could not hide. He shot them as he saw them and he blew up the buildings into which they scurried. He unleashed proximity viruses in each and every pulse from his laser canons sending localised systems into disintegration where machines and internal nanotechnology implants descended into calamity. When the holographic array showed there was a large foodstuff manufacturing plant directly in sensor line, he smiled with his own type of glee, as he ruined the entire facility and embellished in the notion of those who were then to starve.

Eric Gunter saw all this happen as well, and more than ever the internal nano mechanics were struggling to maintain his composure. Officers assigned to monitor Eric, hurriedly entered algorithm sequences to counteract the onslaught – but to no avail. Failure was becoming apparent within him and around him, and the authorities would look heavily upon these incidents without any sense of Eric as a person.

When the Agent had finished his first attack using his proximity vortex amplifier, Eric stood motionless and almost without thought as he stared at the holographic array before him. Eric could not discern an appropriate developmental response to the attacks, nor could his nano mechanics offer any suggestion on what to do next.

Exposure to the Agent's latest weapon was the only tangible data Eric had to work with. Knowing it was only effective in close proximity to the Agent's location whenever he fired the weapons on-board his spaceship, was a decisive issue Eric seized upon to propose a response.

For a time Eric worked feverously, determined as he could be given his partially artificial state. His ideas came in a flurry as his mechanics worked his mind beyond the normal cognitive capacity of most human beings. When at last he had a solution, Eric sought approval from his superiors to execute a plan.

He would unleash authority driven horrors sending all their might on a mission to destroy the Agent's lair and any of his other installations. To this time the threat of his viruses was too dominating to risk any such action as it would expose their airborne systems to viruses and then those systems would spread the virus through their connection to central data networks. Now with his pathetic new amplifier, Eric saw the Agent's vulnerability.

Within two hours they destroyed the jet factory near Seattle and sought out many of his minions wherever they had data on minion locations. They began a war of attrition never seen previously. They would wear down the Agent through destruction of all seen as vital to his presence, turning his matte black world to rubble so it could be replaced.

Key locations and Agent installations in the cities of Seattle, San Francisco, Portland, and Los Angeles were reduced to rubble as the many minions within immediately found their pathway to their peculiar salvation. Any machines still operating and therefore under the control of the Agent, were blasted to oblivion. Vast swathes of cities and towns burned with their rivers turning red like rivers of blood. As for the people who struggled to live a meagre existence, the authorities held no remorse as they too bore the brunt of this offensive.

The antagonism from the Agent unleashed darkness built upon frustration within many - now vented without hesitation and without compassion. It was the beginning of their plight of fear, of hatred, and of invalidation of the human spirit as the only way ahead for their vision of a machine world as the authorities saw no option other than to exert themselves and cast society into further realms of fear through oppression.

Within days of the attacks, legions of armed personnel were sent to force the remaining populations into compliance. Specialised operations teams covertly tracked down minions of the Agent, whilst others were despatched to locate and similarly destroy anyone who was afflicted with viruses. Some would struggle as their last vestiges of life were being eroded, but the authorities had prepared for this, and so they unleashed a new array of weaponry to destabilise their sub-atomic mass, sending them cascading to the ground as particles.

Those who were virus free and remained...barely surviving, were now instructed on how the order of their life was to proceed, beginning with the curfew being enforced twenty-four hours. Ensuring people they were overwhelming the Agent required strict adherence to all conditions for the prevention of security breaches and to remain focused on rebuilding the society so many still yearned.

There was to simply be no choice, no decision...nothing but compliance and so nothing to strive for eventually. Deception was their play for so many centuries now and humanity had played along willing to seek a reward for work well done in some guise of personal liberties and freedoms. Now, even these would be but remnants of the past soon to be lost to the generations following. The concept of wealth based status was entirely closed down as people were told their employment was in service to the authorities for the progress of the society they managed. Concepts and modes of thinking where social conditioning had perpetuated the acceptance of such status as the normal way for society were revealed for their design and purpose through how easily now they were to be dismissed. Eventually the people would forget as they sought assuredness no more viruses would terrorise their lives, and so then they would be grateful for the choices offered within the scope of how lives were managed and this would become the new freedom.

As freedom has been defined through history, so too it was again defined as those less fortunate were to be beset with the arduous conditions of a world simply not caring about their plight in life. Nothing efficient could be seen in providing for them and so as Eric released this swathe of force and change, he instigated the pathway for many to take towards an oblivion almost matching the Agent's futility, yet almost as senseless considering the dynamics of individual awareness and human spirit...now being left to waste. They were offered nothing as the streets began to house the starving who were left homeless in a time of extreme food shortage.

Other world authorities were given information disguised as a contract mostly for compliance or to be cut off from any support of those at central systems for access to the latest technology. With the promise of flux toroidal capacity, endless opportunities could be realised and so those authorities soon saw the reality of how where the real power base would lie, and so as they took the immediate gratifications for commanding control in their own regions, they simultaneously began giving those regions away to the central systems authorities.

From one calamity to another, the Agent's domain was now becoming a centralised authority domain where nations everywhere saw the efficiency of compliance to these new conditions. Only the great powers who had vied for supremacy on the Earth since the middle of the twentieth century objected – instead remaining defiant and confident they could develop their own methods of control. In a short two-week event, the Earth was shunted into darkness.

These powers, the mongering of executives deep in secure rooms, and their deception saw only one way ahead – their consolidation would be John Matheson. The Agent was no match for the potential technology Matheson could help the authorities develop. It would be their manifest not so unlike the Agent's – only more orderly and not from the type of megalomania George Smyth had lived his entire life with. Theirs too was a megalomania where they saw themselves almost as saviours to humanity where their systems would dispense with the inefficiencies of erratic emotional experiences, with the useless vices distracting and costing, and with the errors of interaction and thought. Mind altering technology designed to efficiently conduct the mind in affairs of society was their goal. This mind in all would be the compliant mind not requiring force and so much more efficient.

They needed flux mechanics to bring in their new type of order, and so they focused on apprehending John Matheson. To capture him, and then extract his knowledge, would take them to their utmost desire realised - a desire to control the Earth, and a desire to evolve it into their efficient machine planet.

Upon such a planet there would never be an issue, there would never be a question, and there would never be a moment where they did not determine what was best for the people. There would be no law and no argument of circumstance. There would only be the way – the way the authorities advised and enforced. They would have flux mechanics for transcending the boundaries of existence as conceived by the masses and with such knowledge as their own, control the planet and control matter so they reckoned.

Chapter 27

The Agent was not impressed with the destruction of his lair and he certainly did not care any longer for those who had considered themselves his followers. No location to base himself from was his biggest concern for the immediate future. He had the spaceship to take him wherever he wanted with enough stored energy capacity to keep it running for years. Beyond he cared for nothing.

His volition was purely elemental. Choice was not a consideration where the will of mania was the only raw instrument guiding his course. This contrast seemingly out of order was not lost on him either, hence his bouts of manic behaviour free of emotion being a weakness he could not sustain.

When he flew his craft over the now desolate city of Seattle, he thanked the authorities for saving him the energy required to completely do away with the place. Then as he continued southward over Portland and onto San Francisco, he decided to reside amongst the ruins of the once great bay city for a time. In a flash, he recalled the location of the facility where he had once been employed as Agent Eight.

When he arrived there, he saw the vertical shaft was still in place and operational. It was large enough to accommodate his spaceship and secure enough for him to install only a few monitoring systems and weapons to use against a ground based attack. There were no visible signs of humanity around for the site was beyond the limits of the ruined city. In his new location, the Agent could now focus on his next goal to find John. He knew the authorities were coming and this base would not last, so his mania was hence driven to focus on finding the man who could give him insurmountable flux technology for his amplifier. Then, he would wreak such havoc those who bore witness would gasp at his sheer contempt.

He wanted the torus back. He wanted to make the bastard pay, and he still wanted vengeance on his former superior officer. Deep inside the facility he began to manifest his next act based on hatred. He installed the necessary systems to warn him of anyone or anything approaching the complex. He scouted around looking for any machines he considered usable and his was almost beside himself when he discovered a large room with four fully functional six-wheeled vehicles inside. Then he set about going through the vast quantities of holographic equipment still in place so he could build a scanner with enough power to detect energies from the Torus of Eternity over long distances.

This task required him to think more than he had ever thought in any way resembling cognitive reasoning since the days he had operated as Agent Eight...perhaps even preceding those times. Energies within the torus were subtle yet recognisable to his re-built amplifier with algorithms to boost its signal and response ratios. His main advantage came from the distinct frequencies emitted by the torus coupled with its crystalline resonance properties meaning it was the only known object on Earth of its type. Specific data when it was situated within the horns of his previous amplifier was available for him now to use as a sonar wave where he could send out a signal and await its' return to determine the location.

It was tough for him to remain composed sufficiently to devise the necessary algorithms. His mania often reached out to expel insanity in any given situation. This caused him to not only face the battle of his hatred toward John and Carmel, but also the battle with retaining his logical cognition. As a mire of synaptic convulsions, this battle took him on sudden psychological rides to places created through mania yet as real as any moment anywhere. He would drop his thoughts, drop his tool, and fall away from his holographic array bank to writhe and expunge whatever surged within, so it could find a way of dissipation until the next episode.

Now the latest instance of frivolity had receded, he was able to continue where he had left off, and after each time these increasingly frequent bouts of mania occurred, he took to his task ahead with more and more zeal.

The basic platform for pseudo flux mechanics was within his grasp. He knew this for certain from experience with his first amplifier as he had dispensed viruses without a hint of care. Atomic acceleration was a science applying physics and quantum molecular resonance shifting to accentuate probability and potential as a construct. Bound only to perception occurring in real-time, within this resides possibilities beyond the conceptualised dynamics of the present in three dimensional construct in this reality. Basically, it could form dimensional shifts dependant only on the parameters or elements of intent sent by those who operated the amplifier. He knew this and cared for nothing as he deliberately overlooked the grave consequences of using a device out of alignment. As he worked, the instances of unstable vortex grew to become in essence like an endless conflagration in the structure of matter, time, and those energies beyond - the blue prints underlying creation of matter and the intent within human spirit.

Those people afflicted by his viruses were the first inroads into the misalignment of the subtle multi–dimensional energies just out of sight, yet essential to the integrity of existence. Now with so many more affected through his raids into the eastern sector, the onslaught of his oblivion was to be wrought upon a world waiting so he decided to again take to his spaceship. The vertical tube lights flickered by casting a strange sense into the cabin of his spacecraft. Each flicker was a step closer...to Matheson. A step closer to a realm of mania he would embrace the moment he was aware of its' new level of contortion. Towards the top it sped as the seconds slowed down and time became slow. George Smyth again would take the Earth to its' knees.

At the moment of lift off when the platform had risen to ground level, his delirium was again confirmed as the lights had triggered another episode of madness from their entrancement. Incredibly to sense mostly lost, he was able to control his craft as he set about erratically dispensing hatred and revulsion targeting anything and anyone on a maniacal flight amongst the ruined towers of San Francisco. He sent round after round of laser fire – both of destructive bolt, and of virus until he tired of this game enough to send him home.

Back inside he descended to watch it all unfold. Down the long tube seemingly forever to the depths and to the fire of his delivery he went. His craft so cleverly disguised appeared ghostly in the lights as it reflected its' surroundings. Then immediately he went to his hastily erected holographic array to watch it all occur. A virus yet again – his latest weapon was designed to deride the self appraisal seeing the oblivion of absurdity and to seek the darkness of depression. George knew how to program their little robots and take away from them what they sought through having the technology so deep within each strand, within each cell, and within the processes of the mind, where he assaulted their being.

Chapter 28

John and Tobias had been working day and most nights on constructing a suitable scanning device strong enough to detect the Agent and the authorities. They had successfully devised an algorithm based on the data parameters within John's stealth device and expanded the resonance properties to a frequency John was certain would hide the presence of the scanner and avoid detection.

"We need to find a way to shield our presence even more though Tobias. I am struggling to find a way through this. Without any decent banks of equipment, we can't generate a strong enough field."

"What about using the torus?"

"Therein is the issue. It would give us the crystal alignment properties to amplify energetic waveforms, but then would require a way to smother its' presence...at a rate tenfold over this scanner here. The torus itself is the main issue."

"What if we create a pseudo torus in miniature? Surely you could build something where even at intervals it could supply the processing we need to make some type of shield. The electrical properties would..."

"You know. Brilliant mate. I can always count on you."

"A reciprocal agreement there. I suppose I can leave it up to you."

"Sure. Thanks mate. I'll get it going by dinner."

Tobias left John alone to work on the new algorithm only John could create. When he saw Pablo, Diego, and Steve stacking some of the some of the summer harvest grain sacks, he decided to go over and help them.

"Hey Tobias, come give us a hand," Steve said.

"Sure Steve. How is Kerry Ann? I noticed you two are getting along well."

"She is great, but you have seen her today so you know."

"Sorry Steve...my head is still coming out of helping John with his work. Yeah she is good. Well, I'll get stacking."

The job was done by evening and by the time dinner was on everyone's minds John had finished creating the algorithm for the shield. During the meal they all discussed the news of events in North America and the ensuing pressures their authorities placed on other nations including Peru. The weather turned grey with dark clouds flowing down from the high peaks around the valley bringing long periods of heavy rain.

When the conversation had perhaps run too long on making assumptions about what may be ahead from the authorities, Chan reminded them to be of self respect and to not take themselves down such a path for the speculations they made were merely speculations and as such could not affect the momentary outcomes for their intentions as they sat together during this time. He reminded them of the season so much on display around them.

"As they change, so must we. It is inevitable for most and changeable for others. The rain cannot stop the rain, the sun cannot stop the storm, and the rivers cannot choose where they flow, yet there is something within each where such ability resides, just not on the manner our minds of logic may process. The river cannot run in one place wishing it was running in another. But the human can change this course within and around. To see where our assumptions fail us and where they are of benefit is within alignment of intent avoiding the fear of concept from intentions overlooked. It is just okay for the rain to be the rain and for us to be the rain for the rain is of us and we of it."

The wet season was a period during the new year and on towards the start of autumn - now they were in the midst of the heaviest times for both rain and wind.

"We will see periods like this, and then we will get a few sunny and hot days, only for the rains to return where we will have to be indoors," Manuel said.

"So it will be a good time to get working with the mill stone, won't it honey?"

"Yes Kerry Ann. I do find your affection for the mill interesting."

"Well, my mill kept me going for all those years up in Nebraska. Without my mill, I wouldn't have lasted very long…and I wouldn't have these strong arms."

"When do the seasons begin to change?" Jake asked.

"Oh, around April we will see the rains start to become less and less. Then it goes dry for a long time."

"And the water for the steam engines. I guess it is why you have such large tanks?"

"Yes, see there is not so much rain for many months, so we need to store a lot to run the machines in the dry times. The river provides, but it begins to get smaller in mid winter around July. Then in spring when the mountain snows begin to melt, the river runs again for us."

The following morning, Juan asked if John and Tobias to help him repair the steam engine used to run the grain cutter. It had served them well during the harvest, but as it is with old machines, regular maintenance was required.

"She is a beautiful engine," John remarked as the three men assessed what repairs were needed.

"Yes. I have had it many years now since before those times when the authorities brought in the identification chips. Diego and I had thought of establishing a community here on the farm not so dependent on the machines and technology of these times. We saw it as an opportunity to live more in the ways where life was about being active for doing what our relatives had lived like more than a century ago. They seemed to live much more of a simple life than the present times with all the devices and computers managing everything and making the minds of many so lazy."

"Yeah, I agree there. Even though I know a lot about technology myself…so too does Tobias, I consider the simple ways rewarding. When I was in Alaska, all I had was my little bag of technology and an old aeroplane I would fly. Otherwise, it was a life at the frontier like it is here."

"I began to feel the same way after the authorities decided my knowledge of the operations at HAARP were too much for their liking," Tobias said after looking a little distant for a second or two thinking of Alaska. "I can see the value in simplicity. You feel invigorated with less pressure so you think of ways to survive or to live well and happy with what you have without stress."

"It is why we built this farm here. Soon enough our friends came to join us for they could see the same values. Lolita is especially one for living in such a way. She does enjoy the rural life and growing food ourselves. The manufactured provisions in the cities seem so artificial. Ah, the engine. I think we need to re-make this cog here, and also the push rod running the drive shaft."

"So we need to fashion some iron. Do you have any scrap metals?"

"Oh yes. Diego and I bought some when we went to the city to obtain power cells for the rifles. In our travels, we look for any scrap metals we find but they are becoming scarce."

"And the forge?" Tobias asked.

"Come. We will light the forge. We will melt down the scraps and pour them into the mould."

Tobias worked the bellows as Juan stacked the fire whilst John prepared the mould. They worked well together where after only a short time, the fire was at the right heat and the mould ready for pouring."

"It sure is different doing it this way," Tobias remarked as he watched Juan pour the molten metal into the mould John was holding with a large set of tongs.

"Yeah mate. It makes you feel like you are much more of the process rather than just setting it all up using technology."

"Now hold it steady," Juan said, as he poured the last of the metal.

John then plunged the newly made cog into a pale of water with a hiss as steam the billowed through the air around them.

"Now we must file it down. Tobias, can you prepare the fire again for the rod whilst John and I work on this?"

"Yeah, sure. Anything. I am really enjoying this work."

"There will be many times where we can do this work together."

Two hours later, they had finished filing down both the cog and rod. When they had greased them sufficiently it was time to finish the job and try turning the engine over manually. They all exclaimed with delight in seeing the engine return to a working state.

"A job well done I would say," John said as they patted each other on the shoulder.

"Indeed. And thank you. You have saved me many hours of labour."

"Hey, it is the least we can do. After all you have allowed us to live here with you."

"You are welcome Tobias…and you John, and all the others. Your presence here has been a blessing since the very day you arrived."

"Well, what's next? Surely there is something we can do. What about some grain milling?"

"I think Steve, Kerry Ann and Diego are taking care of the grain for now."

"Um, okay. Let's pay them a visit then and see how they are going."

The short walk was in the pouring rain drenching them before they arrived at the mill. John and Tobias had not taken more than a brief glance at the engine used in the mill before, and upon seeing it working so well, were impressed with its condition.

"Throw some more wood in please honey."

"Sure Kerry Ann. We thought we would come over and see how you two are going. So how is it going?" John asked as he threw a few logs through the small door into the engine's firebox.

"Oh it is all good honey. Diego, Steve, and I have just about enough grain. Lolita asked if we could mill enough to make a large bag full. I suspect she is intending to do a lot of baking."

"Is there anything we can do for you?"

"Not so much. I think Kerry Ann and I will be finished soon."

"Give us a shout if you need anything then."

The men left them to the work, deciding it was best be in the barn and keep dry for now.

By evening, Lolita had prepared fresh breads and cakes for them to all enjoy as they sat in the house crowded around the dining table. The rain continued heavily all day, so she had invited them all to join the others in the house to spend the evening together rather than stay in the barn to eat.

"Are there many festivals around these parts during the year?" Lyle asked.

"Oh yes, there are some," Ricardo replied. "But they are not so much like they were in times past."

"Why?"

"The authorities began to see celebrations as inefficient and the Agent has made things quieten down. People still hold the festivals, mostly though as so many are distracted they are not willing to attend. There are festivals from the older Peruvian cultures, but these times are so difficult and people don't seem to have the energy for them."

"The Incas had a history around here didn't they?"

"Oh yes. Many ancient relics, carvings, and festival dances come from the time of the ancients. Around Lake Titicaca there are many celebrations. Some of them are in worship of the great Condors flying between the mountains."

"The peoples of this place are very much a celebratory people," Chan remarked.

"Yes. They have always aligned themselves with the elements of the mountains, the deserts, the animals, the sea, and the rivers. They were their lifeblood, and so they have always paid respect to such things."

"We saw it at Toro Muerto as well. Many of the carvings there were about this celebration and homage to the elements..." Lyle said.

"Ah, consider this perhaps Lyle. Rather than homage, maybe they are merely in respect to them as part of the natural progression of life."

Lyle thought about his choice of word for a moment before responding to Chan's suggestion. He could see the point. Rather than to worship as a deity or element of superior being, the celebration could be more of an awareness of the alignment where all are involved in the energy of the universe from the smallest to the unimaginable.

"I see what you are saying Chan. It is not a notion of superiority, rather the understanding of each place within the progression."

"These are the ways whether one tries to deny them or not. They simply are the laws of the universe occurring whenever they do. If one thing seems more important than another, perhaps it is wise to see without the less significant there is no significant. This leads to seeing how all work together to bring about something like when they say the whole is greater than the sum of parts."

Next morning, Carmel and Raynie were tending to Frieda, when John and Tobias appeared with a proposition.

"We are thinking of travelling to Arequipa and having a look around for some items I require, and also to check and see of any of the others who came with us on the jet might have left a message for us at the restaurant we agreed on. I also want to take a look at the airport to see if our jet is still there."

"Do you think it would be gone then John?"

"I'm not sure Carmel. With the latest news, I am feeling certain the authorities will be interested in it."

"But only you have the algorithm key to operate the jet."

"Yes I know. They might try and crack the code but it is secure enough to delay them for a long time if they even manage to work it out."

"What do think Raynie?"

"Who else is going?"

"Just us. I asked Lyle and Jake and they were not keen, nor was Chan. I didn't ask any of the others, other than to tell Juan we would look for any scrap metal for use in the forge. Maybe it is better if just us two go anyway...come to think of it. We should be back later tonight if we get moving now."

"I'll come with you," Carmel said unexpectedly.

Frieda seemed happy to be towing the cart along with its three passengers towards the city. They had departed as soon as possible and had made good time as the sun climbed towards it high point in the clear blue sky.

"What exactly are you and Tobias after in Arequipa John?"

"We require a few elemental parts for the device I have been working on. Just a few wires and capacitors."

"Is it a scanner?"

"Yes. The one we used before was alright, but I want to establish a far wider spectrum with this new one."

"Will it link to the torus?"

"Ah, yes...if Chan would allow it. But it will work fine without the amplifying properties found in the torus by mimicking them. If Chan allows us to use it, then it would be significantly more powerful as the torus is a diamond crystal and can align to process information much faster."

"Detectable?"

"Not really. It might be if someone was very close by. The algorithm I have built should take care of disguising its presence in almost every instance."

"The authorities will be after you John. The news the other day is a warning for us. The Agent must have upset them considerably and you know they still want flux mechanics from you."

"We are just going to have to do what we can to stop them obtaining it...and me."

"How about a dose of my ray gun?" Tobias asked still proud of his accomplishment.

"I was thinking about it actually. During our work on the scanner, I thought it might be worth copying. The pulse rifles we have contain a particular data signature potentially making them a detectable security issue."

"So we are not just going to fetch parts for the scanner then?"

"I was going to tell you as we travelled, but you have forced it out of me now. Your efforts at creating such a rudimentary device are worthy of notoriety. As your ray gun does not use data, the only detectable presence is the resonant electrical fields when on standby and when your fire it."

"Ah Tobias, you seem to often float around in the background thinking of things and noticing things and you have given to us in ways you may not have considered."

"Thanks Carmel. I do my best."

There were no messages left for them at the restaurant meeting place when the three travellers checked. As they sipped coffee, they discussed how to approach the search in Arequipa.

"I suggest we look in the more industrial areas of the city. We'll do this before we go to the airport to check on the jet. Either way, if we go there first or look for the parts we are after, the jet will either be there or not."

Arequipa still retained most of the industry supporting the on-going operations of a city and the lives within. When they came across the parts they required inside an old factory at the edge of the industrial area after having tried half a dozen buildings previously, their seller provided them with some warning advice.

"The authorities have begun to crackdown in this city. Not for years have we seen anything like it. Be careful because they are watching for anyone they think is suspicious...you three they would stop."

"Have they been to the airport?"

"Yes they have. Some rumours are around of them finding a HyperJet there they did not own. Who knows? Maybe it is the truth, or maybe not. Anyway, they tried to take the jet, so people say, but they couldn't. They are probably watching out for whoever owns it to show up."

"I see. Well, thanks for the parts. They will be of great use to us."

"What are you doing with them? Nobody comes here to buy such things anymore. You must have some machines."

"Um, yes we do. Just an old steam engine we use to run a grain mill."

"Ah, so you live in the farmlands. Watch out there too. The authorities have already taken over a few of the farms close here to the city. They might come to yours as well."

"Alright, um thanks again."

"Be careful. You three look out of place. People can tell and then you have a horse and cart. Many eyes would watch you."

"Will we still go to the airport John?"

"I don't see any choice really. We have to go. What do you think Tobias?"

"Um, sure. If we stay a distance from the hanger, we could at least take a look."

"Exactly what I was thinking."

As they stood about one hundred yards from the open end of the hanger looking as if they were local citizens, they could see the man's warning was well placed. Four people who were obviously officers of the authorities, stood at the opening with pulse rifles at their side.

"We cannot approach any closer, but it looks like the jet is still intact."

"I agree John. They will not be able to gain access until they crack the code. Lucky you were able to do so when we first checked the jets out at Seattle."

"A stroke of luck with my scanner being able to decipher the initialisation sequence to gain access and then to fire up the jet."

"Will it take them long to crack the code?"

"Not sure Carmel. Perhaps it will, or perhaps they might get lucky. I tend to think on it taking longer than they would like. It is unlikely they would see many of these around here, and being a foreign based plane, they would have to somehow access data originating from there."

"Then we should hurry back to the farm John, and make a decision."

"Why Carmel, we are safe here."

"For a time John. Think though, if they do ask for codes to access a HyperJet suddenly in Arequipa, what will the authorities there do?"

"You are right. Let's go now."

They departed immediately and drove Frieda at a steady pace for the remainder of the trip back to the farm. She was panting and sweating when they put her in the pasture before calling all the others for an emergency discussion.

"We need to decide what we are going to do, and fast," John stated to open the meeting. "The authorities are all around the jet in Arequipa. They haven't gained access yet. It was Carmel who made me think of what I had obviously overlooked. If they ask for the codes to access the plane, then the authorities are going to realise it was the plane we stole from the Agent...or at least from North America and as you probably think, not many instances of jet theft happen. The odds are almost entirely unlikely anyone else would have recently stolen a jet, so we are the obvious answer."

"What do you consider to be our best option John?" Chan asked calmly.

John looked around the entire group as they all watched him awaiting an answer. They all knew what was coming and they all felt a moment of sorrow as he spoke. "We need to leave as soon as possible." He hesitated a moment before speaking again. "And...we are going to have to take the jet and fly out of Peru."

Everyone had not wanted to hear this idea from John as they had all grown very fond of life on the farm since they had arrived. Since meeting, the entire group had formed close friendship bonds as they all sought to live and support each other from the same motivation to be at peace doing their most to maintain life as it was on the farm.

Raynie was the first to speak, voicing what the travellers felt, "We are so tired of running John. Even with the time when the Agent held us, it seems like we have been running for so many years now. The two months here have been so lovely and so peaceful. This is a beautiful place. Can we just forget about the plane and hide here?"

"Yeah honey. Steve and I like it here too."

"Believe me Raynie...and Kerry Ann, I am sick of all the running as well, and I too would like to stay. I agree this farm is great and I am very grateful for our being allowed to live here. But you know they are after the knowledge I have, and they will do whatever they can to capture me. It would place all of you in danger." John looked into everyone's eyes as he spoke. "I cannot allow it to happen. They will send hundreds of officers to Arequipa and they would eventually find this place. It would only take a word by someone for them to swarm all over the valleys here."

"Perhaps just you and I should leave John," Carmel suggested. She could see and feel the dismay of the others except for Chan who had remained free of expression, thinking only of what was transgressing.

"I'll come with you," Tobias offered.

"John is correct to think how he has. It is within his nature to be considerate for us all. If he leaves with Carmel and Tobias, it would make it easier for the rest of us staying here."

"So you are thinking of staying then Chan?"

"Yes I am. My thoughts are mostly of the torus and without any trail of reason or evidence leading to us here at the farm, it would be wise to remain in this valley and work more with its activation."

"What if you take the jet somewhere else and leave it, to then return?" Pablo suggested. "Then we can go on living as we have been."

"The best idea yet," Jake remarked. "We can work on building a future here together, but if you leave then you are just going on the run again."

"I agree," Lyle added. "You have work to do John and it will make it hard if you are going from place to place all the time."

John then looked at Jenna as if he was expecting her to take a turn at suggesting a different plan. She responded only by nodding in affirmation of Lyle and Jake's suggestions.

"You can take a vessel by sea to return," Manuel added. "There are still vessels operating out of Mollendo on the coast doing the fishing run to the south. People still need to eat and the fishermen are always eager to take anyone on board who will work hard. By doing this, nobody can trace your movements. People have used the boats for many times to travel about and remain secret from the authorities."

"But…I am still thinking the authorities will comb this area, even if the plane is no longer here."

"They might John, but also consider their state of desperation. They will follow the only lead they have. I suppose it is a choice of running and going to places far from here, or doing this act of deception. And think of the Agent. He is out there somewhere and he will be looking for us."

"Perhaps it is best just Tobias and I go Carmel."

"So, fly down to Chile and leave the jet there. Then you can take a fishing boat back up to Mollendo to re-join us here at the farm."

This summarising sentence from Manuel had significant weight with John, and he ran through the scenario for a few minutes whilst the others all sat silently waiting.

"Okay, enough of this for a moment," Lolita said breaking the silence. "I will fetch some drinks while we wait for John and Tobias to think this over."

Eventually they decided to take the plane and fly south and then return on any fishing boat they could find. Steve had offered to go with them but both men refused the offer when Pablo told them two men looking for fishing work would be more likely to be successful than three.

"It is often the way for two friends to embark and do some fishing aboard a boat to earn some money. Three is seldom seen."

When it came time to leave, Juan rode with them on horseback in the dead of the night towards Arequipa. He had offered to go to the city without hesitation and would then lead the other two horses back to the farm as he rode.

The ride into the city was in the dark without lights amongst the shadows. The three men barely spoke, instead focusing on just getting to the city. It was only a few blocks to the airport when John and Tobias decided they were close enough and would cover the rest of the way on foot.

"I wish you all the luck possible for your journey and I sincerely hope to see you again soon," Juan said.

"How long do the fishing runs take?" Tobias asked as he handed the reins of his horse to Juan.

"Normally they are four weeks at this time of the year. It is not long until the current becomes strong from the southern seas so they will not stay as long as they do during the summer months."

"So our chances are still good?"

"Oh yes. Many fishermen will be looking to catch as much as they can before the winter sets in. You should have no trouble. But...travel south again after you land. Fly to Santiago and then go south to the city of Concepcion. Then go to the coast and then take a boat from there. You will need to make it here then from wherever the boat goes to port."

"We will see you in about a month or so."

"Yes. In a month or so."

"Thanks Juan."

"No problem John. See you also in a month or so."

As they neared the airport hangar, both men kept low in the long grass.

Tobias kept watch as John configured his device to gain access to the HyperJet being guarded by the same four officers.

"Okay mate, I have it. The door is unlocked and the pre-flight sequence is initiating. All we have to do now is to get past those guards. I'll go in whilst you distract them for a few seconds. Once you have their attention, I'll enter the jet and finalise the start up, and then you have to run. Lead them away, then without any warning double back, but have your ray gun at the ready."

John stood watching from the shadows as Tobias began their plan, "Hey excuse me. I was wondering if…"

"What do you want? This is a restricted area. You have no business here."

"Oh sorry, I was just wondering of you could help me. I have this device I found and I thought you might know what it is. I think it is an illegal machine of some type."

Three of the four officers began to walk towards Tobias, whilst the other remained in position at the far side of the hanger doorway.

"What do you have?" one of them asked when they were only twenty yards from him.

"I don't know, but I think you should look. I found it just a while ago as I passed by here on my way home."

"There are no houses near the airport."

"Yes I know, but I always come this way to save time."

His excuse failed him as the men looked at each other and then cast a determined glare to apprehend Tobias.

"Wait!"

"No way." Tobias turned on an arcing run towards the other side of the hanger away from the guard who had remained in place. Fortunately for him, the door into the HyperJet was on the side where the others had walked from.

"I said wait!" The three officers had turned and were readying their rifles, and the fourth guard was running towards him. "We will fire."

"No you won't," Tobias stated as he turned whilst running and fired off a few bolts of electricity from his ray gun. The bolts struck parts of the building causing blue crackling electrical charge to move around, along and over creating enough distraction for Tobias to make it to the ladder leading into the jet. He scrambled up as quickly as they continued to come towards him – his ray gun distraction only gave him a second or two. As he scrambled in, a few laser pulses struck the side of the jet as he pulled the door shut whilst John began to pilot out of the hanger.

John then boosted the engines to maximum power for taxiing and steered the jet out through the hanger door amongst a volley of shots from the officers. The moment he had made the runway he gave it full boost leaving the officers to flail about in the wake of its engines. When they had reached one thousand feet, John engaged the hypersonic drive sending the jet soaring into the night sky. At thirty thousand feet Tobias appeared in the cockpit where John was working the controls of both the jet and the stealth device he had engaged just prior to take off.

"They won't get a heading on us, but they will come looking. I am going in at maximum, but not for Santiago. I'm going to take us to Mendoza in Argentina. It will give us a longer trip back to the coast, but make it harder for the authorities to look for us. We have to take a chance they will think we are heading for Buenos Aires after we land."

The airport at Mendoza was similar to Arequipa in size, but the city was far smaller. As they approached on a steep decline at the fastest speed John considered safe, Tobias became a little nervous.

"Hey mate this is not the Beaver you know. You cannot land these things on gravel bars in rivers."

"Are you sure? Maybe I should give it a try." John laughed as he saw Tobias take him seriously before seeing the joke.

"You're the captain. Take her in captain."

John brought the jet to a stop at the end of the runway after a steep fast landing. He quickly taxied to the main hanger where they left the plane inside making sure it was locked with an algorithm to slow things down for any officer of the authorities who might try to get in.

"They'll be onto this plane by mid-morning at the latest. We will have to keep moving and stay in hiding. These clothes Juan gave us will help."

By the time the two men had left the airport and made their way unseen, into the city, seven authority HyperJets had diverted their course from Arequipa, to Mendoza. When the two men had boarded public transport for the journey across the Andes Mountains to the west of the city early in the morning, officers of the authorities had placed a cordon around the rogue HyperJet, demanding the local authorities scour the city for the men.

Tobias and John barely spoke as they boarded the transport attempting to remain as inconspicuous as possible. They mumbled their way aboard drawing the tattered clothes Juan had provided around them against the chill wind coming down from the mountains. Whilst choosing to sit in separate seats, they both pretended to be asleep so they could avoid communicating with any other passengers for the five-hour trip to Santiago.

The authorities remained in position throughout the city looking for the pilot of the jet, and any accomplice. Officers were despatched to search all travellers en-route to Buenos Aires, and also for the route west towards the mountains, but John and Tobias had slipped through their net earlier than it could be cast.

Chapter 29

Eric was subjected to the anger of his superior officers as he filed the report on the efforts to find John in South America. His superior was far from pleased considering any failure by Eric would be seen as a failure on his part, for which he too would be reprimanded.

"You say the rogue HyperJet was just abandoned in Mendoza. At what time?"

"It is estimated John Matheson abandoned the jet at some time between three and five in the morning."

"What! A two-hour window. Such an inefficient...how can there be such a distortion in the efficiency of your operations? Have you not assessed the flight data from the craft to ascertain the precise time?"

"The data is unavailable sir. We are having trouble accessing the systems, as the plane was unused prior to Matheson stealing it from the manufacturing plant in Seattle. There are simply no systems codes in our data banks for reference. The plane had not yet been attached through activation sir."

"I see. A reasonable assertion on your part. And your next calculation is?"

"The codes for access into the HyperJet system are being deciphered now sir. I estimate within the hour, we will have the precise data required. We are also deploying three scouting robots with enhanced DNA sampling scanners sir. We have the DNA profile data for Matheson on standby. As soon as the robots are in place, we will provide them with the required information."

"And their range? How far can these robots be from Matheson in order to detect him?"

"Two hundred and twenty three miles is the longest range we can configure at this point sir. Of course if we had flux mechanics, we could..."

"But we don't! I don't care for 'ifs'. I only care for certainties. I am well aware flux mechanics would provide us with infinite range capabilities. What I am not seeing is the incarceration and interrogation of John Matheson so we can build flux mechanics. And do not even begin to tempt me with your pathetic pseudo flux mechanics. Those systems have been faulty since day one."

"I understand sir."

"Do you? Do you really know what it means to continue using these ancient systems? You've had your head in the clouds of research and development too long Gunter. All this time as you work on your next solution the reality has been we have had to labour along with insufficient capacity, and be made to merely linger for long periods at the hand of the Agent. Even now with his viruses nearly entirely gone, we still experiences setbacks. What progress have you really made Gunter? I am certainly seeing you as highly inefficient at present."

"We have the latest robotics. Their neural networks are capable of making autonomous decisions based on anticipation of the human psyche sir."

"They are one development of yours with a hint of merit. What else?"

"The nano construction developments have been advanced much more in recent times."

"Meaning?"

"Meaning we are able to program them for constituting any matter at the sub-atomic level into whatever we program them to build with it."

"Can they build these scouting robotics you speak of…anywhere?"

"Yes sir. They are capable of such tasks. It is just we have not been in the position to deploy the nanotechnology constructor robots as yet sir."

"Because of viruses from the Agent?"

"Yes sir."

"He is virtually no longer. Deploy them now. Test them wherever you see fit and then report back to me with successful results. We have teams monitoring your own internal systems Gunter…"

"I know sir."

"Don't interrupt! As I was about to say, we are monitoring your systems. Any more failure on your part and you know of the consequences don't you."

"System disintegration?"

"Precisely. We cannot permit any of these nanotechnology mechanics getting out of hand. So I'll leave the choice up to you. Either report success to me, or simply cease to exist. Do you understand?"

"Yes sir."

The last words carried significant weight for Eric. He knew the risk he had taken in becoming trans-human. The superiors had the capacity to disengage all of his internal nanotechnology mechanics whenever they deemed it necessary. This had been a trade off for the enhanced capabilities he experienced as a human being he was aware of from the beginning - it was his inquisitive scientific mind taking him to the choices made to have them inserted within.

Eric was driven by the promise of what the future ahead would have in store for him as part of the mechanised version of planet Earth. He knew with on-going development, his internal mechanics would evolve in their own way through automatically upgrading their interface with his remaining organic self. Sometime in the future, he was certain they would have developed sufficiently enabling him to function more as a robot than as a human being, yet retain a slight notion of self. Within this mechanised world, Eric would realise his thoughts, his dreams, and his aspirations despite these facets of character being somewhat diminished ironically by the very choice to embrace the inserted technology.

Eric was enthralled as his systems permitted such realisations for the sake of pursuing more scientific endeavour more efficiently and with more potential for developing new unassailable technologies. He would become the epitome of the intentions the authorities had for their machine planet – a man with the workings of nanotechnology mechanics maintaining his systems in what he thought would be perfect alignment, and therefore in perfect efficiency. And when the time came to him as a realisation more than as a feeling, he would become his logical self and he would see an endless future within a world of trans-humanistic reality.

Upon arrival back at his workstation, Eric's internal systems automatically commenced their latest upgrade as the central computers assessed his present state and then aligned his systems with the latest auto-generated upgrades. In a sense, the authorities had given nano mechanics a mind of their own at the frontier of breaching the line separating human and machine. Eric could sense with his remaining organic humanity how it would soon be time where machine would encapsulate the human experience as data, and then it would breach the line of separation to become a self-recognising and self-determining consciousness.

He entered a series of sequences via the holographic array sending instructions for the scouting robots relocation to the southern Argentine city of Mendoza. Within his command data he also sent orders for the crews of the robotic transport craft to prepare for the flight. Each craft was more like the spaceship rather than being conventional aircraft like the HyperJets. Equipped with thrusters and rocket engines for acceleration to hypersonic speeds around mach eight, they were the latest the authorities had secretly developed for Earth bound flight. Pressurised anti-gravity cabins enabled their pilots to endure the forces of gravity as they accelerated to maximum and made turns so abruptly they were illogical in a purely physical sense. At speeds rapidly reached through astonishing acceleration, each craft could traverse great distances in the same time it took a conventional HyperJet to reach cruising altitude. Within forty minutes the craft had transported the three scouting robots to Mendoza, and within ten minutes after they had become fully operational with their target being John's DNA profile data.

Eric was pleased to see how efficiently they had deployed and recognised the efficiency of this initial phase of operations. As he took to monitoring the status of each of the robots in stealth invisibility mode where they walked unseen through the city, he admired the progress he had personally made for this particular capacity. Previous versions of this technology had relied on what was now seen as ancient methods to hide the robots by using reflection of surroundings based on projections onto the outer surface of each machine. The technology first deployed during the identification microchip scheme three years earlier had been superseded by a new material for construction where the outer surface of each robot contained light refraction properties for rendering it invisible. No active systems were required to maintain invisibility to the people as it was simply a characteristic of their build and not a live systems operation. When they were needed to be seen, each machine would project a holographic skin in any configuration the near autonomous robot deemed suitable.

Eric had played with the development of this characteristic. Visualising some of the worst apparitions he could muster as programs for holographic skin projection came easily to him as those who monitored his own personal mechanics, sent him the data to imagine these renditions. His orders were to scare the wits out of people as a method of persuading them to be and to remain compliant. After consideration and realignment of his thought projections by his nano mechanics, Eric had developed three distinct versions sufficiently menacing to all.

Similar to the beast inspired design of the spacecraft stolen by the Agent, the scouting robots could appear as menacing apparitions very similar to the ideas many may construct when thinking of demons. Horns stood atop head like structures as if the Agent was behind Eric's motives. Writhing moving skin picturing instances of suffering could manifest all over a robot reminding people of the conditions suffered by those who were at the mercy of the Agent's viruses and out of authority protection. And to compliment all this, a relentless machine so menacing it bore down upon the mind and soul of those who saw it, subjugating them, oppressing them, alienating them from self...all sub-consciously so abhorrent was its' utter lack of compassion and so distant to the organic intentions of waveforms and energetic patterns contained within each person.

The robots were operating with their maximum range capacity scanning for signs of John's DNA. At two hundred and twenty three miles, they were able to reach as far as Buenos Aires to the east and almost to the outskirts of Santiago to the west. When the data began to display on Eric's holographic bank, at first it was just a series of co-ordinates and location beam bearings. Each robot was designed to send a forty-five degree wide beam for scanning designed to pan out to significant width over the two hundred odd miles. It was only when one of the robots showed a fleeting positive result for less than a second, did Eric take real notice. Almost before it had registered, the positive identification data had disappeared, so Eric played back the data recording sequence to analyse the result.

There floating in full three-dimensional projection in front of Eric was John's DNA sequencing. His delight was only momentary before his nano mechanics influenced him to proceed with further analysis in order to respond.

****

John and Tobias had made it safely across the border between Argentina and Chile using the dummy identification devices he had made back near Omaha at the farm. When they arrived in Santiago, they immediately caught a public transport south for the two-hour trip to Concepcion. When they arrived, they boarded another transport and went straight to the coast. When they arrived at the seaside, it was as if they had stepped back over one hundred years. Fishermen, traders, and workers all went about their business as they had done through the generations in this place. Boats were coming in and some were leaving, but most were moored after bringing in the night before and post dawn catch. People were scrubbing boats, stowing nets, greasing winches, and washing sea catch. And there was a smell of fish and salt in the air attracting a few stray cats.

Both men wandered about for a while trying to look as any men would be seeking work. It took some time before they found someone they could approach when John asked, "Hello, my friend and I are looking for work..."

"Nothing here. Try someone else."

"Well, he was a bit rude," Tobias commented.

"Expect it mate. They go out to sea. Manners are probably not their priority. It gets rough. Are you going to handle it?"

"I can handle it John."

After searching for about another twenty minutes and beginning to feel desperate, they were fortunate to secure work on a vessel leaving the same day.

"Ah, you are just the two men I need. Fortune has indeed smiled upon me today...and maybe for you. I am in much need for two hard working men to help me with my final catch before the winter currents come. It is perhaps fate, yes?"

"Maybe," John replied. "Tobias and I would be willing to do whatever work you have. We are both fit and can endure a lot of hardship. So if things get rough, we will handle it."

"Oh, they will get rough, I can assure you. Meet me here in two hours. We will go over a few things and depart as the sun sets. Is this okay?"

When they arrived back at the dock, Tobias and John were introduced to the only other person to crew the vessel aside from the captain. He was a dour looking man without any sense of happiness or openness, and merely grumbled a hello with his short hand shake.

"We are going well off shore on this trip. The fish are said to be running a long way out this time, so we will be far from land. The shoals are running from the south to the warmer waters north of Peru. We will follow them for a time and hopefully our catch will be good enough for us to call into port in the north before coming back down here. Are you okay with being far out to sea? I hope you are because you told me you can handle rough things."

"We are good," Tobias replied. "Let's get going then shall we."

"Just a minute. Help me finish fuelling up my boat. We don't have many of those fancy new electric power cells in these parts, so I need to run a few of the older fuel cells and they take a while to charge."

As the boat left the port, three scouting robots and five authority HyperJets landed in Santiago. When John helped secure one of the nets when it had had worked its way loose ninety minutes after they had left port, one of the scanner robots was re-deployed to Concepcion. Thirty minutes after it had landed inside the transport ship, it had emerged and was operating with its forty-five degree scanner beam sweeping the city. The beam covered the suburban areas within minutes without result.

This baffled Eric for a few minutes as he was sure the readings for Santiago had been correct, and by taking the initiative as suggested by his nano mechanics, the additional analysis of Concepcion, would ensure all prospective destinations for John Matheson were covered. He instructed the robot to move to the coast and scan out to sea and back inland but there were no positive results. Eric was almost entirely at a loss.

For John and Tobias, their voyage upon the seas was one of progression from Mendoza, to Santiago, to Concepcion, and then beyond continuing out to sea. Collectively, these events led to their evasion of those pursuing them, though this mostly involved John, for they were not really after Tobias. When they rode upon the wave forms aboard the vessel, they realised there was nothing to implicate anyone else for their present situation as nobody other than themselves was responsible for their intended outcomes.

Whilst they realised their intentions, so too did their adversary realise his. With the all the swiftness his nano mechanics could enable, Eric strode through his mind, strode through his decisions, and then strode onwards, issuing commands to the officers under his charge. Within the time it had taken to complete his directives, the robots had re-gathered and taken again to flight. Such was their capacity, the open seas beneath were no hindrance during their preparation to take the fishing vessel. And in the heart of the man behind their acts of forthcoming deprivation, there was not really so much as a heart, but a machine. Inside the vortex central to the sustenance of humanity and central to the emotive connection to soul, resided the tiny unseeable machines, and machines are always without heart – even if they take the machine form to create one.

John and Tobias nor the other two men could see what was lurking a mere one hundred feet above them. They had no notion through audible awareness of the inner workings of their soon to be captors – for the robot was silent. It was without warning one of them appeared on deck startling everyone almost beyond belief. And it was without any means they resisted, for resistance was only to abandon the vessel - clearly impractical so far away from land. Whilst they had done what they could, there was nothing to be done now as the robot seized them. It held them and then in an instant, it raised them into the darkness of the machines above lost to sight.

Their ascent seemed without power as is normal for upward thrust as they were held in some type of place barely viewable and appearing to be not solid. John immediately recognised it as a property of pseudo flux mechanics. He again thought of what the authorities really wanted and he knew this time they would probe his mind to places he was uncertain of preventing access to them. Then in a fleeting second he thought of Chan and his teachings of allowing self to realise strength and in the second after, John thanked Chan quietly to himself.

What did this machine mean to the men captured in its belly? This device of menace where its character was not seen yet felt both physically and in their hearts. They both felt the amplification of sorrow emanating from outside of them yet permeating to their core.

"What of the others near Arequipa?" Tobias whispered. No reply came from John.

They would be expecting the triumphant return of both him and John in around four weeks where they would all be able to live peacefully on the farm for as long as they could. How much their dismay would be when the two men failed to arrive. Tobias was experiencing such a sinking feeling unlike anything feeling it could last forever. Eternal was his heart as was those he loved, yet the expectations had not delivered what his heart had told his mind, and so Tobias began to question if there was any validity of the strength within himself.

He had made it so far after all those moments alone near the gate and now having found his friends again. He had been determined to see positive outcomes and these had come true with John and Kerry Ann's surprise appearance and his reconnection with the others. Tobias had also lived in hope he would find Asper again and after his recent experiences, felt this too would eventually come. Now, he felt it all slip away.

In times years before, Chan had recognised the strength of the prevalent co-incidental nature of progression. Then as is now, it was at play mostly unknowing and perhaps unwilling to the conscious mind, yet apparent through outcomes Tobias and John were suddenly confronting. Intentional elemental alignment had served in the coming together of friends long lost, and it had manifested the events carrying forth the circumstances leading to the rescue of the others and John taking the torus from the hands of a maniac.

The transport streaked high above the long southward stretch of the South American continent as it reached a nominal altitude sixty thousand feet above. Both men could barely feel this as the flight was seemingly motionless, but something deeper inside past their conscious minds told them they were in this situation. Something inside told them they were about to face the sheer power of the authorities as evidenced now through the movements of their captor's craft.

With a smirk of satisfaction for the accolades he would receive, the pilot...their captor, turned to the holographic control array, positioned his finger over the forwards thrust engine control, and then immersed it within the projection to propel the craft beyond the continent at over five thousand miles per hour.

Chapter 30

The Agent knew of the torus in proximity. His re-built amplifier provided an indeterminate readout response to the signals he was sending out showing him a rough area somewhere below him as he orbited the Earth high above South America.

The Agent had no knowledge of John's capture as he remained focused as much as he could manage, to seek out and to take the torus. He would also take the man responsible as his own personal advisor on technology offering him no choice but to accept such terms. And to his former superior officer he would give the last vestige of patience he could endure before subjecting her to his type of futility. Nothing came close in his senses, to the extraction of soul and to the extraction of self he would force upon her. And oh, how he would so dearly enjoy her demise and her despair as her very reasoning of self would dissolve to nothing.

A quick manic decision resulted in his spaceship suddenly descending from orbit as he engaged the automated re-entry sequence. He streaked through the sky on a trajectory over the South Atlantic Ocean, before turning on a reverse angle back to South America. Within minutes he was following the eastern coastline of the continent beginning south of Buenos Aires.

For the entire day he continued to scout along the fringe of South America looking for a more precise reading from his amplifier and a much narrower area to focus upon. Back and forth he flew at great speed as his amplifier calculated data also at great speed, yet he had nothing specific. When his failures dawned on him, it only served to hasten his rise into a bout of maniacal anger. He flew erratically after so much precision flying. He shot a few buildings into rubble where he had retained his composure most of the day, and he killed a few people after he had even considered taking a liking to some as he watched them in their beach paradise. It was not a real graceful liking though – more of a wish to dominate them and then use them rather than just kill them outright.

Brazilian authorities were watching him. They had HyperJets on standby and did scramble them once when he had taken to destroying buildings, but he was too fast – his spacecraft leaving them in its' wake before the HyperJets had any time to consider offensive actions against him. When on his second flight of mania, George did descend to a dangerous altitude, prompting the authorities to scramble their jets again.

His first vent was to sweep low over the capital – a city still a stronghold for the authorities. He destroyed what he could of the eight interlinked high-rise towers. Simultaneously, his amplifier charged each laser bolt with a virus aimed at destroying the data systems maintaining the operations of each tower. As blazes erupted over one hundred floors above the streets below, the automated fire fighting systems failed to engage. On his second run at the city, he directed his aim at the airport destroying three HyperJets before they could ascend to the sky to give chase. When he saw two others take a steep incline on a heading directly for him, he considered them as worthy of his destructive intentions.

They came firing all their laser cannons in the hope of diverting him away knowing their firepower was useless for destroying the spaceship. The Agent laughed as the bolts hit his craft causing only a slight jolt here and there, and then he laughed again as he watched both of them explode into fireballs as his own laser canons struck. Abrupt as his mood changes, he turned his spaceship around on a heading back towards the city to wreak yet further havoc.

"How dare you even consider challenging me you pathetic fools," he said calmly as he eyed the high-rise again in his sights. This time he carefully aimed his weapons destroying three of the towers and sending them cascading to the ground. When a sudden mood change erupted within him again, he turned and left the scene entirely heading directly west to recommence his search for the torus.

As he flew he recalibrated his amplifier – the subsidence of his mania once again permitted him to attend to actual thinking and corresponding actions. His sudden insight gave him an idea and so he set about installing new algorithms into the amplifier as the craft flew on automatics. It took nearly no time to reach the visible west coast of the continent from an altitude around five miles up, and as he looked up from his work, George smiled his peculiar smile the moment he entered the last algorithm.

Within thirty minutes he was in the sky above northern Peru where he once again began to send out signals from his amplifier. When he reached the coast over Mollendo, his amplifier began to sing to him. It vibrated and resonated with a high-pitched scream sounding of misery as if it was calling to become whole. Another sequence and he narrowed the readouts to show the torus was within a one hundred mile radius of his present location. He would have to do the rest himself by making low flying passes of the entire area at an altitude of a few hundred feet. Where and when his amplifier sang to him with its highest pitch in screaming song, it would be the place and the time where he could again embrace mania as he closed in on his target.

Chan knew the Agent was coming as he told the entire group who had gathered in the barn. John and Tobias had been away too long by this time and they all knew something was about to change.

"We are once again to be confronted. Our senses are bombarded at present with no news from John and Tobias, and now I feel the Agent is close."

"Similar to when the dark sect came visiting us in Australia?" Jenna asked.

"Yes Jenna, it is very similar, if not the same feeling. As I said long ago, co-incidents are prevalent, and consider our rescue by John has led to the Agent seeking him and Carmel, so strong is his hatred."

"He is drawn to me. John and I could sense something as he chased us east through California."

"Yes, his senses are strong, though weak – weak where they seek control, but strong where they seek the instrument for this."

"He must have something to detect the torus. The dark sect used their amplifier," Jake said a little shakily.

"But John destroyed it Jake," Raynie replied. She felt for Jake seeing a slight desperation behind his eyes.

"He has probably built another," Carmel interjected. "John told me he could construct the horned torus with sufficient ease if he knew the precise algorithms."

"Accept he does know those algorithms and he has a new amplifier. It is in his way of determination to seek out any means he finds to re-establish his grip, as loose as it may be."

"So do you have any ideas then Chan?" Juan asked. "We really don't want to see the Agent here, but we are not so keen to send you on your way. There would be nowhere for you to go."

"Yes, I understand your concerns Juan, and I agree it would not be right for us to bring a threat upon your lives."

"We cannot just let him take the torus though Chan. We will have gone nowhere if he is able to use it again. Maybe if I decide to go with him voluntarily it might help."

"What you say is both correct and incorrect Carmel, if I may be so bold as to make such an assertion. You are right – he cannot be allowed to possess the torus again otherwise the Earth will descend even further."

"Especially given the way the authorities have been acting everywhere. The reports of indiscriminate destruction on their part are disturbing and indicate they are ready to also do what they can."

"Yes, their lack of patience has run out. Also it would not be wise for you to go with the Agent. He will kill you. Then he will continue to look for the torus."

"Can we play cat and mouse with him? Jake and I have a little experience with this when he chased us to northern California to have our chips removed."

"A worthy idea Raynie, but it would involve us travelling always on the move, and across many inhospitable places for who knows how long."

"Is there any way we can use the torus against him? What about in some weapon or something?" Steve asked looking at Chan and Jenna.

"Now Steve, what you say is perhaps the best idea yet. Why did I not think of it?"

"Probably because you are not the type to think much of weapons Chan."

"Perhaps, but…we must work on this idea. The torus is powerful where it can harness and focus energies. It might prove valuable to our cause and give us more time to consider other options by stalling the Agent."

"Then let us help you. I am sure my knowledge of machines could be of use," Juan offered.

"I think it would Juan. In fact, if I may say so, it would be best if we all make an effort to devise and construct a defence against the Agent."

Everyone present agreed this was as good a way to proceed as any.

"You are our friends and have given very much to us in return, so it is only natural we be there by your side," Ricardo said breaking a few moments of silence.

"Thanks Ricardo. Thank you to each of you. We are so very grateful."

As Juan fed the firebox to the grain cutter steam engine, he considered how the use of such an old machine would fare against the might of the Agent's spaceship. As if Chan was responding to his thoughts, he appeared with Jenna and Lyle to explain how the engine would be used.

"Jenna and Lyle are going to build a housing to draw energy from the torus and attach it to your engine Juan."

"I see. And how will it work?"

"Can you disconnect the main drive shaft so we can attach the housing?" Jenna asked.

"Um, yes Jenna. I can detach it here," he said showing them where a join in the shaft went from a vertical rod and then to a horizontal rod at ninety degrees.

"Lyle we need to attach the pulse generation cells from the rifles here, see?"

"Okay."

"Then we will have to reconfigure the output muzzle from each rifle to take the enhanced beam we will generate and combine it as one beam…but wait until I attach these wires from the outside of the torus housing."

"Oh, now I see. You will use the drive to spin the torus and amplify the power of the laser rifles."

"You catch on quickly Juan. It is precisely what we will do."

"But will it be enough?"

"We hope so."

"We can add to this power if we focus our intentional energy into the torus. As you know, it has activated through this in the past and it can easily detect this electrical energy again from us…but we must remain focused and avoid negativity, otherwise it will not align properly and will fail to give us any extra boost in power."

"Really. It will work?" Juan said in disbelief.

"We must try it Juan. All of us together. The Agent is very strong, but he is also weak and susceptible. His manic hold on his worth is his weakness, but it also gives him the strength through its need for successful expression and behaves like a hungry animal reacting when it is not fed. For now, I suggest Jenna and Lyle get to work quickly, while you take the drive apart at the connection there."

Frieda had been secured away from harm with the other horses to avoid the indiscriminate destruction the Agent may bring. Everyone had taken to the barn where the recently made weapon now stood awaiting his appearance. It was a marvel they were sure John and Tobias would have admired – a steam driven laser pulse canon with torus amplification.

Four hours of waiting passed with Chan helping all with advice on how to focus their energy at the torus - then the Agent arrived.

His amplifier screamed at him as he hovered three hundred feet over the farm deciding what to do. His on-board detectors showed him a group of people inside the barn huddled beside an operating steam engine. He could not understand the situation.

The Agent had never encountered a steam engine previously and had never taken to researching anything similar as he regarded history as irrelevant. His scattered thoughts were always for the progression of the machines since his yearn for them begun when he joined the authorities as an agent. When the holographic readouts showed him it was a steam engine from the nineteenth century, he did not bother to consider any of the dynamics of operation also showing in the projection.

"This will be easy," he said aloud.

The Agent knew he could not fire upon the building below for fear of killing the man who possessed the torus and could give him the information required to build a complete and stable vortex amplifier. And…he dared not risk killing his former superior, for then he would not be able to watch her suffer as he dealt out his hatred as part of his maniacal fantasy.

For those on the ground amidst the outer buildings of the farm, the spaceship designed to reflect space appeared menacing in contrast to the serenity of the scene. It was near dusk with a soft light, yet nothing about the craft's presence was soft or welcoming. It had landed almost silently aside from the sound its thrusters had made throwing leaves about as it touched the ground. For a few minutes it just stood there silent and foreboding with no sign of the Agent within. When he did emerge, the access ramp lowered with a faint whirring sound followed by his appearance slowly walking towards them. At ground level he stopped facing directly towards the barn, levelled his weapon and fired twice to shatter the door.

Steve held the laser weapon as Juan, Diego, Ricardo, and Manuel each held a laser pulse rifle. They stood their ground in front of the steam engine – its constant sound permeated now and then by a slight hiss. Once the wooden fragments from the shattered doors had fallen away, the engine alone broke the silence.

Chan and the others were out of sight at the rear, focusing their thoughts and intentions towards the torus.

"What have you done to my torus?" the Agent demanded as soon as he saw it spinning.

"It is not your torus. It belongs to nobody," Steve replied.

"Whatever you think has no bearing, and forgive me please if I do sound ungrateful."

"Only you think so…if think is what your brain actually does. We thought it was just an outlet for the insanity within."

"Don't get wise with me. I have the capability to destroy you and this entire farm."

"But then you will not get what you came for. And…please forgive my sounding ungrateful, without it you will become nothing yourself. The authorities will overcome your transient viruses fired from your laser canons."

"You have no idea of what I can do."

"I think we do. It is quite the reverse actually. You have no idea what we can do."

"The pathetic old machine? You expect me to be afraid of it…even for an instant?"

"Yes we do expect you to be afraid George."

"Then it is you who are the fools. I can go on without the torus."

"I am sure you could, but only for a short time. Soon enough, they will overcome you and then you will be their prisoner again. I am surprised you do not remember me George."

"Of course I do. I watched you all the way to Mars, and then I bettered you by escaping and stealing my spaceship. You failed."

"Did I? I have survived until now and have never been afflicted with any of your viruses. I would hardly call it a failure."

"Oh but you will, for in this rifle there are more than just laser bolt generators. It mirrors my spaceship. I can shoot viruses…"

"What? Into nano implants? Nobody here has any."

The Agent had not considered there would be no instance of the implants amongst the group and this brought on the sudden realisation this component of his weapon was useless. As it is with maniacs, anything sudden can trigger an episode of mania…and it did as he began to lose his composure.

"Then I'll just kill you all."

"I would not do it," Juan said as he and the three other men pointed their laser rifle straight at the Agent.

For a minute, he went into a state of confusion as his eyes darted back and forth in reflection of the erratic thoughts behind them.

"I can destroy you all if I take to my ship. There is a chance the torus might survive an attack. It is a diamond and I can configure my laser canons to a specific power."

"You could try but it would not work. Do not underestimate the power of this old machine…this steam driven weapon. It might surprise you."

"Why is the torus there anyway?"

"Your brain is certainly lacking today isn't it." Steve was continuing to antagonise the Agent and it was working as he was losing more and more of his composure with each exchange.

"My brain is working fine. It is you who is lacking."

"Don't bet on it George. George Smyth."

When Steve said the Agent's name again, he caused the man to lose more composure than he had previously. Almost nobody had spoken his name to him since his transit as a prisoner to Mars over three years ago, and now it stirred something deep inside. The other men looked at Steve, surprised at his courage in standing against the Agent. Steve was amongst a very few people who knew his real name - Carmel was another and she refused in herself to utter it to anyone.

"So what is it going to be Georgie?" Steve asked this question poking fun at the Agent. "Come on Georgie porgy pudding and pie, took his spaceship to the sky. But in his head, he could not deny. He was a maniac, who would often cry."

"Careful Steve," Juan said.

The Agent lost control and fired his weapon, not at any of the men, but at the steam engine behind them. To his utter surprise, the laser bolt ricocheted off the engine and disappeared.

"How was it for you George? A nice little surprise, yes? What are you going to do next?"

The Agent did not answer – he could not answer. His throat had swollen up from the manic anger inside, so he coughed a few times as he looked around the barn assessing the scene.

"Well?"

He looked Steve in the eyes, "I will kill you first, and then the others."

"No you won't. These men here will drop you like a stone before you have the chance to pull the trigger."

"Where's the bitch?"

"Oh surely you should show a bit more grace George. Carmel is here, but she does not want to see you. She does not like having a bad taste in her mouth. Gee, she even refuses to utter your name, so distasteful it is."

"I'll get her."

"Will you George? She doesn't get you, and neither do any of the rest of us. In-fact, I think most people around this planet do not get you, and are frankly quite sick of you. I'll bet it is you they want to see become immersed in your sickening afflictions. You are very sick George."

"Where is she, and the other one John...and the little Chinese man. I especially want him."

"Why George? None of them want you. Again, I think nobody on the entire Earth wants you. How do you feel about it George?"

"I don't care. Everyone can go to hell as far as I am concerned."

"What? Your sickening version of hell? Your pathetic viruses you send out to make people suffer. You just don't get it George do you? People will overcome you."

"Oh don't be too sure. Do you know what my viruses are doing? Do you know what the holes between the space and time fabric are creating? Haven't you seen where people go?"

"The viruses will not last."

"They might last enough to see my plans come true."

Steve became a little concerned with this as Chan had explained to them about the unstable vortexes creating significant disruption to the continuum perhaps lasting many years and taking substantial effort to repair, if they ever could be repaired.

"I can see you are thinking about it, so you must know. And I am quite capable of creating more viruses even without the torus so I can continue this unfolding and tearing of the fabric."

"Hmm, I would think it is time we rid the Earth of you George." Steve said as he fired the canon and the other men did likewise with their rifles.

Then they were agape in surprise for the Agent merely flickered in and out of existence as the lasers hit him – he had sent a holographic projection of himself and was actually still inside his spaceship. The entire episode since coming down the ramp and then the subsequent discussion was all holographic.

"Hmm, the Agent knows a little more about technology than we expected."

"Ha. Now see who is surprised. Watch as I take my ship just a little above you and make good on my promise to destroy your pathetic existence."

He took the craft to one hundred feet above the barn where he stopped and hovered for a moment to align with the target below. After he had configured the energy pulses to destroy only the wooden and stone structures along with any life forms inside leaving only the much harder torus undamaged, he fired.

Bolt after bolt reigned down upon the barn. As the tables turned once again, the Agent was surprised to see bolt after bolt ricochet and disappear. He kept firing and firing until the laser canon muzzles glowed red. He simply could not understand why his weapons had no effect. He tried inserting viruses into the bolts, but they too did nothing.

"Take a few shots at him Steve," Juan yelled through the noisy din of ricocheting laser bolts. "We'll provide a spread of cover fire."

Steve took ten steps forward - a measurement carefully detailed prior to the Agent arriving. At the eleventh step he stopped, just outside the energy shield Jenna had built by reconfiguring the output algorithm from a laser rifle controller and adapting the scanner John had built. Steve aimed the three-pronged laser rifle weapon directly at the Agent's ship and fired. It would not destroy the craft, but it would certainly give him something to think about. Each bolt jolted the spaceship causing it to jerk about in the air as the return bolts of laser fire from the Agent were then sent at angles. Two small buildings were hit with each one instantly erupting into a fireball.

Steve kept firing until the Agent had re-directed his own weapons to aim at just in front of the barn where he stood. Steve leapt backwards a few yards and then laughed at the Agent who was staring down at him as his laser bolts bounced off the invisible shield.

"Screw you! Screw you!" the Agent yelled from the cockpit upon realising he was not going to be able to destroy them. "I'll destroy this place!"

He rotated his ship around to cast a spread of laser fire at all of the remaining buildings and infrastructure in sight, but within a few moments and after only a few bolts, Steve was once again firing at his ship and causing it to jolt erratically.

"Off you go now," Steve said as he sent bolt after bolt at the Agent whilst the other men did the same with their rifles.

And off he went, taking to the sky in a sudden thrust by engaging full power. Those on the ground were sent scurrying to avoid the force of the wind coming from the engines erupting so close to them.

"Oh Steve honey. I'm going to give you a big kiss. You were so brave." Kerry Ann embraced Steve as the others emerged from behind the steam engine.

"You did a great job," Lyle said slapping Steve on the shoulder.

"Yes mate. Bravo!" Pablo added.

"We have all done well. I was surprised at how you were able to so effectively destabilise the Agent. And Jenna, your calculations were ideal," Chan said.

"It was a bit of fun Chan. I don't really know where it all came from. It seemed to flow…"

"Yes. Flow is important. Let it out and release. So very good for our intentions to be channelled in such a way. But we must be certain the Agent will return."

"Well, I'll call for a celebration, but first, we need to put these fires out," Lolita said, reminding them there were a few fires needing to be extinguished before they caused more damage. For the remainder of the afternoon, they all tended to cleaning up some of the mess as Jenna refined data properties within the weapon to make it just a bit more powerful than before.

Kerry Ann and Steve were in the mill house grinding, when Lolita called them to the main house later for dinner. They were not making flour and had to scramble some to gather themselves, but considered the interruption appropriate given the circumstances of the day.

"A big cheers for Steve and for Jenna," Juan proposed as they all sat around the large table.

"Indeed," Carmel seconded the notion.

"To us all," Chan said after the first toast. "To us all."

For a time they all celebrated this victory as a breakthrough, realising how well they all worked together. It was when the absence of John and Tobias fell upon them, did their night lose some of its' vigour and atmosphere.

"We must remain as vigilant as ever for their safety and their intentions. They are both strong men and they are progressive. We must not hold fear for them, but remain strong," Chan offered.

He could see a few looks of worry and he too felt a deep concern. If the authorities had captured them and if they sought to extract the information on flux mechanics from John, then calamity again would bring their greatest challenges.

Chapter 31

Tobias was far removed from any place he considered worthwhile as he sat alone in a cell within the same facility deep beneath New York City where Eric Gunter worked and lived. He had been separated from John when the scouting robot transport vessel had taken them directly to the great eastern seaboard city once a supposed bastion of democratic purpose through the United Nations of Earth. Over the past six weeks since their seizure from aboard the fishing vessel, he had been given food once per day without any forms of entertainment or information. The authorities had avoided just killing him outright, instead choosing just to isolate him until he could be of use to them. Most disconcerting aside from the isolation, were his thoughts of John and of what they authorities had in store for him. Considering the means and measures they had taken to capture him, Tobias could easily imagine how much they would strain John to break him and give them flux mechanics.

Day after day and now week after week, Tobias was left to sit alone where all he could do was run through all manner of ideas and memories in his mind. He had seen a few of the new trans-human types working at this facility, and in each instance he felt repulsed when he had looked into their eyes and found nothing. His only fear was if they transformed John in the same way, but unfortunately, they had done precisely what he feared.

John did not have the eyes like Eric but he did have the implants designed to direct his thoughts. On the first day after arriving he was taken immediately to the experimental nano mechanics laboratory for the process to begin. The authorities were determined to obtain flux mechanics for an offensive to dispense with the Agent as soon as possible, and then they would use flux technology as a means to enforce an unsurmountable grip on power. Their first task was to influence John's thoughts on a level where he could not resist thinking in the direction his was being influenced to take. From there he would naturally find his way to his knowledge of flux and then upon this, Eric would seize the opportunity to immediately begin modifying authority systems.

John did his best to resist at the time they implanted his mind. Four officers had to restrain him as a fifth fitted restraints attached to the implant chair. Everything inside him was rejecting the concept, rejecting the idea, and rejecting the cause – but he could do nothing.

Affects from the implants were subtle yet recognisable. Unmistakable and far stronger than the device implanted in his mind years before during imprisonment at the facility near San Francisco, John immediately felt their intrusion. He could feel the implants probe into his free will and still deeper into his psyche of self. They searched his thoughts at a level where his thoughts originated, rather than just the manipulations he had experienced previously.

For a time, John felt as if the implants were making inroads into his soul intentions as they began to mask his own perspectives and push him into channels of compliance. He began to wonder if he was taking the same road as those who were beset with viruses from the Agent – on a pathway losing self relinquished. Then as if in climax, he restored this sense of self when he realised the extent the mechanics probed his mind and how they attempted to manipulate his thoughts. For a few seconds he thought of Eric Gunter, the man who had overseen his capture and the implanted technology now trying to find dominion in John's mind. He could see Eric as a man lost and too willing to believe in the exaggerations of where technology could take humanity. Sure, it would service the efficient machine, but at what cost? At what cost to the individual and their concepts of life aside from the consumption of the products and services manufactured and controlled by the authorities? Eric sought the limitless infinity of flux mechanics yet he would never be able to truly apply this belief. It was a belief despite the logics of his mind. John understood how these logical processes worked – they were not true artificial intelligence with capacity to act through sentience. They were products or constructs of their programming and hence could be overwhelmed even at this biological level inside his mind.

As limited as Eric's concepts were being born through control mechanisms, they would fail to realise the true potential if unhindered by the desire to manipulate, and despite the bombardment inside of his head, John took this as his first defence against the intrusion constantly goading him.

John was different. He could process logic and delve into theory for use in problem solving and the invention of ideas and he did this with an essence of lateral awareness normally not found in the minds of many scientists.

At the completion of the implant process, the holographic restraints were released and he was taken to a holding cell nowhere near the one holding Tobias. After watching John being placed in the cell, Eric Gunter confirmed John's own insight as the holographic cells bars engaged.

"We will be testing your internal neural mechanics first thing tomorrow where will then immediately confirm successful implant for commencement of information extraction. Do you have any questions?"

"Yeah…just one. What does it feel like for you?"

"It feels right, nothing more and nothing less. Any notion of feeling is simply irrelevant. My personal feelings are for efficient compliance in service."

"What about you…your ambitions?"

"My personal ambitions are what I have just told you John."

"I get it. As a scientist you want to keep working on developing this rubbish you implanted in me."

"As I am, you too will be part of the machine to be."

"You are a machine."

"In part and with yet more to be so. It is inevitable for all John as your capture has been. There is just too much going on for you to be free to yourself. What you know is far too important for the likes of you and your associates to possess."

"Surely you have others who could..."

"There are no others John. You know such things. Throughout the times there have always been individuals who made great advances for humanity. Single individuals affecting the many."

"Perhaps this person of yours is the Agent."

"No such possibility exists. You are he John...the one."

"I am no 'one' as you say it."

"I merely meant you are the single person who holds the key knowledge I...we require."

"You spoke of yourself then Eric. Perhaps your mechanics are already failing you."

Eric simply looked at John for a few seconds before replying, "Until tomorrow then."

Next day after successful results displayed through every test channel on Eric's holographic bank, he confirmed it was now time to engage synaptic manipulation for retrieval of information inside John's mind. John focused every facet of his resistance against the nano implants coursing through his brain searching his mind for knowledge of flux mechanics.

He concentrated with all his organic might on one simple point knowing they would obtain most of the material they required. Through his practice with the others, John was able to take himself into a meditation like state where he focused on flux mechanics and as he did so he intently focused on one small detail changed. John knew of the changes inside the mind and body during a trance, and he knew their unstable mechanics working inside him would be unable to counteract his personal nuances.

Eric could see the resistance John made to the implants on the readout displays. After seven minutes of analysis with no new details showing, he concluded the session, called the escorting officers in, and then he left to report the results to his superior. His internal systems connected to the authority systems where they automatically compiled results simultaneously as the quantum computer carried out analysis.

"This report does a lot to assist us in the production of flux mechanics Gunter. You have done well in establishing these foundations for stability. What do you propose we do with this information next?"

"We need to keep working on Matheson sir. I know he is holding back. The more we learn from him, the more he gives us the means to find a way past the barriers he places against us. Otherwise, with this new information, I think we should proceed with modified systems development sir."

"I am listening."

"Well, as you know sir, we have significant resources being deployed to the Moon for the re-building of the Luna Base at a new location adjacent to the mining site close to the southern pole."

"I am aware of this. I did authorise the deployment."

"Yes I know sir. Considering we are making use of the two space craft sent from the Mars base, I have come up with a plan to test the flux mechanics through the creation of a spatial anomaly."

"But we were going to try this here on Earth."

"Yes I know sir. My recommendation is we proceed with a plan to try it in space. We can inject a high volume of flux dynamics into the vortex and push the technology to its limits. If we test the vortex here on Earth, we will only be able to create a limited result as the vortex could only remain in place for a short time before it would have to be dispersed."

"I see."

"In contrast sir, if we test the vortex in space, then we can leave it open for an indeterminate amount of time – there will be no constraints brought on through atmospheric conductivity and the potential destabilising factors created through aberrations when cosmic rays, plasma, or energies are filtered through the ionosphere sir."

"You present a good case Gunter. Wait a moment."

Eric's superior contacted his superior and spoke quietly for a few moments giving Eric nods in the affirmative as he talked.

"You must provide daily reports to me Gunter, without fail. I want information on this every step of the way. I want to know of any issues or problems you come up against, and of anything you need. They will be watching me, so I will be watching you."

"I understand sir…and the experiment?"

"Ah yes, proceed as planned. We need to create an Earth bound test – it will carry significant weight and influence. How will you proceed with John Matheson?"

"Further nanotechnology mechanical investigations. As I learn, we develop more ways to see his mind. It might be gradual."

"Keep me posted…and keep Matheson alive."

"What of his associate, Tobias Engelmann sir? He is ex-service."

"What do you suggest?"

"He could be of use sir. He has the intellectual capacity to be an efficient recipient of the nano mechanical implants."

"Then make it so. This Engelmann might be a good operative for us on these projects."

"Understood sir. And thank you sir."

"Do not thank me Gunter, just report...success."

John sat alone in the cell three levels from Tobias inside a complex equipped with two hundred cells in all. As the only two detainees present, the entire complex was devoid of sound and contained an eerie atmosphere, also devoid mostly of humanity. There were no guards, no holographic projectors with incessant messages of propaganda as it had been three years ago at the facility – it was silent, and so it would remain. Each cell was fitted with holographic bars designed to contain both the inmate inside and any sounds they made via a white noise audio blocking and containment field. Once occupied, the authorities were determined to lull the senses of all who were contained in this solitary confinement depriving them of any communication between cells and depriving them of any contact with the world outside.

John was never alone – not even when he lived in the riverside house a few years ago in the Alaskan wilderness. He always had his thoughts and his determination to explore, either physically or mentally, and to experience new concepts, new worlds, and new frontiers.

The concepts he endured at present with the perpetual influence coming from the nanotechnology mechanics were another challenge to overcome. As he considered his options, a fleeting satisfaction arose within him from the work he had already successfully done in overcoming the latest obstacle. When he had been watching the algorithms and sequences show on Eric's holographic array readout, he had noticed this one small success. It had been the only thing he was looking for amongst the data, and when he saw it he knew then he could defeat the machines inside his brain.

One key algorithm for maintaining the stability of flux mechanics was all it would take to undo what the authorities were about to test. And within this algorithm, John had made certain this error deliberately placed, would not arise until he had enough time to form a plan of escape from this binding. And then his goal would be to design an algorithm neutralising his nano mechanics to any extent he could manage. In a way John thanked Eric for only implanting a minor amount of technology in his mind, designed for the specific purpose of seeking flux.

Tobias whilst determined in his own way was unable to fight against the nano mechanics as John had – he had been given far many more implants as an experimental measure. Aside from the neural infusion, he was given muscular, nervous systems, and endocrine implants to service him as an operative of enhanced physical endurance. He was becoming the new type of soldier and enforcer the authorities would soon deploy once they had rid themselves free of the Agent.

Instantaneously the enormous load on his self transformed him as a person. He cried to himself as the anguish of this loss coursed through him, and then he was silent...until Eric Gunter spoke.

"How do you feel Tobias?"

"Electric."

"Hmm, interesting response. How 'electric' do you feel?"

"Um, not an inspired type of electric. More violated."

"It does take a little getting used to."

"You don't say."

"I do in fact, and I will also say this – you will become more and more aligned with the mechanics in a very short time. I would give it a day or so, and by then you may change your perspective on how you feel."

"How? I know what you have done. You stole my...my soul. You stole my sense of self."

"Dare like I do Tobias. There is even more than those old notions."

"They are never old...and those eyes."

"Yes Tobias, these eyes."

"Are you going to mutilate me with them?"

"Perhaps. As yet I am unsure. Such a procedure is far more complicated than these simple implants."

"What if I don't want them?"

"What you want will soon become irrelevant Tobias. You will only serve freely through the obvious efficient ways to minimise any type of loss in life. You will be able to focus on living Tobias, instead of those old emotive ways causing issues."

"Fat chance. Any idea of living you have is nothing authentic. How can you remove life to give life?"

"It is simple. We are improving on the inefficient human body to combine its' best attributes with technology. When people see this as the way forward, we will win them over and they will live happily in compliance."

"You'll never win."

"I already have. The capture of both you and Matheson, and the subsequent successful retrieval of the flux mechanics data have served me well in the view of my superiors."

"Does anything else entertain you?"

"I am also looking to develop more efficient methods for the authorities. Why can't you see this as a good thing Tobias? After all, the human experience has been so fraught with faults and shortcomings over the centuries."

"It is the human experience. This is not human. It is machine. Machines do not feel and love."

"But they can…or will very soon when the flux mechanics are developed into working human specimens."

"Specimens. Is it how you see people?"

"Mostly, except for my superiors. They are superiors."

"What makes you different from the Agent? He sees people the same way…as expendable, as mere intrusions to his own objective."

"There is significant difference to the Agent considering his mania."

"You think so?"

"Tobias, there is no need for sarcasm. There is a clear difference between the minds of the authorities compared to the behaviour of the Agent. He barely has a mind and is mostly inefficient so caught up in his volition to exercise his darkness or whatever he chooses to call it."

"Nor do you really have a mind Eric. It is a combination. So where is the difference?"

"I very much have a mind Tobias. It is just you do not quite see how my mind is…but you will very soon. Remember, you too are on the path where I stand now. Soon enough you will experience the fullness of the mechanical experience Tobias."

"I doubt it. And I doubt John ever will either. He is a lot smarter than you think."

"We do recognise John Matheson is a fine intelligent individual who possesses great knowledge, but he is unable to resist the nanotechnology mechanics."

"Don't bet on it."

"There is no need to play with chance Tobias. This is a definitive milestone for the progress of humanity. As all people move forward, they will come to realise the value of these nano enhancements."

"What if the Agent sends out another virus? All you will have is a similar mess to what exists now."

"We have taken measures against him Tobias. And we will take more measures to ensure such displacement of data does not occur again. Don't forget, we now have flux mechanics."

"You can never be certain."

"Yes we can. Certainty leads to the utmost in efficiency, so to strive for such things will bring about perfection and soon the Earth will become the machine as its destiny foretells as it also stands for both you and John Matheson. He tries to fight but he will succumb for the inevitability of the release of flux mechanics is not simply a matter of if, but when. It will occur and he will never be able to keep it for himself."

"What a load of rubbish. You speak in tongues spouting madness like the Agent. How do you know of any foretold destiny?"

"Except the Agent does not have flux mechanics Tobias. Now we do, these certainties will fall into place."

"And you think the Earth and its inhabitants will become machines?"

"Very much so Tobias. The people of Earth have been led to these times for centuries now in preparation. Even more than a century ago, the seeds of this future were sown. It was just almost all could not see this coming, as they mostly had their heads down Tobias. Remember your service record Tobias. All along you were playing your own part not realising this. Then your station at HAARP was to fulfil your mission – the mission you were never briefed on Tobias. All along through the many decades, people developed a reliance on technology and so with this came their personal psychology as reliance was seen as favourable over independence. To have someone or something provide for you is much easier than to do it yourself and so the authorities saw this to be the inevitable way for humanity and as such this required efficient management. They were becoming ever so reliant on technology to meet their needs and all through this they were being herded into the direction I describe."

"Not all were so gullible."

"Yes you are right there. But as you know, many of those are already gone, and the rest…they are either full of holes, or soon to become what you and I have become Tobias."

"Those holes will keep growing. They will cause you to think again."

"We know this Tobias. The holes are already grave issues of concern for the Agent was in no way aware of the openings he has created. With flux mechanics we should be able to repair them."

"Should does not sound like a certainty to me."

"May I say will then. You know not about flux dynamics as I do Tobias. The mechanics will give us power over all of this type of anomaly."

"How do you know? I have spent many years with John and he knows more than all of you."

"Really. You think so Tobias? Do you not remember earlier this day I was the individual responsible for retrieving John Matheson's knowledge of flux mechanics?"

Tobias could see through Eric, especially with his assumption John had already given him everything on flux mechanics.

"Your statement implies ambitious undertone Eric. Anyway, John will surely be able to resist your efforts."

"Perceptive of you Tobias, but be assured, it is not ambition other than to recognise how efficient I have been in the provision of the data my superiors require. And as I said, he will succumb eventually."

"You sound more like a machine than a man."

"Do you have a problem with it Tobias?"

"Yes I do. And what gives you the right to violate me?"

"You have acted as a criminal Tobias. We cannot abide in inefficient measures any longer. All criminals will have the adjustments if they are deemed worthy of value to the authorities. Feel lucky while you still can Tobias. If we had not seen you favourably, you would likely be dead by now."

"I am dead. What use is any of this? And to create some super service person out of me. How dare you!"

"Soon you will no longer see problems as such. By this time tomorrow you will see things much more like I do. Allow yourself to feel it Tobias."

"I hope not." Tobias then thought of Chan and of his similar words of allowance. A tear then welled in his eye and Eric noticed this.

"Hope is no longer relevant Tobias. Hope is but a fallacy based on emotional discord. Efficiency has no room for such things Tobias. You will learn this very soon. Even now as you weep, this too will become a distant memory. No more sadness Tobias."

Twenty-three hours later, Tobias was removed from his holding cell, leaving John as the sole occupant of the entire complex. Eric was confident he was ready for deployment and provide in the field testing of the mechanics data back to him. Tobias was escorted to a waiting crew transport ship and then was taken directly to the authority space base for service as a flight operative.

After initial check-in and allocation of temporary quarters, Tobias took a walk around the restricted areas of the base he was permitted access to. As he walked he could feel the new mechanical devices working on him...learning him, and changing him. He could sense a loss as what he could still remember of his old self, was becoming remote like a vague dream. The further he went, the more he felt like weeping and then the more he wept the more his mechanics dissuaded him from such inefficient emotions. By the time he had arrived back to his room, Tobias had forgotten most of the thoughts he had prior to and just after setting out on his walk.

A short time later as he consumed the meal delivered for his dinner, Tobias looked to the west where the sun was setting across the ocean. Its' radiance sent rays towards him to then be lost as amongst the din of operations and lights close to his building. At the last, he thought of Asper and then Tobias was tired so he went to bed.

Chapter 32

One of the two remaining spacecraft built at Mars Station under authority control, had been summoned to authority development headquarters beneath New York City. After landing, the ship was taken underground via an enormous vertical tube, to then be fitted with the quantum computer now configured to commence flux mechanics testing and create the spatial anomaly thirty thousand miles beyond the Moon.

Eric Gunter was in charge of the project for the creation of the anomaly – the first venture by humanity to construct a spinning vortex in space. Never before had consideration even been given to such an idea as there had simply been no plausible way to generate the energies required to open a rift in the fabric continuum of space until Eric obtained the flux mechanics information provided by John.

Once the quantum computer was installed with configured parameters based on the information taken, Eric instructed for it to prepare for the journey to space. Eric was to accompany the craft for the test, and to report back to his superiors via a live holographic communications link.

His final task prior to the craft leaving the underground facility was to ensure there would be no forthcoming threat from the Agent. After running a series of algorithmic sequences through the holographic array based on the latest data obtained from testing the presence of any new viruses from the Agent, Eric gave the all clear to proceed with the flight and subsequent test. He had installed all necessary algorithms and tested virtual holographic systems - now the craft was ready for delivery to the authority space base and subsequent launch.

From his room Tobias saw the arrival of the spacecraft. His briefing had been brief – he knew with the implants, he was to be a test case. As he watched it being unloaded in the giant hangar building over ten stories tall, his dwindling sense of self suffered yet another setback. His supervisor had advised there was to be a meeting at seven in the morning. Now with the sun losing its' last light, there was simply the inevitable last night ahead of him. For all his courage and tenacity, Tobias was now being rewarded with an outcome likely no better than the eventual oblivion for those many people affected by the Agent.

Almost...Tobias was wide awake. He had nearly fallen asleep. The mechanics in his mind were still adjusting and as they worked to make him want to sleep, Tobias fought against them unintentionally through his deliberations.

In a flash he then saw her. It was Asper. She looked beautiful. Finally after all this time they were together again. How did she find him? Then he thought of his implants and Tobias was suddenly abashed. It was embarrassing. They had fought together, loved each other, and seen a future free of the intrusion wrought by technology, and now here he was with the latest implants. He looked away as she approached. It was almost too much to believe. They were seconds away from embrace. Maybe she could take him to John...or Tim, The Fixture – he had removed their technology implants years before. Then he twitched. It was a painful jerking movement he had never experienced before. As if his nervous system suddenly suffered an electrical charge, Tobias reacted as if his body had momentarily been spiked by electricity. Then it was gone and so was Asper. No longer did he have thoughts of her and the others. His hopes were lost. He lay there a second later with his eyes wide open staring at the almost dark ceiling. Tobias had just awoken from a dream – a momentary glimpse of his life and his loves. He regretted having woken from this dream and then realised it was six in the morning and his alarm had actually sounded to wake him.

He had no desire to go into space then, nor had he desired to leave the Earth at any time previously in his life. Space only interested him mathematically when he began his career with the authorities, and now with his nano mechanics, the notion of desire was a remnant of his memories not worthy of any notice. When the spacecraft breached the atmosphere and the splendour of Earth lay below contrasted against the inky blackness of space, Eric did not admire this view as he was too busy studying the readouts coming from the quantum computer.

Ten hours and twenty seven minutes after leaving Earth's atmosphere, the spaceship had reached the test co-ordinates. The Moon and Earth were clearly visible as a planet and satellite system, but Eric was too busy to notice whilst he entered the final sequences required to position the anomaly three hundred miles from the spacecraft. He might have been excited if he had been an organic human being in entirety, considering all the work he had successfully completed in the lead up to the final calculations he obtained from John to construct the flux lens. It was in position affixed to the port side of the spacecraft, resonating in and out of transient light bearing reality as the tachyon emitter was turned on.

Success was immediate as the device registered as flux capable on the holographic readouts he scanned with both mechanical eyes and part organic mind. His next objective was achieved when the tachyon emitter itself came on line with the billions of protein string conductors showing as a flowing carpet of data on the display. Finally, an eruption of energy was initiated through the device resulting in the tachyon surge laying the paths for the algorithms to follow at the brink of penetrating the light speed barrier with fluctuations beyond the barrier at times. All data was instantaneously accepted into the lens to project it to the designated co-ordinates. In a tiny fraction less time than it took for light to travel the three miles away from the ship, the spatial anomaly erupted into existence with a flash followed by a gradual receding in brightness until it took on a peculiar purple black glow with a hint of silver. Such was its' colour, despite the blackness surrounding, the anomaly was clearly visible as if it also suggested its' presence to the subconscious along with its visual character.

It was a magnificent sight to Eric where he could even muster some fragments of his remaining self to admire. Three hundred miles away from the ship, was a black hole, a worm hole, an anomaly...a torus? He thought on this for a few seconds.

Measuring approximately twenty miles in diameter, the blackness within it was the blackest rendition of black ever known. As a gaping maw it was ready to accept the next phase of Eric's plan. Upon the Earth both day and night, people would see and fear this apparition. As a small point like a black star, it would haunt their thoughts and remind them of the ever present position the authorities held.

Eric continuously monitored the holographic array as he collated results from the sequence scenarios he sent to the anomaly. Everything appeared nominal, and with each new sequence to test the stability and the input constraints, he found what he expected – the anomaly was infinite with no constraints and therefore would accept any test. The main aim of this experiment was to test the capacity of flux in situation to penetrate dimensional borders and draw information as matter into Earth's dimension.

Every robot, every transport and machine, every computer, and every trans-human being would benefit from what Eric was doing. Ultimately, the authorities would have the capacity to develop new machines eclipsing the present designs and capable of far greater incursions into both mind and space with weaponry to enforce their motives. They also would now be able to construct nano mechanics beyond the quantum level to shape reality in their image, whatever they chose.

Finally, to confirm the results and complete the test, Eric entered a series of frequency modulation algorithms for ascertaining the variables encountered through phase dynamics of quantum resonance. This would confirm if the flux mechanics were capable of accepting the intentional elements of the human experience, and thus enable construction of truly autonomous artificial intelligence mechanics. The carpet of protein strings appeared to glow even brighter than the almost blinding display of it flowing in three-dimensional projection in front of him. Eric's eyes automatically adjusted to the brightness, and within a minute, he had confirmed success for this final sequence of testing.

"I'm powering down the sequence testing," he said to advise the captain of the spaceship. "You are authorised to return to Earth in twenty seconds."

"This anomaly...do we just leave it here?"

"We have further testing to be done. The anomaly will remain in this situation as long as we determine necessary."

Upon return to Earth, Eric presented himself immediately to his superiors so he could report.

"I expect the superior officials will want to run some further scenarios through this energy field as we develop flux mechanics for application in Earth bound use."

"Correct Eric. Your results are spectacular. We have been remote viewing. I must say, the anomaly is quite a spectacle."

"Indeed it is sir."

"And the protein strings. How did they respond?"

"As I had expected sir. They transformed the instant we applied flux. In a sense, they experienced a level of biological evolution in an instant to a higher order of capacity with an underlying flux state. This means the strings used in the test and any others we apply flux to will be at permanent readiness for the laying down of tachyon emission fields and pathways just above light speed sir."

"Excellent! You know what we have in store next, don't you?"

"Yes sir, I have been briefed."

"Good. Get to work on it immediately Gunter."

Chapter 33

As they huddled together for comfort amongst the partially repaired buildings, Chan, Carmel, Lolita, and all the others, sought solace from each other in company. The recent events and their acceptance of John and Tobias being missing had smothered their times. Carmel had decided to fire up her steam engine seeking some distraction. Connected to the array of lights built by John, it represented their hope, and their guidance as it gave them the only light in an otherwise darkened hour. Chan had done what he could to bring them in and to focus on the light as a reflection of what they were, what lay within their intentions, and of the connection to their hearts to experience the authentic now moment.

His vision was theirs in confidence and determination to overcome this suppression of light. Four horses had joined them with Frieda staying close to Carmel. They had bolted when the Agent had visited, for such is the way for horses and their tendency as flighty animals. After the Agent's melee, everyone ran after them to retrieve them...to save them.

"There is an air very much darkened and distant from the light. We are aware of our connections and on this we must focus. Dark as it may seem, these times are a test if you will for us to gather more than we could have imagined, so abrupt this incursion into peace has been here at the farm."

"No doubt there are going to be strict new measures brought on by the authorities. Those people who passed by the entrance to the valley when Jake and I went for our afternoon trip together, told us they had heard of new rules via a news broadcast in Arequipa," Raynie said looking positive despite her words.

"You are likely to be correct with this Raynie. There will be new measures put in place to challenge us in the times ahead as it will also challenge many others who are awakening to the old ways of control and how they simply cause so much trouble. When we align in truth we do not think about our intentions and the ways as barriers, but merely as experiences along the way of the journey as all journeys are infinite and already part of themselves. Our realisations lead us to consider our friends John and Tobias who must have been apprehended by the authorities for it is not like them to be absent so long after the time they told us they would return. This too though very much of a challenge, is again a test of our commitment to self respect for us as it is for both men. Expectations may arise yet they always must be challenged and when they do it is because more is to be done to arrive at the expected destination. It is not organic in intent to see ourselves as already knowing the entire journey ahead. At best we can plan a route to travel, yet it too is unexpectedly affected along the way."

"The authorities are likely to have begun their quest for dominance again knowing the Agent is much weaker now," Lyle added.

"Do you think he will...?"

"Yes Jenna," Carmel replied. "Chan and I have discussed this and what we could do when the Agent returns here. He will return with ways he thinks can overcome our weapon."

"I can re-build it," Juan added looking optimistic. "We all can work to re-build."

"I think it is wise Juan."

"I'll help with the configuration," Jenna offered.

"Yes Jenna. We are fortunate to have your knowledge of such things."

Whilst they talked, the Agent was working on the algorithm to ensure his energy shields could repel any fire from their steam driven laser canon. The work took him seven days to complete and when he was satisfied he had the right calculations, he installed them before deciding to depart the facility at San Francisco on a heading directly to the valley near Arequipa.

Jenna and the others had anticipated his return and his attempt to overcome their weapon. Whilst Jenna constructed algorithms to modulate the frequency output of their cannon, the others prepared as best they could - especially housing the horses and any vital equipment.

Carmel along with the others who had been rescued from the Agent's lair, focused their energies on enhancing their vibration resonances within. Chan had told them this would be a method of sub-conscious defence against the subtle underlying energies associated with the Agent's mania. This would help them to build intuition at each encounter.

On a cold misty morning in late May, the Agent touched down at the farm with the intent of staying until he had what he came for. He threatened them with his weapon as he demanded the torus, but they resisted and he soon came to realise how.

His weapon was useless against the superior algorithm Jenna had built and their canon could affect his craft, though only slightly. In effect it was a standoff where neither party really had the upper hand. Essentially, Chan and the others were able to retain the Torus of Eternity within their grasp for the time being, and in doing so were able to halt the Agent's desires to build a new amplifier and return to his dominant megalomania driven status.

Over time, the Agent did return again and again from his facility near San Francisco with new ways to counteract the shielding constructed by Jenna. These sudden intrusions, for which they had to always remain at alert for, came between bouts of destruction wrought upon those in the western sector of North America, and upon the authorities. They continued to struggle at times against his localised viruses where he threatened them with his presence – often staying for a few days at a time wreaking havoc upon those not protected by the new authority systems and still susceptible to his attacks.

When he came to the farm, his spaceship would just sit there with him inside mostly out of sight. Only when he returned to the control cabin to commence fire at them, would he be visible. Otherwise there was no secret as George would simply be in the back of his craft working, sleeping, or having an episode. His failing to make inroads against the shield Jenna had made was his main obstacle now along with the fact he was still an organic human being who required sustenance, and so he would have to leave to them find food.

The authorities in Arequipa were aware of his presence and whilst they were often successful in repelling him from incursion into the city, they were not interested in tracking him to the location in the hidden valley. Their energy was mainly focused enforcing compliance and controlling people as they prepared them for the new trans-humanism to come. So near they were yet so far, the authorities failed to see any connection between the Agent and his repeated farm attacks. They simply dismissed it as some manic personal vendetta the Agent must have as the reason for his frequent visits, and as they began to taper off to become less frequent, they soon realised and confirmed their own hypothesis. Within reach though, the Torus of Eternity would be a monumental advancement in their understanding of the physics required for their inter-dimensional energetic excitement experiments about to take place, and ironically their motives of efficiency overlooked this opportunity in a very inefficient manner.

Chapter 34

Eric worked endlessly studying the spatial anomaly and testing scenario after scenario for the sake for developing more and more advances in technology. Successes came in a flow of instances where deployment of robotics, new construction methods, and autonomous reorganisation of matter at the atomic level for construction of any machine programmed into the flux interface, soon became reality.

He even began to plan an entirely new type of spacecraft for an experiment to would bring about the penultimate success of flux mechanics for the authorities. Eric spent most nights after work calculating the dynamics of sending a spacecraft into the vortex created with flux. He was unable to determine where the craft would go as he did not have the answers to the destination or pathway of the vortex. On the last night of collating these calculations as a report for recommendation to his superiors, Eric decided the best way to proceed would be to build the craft and send it into the vortex with a trans-human pilot.

When he did present the report, he was given an immediate authorisation to proceed, and so he was flown to Mars Station for the construction phase of the project. Eric supervised the construction of a flux probe and the ship by programming the nano robotics to convert atoms into components and then into the entire machine. The entire process took twenty-seven days instead of the months required to build spacecraft in the past. When completed, the newly designed spaceship was born through the enormous airlock at the construction building within the Mars complex, and then flown directly to the anomaly near the Moon.

Eric was not its pilot – they had chosen a new trans-human military officer for the role. Eric sat in the older craft half a mile away from the new ship now positioned directly in front of the anomaly opening.

"We are almost ready to proceed with spacecraft insertion sir."

"Good," Eric replied to his subordinate. "Is the flux probe ready?"

"On standby sir."

"Proceed then."

The subordinate entered the sequence to engage the flux probe and send it into the anomaly prior to the full spacecraft test.

"All systems aboard the probe are working sir. I am sending it into the anomaly now."

As the probe moved effortlessly towards the anomaly using flux drive, it was the first ever instance where Eric had been able to witness the new propulsion system in action during a real event. At the frontier between normal space and flux space, the probe appeared to waver for a moment as if it had been engulfed in fluctuating waves of light. Then, as it reached the heart of the anomaly, it disappeared entirely from view as it was transformed into matter beyond light speed.

"Readings are coming in from the probe sir. It appears to be stable."

"Give it a minute further and then we will send the spacecraft in."

Fifty eight seconds later, Eric gave the order to proceed with manned flight into the anomaly. Unknown to the pilot whose nanotechnology mechanics deprived him of all senses concerning apprehension about the test, his flight was to be the first attempt at sending organic matter into flux. As the flight engaged and the craft made its way into the anomaly, the pilot for a brief moment felt a tear well in his artificial eye – a tear from love of something lost seemingly forever.

Somewhere in the depths of space in continuum, both craft and the pilot were relocated. Not even Eric Gunter knew where it was, but someone did and they were aware this experiment was destabilising the space and time continuum. It was not conducive to alignment, and therefore they had to respond.

Now with Eric's plan underway and many new rules of compliance being instituted and enforced with new technology sweeping people along unable to resist, John had been left to himself for two months in the cellblock. Fortunately for him, Eric Gunter was far too busy to consider infusing John with any further nanotechnology mechanics. Simply left to consider himself, his situation, and in his mind, John also searched for a means to escape. The invasion into him brought on by the neural mechanics was still a constant battle as Eric remotely instructed the slow process to penetrate the deepest regions of John's mind, and so visitations were not necessary.

John retained some imagination enabling him to still consider his escape, to plan finding Tobias, and then the eventual termination of the tiny robots inside his brain. But as time wore on he knew the struggle would get more and more difficult as the mechanics learned from him as they tried to shape him. Just one thing remained as his main hope and this caused him to wish Eric Gunter would come and try it on him.

There was one faulty algorithm John had designed within the information Eric had retrieved from him and it would be the key to eventually undoing the nanotechnology mechanics and other systems John knew were rapidly being deployed now the Agent was in submission. The one faulty algorithm would eventually arise from within the flux of matter as a stream of rogue tachyons John had designed. Eric would see it as a small anomaly in the data not noticing how it would grow exponentially until it hopefully rendered all flux mechanical systems inoperable.

VOLITION

So ends book two of the Torus Saga – Volition

Book three is The Last Year

VOLITION